Aged sixty at his death in 1972, Ronnie Delderfield was best remembered for his very amusing play about life in the RAF, *Worm's Eye View*. But to countless millions throughout the world his name came to be synonymous with the long, intricate and sensitive novels that he came to write in his late years.

GIVE US THIS DAY was the last of these, the last in a series that truly began with the publication of THE DREAMING SUBURB in 1958 and really sprang into popular focus with A HORSEMAN RIDING BY in 1966. Together with its sequel, THE GREEN GAUNTLET, that book chartered the progress of British life and manners in the inter-war years. And its success gave the author the impetus to look further back in time. The result was the trilogy of books of which this is the last part. GOD IS AN ENGLISHMAN began the saga, introducing to the reader Adam Swann in the middle of the Victorian era. Then came THEIRS WAS THE KINGDOM which took the narrative down towards the final years of the old Queen's reign. And interspersed with these books was Ronnie Delderfield's appealing look at school-life in the inter-war years, TO SERVE THEM ALL MY DAYS.

The whole adds up to make for a panoramic vision of the British Isles that may come to stand the test of the next few decades. For Ronnie Delderfield was in essence a storyteller of genius, a teller of tales in the market-place, practitioner of an art that will always be popular and always be influential.

Reconnaissance

Book II of
Give Us This Day

R. F. Delderfield

CORONET BOOKS
Hodder Paperbacks Ltd., London

*The characters and situations in this book are
entirely imaginary and bear no relation to any real
person or actual happening*

This book is sold subject to the condition that
it shall not, by way of trade or otherwise, be
lent, re-sold, hired out or otherwise circulated
without the publisher's prior consent in any
form of binding or cover other than that in
which this is published and without a similar
condition including this condition being
imposed on the subsequent purchaser.

Printed and bound in Great Britain for
Coronet Books,
Hodder Paperbacks Ltd,
St. Paul's House, Warwick Lane,
London, EC4P 4AH
by Hazell Watson & Viney Ltd,
Aylesbury, Bucks

ISBN 0 340 18819 7

For May

Col. Edward Swann = Monique D'Auberon
1789–1879   1789–1830

Adam Swann = Henrietta Rawlinson
b. 1827   b. 1839

Stella = (1) Lester Moncton-Price
b. 1860
(2) Denzil Fawcett

Robert = Dolly   Martin   John   Victoria   Richard   Daughter
b. 1882   b. 1882   b. 1884 b. 1887   b. 1888   b. 1889

2 daughters   1 daughter

Giles = (1) Romayne   Joanna = Clinton   Hugo = Sybil
b. 1866   Rycroft-Mostyn b. 1867   Coles   b. 1869 Uskdale
(2) Gwyneth Powell

David   Son   Valerie   2 sons   Mary   Humphrey
b. 1900 b. 1902 b. 1889   b. 1901   b. 1902

THE SWANNS OF 'TRYST'

Alex = Lydia Corcoran
b. 1861

Deborah Avery = Milton Jeffs
b. 1855
(Adopted 1863)

Deany
b. 1898

George = Gisela Körner
b. 1864

Rose
b. 1888

Garnet
b. 1900

Max
b. 1886

Rudi = Evie
b. 1887

Adam
1889

Henrietta
b. 1896

Baby
b. 1898

Sam
b. 1908

Helen = (1) Rowland
b. 1870   Coles
        (2) Rory
            Clarke

Edward = Gilda
b. 1878   Wickstead

Margaret = Huw
b. 1879   Griffiths

Gillian
b. 1909

SWANN·ON·WHEELS
REDEFINED·REGIONS

SCOTLAND

Glasgow   Edinburgh

NORTH
EAST
REGION

Whitby

IRELAND

Belfast

THE
POLYGON

Dublin

Manchester

THE
FUNNEL

Macclesfield

Newark

Beddgelert

WEST   Derby
MIDLANDS

Norwich

Birmingham

THE
MOUNTAIN   Worcester
SQUARE

THE LINK

Pontnewydd

THE
SOUTHERN   London
SQUARE

Cardiff

Tonbridge

Barnstaple

Salisbury   THE KENTISH
TRIANGLE

THE   Taunton
WESTERN   Exeter
WEDGE

TOM
TIDDLER'S
LAND

Truro

Contents

PART FOUR

Reconnaissance

I

In the Beginning There Was George . . .

THE TRANSITION OF SWANN-ON-WHEELS FROM A horse-powered network to a haulage system served by a fleet of mechanical vehicles, supplemented by horse teams where the terrain was more suited to hooves than tyres, was effected so quietly, and so smoothly, that it never qualified as a nine-day wonder in the trade.

Briefly, in city coffee houses frequented by shipping men, and in the loading yards of midland and northern factories, it was seen as a typical foray of that old fox Swann, who had been trying to corner the national hauling trade from the day he recruited his ruffianly army of unemployed coachmen and Thameside waifs back in the 'fifties. Briefly because the 'fifties themselves were now viewed as an era not far removed from that of Stephenson's Rocket.

Swann, they recalled, flaunting his banner-with-the-strange-device, had always been an innovator so there was nothing remarkable about his overnight conversion to horseless carriages. He would likely burn his fingers but he could afford that, having exacted his percentage from almost everything carted over county borders during the last forty years. Even those among his rivals who actually owned a private motor and bumped their wives and families down to the seaside at weekends, considered that he might, for once, have over-reached himself, especially when it got around that he was designing and building his own transport. But that again was to be expected of a man who had always been a jump ahead of his competitors and who still qualified as an eccentric in a world where eccentrics we~e rare and becoming rarer. After all, no one could challenge Swann's record as an amateur whose enterprise, launched with a hundred Clydesdales and half as many waggons, had gone on to become a household word in a single generation, and there was no denying the horseless carriage had come to stay. Only a small minority of merchants refused to entrust their goods to these clumsy, vapour-trailing equipages, that people were beginning to call 'lorries', once their overall performances were seen to be fairly satisfactory. A majority, remembering Swann's reliability and punctuality, were content (though not over-eager) to renew their contracts, reasoning that Swann and his successors must know their business or how could they have survived the cut-and-thrust of the last half-a-century, when something revolutionary appeared on the world's markets every day of the week.

This then was the impersonal verdict on the transition. It was otherwise from within, where initial opposition to the change-over had been so resolute that it had been seen as a board-room mutiny. Here, indeed throughout the entire network, there had been a ransacking of conscience and personal prejudice that was regarded as a rich private joke by the minority that had voted in favour of George on what was accepted by Swann veterans as 'The Watershed' That is to say, the period immediately prior to George Swann's famed cross-country jaunt with a six-ton gun-turret aboard, a feat that set every transporter in the country by the ears once they had digested the relevant logistics. The conversion was unanimous and all but immediate, and perhaps Jack-o'-Lantern Coles summed it up best in a Biblical parody of the incident that enlivened the otherwise dull speeches at the firm's annual dinner, in December, 1905. It was an occasion when the commissioning of the hundredth Swann-Maxie was announced by Scottie Quirt and Coles said, proposing the customary toast to the firm: "In the beginning there was Adam. And Adam begat George. But George did much better in that *he* begat the giant Maximus, and Maximus begat the Swann-Maxie that did multiply until it darkened the countryside. But the elders of the tribe murmured against such begetting and took counsel among themselves, saying, 'It is not seemly in the sight of the righteous that so great a strain should be placed upon our pockets.' Yet George set his face against them and persisted. And it came to pass that they were convinced in spite of themselves, and took counsel one with the other again, saying, 'We have sinned and will go forth in sackcloth and ashes manifesting our fault. For this man has found favour in the sight of the Lord and we will henceforth bow down before him and do his bidding . . .!'"

It was recorded that even Young Rookwood smiled (he had never been known to laugh) but the others, Godsall and his fellow doubters, were more generous. Few annual dinner speakers had received such a weight of applause and laughter as Clint Coles, when he sat down and reached for his glass of hock. Converted they were, and to a man, but some went even further, becoming, as George told Adam after the 1906 New Year conference, 'More Catholic than the Pope.' And indeed they were, inasmuch as they were clamouring for vehicles much faster than Scottie could manufacture them. But notwithstanding this, George rejected his father's advice that he should put the patent out to tender among the two hundred-odd registered motor manufacturers now operating in the country.

"No, *sir*!" he said, with emphasis. "Swann-Maxie remains a private company in our name, although it's officially registered under the title of Swann & Quirt, Scottie owning forty-nine per cent of the stock. From here on we sell ourselves all the transport we need, even if we have to dribble it out piecemeal. That way we not only save money, we modify week by week, using our experiences on the open road as blueprint material. Ten

years from now, five maybe, four-fifths of those manufacturers will be broke and out of business. You recall
what happened at the tail-end of the railway boom,
before you set up in business?"

"I remember very well. There were two hundred bank-
ruptcies in as many weeks but there's no real comparison,
is there? The founding of a railway company called for
heavy investment, mostly for rights of way and a motor can
drive anywhere it pleases on established highways."

"I'm saying the majority of those pioneers are amateurs," said George, and when Adam reminded him that
both he and George had been amateurs in their day he
said sharply, "Not in that sense, Gov'nor. We mapped
our markets in advance. That's more than you can say
of this bunch. Most of 'em are financed by loan sharks,
who make damned sure they skim any profit that emerges.
Half of 'em are working in back street stables, buying their
materials retail from blacksmiths and coach builders, and
all of 'em, without a single exception so far as I know, are
concentrating on the joyride market."

It made sense, as George's pronouncements usually did
on reflection and Adam, who had never stood in awe of anyone during twelve years' soldiering and forty years' trading,
confessed to a certain awe of his son when he gave Henrietta
a summary of the discussion that same night.

"I once thought of him as a chip off the old block," he
said, ruefully, "but I'm well on the way to revising that
opinion. Before he's done the trade will think of him as
the block and me as the chip."

It irritated her to hear him talking like that, even in
praise of his own son, for she could never see him as anything less than an oak among saplings.

"He had two advantages you never had. Almost un-
limited capital, and a father egging him on," she said,
sharply, and was rewarded by a self-satisfied grin on his
face as he reached over her to extinguish the bedside lamp.

"Ah, something in that."

*   *   *

By early summer of that same year he had a. much sharper reminder of the debt George owed him when the new Swann maps appeared in the annual brochure. For there, set out for all to see, was the twentieth-century image of Adam Swann's earliest essay in commercial cartography, reproducing so many features of the original company maps, now framed and exhibited in the Swann museum at The Hermitage. For the revised theme of the network now was re-regionalisation and George, he noted, had even restored some of the first names bestowed upon regions by Adam, in 1858.

He carried the brochure away to his perch on the knoll overlooking the southern boundary of the estate, as intrigued as a lad with a complicated mechanical toy. One by one, superimpositions of the new upon the old emerged as though he was looking at George's fleet of mechanically-propelled vehicles through the legs of a hundred Clydesdales, symbol of all the muscle, blood and bone that had hauled his customers' goods from one end of the country to the other.

For to Adam the familiar tracings of old routes and boundaries of the network were clearly visible under the firmly drawn lines of the new frontiers, dictated not by railways, as in his day, but by the factors that had governed the path of the gridiron in Stephenson's day.

First, Zeus among them, was geology, the innumerable stratas of chalk, greenstone, Lias, Trias, Permian, oolite, basalt and granite that had prescribed the movements and habitats of men in these islands since the beginning of time and still, for all man's new technologies, called the tune and regulated the pace.

Then came temperatures and rainfall, and the use man had made of the land in his nonstop wrestle with the elements, and after that, on the heels of climate, came crops, mineral resources and the new concentrations of electrical and industrial power and population.

It was as though he was looking at a potted history of transportation and in the siting of George's new depots

he could detect pointers to all the problems and frustrations of man's fight against gravity since stones were
dragged across country by weight of muscle for the
erection of cromlechs and the building of pagan temples.
But, once he had absorbed the general message of the map,
he was able to distinguish the domestic patterns that had
emerged and found here food for speculation in the way
George had set about carving up the realm for the con-
venience of Swann and Swann's customers. Some basic
conclusions leaped from the page but there were others,
born of stresses unknown in his day, that he had to search
for.

It was quite clear, for instance, that terrain had
reprieved the horse in many of the areas of the west and
north. In the old Western Wedge, so prolific in humps,
bogs and untamed heathlands, the horse still reigned and
would, he supposed, continue to reign for a long time yet.
Only two depots, Exeter and Truro, fielded a few motor
vehicles designed to operate over short distances and the
same was true of the Mountain Square, with its main
depot shifted from Abergavenny to Cardiff. It would be
a long time, he mused, before Taffy took horseless carriages
for granted, save in the extreme south of the principality
where all its heavy industries were located.

Further north, among the Cumberland and Westmor-
land fells, few if any Swann-Maxies would run, whereas
north of the Tay, horse power, in the old-fashioned sense,
would hold its own, probably until he and George too
were dust in the churchyard down the road.

Yet here and there, in areas that Adam recognised as
a terrible challenge to the newcomer, George had com-
promised, siting branch depots, furnished with teams
transferred from elsewhere to supplement and link Swann
hauls on either side of high or soggy ground.

The Pennine depots were a case in point. At six centres,
both east and west of the Pennine Chain, George had
marked out territory where teams could be summoned at
short notice to bridge a difficult stretch, and when they

were not so employed they would doubtless earn their oats on shorter, local hauls. All down the eastern coast, clear across the old Southern Square, and over the whole of Kent, the motor vehicle predominated, but the Cotswolds, the Northern fells and the Fens were served by emergency depots. Only Ireland, where the pace was slower, was all but denied power-driven vans. Belfast had two and Dublin three. The other ninety-five were shared, unequally, among English and Lowland Scottish shires and the industrialised regions of South Wales. As Adam refolded the pull-out map inside the brochure, he wondered how impressive an ascendancy George enjoyed among those quarrelsome privateers, so jealous of their individual rights and privileges.

2

He was right to ponder the question. Under the reconstruction, George discovered, the managers were not only greedy for vehicles but for territory, and the right to nominate managers of the sub-depots sited within their frontiers. The preparation of the short lists for these, and for the new territories, demanded a deal of thought, private enquiry and tact, and even when they were approved there were mutterings all round.

There were now thirteen areas, eight of them with all but unchanged frontiers and in the main he left the suzerainty of these severely alone.

Bertieboy Bickford still ruled in the west, Young Rookwood in an enlarged Southern Square and Godsall in the old Kentish Triangle, where his influence was undisputed. Similarly Jake Higson, he who had adopted the kilt, was left master of Scotland, and the ageing Dockett, who had at last abandoned his fence-squat, was still in charge of the Isle of Wight, otherwise known as Tom Tiddler's Land. Spectacular gambles, however, had to be taken with new personnel appointed to oversee the new territories and the two biggest of these showed up in The Funnel – a two-hundred-mile wedge tapering north from Southern

Square to the plain of York and the Polygon territory, where the Lancashire cotton and Liverpool shipping industries were paramount.

Casting round for a promising master of these George remembered his brother Edward's contribution to the now historic snail-crawl from Bromsgrove to the naval dockyard at Devonport, and on impulse he took a night train to Cardiff, where he found Edward superintending repairs to a ditched Swann-Maxie that had fouled a gateway a few miles from the depot and had to be towed home by horses. Edward said, emerging from beneath the chassis with a broad smear of oil on his forehead, "I've been thinking of you all morning, George When are you going to set up a driving school, and put these damned mechanics through a running repair test? Pritchard can handle a vehicle well enough but he's got no more idea about what makes it tick than a South Sea Islander."

The remark, and its portentous implications decided George in a decision he had been considering ever since reorganisation.

"That's an idea that's been playing hide and seek in my head ever since we made that run, kid. I'll get about it as soon as I can clear a space on the desk. In the meantime, however, wash your face and join me in a beer for I've a proposition to put to you," and they went across the road to the Prince of Wales' Feathers and ordered two pints from the wood. With Edward one never had to approach a subject deviously. He said, after the first draught, "You've served a long enough apprenticeship in the backwoods, Edward. How do you feel about taking charge of The Funnel?"

The boy pondered, emptying his tankard slowly and all but scowling into it, another trick he had inherited from his Grandfather Sam Rawlinson who invariably frowned on the prospect of a bargain sale, probably because he had a conviction that this might bring the price down.

"That's a big bite, George. It's seventy per cent self-propelled, isn't it?"

"Around that. There are something like twenty teams at auxiliary depots, east of the high ground and Fens."

"Would it mean doing young Wickstead out of the job? It's his beat mostly."

"No, I've got plans for Wickstead. All I'm asking is, do you feel up to it?"

"I could do it."

He was always, George reflected thankfully, a man of a few words but those few were almost invariably to the point. And so it was arranged, and Edward, at twenty-seven, found himself responsible for as much territory as veterans like Markby and Rookwood. It was an impressive step up the ladder and meant promotion for others, too. George took his brother's advice and put Bryn Lovell's two half-caste stepsons, Enoch and Shad, in joint charge of the Mountain Square. Both were native Welsh, with Welsh prejudices and fluent command of the Welsh language. They seemed to be the logical choice, for each had acquitted himself well as a sub-depot manager.

He took a somewhat similar gamble with less confidence on the eldest Wickstead boy, who had all but succeeded his father in Crescent South and Centre, for Tom Wickstead was ailing now and Edith insisted that he conserved his energy. This territory, largely flat, composed of the Eastern Region and the old river lands that Adam called The Bonus had been incorporated in The Funnel. But a large new region had now been created to the west under the title West Midlands. Luke Wickstead, son of 'Edith-Wadsworth-that-was' (some of the old hands still regarded her as the Old Gaffer's ex-mistress) had shown an aptitude for motor transport. Out here, where a score of Swann-Maxies served the engineering plants of Birmingham and the Potteries, George reflected that he would have plenty of scope to prove himself.

He found room, in the reorganised network, to advance his own family. Max and Rudi, his two elder sons were promoted from sub-managerial posts to work under the general supervision of Scottie Quirt in The Polygon, now including the hilly region, The Chain, to the east. Rudi as general manager with the promise of eventual succession and Max, the more mechanically minded of the two as improver in the motor plant at Macclesfield. Gisela was delighted, although her maternal pride in the boys prohibited any overt display of pleasure.

"Your grandfather would have approved wholeheartedly of what's happening clear across the board," George said to her, chuckling and then, recalling, as he tended to do these days, the many hours they had spent tinkering with that cumbersome ancestor of the Swann fleet. "That was the beginning of it all, Gisela – you and me, the Swann-Maxie, the whole box of tricks, and it doesn't seem all that time ago. Do you remember jumping out of that tree during a game of hide-and-seek on Lobau, when I was skylarking with your sisters?"

"Why should I forget? It was the first time you acknowledged me as a woman."

It wasn't strictly true, of course. His real awareness of her came a little later, when that crafty old Austrian grandfather of hers had despatched her to his room early one morning, in the fervent hope that he would seduce her and marry her in preference to one of her pretty sisters. The plot, if it really was a plot, had succeeded and they were married within weeks. He would give something, he reflected, to resurrect old Max and discover how much reluctance he had to overcome on Gisela's part for that little piece of stagecraft but it was not the kind of thing he cared to discuss with her even after this lapse of time.

The mere memory, however, quickened his appreciation of her that same night, when the house was quiet and he lay in bed watching her prepare for bed, noting her singular neatness and precision in her every movement, in the way she folded her petticoats, brushed her long, chestnut hair and gravely contemplated the clean nightgown she took from a drawer. The gentle fragrance of lavender reached him as she slipped it over her head and switched off the light, for George, alone among the Swanns, had installed domestic electricity the moment it became available. He thought, as his arms went round her, 'By God, I had my head screwed on when I married a Continental! How many English women would have buried the past, the way she buried Barbara Lockerbie? That nonsense is eight years behind us now and she's never once hinted at it,' and if Gisela Swann wondered at the display of spirits in the way he handled her, or the genuine affection inherent in his long, contented sigh when, cradled in her arms, he dropped off to sleep, she made no reference to it. She was a very placid woman, with a rare disposition to come to terms with fate but perhaps her mildness stemmed, in the main, from what she recognised as her extreme good fortune. After all, she had exchanged the dullness and obscurity of village life in her homeland, for partnership with a demigod. It was no wonder, therefore, that she enjoyed a happy relationship with her mother-in-law, Henrietta. Adam would have said that in this respect, if in no other, they were as alike as two peas.

*   *   *

There were still one or two stray ends to be tidied up before the Swann facelift was complete, by the spring of 1906. Someone had to be found to oversee The Link, a long, narrow strip of territory connecting the Western Wedge with the Southern Square, The Funnel and the West Midlands, an appointment that would call for tact and flexibility, inasmuch as its next-door neighbours included two new boys, Edward and Young Wickstead, and the proud, touchy Rookwood, who would be inclined, George thought, to bully inexperienced younger men operating on his borders.

He finally settled on Coreless, the energetic middle-aged Northerner, who had voted with him when a majority had opposed him, and when Coreless called in at Headquarters on his way to take up his post at the new Gloucester depot he said, "Word in your ear, Coreless. Keep a fatherly eye on my kid brother, Edward, and Young Wickstead. You're round about my age, aren't you?" When Coreless admitted to forty-four he added, "Just so. I'm forty-two. Old enough to enjoy playing Father Christmas to youngsters like Edward and Wickstead but young enough to remember that at their age I thought I knew all the answers. They might need guidance from time to time. Give it to them if they ask. Otherwise let 'em make their own mistakes and learn from them, for I'd sooner them lean on you than on Rookwood.'

"Rookwood's a top-class man, isn't he, Mr. Swann?"

"Aye, he is, but he knows it, and is inclined to patronise. Even me if I give him half-a-chance. It's often that way with those who came up from the bottom rung, as he did."

Coreless nodded and the nod told George that he understood him completely. Close co-operation was vital to all of them.

'I picked the right chap there,' he mused, as Coreless's hobnailed boots clattered on the tower stairway. 'Maybe I'm developing the Old Man's knack of deputising, and it's time I did . . . for years now I've been disinclined to trust anyone even to lick my stamps,' and he turned to his two remaining problems, recruitment for trainees in the Swann-Maxie depot at Macclesfield, and the more pressing decision concerning the power structure of regional depots, with three disparate sources of income – routine haulage, house-removals and the ever-expanding demand for hired vehicles for holiday excursions known, in the network, as 'The Beano Trade'.

In consultation with Edward he had a half-approved solution for the first problem, so he spent a day concentrating on the latter, weighing the pros and cons of separating the three streams and putting them in charge of individual stewards or leaving one man to co-ordinate all three, as in the old days. He finally chose the latter course and when he explained his reasons to Adam the Old Gaffer approved.

"Never saw a battle won by three generals," Adam said. "Specialists are all very well but a specialist sub-ordinate, aware that the boss is wholly dependent on him, is inclined to get uppity and you can see where that could lead when it comes to priorities. Let one man run the whole circus. He's the only chap qualified to decide whether the acrobats, the lion-tamer or trick cyclists go to the top of the bill. I never did trust that breakdown system you tried after you took over. It looks well enough on paper but it had a fatal defect." And when George enquired what that defect was he said, with a grin, "It puts too much power in the hands of Headquarters who like to play one man off against another. Saw it happening but I wasn't the one to point it out. It's your show now, yours and Edward's and all those downy-whiskered colts you're pushing forward."

He said nothing to his father or to Henrietta regarding a plan he had to offer jobs to two of the Fawcett boys, having a premonition that it might stir up trouble over at Dewponds. He meant to take the risk, however. There was no harm in presenting his nephews with a unique opportunity, and at the same time enlarging the family's hold on the firm for there was no knowing how long he could carry a clear majority with the board. The vice-roys had mutinied once. Under the stress of a crisis, or a series of crises, they might do so again.

He walked the two miles separating 'Tryst' and his sister's farm one blithe May morning, when the Weald looked its best in late spring finery and even George, not one to appreciate pastoral pleasures that would have gladdened the hearts of his brother Giles, or his youngest sister Margaret, could not fail to benefit from the bene-diction of his surroundings.

The belt of woodland to the north-east of 'Tryst' was in full leaf after a long spell of mild weather. Larks sang over the paddocks and every hedgerow sported its galaxy of wildflowers, few of which George could have named. It did occur to him, however, to wonder whether boys born and raised in these surroundings would take kindly to working eight hours a day in a northcountry machine-shed, with its incessant clatter and reek of oil and tortured metal. He thought, 'My intentions are good enough but I daresay all I'll get in return is the length of Stella's tongue,' and he was not so far wrong.

Encountering his sister in the farmyard, where she was superintending the replacement of a worn-out windlass, he noticed the entire absence of sisterly warmth in her greeting. She said, impatiently, "You, George? Wait on a minute, I must see to this first. We can't do without well-water. The pond is dry after so long without rain," and he stood by, watching her with amusement as she berated two farmhands who were making slow and clumsy work with the fitting.

The abrupt transition in the character of Stella since her second marriage, that had taken place when he was still at school, had always intrigued George. Indeed, he found it difficult to equate the two Stellas for, unlike the younger Swanns, he could remember her as a seventeen-year-old county belle, riding with haughty glance to the local meets, where every buck in the field was a would-be suitor. He recalled her mincing ways and her sharp outbursts of temper when things were not to her liking, and had not been much surprised by her marriage to Lester Moncton-Price when she was eighteen. What had startled him more than somewhat was the dramatic change that the foundered marriage had wrought in her and how, within weeks of taking up with young Denzil Fawcett, and helping him rebuild his farm after the fire in which his father was killed, she had adapted to the life. Just as his own viceroys in the regions found no difficulty in switching their allegiance from horse to motor, so Stella had shed all the trappings of a fashionable woman overnight and become a particularly homespun housewife, happy, it seemed, to work a fourteen-hour stint for a reward that one of his junior managers would have regarded as inadequate. She had changed physically too, putting on at least three stones in weight, and getting her once delicate skin gypsy brown in sun and wind. Her voice, pitched low and rather sweet in her childhood, had taken on a sharp, nagging note, and her exchanges with Denzil and the local farming community had introduced into it traces of a Kentish burr.

He was aware that his mother and old Alex (Alex would not have acknowledged her as a sister at this particular moment) had been bothered by the change but Henrietta had adjusted to it over the years and Adam, in his wisdom, let well alone. George knew that his own wife, Gisela, was fond of her sister-in-law but that was predictable. Gisela, too, at heart, still reckoned herself a peasant. What George did not know, and told himself now that he was unlikely to find out, were the underlying factors that had contributed to the change and now, watching her, he pondered them yet again, so deeply indeed that he hardly noticed when his sister was done with her supervision and saying, briefly, "Come into the kitchen then. I can give you a mug of cider if you care for one," and he followed her meekly, entering the big stone room where, summer and winter, a green log smouldered in a fireplace wide enough to roast the traditional ox.

She said, drawing him home-brewed cider from a cask, "Is it a message from mother?" He said no, he had a proposition to put to her and Denzil concerning the boys. "The two middle ones," he added, hastily. "Martin and John." They were no longer boys, he reflected, Martin being twenty-three by his reckoning, and John less than two years his junior, but everyone seemed like a boy in his sister's presence; even Denzil, her husband, who was about forty-six.

"What about my boys?"

"I've been wondering . . . this isn't a very large farm, and a good deal of your acreage is rough pasture. Robert, your eldest, will take over eventually, I imagine. It seemed to me that you might like to place them."

Stella looked very surprised and then equally

disapproving, squaring up to him, both freckled arms on heavy hips. "*Place* them? How do you mean, *place* them? They have a place, haven't they? Right here, working for us."

George said, patiently, "I know that, Stella. I've seen them about in the fields but four sons, on a farm this size, it doesn't seem very practical. I'm no farmer, of course, but everybody knows agriculture is in the doldrums. You can buy farms two a penny in some counties since they began bringing in all these refrigerated Australian and New Zealand products, and buying up millions of bushels of wheat from Canada. Ask Denzil if you don't believe me."

She continued to eye him, with vague hostility. "I didn't say I didn't believe you. But you haven't seen me over at 'Tryst' seeking charity, have you?"

"Damn it," he said, half in mind to tell her and her sons to go to the devil, "I'm not here offering charity! You've got a claim on Grandfather Sam's money, the same as the rest of us, and it's no secret that the Gov'nor makes you an allowance. I'm not talking about money but careers for the younger boys. If you don't care what becomes of them ten years from now then say so."

Denzil Fawcett clumped into the kitchen, nodding briefly in George's direction. George had a swift recollection of Denzil as a youth, walking with long strides and head held high, through a rainstorm to one of his father's pastures east of 'Tryst'. He now looked like a man in his late fifties, with slumped shoulders and grey, balding head. Farming aged a man, George thought and it encouraged him to press on. He said, "I'm here to offer apprenticeships to two of your boys, Denzil. They could learn the motor trade up north and get in on the ground floor. Stella doesn't seem taken with the idea. How about you?"

Denzil glanced at his wife and in that glance, George thought, was the story of their marriage. Lifelong incredulity on Denzil's part, that he had brought home a prize like Stella from the grand house over the hill, complete renunciation of her past on Stella's part, who must, he reasoned, have suffered dismally at the hands of the Moncton-Prices.

"You'm hard agin it, m'dear?"

"Aren't you? The boys' place is here, with their family and acres. Helping you as you get older and slower."

"Arr," he said, thoughtfully, "that's so," but then, to George, "The motor trade? Will that ever amount to anything, George?"

"Good God, of course it will! It'll practically take over ten years from now In your trade as well as in mine. Why else would I have invested a hundred thousand pounds in lorries? It's not a passing fad, man! Why the devil can't everybody see that by now? I had the same job convincing my managers but it hasn't taken them long to decide I was right."

"A 'prenticeship," he said, thoughtfully. "You'd mean, I take it, to learn the trade. But how about after? I mean, who would be likely to employ 'em in that sort of work?"

"I would, if they showed an aptitude. I'm training drivers and mechanics. We'd teach them all we know. After that it would be up to them. My guess is your boy Martin would take to it like a duck to water. I remember how he used to come over to 'Tryst' when I was working on the old Maximus and watch the wheels go round. It was remembering that that made me think of them."

There was a heavy silence in the room. The sap in the green log in the grate hissed an accompaniment to the ticking of the grandfather clock. Stella still had her upper lip clamped over the lower but Denzil, judging by the furrows on his forehead, was thinking hard.

"Would they get paid for larning?"

"Not much. They'd get board and lodging, guaranteed by the firm. And ten shillings a week for pocket money."

"And afterwards? When they knew what they was about?"

"A driver mechanic in the network earns fifty shillings a week, plus overtime. He can soon double that, however, providing he's up to his work. We're expanding all the time. I hope to have two hundred vehicles on the road within two years."

"It's still wrong! Wrong and unnatural!"

This from Stella, red in the face now, and having some difficulty in restraining herself, but Denzil looked at her mildly. "Maybe so, maybe not. You say what you think any road."

"I've told you what I think. Time enough, whether or not things pick up here, as they may and should, we won't be able to keep Ben Gaskell on as a hired hand. And old Trescoe is about finished, what with his rheumatism. What'll we do then, with none but you and Robert and young Richard to farm four hundred acres?"

He said, without looking at her, "That's not the point, m'dear. I don't offen run counter to you, do I? But there's some sense in what George says, for things coulden be worse for farmers. How can we compete with all this foreign muck they're dumping on us every day o' the week? As long as there's Free Trade it'll get worse instead o' better. Maybe we owe it to the boys and I reckon I'd like to sleep on it."

"And talk it over with them if I were you," George said, although something in him responded to the despair in the man's voice and manner. It must be hard, he thought, to see a traditional way of life foundering month by month, with markets shrinking and roots, hard down in the land for a thousand years or more, wrenched up by technologies that, to a man of Fawcett's disposition, must seem as alien as Black Magic. Maybe an answer lay in the adaptation of farms and farmers to the mechanical age, with purpose-built vehicles taking the place of their clumsy ploughs and lumbering, boat-shaped waggons. But this was years ahead, and men who had worked the land with their hands all their lives would be slow to adjust to such a revolution, even slower than would a transport man like Bertieboy Bickford in the far west.

He rose, draining and setting down his cider mug.

"Think it over, both of you. The offer is there. All you have to do is to tell me yes or no," and he went out across the yard, scattering hens who were scavenging there.

Denzil and Stella sat on, silent for above two minutes before Denzil rose and crossed the kitchen, laying his gnarled hand on his wife's shoulder.

"We can't stand in their way," he said. "It woulden be right. Neither of 'em could ever wed on what I pay 'em, and I know how I would ha' felt about that wi' you in mind. They'm both courtin', baint they?"

"Farm girls," Stella said. "Girls reared on good farms over in Lee Valley, but . . ."

"There's no 'buts' about it then. We'll have to let 'em go if they've a mind to go."

He went over to the open window and called Ben Gaskell, still wrestling with the windlass. "Leave that, Ben. Find Martin and John, and zend 'em to me and mother. And tell 'em to look sharp about it, I've something to zay to 'em!"

He went back to where Stella sat by the smouldering fire and stood before her. They had ridden out a number of crises over the years, resolving each as partners in accord, but here, for the first time since they had rebuilt the farm together, was something he had to face alone, shouldering her prejudices to one side, and deep in her heart she understood his motives. They would never fail utterly, and sell up as some of their neighbours had done since the agricultural slump set in like a blight. She had savings of her own and access, as George had reminded her, to capital, but this was irrelevant. In their twenty-five years of marriage he had never once sought help of this kind from her or her family, and she had never offered it, realising that his countryman's pride was as precious to him as the house they occupied and the acres he and his ancestors had farmed for more than four centuries. She took his hand and pressed it to her cheek, holding it there until she heard the scrape of her sons' boots in the yard.

2

Swann Whirligig — 1905/6

ADAM SWANN, IN A WHIMSICAL MOOD, HAD ONCE
likened his family's march down the decades as a tribal
migration, headed for the uplands. More objective observers, and there were many about the city and the big
provincial centres, where money and goods changed hands
in volume, saw it rather as a spring gushing from the old fox's
enterprise in the 'fifties, and building rapidly to a broad,
swift-flowing river in its progress towards a collective
destiny. Or perhaps as a tide, beating on a coastline where,
ultimately and given luck, it could change the map.

For the Swanns, confound them, seemed destined to
advance on a singularly broad front, and before the new
century had got its second wind around the fall of the year
1905, they were recognised as a power in the land. Not
only in the field of transport (almost from the beginning
they had offered a formidable challenge here) but in
areas where rival trading clans sought no advancement,
that of older, more staid professions, like the armed services and administrative spheres, and even out on the
periphery of the national scene, where the vanguards of
social reform ranging far ahead of the national conscience,
now emerged triumphant at the polls.

As in the flow of all tides and rivers there were stretches
down the years when the thrust of the current lost impetus,
spending itself in puny forays mounted by individuals,
often at odds with one another. Such a period had been

Adam Swann's recession in the early 'sixties, when he and his concerns came close to foundering. Or when, in 1865, he was out of action for a year after the Staplehurst rail disaster. But soon a sportive fate would take a hand in affairs, presenting some challenge that taxed the wits and the stamina of the tribe to the utmost. This had happened, after a long, smooth ride, in 1897, when George Swann wandered off course and the hub of the empire went up in smoke, leaving its spokes in disarray.

But the Swanns, it seemed, were seasoned survivors and these occasional setbacks put them on their mettle so that very soon, in no time at all it appeared to observers, they were in the forefront of the battle again, having used the check to marshal their reserves, mount a series of new attacks in unexpected sectors and push forward as a unit on several fronts.

Then competitors in all their chosen fields acknowledged their merits, numbering among them resilience, original thinking and, above all, the obstinacy of the British squares at Waterloo.

The period immediately following George's display of what mechanically-propelled vehicles could achieve when handled imaginatively, was high noon for the family. Some of George's will to succeed had been siphoned off and distributed among other members of the clan and retainers. Thus 1905 was a time of triumph in a variety of sectors, beginning with the appearance on British roads of over a hundred power-operated vehicles, the very first of their kind, and ending, in December of that same year, with the arrival of Giles Swann at Westminster, as the member for Pontnewydd. But between these two triumphs were a number of smaller victories that could have been grouped under the heading of Domestic Retrenchment.

*   *   *

The first of these modest victories occurred in the early spring of the year and its Boadicea, so to speak, was Helen

Coles, *née* Swann, widow of a decapitated missionary and unsung heroine of the Peking Siege.

It assumed the form, in the eyes of Joanna, her sister and sponsor, of an enchantment for nothing less, in her view, could have accomplished such an unlooked for event. It was as though the malign agency that had reduced Helen to such dependence on her sister when haunted by nightmares of one kind or another, had suddenly relented; or, more probably, been sent packing by a sentimental genie with a sense of humour. For Helen Coles, the pale, brooding widow of a year or so ago succeeded, against well-nigh impossible odds, in capturing Dublin's most eligible bachelor.

Joanna was never quite sure how it came about or why Rory Clarke, most turbulent of the Dublin fillibusters in Westminster, should have been bewitched by a woman five years his senior, when he might have taken his pick of the Dublin belles, most of them pretty, a few of them both pretty and handsomely dowered.

Rory, younger son of Tim Clarke, the vintner Joanna had enlisted as a Swann regular, was a dashing, slightly Byronic man for whom a brilliant political future was forecast, and the two were introduced to one another at one of Clarke père's soirées. Their conversation, on that occasion, was confined to the exploitation in South Africa of Chinese coolies, imported as a source of cheap labour; not, one would have thought, a very promising springboard for a romance. It happened, however, that circumstances favoured the encounter. Rory was in search of a new stick to belabour the British Government, and Helen Coles was the only woman in Dublin with first-hand knowledge of Chinese affairs, so that no other woman present could compete for his attention.

The very next day Rory sent his card round to Joanna's, together with an invitation for a carriage drive the following Sunday. Predictably Joanna was included in the invitation. Equally predictably, somehow scenting a miracle, she persuaded Helen to go unaccompanied.

From that point on progress was spectacular. Something in Helen's new-found stillness (and possibly her aura of tragedy) made a direct appeal to Rory Clarke's Celtic imagination. Bouquets and invitations began to arrive at the house almost daily and soon Dublin was scouting the possibility that Rory Clarke (the new Parnell some were already calling him) had succumbed to the charms of a thirty-four-year-old Englishwoman, who had been romantically involved in a welter of bloodletting on the other side of the world.

At first the neglected matrons and young eligibles of the Irish capital viewed the prospect of a romance with dismay, reflecting that an Irish champion had no business gallivanting with the English, but then certain unseen pressures began to be applied. First by Rory's soldier brother, who had no patience with the quarrel between the Irish and Dublin Castle, then by old Tim himself, who had taken the trouble to inform himself of Helen Coles two likely sources of income, her father and her father-in-law, the famous pill manufacturer. He also discovered, as a kind of bonus, that Helen, on remarriage, would have access to a trust fund from her maternal grandfather's fortune, derived from cotton and the Suez Canal shares.

Yet these were not deciding factors in Dublin's ultimate approval of Helen as the bride-in-waiting of her most promising son. These had their roots in the Irish sporting instinct, for who could fail to respond to the run-up of such an unlikely outsider, who had somehow contrived to lead the field in the Clarke matrimonial stakes?

And then, for Joanna, came a miracle within a miracle. Under the sun of Rory Clarke's tempestuous courtship Helen not only revived but reflowered, recapturing some of the sparkling good looks and high spirits of her youth at 'Tryst', to which was added a maturity and dignity that won approving nods from the senior section of society. Her appearance, in Joanna's view, changed almost overnight. When she had gone to her that night and assessed the damage caused by her marriage and dismal experiences abroad, she had been sallow, hollow-cheeked and listless in movement and manner. She had never been as pretty as Joanna but she had large and expressive grey eyes, a good complexion and, in those days, a trim, athletic figure, moulded by her youthful passion for lawn tennis and cycling. But her best feature had always been her hair, dark brown and thick but very soft in texture.

These starting-out advantages had been sacrificed by her years in the tropics. Hardly a trace of her original sparkle remained when Joanna talked her into a therapeutic frolic with the tipsy Jack-o'-Lantern, and when that sparkle returned in full measure Joanna reasoned that the change could never have been accomplished by a few sweaty moments in Clinton's embrace. Indeed, no appreciable change was apparent in the interval between that occasion and her first meeting with Rory, and yet, little by little, it became apparent that something had been achieved after all, for when they returned to Dublin Joanna noticed that Helen's apathy had changed to a kind of stillness, while privately her sister admitted that her recurrent nightmare had ceased and she was now sleeping and eating normally.

The knowledge made the goodhearted Joanna glad, despite a lingering doubt that Clinton had not been hoodwinked, for she sometimes caught him looking across the table at his sister-in-law with a vaguely puzzled expression, as though there was something about her that eluded him. It would, please God, continue to elude him. Men, Joanna was aware, often joked in their coarse way about all women being identical in the dark but perhaps they deceived themselves in this respect. Perhaps something, smothered under those fumes of alcohol, some awareness of physical unfamiliarity in the woman he had held in his arms so briefly, remained in the morning, when he awakened to find his wife beside him and in an unusually thoughtful mood. If it was so she did not let it bother her overmuch, or not after the forthcoming wedding of

Rory Clarke, M.P. and Mrs. Helen Coles was announced in the Dublin and London papers. One way or another her sister-comrade had been restored to her, whole and healed, and Joanna was never one to quarrel with luck.

2

Adam received the news that his daughter was to take a second husband with reservations. He knew all about the Irish fillibusters at Westminster and was scornful of their tactics. It gave him no confidence that, when, as he predicted, they gained their precious Home Rule, they would govern themselves any better than they had been governed by the British, but he was glad that Henrietta welcomed the match, realising that she had never really ceased worrying about Helen since hearing that story about the girl shooting a man in cold blood and exulting in the deed. She said, "It's positively the best thing that could have happened, Adam, and it doesn't matter a dropped stitch if Clarke is the firebrand you say he is. The fact is she'll be settled again and it's not too late for her to hope for a child to take her mind off her troubles."

That, he reflected with a chuckle, had always been Hetty's way with difficulties of any kind as far as her daughters were concerned. Children represented continuity, and continuity to Henrietta Swann, daughter of a pushing mill-hand and a penniless Irish immigrant, was paramount. Also, he supposed, with another chuckle, the act of begetting them, for no woman in this self-righteous day and age, could have approached that with more enthusiasm. He contented himself with replying: "Well, they're an enterprising bunch, I must say, when it comes to choosing partners. Just tally up our in-laws and try and find the common denominator. We've got a farmhand, a general's daughter, an Austrian peasant, a millionaire's daughter, the son of a pill manufacturer and that social lioness who gobbled up old Hugo. Now,

39

to add variety, Helen is giving us a ringside seat at Donnybrook Fair. And we've still got young Edward and Margaret in reserve. What's brewing in that direction, I wonder?"

He was not to wonder long. News came via Giles that same season that Margaret, postscript of the tribe (conceived, he recalled, the night they buried the old Colonel, in 1879) had found a cogent reason for prolonging her stay in the Welsh valley and would almost surely, or so Giles predicted, marry a Welshman, "Without," as he described it, "two halfpence to rub together."

*   *

Her youngest daughter's shy but prolonged renunciation of the social scene, her seeming inability to make an impact on any one of the eligible young males her brothers had introduced into the house over the years, had been a source of concern to Henrietta for a long time. She reasoned that Margaret, at twenty-five, was in a fair way to becoming an old maid, totally absorbed in what Henrietta thought of as time-wasting pursuits, of the kind once recommended to young girls to keep them out of mischief until a suitor came knocking at the door. And this, in her view, was quite unnecessary, for Margaret had claims to be considered the prettiest (she was certainly the most feminine) of all the Swann girls. She had the kind of face that would retain its youthfulness into middle-age, perhaps even later, a delicate pink and white complexion, despite hours spent outdoors in all weathers, a gentleness of disposition that none of the other Swanns, male or female, possessed, a low, pleasing voice, an equable temper, a quick, shy smile and a trim figure, all of which, in her mother's experience, were qualities young men sought when they came looking for a wife. She had, in addition, two characteristics that were even rarer in girls, especially pretty girls: intelligence and the good sense to conceal it, for it was Henrietta's experience that young men were frightened off by signs of intelligence in a woman, indicating, as it usually did, that they were bad listeners. And yet, as the years passed, nobody came asking and, what was worse, Margaret showed no disposition whatever to worry about her lack of suitors. She was quite content, it seemed, to enjoy her endless love affair with nature, to woo and be wooed by spring landscapes, cloud movements over the Weald, the song of the wind in the larch coppices bordering 'Tryst' to the north, or the older woods that crowned the spur behind the house. She had a predisposition to wear clothes until they all but disintegrated under the tug of briars and hedgerow and her shapely hands (hands that her sisters envied) were usually stained with paint when she answered the lunch bell summons.

Adam, and Deborah, maintained that Margaret had a rare talent for painting pastoral scenes but Henrietta, whose ideals in painting were battle scenes, reproduced in the *Strand Magazine*, was not equipped to evaluate her daughter's artistic potential, for this she would have said had nothing to do with the three essentials in a young woman's life – finding a husband, founding a family and keeping both contented.

It was her doubts concerning Margaret's future, indeed, that encouraged Henrietta to persuade Margaret to accept Romayne's invitation to pay a visit to South Wales and lend a hand with the children. Romayne, who had recently miscarried another child, was in poor health at a time when Giles was fully stretched preparing for the forthcoming General Election.

Henrietta reasoned, no doubt, that Giles, centrepiece of a political arena, would be acquainted with any number of bachelors and perhaps, who knew, a comfortably-off young widower or two. He was, moreover, a kindhearted boy, who would surely do his best to promote any promising friendship, so that she was all agog when Giles wrote in the autumn of 1905 that he was visiting 'Tryst' during a dash to London, 'and would pass on some intriguing news concerning Margaret's debut in the valleys'.

Henrietta could place but one interpretation on this and when he appeared she whisked him into her sewing-room before Adam could bombard the boy with political queries. She said, closing the door and leaning against it, "Tell, then. Tell! That bit about Margaret? Does it mean what I hope it means?"

Giles smiled as he peeled off his overcoat. The relationship between him and his mother was unique in the family. She had always stood in awe of him, even as a child. He was so scholarly, so dangerously knowledgeable about life and people, holding a kind of balance between the clamourings of eight sisters and brothers, a tolerant referee no one cared to dispute. In some ways he seemed even older and wiser than Adam who often, Henrietta had noticed, deferred to him. Giles, for his part, saw his mother in the light of an amiable and impulsive elder sister, but there were aspects of her that he admired, notably her courage and resilience. He said, kissing her, "Oh, it's nothing sensational. Only that she seems to have taken a fancy to one of my party workers. A splendid young chap called Huw Griffiths. They go everywhere together and a day or so ago the poor chap came to me quite lost for words, very unusual for Huw. It seems he thought he should ask my permission to propose."

"Good gracious! And you don't regard *that* as sensational! With Margaret twenty-six next December? What did you say to him?"

"What could I say? I told him it was up to her, to both of them. As you say, she's surely old enough to know her own mind. If she had been younger I should have shuttled him to father. As it was I advised him to throw his hat in the ring."

"But what kind of man *is* he, for heaven's sake? I mean, how old and how eligible? And what does he *do*? Surely even you realise these things are important to us?"

"To you, I daresay. Not to Margaret. She's in love, I think, not only with Huw but with his valleys and the people who live in them. She's even taken to painting pithead scenes and they're very good to my mind, full of truth and humour . . ."

"Oh, *fiddlesticks* to what she's painting!" Henrietta exclaimed, impatiently, "tell me about this man Griffiths. You said 'a splendid young chap'. Splendid in what way?"

"Well, as a party worker for one thing. He's an excellent off-the-cuff speaker and a good organiser . . ."

"Do you mean he's a member of Parliament?"

"Member of P . . . ? Old Huw? Lord, no, nothing like that. He's a miner. About Margaret's age."

"A . . . a . . . miner? A coal-miner?"

"Yes. A big, strapping chap, with hair as black as the coal he digs and a tribe of younger brothers who worship him. They all live in a cottage and look after their mother and one little sister. His father is dead, you see — silicosis, poor devil."

"What would he earn?"

"Oh, about thirty shillings a week, but he isn't likely to stay down the pit. He attends evening classes when he's on day shift and sooner or later he'll get a job on top. I might even persuade him to leave the pits altogether and become my agent. Old Bryn Lovell is getting past it and we're looking for a younger man. If he and Margaret did marry I daresay he'd be tempted. We've got a good organisation and could pay a full-time agent three pounds a week."

The shattering unworldliness of the boy checked her outcry. His values were so alien to her, and no more welcome for being so innocently stated. Looking back over the past she realised that this had always been so with Giles, strangest and most complex of the brood, a boy who, she recalled, always seemed to her to inhabit a different planet from her and the rest of them and even, to an extent, from Adam, the wisest man on earth. And yet, in this kind of situation, there was no place for other-worldliness. She said, gulping down her disappointment, "Margaret can't be serious. You just don't understand these things, Giles. She's probably bored down there and just . . . well, flirting a little. I suppose even that is encouraging in a way, for it's never happened before. But I do think it's time she came back, before she gives that young man silly ideas. You tell her from me I want her home, do you hear? And now here's your father, and you'll be talking politics nineteen to the dozen until luncheon. I'll go and see to it now," and she withdrew into the hall before he could reply, calling to Adam, who was pulling off his gardening boots in the porch, "Giles is here. He hasn't long, he says."

That was the way of Henrietta, faced with unpalatable facts or even trends. She had a trick of reversing them, of picking the meat from the bone of some grisly-looking morsel and persuading herself that it must be good for something, although she wasn't sure what and would have to think about it. If Margaret had taken up with a miner of her own age it must mean that she was becoming aware of herself as a woman and that was hopeful, for it meant that with her daughter safely restored to her own circle, she could begin looking about for a real husband before the girl became restless and out of sorts, as was the way of unwed and uncourted females once they reached their mid-twenties. After lunch she would give her mind to the matter.

*   *   *

Margaret Swann's renunciation of her former lover, the soft, unchanging Kentish countryside, had occurred within a week of setting foot in the mining valleys. She did not understand what agency brought about such a betrayal, only that some gaunt, looming stranger, brooding but infinitely persuasive, rose out of the mountain under her feet and tugged at her sleeve buttons, bidding her look, ponder and absorb. For here was something unique in her experience and far more soul-stirring than any pastoral scene, with its eternal half-tones of green, brown and gold, its regulated light and the plodding figures seen about its fields and coppices.

Here, her accoster insisted, was vitality, adventure, challenge and an ugliness capable of crippling the spirit if you let it. But you didn't, seeing it for what it was, a stark setting for comradeship, laughter and compassion among all the teeming families inhabiting the terraces that seamed the steep slopes of Pontnewydd bowl. Here was greed, certainly, and probably all the other deadly sins, but they were on the defensive, despite occupation of the landscape reaching up to the rain-heavy sky behind the town. Within this arena, a cheerful, beleaguered garrison manning a battered citadel, were people, a multitude of Joneses, Evanses, Pritchards, Powells, Howells, Morgans, Reeces and Owens. And, of course, Griffiths, like the Griffiths of 107, Bethel Street, where the branch of the tribe lived.

It all began, in fact, within a stone's-throw of the open end of Bethel Street, where it joined the track leading out of the town to the fold in the hill where Giles and Romayne had their stone-built house. Not half-a-mile from the pit that provided some kind of justification for all this clutter, clinging to the side of the hill. Climbing up from the cluster of little shops on the floor of the valley she could just see the winding gear crowning the summit, with its huddle of sheds and sidings and its single rail track that reflected the last rays of the afternoon sun, playing catch-as-catch-can with the clouds.

Huw Griffiths was coming off shift with about a dozen other miners who lived in Bethel Street and she recognised him at once as the impressive young man who had attended last Tuesday's committee meeting in Giles' parlour. He was, she would judge, an inch over six foot and his shoulder span, for a man with such a slender waist, was impressive, but it was not his undoubted masculinity

45

that had imprinted him on her mind but his smile, that was ready and very winning but, at the same time, slightly tremulous, the smile of a child who wasn't sure if he would win some permission he sought, or excuse some fault for which he was about to be blamed. For Huw Griffiths, a man in his mid-twenties she would say, looked no more than thirteen when he smiled and he was smiling now, having seen recognition in her glance across the width of the narrow road. He crossed over to her, his great, clodhopping boots striking harshly on the rocky surface of the track and lifting a filthy hand to an almost equally grimed forehead, said: "It *is* Miss Swann, isn't it, now? I'm Huw Griffiths, the candidate's senior steward. You opened the door to me Tuesday's meeting, Miss."

"I remember you very well, Mr. Griffiths."

Although reckoned shy by Henrietta and others who did not know her well, Margaret Swann was never embarrassed by strangers. Men, young and old, had been coming and going all her life at 'Tryst' and she noted them all, for her eyes were trained to record tiny details and idiosyncrasies about people as well as those of petals, leaf patterns and sun-shadows on gorse and bracken. Besides, there could be nothing to fear from a man with such a childlike smile and she smiled back as he went on, seemingly encouraged, "Might I ask a favour, Miss? I've some draft leaflets, you see – for the candidate, they are. Promised for tonight but there's an evening class, see, and I've scrub-up and tea ahead of me. Our place is only a step and if you'd be so kind . . ."

"I'll take them, certainly, Mr. Griffiths," and she fell into step with him, lengthening her stride over the uneven surface of the road and saying, for something to say, "What exactly *is* senior steward, Mr. Griffiths?" and his smile widened. At the corners of his mouth tiny furrows overlaid with coal-dust seemed to wink large black stars on a white ground. The smile fascinated her so much that she hardly heard his small joke in reply.

"Just a handle. To make a man feel someone, you'd

say, Miss Swann. The candidate's like that, you see . . ."
He referred to Giles as though he was a stranger to her,
"he likes to haf everybody in there with a part to play.
Not just himself, like all the others."

"What others?"

"Oh, the party bigwigs, those who come yer to speak,
you know."

"But what do you do, Mr. Griffiths? Write leaflets to
put through doors?"

"Ah, no, I only copy them. It's practice, you see, for
I'm not much at writing yet. But I can talk when I've a
mind to." He expanded then deflated himself with
another smile. "All I do is go on ahead to meetings and
put out the chairs. Stand by for hecklers too, but the
candidate isn't one for clearing the hall, not unless things
get too rough, mind. Any old job handy, I reckon, that
would cover it. Here's our place, Miss," and he stopped in
front of one of the redbrick dolls' houses, identical in almost
every detail with all its neighbours, save that its knocker
gleamed as though it had just had its daily polish.

"I'll get the leaflets . . ." but then, hesitating, "Won't
you step inside, Miss? It wouldn't do to leave the candidate's sister on the doorstep."

She moved in ahead of him, into a narrow strip of
passage formed by planks partitioning off the parlour,
then, one step beyond, into a kitchen filled with people
half-seen through a cloud of steam and drying washing.
He squeezed past her, blocking the way. "No, no, Miss,
not in there. Mam and the kids are home and my bath is
laid out. Into the parlour, please."

She turned and he reached over her shoulder to open
the parlour door, revealing a room about eight feet by
ten, stuffed with furniture. Inside the tiny house he
became a giant but a giant moving over familiar ground,
so that every movement was pre-judged. "Take a seat,
Miss," and she sat on the one red plush chair, its back
protected by a lace antimacassar, while he sidled out again
and she heard him subdue a sudden babel from the

kitchen, hissing them down as though her presence had converted the kitchen into a chapel. "*Ssh*, Mam! Shssh, Miriam . . . It's the candidate's sister. . Mustn't keep her waiting . . ." and after that a long hush, broken only by whisperings and stealthy movements on the other side of the wall.

She looked about her with the keenest interest. The room, vastly overcrowded as it was with table, chairs, a large green plant pot containing a huge aspidistra, knick-knacks of the kind she had seen won as prizes at Tonbridge Fair, and an assortment of wool mats worked in all colours of the rainbow, was none the less cleaner than any room she remembered. It was, she supposed, the holy place of the house and very seldom used, for it felt cold and damp in contrast to the street and steaming kitchen. Family photographs decorated the walls, dominated by an oak-framed portrait of a thickset man about forty, wearing his Sunday best and gazing down at her as though hypnotised by her presence. The eyes and the heavy square jaw betrayed him as Huw Griffiths' father, and she wondered where he was, concluding he was probably down the mine on the night shift.

And then, as she sat taking in the contents of the room, and relating it to all she had seen in the few days since arriving here, there came to her a revelation, of the kind she had read about in social and religious tracts, where people renounced one form of life for another, turning themselves inside out and seeing everything about them from a strange new angle. It had to do, in some mysterious way, with her painting, so far wholly concerned with nature, with rich, colourful, unsullied things that flowered and gave off a wide variety of scents, with solitude and stillness. But now, in the presence of these drab, mundane things, most of them lacking colour and form, and with the memory of the scenes outside, dominated by the skeletal winding gear crowning the hill, she had an awareness of stirring from a long, drugged sleep into full and vibrant wakefulness and the desire to capture the experience in pencil lines was so strong that her hands itched for crayons and paper. For here was a new world, with a million subjects awaiting her brushes, subjects of the kind generations of genre painters had found compelling in the past but had never, so far, seemed to her worth reproducing. She could hardly wait to get to her portmanteau containing the materials she had brought from 'Tryst' and stood up, fidgeting with her gloves as he edged himself into the room and handed her a bundle of leaflets tied with string.

"Sorry to keep you waiting, Miss. Nothing's easy to find with so many under your feet. Under Miriam's bed, they were, of all places," and he turned on her that slow, bewitching smile so that she thought, 'I'll capture that too before I'm many days older . . . that smile, against the background of a house like this in a town like this. For that's the essence of it — warmth and cheerfulness dominating squalor and overcrowding, and everything else these people have to put up with . . . Yet not letting these things run away with them, keeping them on a tight rein, just as his mother keeps this place spotless, with all that dirt coming into the house from the black mountain yonder . . .'

She said, facing him as she tucked the leaflets under her arm, "Will you be coming up to Mr. Swann's house in the next few days, Mr. Griffiths?"

"Why, yes, Miss. We've a committee meeting there tomorrow, after tea. The agent, the secretary, the treasurer and the committee men who make out the roster for street-corner meetings."

"When you've done talking will you sit for me?"

"*Sit* for you, Miss?"

"I'm sorry. Let me explain. I paint, you see, and I'd very much like to paint you, Mr. Griffiths. You, holding my brother's little boy David, perhaps, but with the pithead in the background. It will be light until around eight-thirty and the sketches wouldn't take long. Would you do it for me?"

He seemed so stunned that she was not sure he comprehended her request but apparently he did, for presently he said, "You want to *draw* my picture, Miss? *Me?* You don't mean *take* it, with a camera? Like Dadda up there."

"No, draw it . . . sketch it that is . . . and paint it afterwards. See, I'll show you . . ." and she put down the leaflets and whipped one from the pile, diving into her reticule for a sharpened pencil she kept there. "Now keep quite still, Mr. Griffiths!" and she limned him with a few bold strokes, catching what he obviously regarded as an astounding likeness in a matter of seconds. "There, like that. Only much better, of course."

He took the leaflet and stared down at it. "Why, that's wonderful! Wonderful it iss! Just like that! Like . . . like a flash of lightning!" The awe in his voice made her laugh, banishing the last of her shyness and the strangeness of the encounter in this crowded little parlour. "I spend most of my time sketching," she said, "but I'm not very good at portraits. I think I cou'd be but I should need a lot of practice. Will you do it, after the committee meeting tomorrow?"

"The candidate wouldn't think it a liberty?"

"Giles? Of course he wouldn't. He'd be interested in a change of subject. He's never seen anything of mine but pastoral scenes, in and about the place where we live in Kent."

"May I . . . could I keep this bit o' paper, Miss?"

"Of course, if you want to. But it's only the roughest kind of sketch."

"Mam and the others will be struck dumb when I show them. We never heard. . . the candidate never said . . . I mean, having a sister who could draw pictures like a camera only better . . ." He fell to examining the sketch again, clearly regarding his likeness as the eighth wonder of the world.

She squeezed past him and he followed her out into Bethel Street. The sun had finally won its day-long battle with the clouds and the row of tiny houses was bathed in orange light. Higher up the hill, and down below on more level ground, a veil of smoke had drawn a heliotrope curtain across the sky. The shouts of children at play came to them from lower down the street. She said, as to herself, 'There's so much to paint about here. Why, there's a lifetime of painting ahead of me,' and then, offering him her hand, she walked thoughtfully back towards the track. At the corner of the street she turned and saw him still standing there, silhouetted against the sky, the sketch in his hand.

3

The nine months comprising spring, summer and early winter of the year 1905 was a flood tide for the Swanns. Change, adventure and enterprise, bringing with them individual and collective advances, ran like a string of Chinese cracker explosions along the Swann ramparts.

Tidings of their forays reached Adam at intervals in the form of bulletins and personal reports and, unlike his wife, he was able, from the serene standpoint of a man of seventy-eight, to ponder each objectively. Some excited him but did not surprise him. After all, it was in the nature of things that George should forge into the future with his fleet of mechanically-propelled waggons, and just as predictable that his daughters, Helen and Margaret, should find men to their liking and go their own way up and down the social scale.

Two subsequent developments, however, one concerning his eldest son, Alexander, the other his son Hugo, found a deeper lodgment in mind and heart. The first because he was still able, even after this stretch of time, to see life through the eyes of a professional soldier, the second because, having come to think of Hugo as a permanent casualty, he was uplifted by the boy's re-entry into the lists.

News of Alex's advancement came in late autumn, when he and his wife Lydia spent a period of leave at

'Tryst' and he was told of his son's invitation to join the counsels of the exalted. At the age of forty-five Alexander Swann, with several wars and twenty-seven years' service behind him, was often mistaken for a run-of-the-mill career officer, advancing by seniority, destined, perhaps, for a colonelcy in a line regiment before retirement. Outwardly, he was very set in his ways and his opinions (prejudices, most people called them) were those of a majority of his colleagues. He looked what he was, too, having acquired a slight paunch and the habit of command, and of strict obedience to the whim of superiors, had imposed upon his voice and manner a certain brusqueness. In addition, somewhere along the line, he had forgotten how to laugh at himself, the one quality, in Adam's view, that could prevent an army officer developing into an animated duplicate of the stuffed dummies he had once used for sabre practice on the drill-ground. But Adam, almost alone among those whose path occasionally crossed that of Lieutenant-Colonel Alexander Swann, was not deceived by this veneer. He was aware that, below the skin, his eldest son concealed a brace of Swann traits that could still rescue him from the mental atrophy that overtook almost every serving officer in middle-age. He had sacrificed the saving grace of laughter, certainly, but he had retained and even developed that professional curiosity that lay at the very heart of the Swann empire, as his obsession with the importance of firepower proved. Urged on by his devoted Lydia he had avoided all the popinjay pitfalls in his twenties, and had become an acknowledged expert on the new Maxim gun and its successor, the heavy Vickers machine-gun. Tirelessly, and often with no apparent effect upon his superiors, he had hawked his ideas around the Empire so that now, whenever the question of increased firepower came up in war games and the inquests that succeeded them, Lieutenant-Colonel Swann's advice was sought by men of high rank. Sought and occasionally heeded, Adam remarked, for he kept a sharp eye on the army's technical advances, particularly since the British, descending on South Africa as though it was another Crimea, had taken such a hammering from a few thousand farmers.

The army, he supposed, was changing like everything else about him and modern technologies could not be held at bay indefinitely by an assortment of polo-playing, pig-sticking fops operating at a safe distance from London. Here and there changes were forced upon them, usually by news of French and German innovations, and now that a man of intelligence was in command of the army spring-clean that followed peace in South Africa, it seemed likely that progress would accelerate to the point where it might have some lasting effect upon the cavalrymen crowding the highest rungs of the profession.

And this, in fact, was more or less confirmed by Alex, when he accompanied Adam down to The Hermitage one November afternoon and told him of his recent interview with Haldane.

Adam, who, since his retirement had spent upwards of two hours a day with his newspapers, was familiar with Richard Haldane, one of the brighter stars in the Liberal firmament, judging him a painstaking and unusually imaginative man. Haldane's thoroughness, however, seemingly went far beyond Adam's expectations, for Alex told him that he had been among a group of home-based officers invited to discuss a particular plank in the Liberal platform, grounded on the near certainty that the Liberals would sweep the Balfour Government out of office at the next General Election.

"It's an open secret," Alex told him, "that if the Liberals win, as seems certain, Haldane will be offered the War Office. How much do you know of him, Gov'nor?"

"I've read some of his articles in periodicals," Adam said, surprised to find Alex caught up in politics. "He seems to have some far-reaching ideas about military reorganisation. German educated, isn't he, and spends a lot of his time at Potsdam?"

"He's very impressed with Germany's military

re-organisation. He admitted to me that we could learn a great deal from the Junkers. Well, not the Junkers exactly, for I imagine they correspond to our cavalry caucus, but from the German General Staff. We haven't even got a General Staff. If Haldane gets the opportunity the creation of one is his first priority but that won't concern me, save indirectly."

"You say he sent for you?"

Alex looked a little foxy and Adam guessed, rightly, that he was debating with himself how far he could confide in a civilian.

"I don't know if I should pass all of it on," he said, at length. "I can rely on your complete discretion, of course."

"If you can't, then God help you, boy," Adam said. "I've stopped hobnobbing in city coffee houses, you know." Then, "You had it in mind to confide in me, didn't you?"

"Yes, I did. Well, Haldane aims at instituting some tremendous reforms in the service. Apart from the creation of a staff he wants to amalgamate the Volunteers and Yeomanry into a single unit called Territorials, with a strength of fourteen divisions and as many mounted brigades."

Adam whistled. "That's a big bite. I hope he doesn't give some of his turn-the-other-cheek Liberal colleagues heartburn. They're against army expansion, aren't they?"

"Oh, I know nothing about that," Alex said, casually. "We chaps aren't supposed to meddle in politics but I must say the chap impressed me. For what he's after is the creation of a highly-trained reserve army, plus the founding of a schools' cadre for officers, to be known as the Officers' Training Corps."

"And that, I imagine, is where you come in?"

Alex coloured, never having learned to adjust to his father's badinage. "It would mean an acting colonelcy. And a chance to pass on what I know about small arms to people who . . . well, to put it bluntly, have had their heads in the sand for forty years."

"Why the devil don't you say what you mean," Adam said, irritably, for he had never cared for circular talking when he was young and found it even more frustrating in old age. "Those chaps you've been canvassing for years aren't just ostriches. A majority only took a commission to avail themselves of an idle life, with strong, social advantages. The older ones are fossilised fools, and you've broken your head against them time and again, so don't pretend otherwise. What answer, if any, did you give Haldane?"

Alex said, as though confessing to a felony, "I . . . er . . . I . . . took a chance. I said I was wholly in favour of all the changes he suggested, and if I was given the chance I'd do my damnedest to teach part-time soldiers all I knew on the ranges. Was I right?"

"You were right," Adam said, "and I'll add something to that. I'm proud of you, boy, for if you had wriggled off the hook you wouldn't deserve another step nor a chance to haul the army into the twentieth century." He scowled at the dreaming landscape. "Listen here, as long ago as the eighteen-fifties I saw campaigns bungled and men butchered simply because those in command of them approached every battle with the tactics of Waterloo and Blenheim. The penalty for that was incurred in South Africa and if we didn't learn from that we might as well concede the next war, if one comes, to the Prussians, the French, the Germans, the Russians or the Japs. I wouldn't put a shilling on us beating anyone but the Turks right now, would you?"

He saw that he had gone too far but he did not regret it. Alex, notwithstanding his obstinacy, still needed prodding when it came to making bold decisions, of the kind Adam had made every day when he was his son's age. It was fortunate, he reflected, that Alex had found that funny little wife of his when he was at the crossroads of his career. He said, remembering her now, "Have you told Lydia as much as you've told me?"

"No. I was in two minds whether I should tell you."

"Well, here's one more piece of paternal advice. Confide in her as you go along and you'll never go far wrong. For if anyone can push you to the top of the tree it isn't Haldane, or anyone like Haldane. It's Lydia, who brought you this far without much trouble. Am I right about that?"

He was relieved to see a slow, rather boyish smile crease his son's face so he went on, "Of course I am. You know that better than anyone! Tell her tonight, boy, and see what she makes of it."

Dusk was creeping over the paddocks and Adam went into The Hermitage museum to retrieve his ulster, shed earlier in the afternoon. Alex followed him in, glancing curiously at the Swann paraphernalia cluttering walls and floor of the building. He said, as though voicing a question that had tormented him all his life, "You were trained as a soldier, Gov'nor, and my guess is you were a damned good one. What the devil prompted you to sidestep the chance of a career like General Roberts' for . . . well . . . all this?"

"I can tell you that easier than I could have told you an hour ago. In my day there were twice as many ostriches and no Haldanes about. Come, boy, it's getting chilly and I've a taste for muffins and a dish of tea."

They went out and across the paddock to the break in the sentinel row of trees guarding the drive to the house; father and son, separated not so much by a span of years as by the gulf between wars fought with lance and sabre and an era when weapons could kill at a range of several miles. Between them they represented, perhaps, a dozen generations of professional warriors and the link, to anyone who knew them both, was still strong, despite Adam's early renunciation of the Swann trade. After all, Alex reflected, he had laid aside sword and lance fifty years ago but he was still, in the real sense of the word, a warrior to be reckoned with.

4

Hugo's news came early in the New Year, although Adam and Henrietta got an advance hint of it at the Christmas reunion.

This had gone smoothly enough this year, for Giles and Romayne, caught up in what promised to be the toughest and rowdiest election since the introduction of universal male franchise, were far too busy to leave their constituency and travel down to Kent.

The breach between Alex and Giles, Romayne and Lydia, had not healed during the last few years and Adam sensed that Hugo, innocent cause of it, was still unhappily aware of the family rift, but the paths of the three brothers rarely crossed these days. Furthermore, even Alex had to admit that public opinion had swung in a wide arc since the mood of obsessive patriotism, at the time of the South African war. People, even important people, were beginning to ask themselves if they had not made fools of themselves in public during that spell of euphoria, and a generous peace with the Boers went some way to convincing the electorate that there was a great deal to be said for Lloyd George's opposition to the war, so unpopular at the time.

The fact remained, however, that Hugo was still little more than a hulk, carted round by that tireless wife of his, and that barking parade-ground sergeant he employed as a watchdog. Sometimes, in the long hours of the night (Adam did not need much sleep nowadays) he wondered about the boy, and how he would fare as the years passed, and faced the prospect of travelling down them as a passenger. His faith in Hugo's wife, however, was considerable, and he listened with the closest interest whenever she appeared at 'Tryst', projecting various plans to achieve rehabilitation. Most of them, Adam decided, were harebrained but he admired her audacity, and the way she explored every new prospect of salvaging Hugo's manhood from the wreck of that shambles out on the veldt.

It came, he learned later, during a pilgrimage Sybil and Hugo made to Netley Military Hospital, in the autumn of 1905, with the object of a final consultation with Udale, the surgeon to whom Hugo owed his life.

Udale was permanently stationed at Netley now, caring for several hundred maimed victims of the fighting, and after a prolonged physical check he pronounced Hugo completely fit but privately expressed some concern regarding the patient's state of mind.

"He's too . . . too *passive*," he told her, while Hugo was making a tour of the wards. "Ordinarily this might not matter, might even be a help and a handhold but not with a chap like Swann. More than anyone I know, he concentrated his entire being on physical prowess, and you'll never capture his interest with any of the usual pursuits of the blind. It isn't as if he had ever been engaged in manual labour, or work calculated to tax his brains. We have to hit on something that will focus his mind on some kind of variant of his former occupation, that is give him a renewed interest in his muscles, sinews and staying power."

"He exercises regularly," Sybil told him. "He's walking and riding every day, and he spends a good deal of his time swimming."

"I wasn't thinking of exercise. He needs to use that magnificent body of his to someone else's advantage." Sybil remembered, during the second stage of convalescence, how insistent Hugo had been on regular massage to counteract a flabbiness encouraged by the helplessness of a man without sight. She said, "Do you do much massage here, Mr. Udale?" At once Udale's quick mind sparked and he thumped his desk, exclaiming, "Why, Lady Sybil, that might be the answer! Massage! Professional massage, and I don't mean on the receiving end."

"He once took a course in massage and spent one day a week at a teaching hospital soon after we came home. It didn't seem to interest him at the time."

"But it might here," Udale urged. "You say he learned the theory? Well, why don't I hustle him along to our gymnasium?" And he picked up his desk telephone, the first Lady Sybil had ever seen, and turned the handle with emphasis, asking the operator to put him through to Corporal Corkerdale at the gym. But Hugo confounded them both, so completely that afterwards Sybil speculated seriously on the theory of thought transference, currently fashionable among some of her friends in Belgravia. The N.C.O. in charge of the gymnasium, learning that Mr. Udale intended to bring a blind officer down for a visit replied, instantly, "Would that be Lieutenant Swann, the athlete, sir?"

"That's who I had in mind. How did you guess?"

"But he's already here, sir. Working on Sergeant Toller's legs."

"*Working* on them? How do you mean exactly?"

"Well, sir, manipulating. He and Toller served together in South Africa, and Mr. Swann told me he was qualified as a masseur and would like to give Toller a going over. Did I do wrong to give my consent, sir?"

"No," Udale said briefly, "you hit the bullseye in one, Corkerdale. I'll explain later," and he replaced the earpiece and recounted the conversation to Sybil. "We'll go down and watch," he suggested. "I've time before my next round."

*   *   *

His tour of the wards, in search of two or three men he had met in the early days of his convalescence, had been depressing for Hugo. Failing to find those he sought – Sergeant Toller, hit in both legs by a shrapnel burst at Modder River and confined to a wheelchair ever since, was one of them – he soon discovered that the pity he generated among the crippled servicemen more than outweighed any comfort or cheer he could dispense. As one young officer put it, rather crudely, "I'm short of one leg and one arm, but what's that compared to your problem, Swann? Damned if I feel like complaining when I meet a chap who has lost his sight. Nice of you to look in."

Someone told him Toller was exercising on the bars in the gym so he let his watchdog guide him there. Toller retained both legs but they were little more than props and the two casualties sat side by side on a bench comparing notes. Toller, having seen Hugo canter the open mile at Stamford Bridge just before the war, showed more tact than the officer upstairs. "You're looking pretty fit to me, sir. You must be taking a deal of exercise."

"Oh, I exercise," Hugo said. And then, petulantly, "It's about all I do these days, Toller."

"I can't get enough," the sergeant complained, "but it's not my fault. The quacks tell me I could get the use of my legs back in time but the fact is . . . well, I'm dog-tired in five minutes, and have to give up, what with that and the pain. It's no wonder, I suppose. I stopped about two pounds of lead out there and it was a bloody miracle I didn't lose both legs. But I might as well for all the use they are. Feel here, just below the knee joint," and he guided Hugo's hand to scarred and pitted areas of flesh where Toller's calf muscles had once bulged. "I was a bit of a miler myself," Toller went on, "never in your class, of course, but I brought home some pots in my time."

"You could again," Hugo said, unexpectedly.

"How's that, sir?"

"You could again. There's no permanent damage to the bone structure, is there?"

"They say not, not in either leg. There were five fractures at the time but they all healed. It's torn sinew and wasted muscle, I suppose. No damned go in 'em, sir."

There was not much Hugo did not know about leg muscles. Ever since, as the boy wonder on the Exmoor plateau, he had submitted to the routine calf massage of his brother Giles and, later, to that of his trained fag in anticipation of some cross-country event, he had been a student of muscles and how they responded to the strains put upon them. In his championship days he had met, in many a stadium dressing-room, dozens of coaches, most of them professionals, who had taught him how to eradicate the stiffness from overtaxed muscles, how to nurse minor injuries and, above all, how to induce a suppleness that was essential to muscles subjected to the strain of a prolonged training session. Legs, for so long, had been Hugo's stock-in-trade and he knew his own as well as his father knew the main roads of the Swann network. His accumulated knowledge told him that what the doctors said of Toller's legs was probably true. All the man needed to walk again was expert massage over a long period, combined with a graduated course of specially-designed exercises using a few simple items of equipment. He said, "I'd like to have a shot at you, Toller. I'll lay you ten to one in sovereigns I could put some real go into those stumps. Given time and plenty of grit on your part," and after a brief word with the gym instructor, he went to work, hammering away at Toller until he shouted for a respite.

He was so engrossed that he did not notice Udale and Sybil enter and stand beside the gymnast who was watching Hugo with interest. Corkerdale said, in a quiet aside, "He's a dab hand at it an' no mistake, sir. We could do with someone like him to chivvy 'em up. And it's not just the way he goes about it either . . . it's . ."

"What else is it, Corkerdale?" Udale, unlike most members of his profession, was a good listener, particularly when confronted with a specialist in one field or another. "Well, sir, it's Lieutenant Swann being blind . . . beggin' your pardon, Ma'am . . . I mean, not letting it gripe 'im, the way it would most of us."

"Go on," said Udale, gravely, and when Corkerdale hesitated, "I'm right in assuming there was an idea behind that idea, wasn't there?"

"Maybe, sir, but who am I to talk about it in front of someone like you?"

"Why not? We don't know everything, we only pretend we do. Tell me what you were going to say."

"Well, sir, it's him being blind. Having someone like that, even worse off than most of 'em, that is, makes 'em sit up and take notice and that's very good for 'em, sir, seein' as how so many are down in the dumps. Do you follow me, sir?"

"All the way, Corkerdale, thank you. We'll see what we can do about it," and he watched Hugo shrewdly, so absorbed in the massage that he was still unaware of their entry, so that presently Udale motioned to Sybil to withdraw.

She put it to him that same night, armed with some figures Udale had given her. In Netley Hospital alone there were close on two hundred maimed ex-servicemen, some of whom were permanently crippled, but others for whom there was hope of regaining the use of a limb or limbs under protracted courses of treatment. Toller was a typical case. Encouraged and bullied, he could, in time, make a fifty per cent recovery and might even dispense with crutches. It depended, Udale insisted, more on his own reserves of will-power than upon outside agencies. "Udale swears that you could bridge that gap, Hugo," she urged. "He tells me that one of the biggest handicaps facing them as regards men with a sporting chance is the unconscious resentment patients feel for those who prescribe their courses, and deluge them with advice, from the standpoint of the hale and active. He's very anxious to take you on full-time down there. We can find a house, overlooking Southampton Water, and the sergeant could drive you in every day. Why don't you think about it over Christmas, dearest?"

He thought about it. Indeed, he thought about little else, ranging the coverts and uplands of the Weald on horse and foot, until there grew in him a conviction that here, perhaps, was a field where he might engage his unused stock of energy that could find no outlet in conventional exercise, taken with no other object than keeping his own body at concert pitch. For by now he had adjusted to his blindness in most ways. Moving in a familiar background such as 'Tryst', or about their home in Eaton Square, he could walk about almost unaided and he discovered that an enlargement of his other senses, particularly those of touch and hearing, had occurred much the way Udale had prophesied. He was not exactly unhappy, but he was confused and indecisive regarding a purpose and self-justification, for until the moment of his tragedy his athletic prowess had been an end in itself and he had never ranged as far as the point where he would be too old and stiff-jointed to compete with younger men. It was as though, all his life, he had been loping up an incline, without asking himself why, yet finding a full measure of satisfaction in the certainty that he could move faster, and with more precision, than any challenger and this supreme faith in his physical ascendancy had persisted right up to the moment he reached the top of that scrub-sown hill and lay in wait for the Boers manning the outpost beyond. Then, in a single moment, he had lost his bearings and paused to ask himself where he was travelling and why, and what was the nature of the trophy they would award him, and in the period since his mind had been mostly a blank, without anything to focus upon other than moments of guilt concerning that dead boy, or the transitory repose he found in his wife's body and the prattle of their child, Humphrey.

He was touched, deeply so, by the kindness of those about him, sensing that patient efforts to convince him that he was still at one with them but he knew very well that he was not and could never be so long as he lived, and that he must face this formidable truth sooner or later. And yet he continued, assiduously, to nurse his body, losing no opportunity of keeping it in the peak of training, for somewhere ahead there might be a use for it and, in any case, it was all he had in the way of capital.

A few rare bonuses had come his way since he had learned how to surmount the worst aspects of his handi-cap, to think beyond the daily challenges of shaving, dressing and eating his food without having it cut up by

Sybil or by the sergeant, and perhaps the most rewarding of these was a heightened physical relationship between himself and Sybil, dating from that first embrace in the tented hospital where, or so Sybil declared, young Humphrey had been conceived. At the time he had regarded it as no more than a release of fear and anger, prompting him to use her body as a buffer for his wretchedness, but when, in more tranquil moments, it returned again and again, promoted by her in a way that never failed to stir him, he came to think of it as a source of solace, freely available as an outlet of tensions within him, and would sometimes try and tell her as much, in stumbling, half-articulated phrases, when he was spent and lying still in her arms. And the wonder of it was she seemed to understand, indeed, to revel in her role as comforter, murmuring over and over again, "But I love you, dearest . . . you're everything . . ."

But there was another, more subtle consolation that was harder to understand and evaluate, and it had to do with his frozen memory of the sounds and scents of the countryside where he had spent his boyhood, for these were now intensified to a degree where he could isolate and savour each of them, identifying the smell of autumn and the stir of spring, and images awareness brought to him out of the past; violet mist in the Bray valley on a still October afternoon, rain blurring the escarpment behind 'Tryst', ripening fruit in the cages and orchards south of the house, rows of leather-bound books in his father's library, the steady surge and recoil of winter breakers on the seashore, the rush of hounds breaking covert when the huntsman sounded 'Gone Away', all kinds of things that had once never impinged on him when he had eyes to see them but were now like old friends helping him along the way.

Yet for all this placid acceptance of his limitations there remained the emptiness of his future and it was not until he sensed, through his fingertips, the flacidity of Toller's wasted legs, that he saw, as it were, a glimmer of light in the surrounding darkness, identifying it there and then into hope of a kind so far denied him. Energy surged back into him then, of the kind that had launched him at such speed down the embattled valley among the remnants of Montmorency's shattered column, and something told him that here, at last, was the elusive secret of regeneration, the use of his own bones and flesh to restore the crippled bodies of other poor devils whose youth and vigour had been taken from them out on the veldt.

He went to Sybil on the last day of the old year, saying briefly, "Write to Udale. And look for that house in Hampshire. I'll work at Netley for as long as he needs me, as long as there are men there who can be helped, even slightly."

"There'll always be someone to help, dearest," she said, gladly, and kissed him, but impatiently, for she did not want to waste a moment in setting the seal upon the victory.

*   *   *

She came to Adam with the news in early February, a week or two after Hugo had joined the Netley staff, with full details of his vocation and their impending move to Hampshire. "As chirrupy as a sparrow," as he afterwards told Henrietta, making no attempt to conceal his own satisfaction. Henrietta heard him out and then had a private session with Sybil, plying her with innumerable questions concerning Hugo and their new base south-west of the Gosport road and overlooking Southampton Water, and when Sybil, with her usual air of setting out on a royal progress, had bustled about her business, Henrietta withdrew to her sewing-room, wondering about her and what strange alchemy had been at work to fuse a woman of that kind with that great son of hers, the splendid young man she recalled so vividly in the days before they shot away his sight. It was a case, she thought, that paralleled Hugo's own pursuit of trophies, for that was how Lady Sybil Uskdale must have thought of him when they met and married. But now, instinct told her, it was different. Something strange and secret had developed between them, that had nothing much to do with Hugo's fame and popularity, but was concerned with a compulsion on the part of that rather overpowering woman to make amends for the wrong she had done him by dragging him off to that terrible war. But there was something else, she sensed, behind Sybil's assessment of him whenever she discussed the boy, or even looked at him, and this was a hint Henrietta could interpret without much fear that she was jumping to a conclusion. Lady Sybil had found in Hugo the kind of fulfilment that she, as wife and mother, had found in Adam all those years ago, and Hugo's blindness, cutting him off from diversions, and making him entirely dependent on her, had proved a kind of boon to both of them, adding something essential to a relationship that had been little more than an arrangement when it began. She thought, 'I never did understand the woman before. I suppose I was always a little scared of her. But I'm not any more, for she's really no different from any of us when it comes down to essentials . . .' And then, whooping like one of those Red Indians in Buffalo Bill's Travelling Circus, Adam hurried into the house, calling for her at the top of his voice, flinging open the sewing-room door and brandishing a telegram that he must have taken from the boy she saw pushing his bicycle up the drive.

"It's from Giles!" he bellowed. "He's in with a thumping majority! Over two thousand, by God!" and she thought, taking the telegram from him and reading it carefully, 'They're such a whirlwind tribe and he's no different from any of them, for he keeps pace with them somehow and that's more than I can do these days.' But she said, trying hard to match his enthusiasm, "How wonderful for him. I *do* hope he likes it when he gets there," and that, for some reason that she did not understand, made him laugh, a fact that underlined somehow the sad but undeniable fact that she was getting left behind with stay-at-homes like Stella and Denzil, in the family's advance into new and frightening worlds.

It was no wonder, really, for things were changing at such a pace, for her and for everyone else who could remember older, more tranquil times, when the social frontiers were fixed and nothing (if you excepted the new railway engines) moved faster than a horse. She remembered that Adam, in one of his jocular moods, had called these changes 'another spin of the whirligig' and they did not appear to distress him at all, even though he was twelve years older than her. Perhaps this was because his newspapers prepared him for them, or perhaps, even without newspapers, he had the temperament to adapt to change. For her part, she found it increasingly difficult, what with daughters finding new and improbable husbands, George rushing about the country on all those horseless carriages, Alex talking about all these frightful new weapons men were using in battles, with Giles becoming a Member of Parliament, Hugo becoming a sort of doctor and every one of them caught up in some cause or invention that hadn't concerned anyone but people like the Royals and Messrs. Disraeli and Gladstone when she was their age. She was sixty-six now, and a grandmother a dozen times over.

She let Adam talk himself out about the election and what it might mean with the Liberals and their allies holding a majority of three hundred and fifty-four over the Conservatives and Unionists, and presently excused herself, going upstairs to try on a green silk dress she had bought for Christmas but had not worn because it was delayed in the Christmas post and hadn't arrived until nearly everybody had dispersed. She held it against her and studied herself in the mirror, a stocky, well-set-up woman who had aged, though she herself said it, very gracefully, for she had never run to fat and her hair still showed no more than a trace of grey. Her complexion was still good, too, and in her eyes was a sparkle that had been there ever since Adam Swann had ridden over the brow of the heath and carried her off, and which would last, she hoped, as long as he was about to share her memories. The reflection in the mirror comforted her somewhat. They might all be much cleverer than she was, and more in tune with the times, but she doubted whether they would look forty-eight when it came to be their turn to be sixty-six and even now none of her daughters-in-law, not even that fashionable Lady Sybil, could hold a candle to her when it came to *style*.

She laid the dress aside and moved over to the tall window, looking down across the new vista Adam had conjured out of the paddocks and seeing, at its northern extremity, the larch coppice bordering the road. It had a bearing on the new family M.P., she thought with a smile. It was there he had emerged from a wayward frolic on her part and Adam's, so long ago as 1865, and today it had the ability, somehow, to laugh back at her across a mile of parkland, as though its treetops were saying, "They know all manner of things you don't, Henrietta, but most of it isn't as important as lessons you learned here, and in the weeks that followed that roll in the hay on a summer day so long ago."

3

The Servile War

HENRIETTA'S AWARENESS OF THE CHANGES AND stresses of the new century could not be dismissed as the prejudices of a woman without education, who had spent most of her life deep in the Kentish countryside. It was real enough, this terrible quickening of tempo, to anyone who recalled more spacious times, and it was not necessary to be an avid newspaper reader like Adam Swann to see reflected, in the strivings and discontents of the Western World, the threat to the entire social order. Thrust, turbulence and challenge were everywhere and the rallying cries of storming parties assaulting strongholds of privilege and custom were heard in every city from Lisbon to Moscow, and loudly enough in places like Leeds and Birmingham to cause countrymen to enquire of one another what devilry was afoot in those wildernesses of brick that had tempted so many of their sons and daughters to forsake a traditional way of life in search of advancement and adventure.

It had begun right here in England, Adam could have told them, and no more than a couple of generations ago, when Stephenson's railroads quartered the nation, giving him his own opportunity to make a fortune, but now, far sooner than even he had judged, the children of the machines had spread south, west and east, preaching their brassy gospel as far as the American prairies, calling to the sod-breakers pursuing centuries-old furrows to make haste to the fair where the pickings were rich and a man's life was not regulated by the seasons and the yield of the amount of soil he shifted by weight of muscle.

No one under forty, least of all a Swann, could be unaware of what was happening in the big world and for the most part they were more than equal to the challenges offered. Only here and there, in isolated pockets like Dewponds Farm, were fences raised against further encroachments and even here, by the spring of 1906, desertion had begun with the migration of the two Fawcett boys, Martin and John, to George's machine shops in the north.

Elsewhere the challenges were met head-on, sometimes fearfully but more often cheerfully, as in the case of George Swann, already accepted in the city as one of the boldest riders in the field. Yet even George, geared to change, and welcoming every short cut that presented itself, sometimes ran out of breath and would pause to make sure of his path ahead. No longer did he see himself as a pioneer, cutting his way through unmapped territory, as in the days when he had driven singlehanded from Stockport to London Bridge with a load of rice aboard his temperamental waggon. Many others were out there, tinkering, experimenting, disputing this and that with backers and public authorities, and it was no longer necessary to preach his private gospel that the horse-drawn waggon would soon be as outdated as a muzzle-loader on the army's artillery range on Salisbury Plain.

The underground railways, stuck with the slightly derisive name of 'Tube', had been a wonder of the age about the time he negotiated his first contract with a shifty Cypriot tea merchant at Hay's Wharf. Now, as if in answer to his fleet of petrol-driven vans, the City of London Authorities had opened the Bakerloo Line and 'tubes' were accepted as a natural means of cross-city travel. A company, conceited enough to call itself 'Vanguard', was running motor omnibuses in competition with the horse-drawn public transport that had proved such a bane to Swann waggoners in Cheapside and Ludgate Hill, although he noted, with a spark of malice, that their vehicles were fitted with iron-bound wheels, and maintained an average speed over a stage only a little above that of the old horse-buses. A few taxicabs had appeared on the streets, not only here in the capital but in places as far north as Liverpool. Three-horse fire-engines, for so long the darlings of every city urchin, were in retreat and some fire-brigades were going over to petrol, advertising their increased speed by clanging bells with a note that struck Cockneys as more insistent than those of their predecessors. There was even an experimental motor exhibition out at Islington that George attended, hoping to pick up a few tips but leaving with a conviction that he was still ahead of most of them. And, on top of that, in 1906, a few sportsmen who persisted in regarding the internal-combustion engine as a rich man's toy, began holding racing rallies at Brooklands and over winding, hilly courses in the Isle of Man.

It was not only in George's chosen field that progress (Adam, perched on his knoll overlooking his quiet acres, was already beginning to suspect that word) was apparent. Those who looked up from the traditional task of net-mending on a hundred quaysides could see Cunard's floating island, the *Mauretania*, at her trials. With a stupendous displacement of 30,700 tons, and a capability of twenty-six knots, she did for sea travel what a hundred and one George Swanns had been attempting on behalf of road transport. A year or so later she crossed the Atlantic in well under five days. And even overhead, in the hitherto untroubled skies, competitors in balloon races could be spotted over Britain, their occasional appearance causing city urchins to pause in their collection of horse manure (a traditional pursuit enlivened, of late, by the noting down of the names of new motors honking their way among the traffic) and whistle their four-note, rhetorical version of the question, 'Seen the *air*-ship?'

So much for transport, to which so many other changes

were hitched, but in wider fields, here and abroad, innovators were hard at work, some of them hell-bent on subjecting the social systems of democracies and autocracies to terrible strains.

Making his first hesitant appearance in the Mother of Parliaments, in February, 1906, Giles was soon aware that the pressures that had contributed to his victory in a Welsh valley were even more apparent on the Continent. Russia, still deep in a feudal sleep, was stirring after the lost war with Japan and blood spattered the pavements of Petrograd when the Tsar's Cossacks, shepherds of a once passive flock, tried in vain to stem the tide of revolution that ended, to the delight of radicals all over the world, in the Tsar's summoning of the Duma to approve what optimists were already calling 'The Russian Magna Carta'.

Nearer home old and tried foreign policies were being jettisoned and replaced by new, to the confusion and alarm of men whose grandfathers had fought Napoleon for twenty-three years with one short break, King Edward, he whom men were beginning to call 'Peacemaker', having succeeded, against all odds, in charming the Parisians and cementing the Entente Cordiale, an alliance designed to apply a brake to the upsurge of Germany after Bismarck unified a knapsack of petty kingdoms into a single, aggressive nation.

Adam, reading of this in his morning perusal of *The Times*, did not put much faith in the cordiality of the entente and this was not because his father had left two fingers on the field of Waterloo. It was because, as a lifelong pragmatist, he had no confidence in the ability of the French to wage a sustained war against anyone, with or without allies. They were like some of the tribes he had fought in his youth, bold enough in attack, but lacking the stamina for a protracted campaign. Any war against a resurgent Germany, he reasoned, would call for more than bugle calls, drum rolls, baggy red trousers and the gospel of élan, preached by paunched French generals at every military academy in the land. He would have preferred an alliance (if there *had* to be an alliance) with Germany, whose faith in lance and sabre had been superseded by the breech-loading rifle as long ago as 1866, and he suspected that his view was shared by a majority of his countrymen. But then, as ever, he would demonstrate his impatience with all foreigners by turning to pages of his newspaper devoted to home-based events, noting that at last the new docks serving the Manchester Ship Canal had been opened by the Peacemaker and his handsome consort, who was said to abominate the Prussians for the way they had served her homeland a generation ago. He noted also that advances in communications were being made across a very wide field and that Marconi's Wireless Telegraph Company was now in constant use by the shipping insurers in the city, and this in a day when the telephone linking his depots along the network was still regarded, by all but people like George and his disciple Edward, as a novelty.

Even nature herself seemed restless in that period, a mere twelve months or so marking the middle of the first decade of the new century. In Chile an earthquake accounted for thousands of lives, and within a year San Francisco was in ruins from the same agency. He thought, turning the pages and scanning headlines, 'I often told myself, in the old days, that I had caught the flood tide of an era but I hadn't. Just the ripples of a tidal wave that will change the face of the world before I've been in the churchyard a dozen years.' But then he congratulated himself on being young in the old century, for the options of an individual had been wide open then and not, as now, narrowed by consortiums and industrial groupings of one kind or another.

2

The social changes that preoccupied Henrietta were not discriminatory, as they had been a generation ago. Then a change of tempo was the business of men and the womenfolk, if they were aware of them at all, awaited the guidance of their masters in these matters, providing they deigned to give it. But even the rampart of male dominance was beginning to crumble and Swann women, dotted here and there about the islands, were among the first to appreciate the fact. Among them Helen Clarke, formerly Helen Coles, who had set Dublin tongues wagging by capturing a handsome groom several years her junior.

Most widows, she supposed, conscious of passing years and the looming menace of fading looks, would have married Rory Clarke with their eyes closed and so, probably, would Helen ten years before he led her to the altar, in the spring of 1905. But Helen, alone among the Swann girls, and almost unique among her contemporaries, had undergone ordeal by fire and the experience had taught her, among other things, to prospect ground over which she had decided to advance.

She did this during the waiting period between the beginning of Rory's storming courtship and the day when, clad in a gala dress of Irish green (as a widow whose previous husband had been decapitated by brigands she could not, she reasoned, wear white without sacrificing dignity) she threw her wedding bouquet from the carriage and set out for the new home Rory's father had given them as a wedding present, a handsome, Georgian building, standing in several acres of land near Crumlin, south-west of the city.

She was now, she assumed, beyond the Pale in two senses, having sacrificed Dublin Castle society by embracing the Roman Catholic faith during courtship, but she almost certainly reasoned that Rory Clarke was worth a mass, deep religious conviction never having been a feature of her upbringing at 'Tryst'. There were aspects of Rory Clarke, and even more of Irish political life, that baffled her during the first summer as the wife of a man who seemed to prize her above his pursuit of political laurels and popular acclaim, but one of the many lessons she had learned during her years in primitive surroundings was to look through rather than at local imperfections, counting only such blessings as were within immediate grasp.

They were, as it happened, many and various during those halcyon days of 1906 and 1907 and chief among them was the discovery that Rory's veneration of her was not, as she had half-suspected, a mere facet of his impulsive, many-sided character. It was rooted in a need to anchor himself to someone sufficiently mature to adjust to his moods and bolster a dignity that he continually placed at risk in his career as professional clown and sustainer of myths; to which could be added, she supposed, incidental roles as conspirator, ballad-maker and several other walk-on parts in the repertoire of the dedicated Home Ruler.

She had braced herself against a cooling of ardour on his part as soon as Parliament reassembled, and he returned to London to do his clamorous stint in the Irish members' attempt to focus attention on themselves and The Cause, but nothing like this happened. Instead he insisted that she accompanied him back across the sea to his head-quarters in Bayswater where, under his active encouragement, she came to preside over a kind of salon, frequented by some of the weirdest people she had ever met, not excluding head-hunting Papuans who were reported to practise cannibalism.

Members of Rory's set whom she entertained at Crumlin and Bayswater did not go as far as the Papuans in that respect but there were similarities for they fed, male and female, upon one another's vanities and extravagances, each competing for the title of Eccentric of the Season. She met and moved among wild-eyed Fenians who had served long sentences in British gaols, professors of Gaelic mythology, poets, dramatists, songsters, orators with and without official platforms, Barcelona anarchists, Welsh activists, explosives experts, courtesans who had seen the Celtic dawn and been purified by it, men allegedly wanted by the police of several countries and a handful of comparatively sober politicians with some pretensions to statesmanship.

They had two characteristics in common. Each of them talked incessantly to anyone who would listen, or even pretend to listen, and all of them seemed eager to achieve Celtic martyrdom and, via martyrdom, a few lines in a Celtic ballad. The shortest road to the second seemed to be a resounding act of violence involving assassination or demolition.

It was no wonder, Helen reflected, that Rory sought tranquillity in the few hours he could spare from such a babel and in these intervals she was strangely touched by his boyish gentleness, and a sensitivity much at odds with the violently extrovert personality he revealed in public.

He was, she discovered, a shy but rewarding lover, so unlike poor Rowley in his response to a little cosseting, so grateful for any active encouragement she gave him when the fearful cacophony had subsided and all the callers had left or had been carted off to bed by the flock of Irish servants they maintained at both houses, every one of them schooled in the handling of stupefied anarchists, poets and mythmakers. And being five years his senior, and a survivor of a real rather than an imaginary revolution, she had no hesitation in taking the initiative on these occasions, especially after she had discovered that his aggressive masculinity (like so many mantles he donned during his working day and convivial evenings) was light in texture. Unlike most of his guests, he had no head for liquor and sometimes, after she had sent the yawning servants to bed and opened a window or two, she would rouse him from a doze on the chaise longue and guide him upstairs. Once here, like her sister Joanna before her, she would help the master of the house undress and let him sleep it off for an hour or so, after which he would awaken, surprisingly sober and restrained, demanding to know where everybody had gone, what time it was, and whether she should be up here ministering to him instead of presiding as hostess downstairs.

She made the most of these few intimate hours, taking her cue, unconsciously perhaps, from her sister Joanna and after, at her gentle prompting, they had made love, she would talk to him about her adventures beyond the seas, native customs, her happy-go-lucky girlhood under the tolerant Adam at 'Tryst', all manner of things that were unlikely, she would have thought, to interest a man whose outward life was dedicated to a fiery crusade. It was impossible, however, after rubbing shoulders with so many fervent converts, to avoid mild infection of the fever and Helen perforce absorbed some of the legends of Ireland's frenzied obsession with the English quarrel. As to forming some conclusions as to how that quarrel should be resolved she soon abandoned that pursuit, for everyone in Rory's circle had an individual solution and she lost herself in the maze of theory and practice they debated one with the other. Alone among their visitors the more mature of the Irish M.P.s seemed bent on maintaining their political alliance with the British Liberal Party and thus obtaining for Ireland a measure of Home Rule. For the rest, methods of ending Ireland's servitude depended on a wide range of offensive measures, all the way from the setting up of an unofficial parliament and refusing to pay taxes, to plots to kidnap ministers of the Crown and hold them to ransom.

In the quiet hours, when he was lying in her arms, she would sometimes coax him to discuss his own theories but he did not seem to have any, beyond a vaguely defined dream of becoming the first president of an Irish Republic, that he saw as a kind of latter-day Eden from which poverty and injustice had been banished, everybody talked Gaelic and national business was confined to celebrations and the exchange of mutual congratulations.

She would think, in moments such as these, of the tremendous gulf existing between men like her father, her brother George and even her brother-in-law, Clint, whose energies centred on money-making, and this charming boy, besotted by his own extravagant dreams and so steeped in the legends of Irish greatness (past and potential but never, she noticed, affiliated to the present) that noble orations replaced ideas and poetry, laced with pathos and humour, the writ of government.

Listening to him the age gap between them widened from five years to fifty, so that he seemed no more than a child, endowed with a rich and colourful imagination fed by tales of giants, dwarfs, magicians, knights and the distressed damsel that was Ireland awaiting deliverance from the fire-breathing dragon across the sea. And yet, coming to know the Irish, she understood very well why they responded to his speeches and pamphlets and why they identified him as a champion in Westminster.

His voice, musical and infinitely persuasive, had something to do with it, and his boyish good looks, too, with soft brown hair falling over a Byronic forehead and eyes that were always full of laughter, even when he was launched upon one of his tirades against centuries of English oppression. It made her wonder, sometimes, why he had singled her out from all the pretty girls of his constituency and she did not find a satisfactory answer until, one night, she put the question directly to him, expecting one of his prolix or jocular replies but getting, instead, an answer as close to the truth as she was ever likely to get. He said, "Because you're real. Because you've suffered and survived and that's rare, much rarer than you realise. For what happened to you wasn't something out of a book or a ballad. You experienced it, horror, bloodshed, the rattle of gunfire in your ears and the fear of death in your heart. I *live* these things but at a remove. How can I be sure I would show your kind of steadfastness if it happened? Knowing you, holding you, makes me believe I might."

"But does it *have* to happen, Rory? I mean, do your people expect to have to battle your way to independence, the way the whites fought to survive out there in China?"

"It's in the cards, Helen. We'll never get real independence without a fight. Oh, the real radicals, like your brother Giles, believe we should and will, but I know otherwise. How do I know? I feel it, here and here," and he tapped his heart and belly. And then he sat up and looked down at her in the early morning half-light and she noticed there was no laughter in the eyes and that he was wearing what she called his 'climax-of-oration expression' as he said, "*When* that happens, *if* it happens, will you be with me or against me?"

"I'm your wife, Rory. Why do you ask me a question like that?"

"Because you're English and your folks are English, and think like the English."

"How do the English think?"

"Arrogantly, overbearingly and inflexibly."

"Could any people be more inflexible than the Irish?"

"Concerning their right to govern themselves? No, they couldn't. But the English take it as their God-given right to govern everybody."

"Yet you married an Englishwoman, Rory."

"I fell in love with one and that's my good fortune right now. But if it ever became a choice I'd turn my back on you, Helen."

The laughter had come back into his eyes as he said this and he capped it by kissing her and running his fingers through her hair, so that she dismissed it as banter at the time. She was to remember it, however, when they returned to Crumlin for the summer recess and the tone of his house parties changed, so abruptly that it seemed to her someone had turned out the lights on all that gaiety, bubble-talk and vainglory at the London soirées.

The hangers-on dropped out of sight, along with the sportive ladies, the ballad-makers and the foreign elements, leaving only a hard core of ex-Fenians and poets, some of the former coarse, unsmiling men, heavy drinkers who never got drunk and some younger men who were teachers and journalists, with the ascetic bearing of young priests obsessed with the sins of the world. And these were quite unlike Rory in that they listened more than they talked. The social climate of Dublin was changing too, she noticed, and certain people, among them the older, more sober element among the Irish members at Westminster, were seldom seen at functions where, only the previous season, they and their wives had played leading roles.

She asked Rory about it when he was on the point of leaving to attend a meeting in the city one fine summer evening and he told her briefly that the party had undergone a severe shake-up and some of the moderates, who still trusted in the promises of the English radicals, had refused to enlist under the banner of Sinn Fein. It was the first time she had ever heard the phrase and she asked him what it meant. "The nearest translation is 'ourselves alone'," he said, and told her the story of the Irish servant who, sent to a fair to sell a horse, was absent several days and returned in a happy frame of mind, replying to every question about his absence and the money by repeating, over and over again, 'Sinn fein, sinn fein'.

"But what's the difference between a member of the Sinn Fein movement and a dedicated Irish Home Ruler?" she demanded. "You're all after the same thing, aren't you?"

"Not quite the same, my dear. And certainly not by the same road when it comes to the crunch. Some of us won't settle for Home Rule as they want it on the Statute Book, with limitations of one sort or another, and most of us are near done with talk. We've been talking, off and on, since 'ninety-eight – a hundred and seven years of talk! What Sinn Fein means to get is an independent republic, entirely separated from Britain."

"I take it you already belong?"

"My love," he said, "I'm a founder member."

She heard herself say, without consciously framing the words, "Is it an exclusively male society, Rory? Are any women enlisted?" and he cocked his head, giving her a humorously searching glance.

"I'd sooner have you with me than against me. Or neutral."

"But I couldn't be neutral, could I?"

"No, my love. Not if those people up north try and block Home Rule and it comes to a fight. No, you couldn't be neutral."

"Then I want you to know I wouldn't care to be, Rory. I was too long finding happiness to risk playing the fool with it."

The statement seemed to release some inner tension in him and he threw his arms round her, ignoring the presence of the coachman, who stood awaiting him on the steps just out of earshot. He kissed her twice on the mouth and stalked out, swinging his suede gloves in that characteristically jaunty manner of his and whistling a bar or two of one of Tom Moore's airs. She stood watching the gig bowl away down the incline of the drive, feeling at once disturbed and released, the way she sometimes felt after he had made love to her. Then, very thoughtfully, she turned back into the house and closed the door.

3

There were establishments less than a hundred miles to the east, on the other side of the Irish Sea, where lords and masters were not disposed to show as much confidence in wives and daughters. Social bastions of one sort or another had been under attack ever since Adam Swann sent his first waggons rolling, and in almost every sphere cracks were showing in the façade of mid-nineteenth-century felicity. One such bastion, however, resisted every attack, the determination of its male garrison hardening with the fury of each successive assault. Unrepentant reactionary or avowed radical, Philistine or enlightened, the inheritors of the tradition of male supremacy closed their ranks against any disposition on the part of their helpmeets to challenge the tribal doctrine in the chambers of the legislature, for here, it was sensed, was the citadel of paternalism. In the home, still so occasional as to be all but unnoticeable, random burrs had stuck in the hedge of Victorian whiskers. A few privileged women, with private means, or impressive reserves of stamina and resource, had secured for themselves a good education and a handful of women doctors, still regarded as oddities, had won the right to practise. Most other professions remained closed to them and even in the fields of commerce, where their services could be secured for pennies, they were mostly confined to repetitive tasks, requiring no particular skills or training. Yet even these trifling advances were regarded, by men as a whole, as straws in the wind promising a gale of frightful proportions if the vents were opened another half-inch. The doctors might waver. The educationalists might preen themselves on a mild display of tolerance. The city gents, with one eye on profit margins, might yield a little here and there. But in the ranks of the lawgivers there was no sign of weakening, if one discounted the lonely voice of the Socialist Keir Hardie (he who had arrived at Westminster a few years ago wearing a cloth cap as the badge of egality) who had astounded the legislators by proposing that the franchise should be extended to women.

It was as far as he got. The parties might hurl challenges and insults at one another on the future of Ireland, on the importation of Chinese indentured labour into South Africa, on workmen's compensation acts, indeed upon any other topic aired, at regular intervals, beside the indifferent Thames. On this one thing there was solidarity. A woman, no doubt, was capable of rising to impressive heights as an individual. One could not entirely discount Boadicea, Nell Gwyn, Grace Darling, Florence Nightingale and, of course, the dead Queen, now reunited with Albert at Frogmore. But no man in or out of his cups could advance the proposition that women, as a sex, possessed the wits to make an unprejudiced decision at the polling booth. They were not intended by nature to shoulder such a responsibility, and that, praise God and John Knox, was that! A few recalcitrants might deem themselves so endowed, might even venture to point out that a woman doctor with an Edinburgh degree was capable of exercising the same degree of judgment at the hustings as, say, an illiterate stonebreaker, with ten pints of ballot-box beer in his belly, but not even the progressive Mr. Asquith would endorse such a heresy, whereas King Teddy himself, an experienced judge of woman's capabilities, would have smiled on the proposition and switched the conversation to the season's prospects at Ascot.

All this being so it was predictable, when one such harpy founded a crackpot pressure group known as the Women's Social and Political Union in 1903, and opened her campaign of militancy aimed at securing women's suffrage, that a growl of anger rose from bearded lips in Highland croft and south-country mansion, followed by a smart redressing of male ranks in every city, town and hamlet of the nation. For this, they seemed to be saying to one another in suburban railway carriages, in horse and motor omnibus, at factory bench and behind a thousand counters – this was the first rumblings of a servile war and would be ignored at the peril of men in possession. This was an issue that cut clear across lines of party, church and rival schools of philosophy, and must be attended to with the despatch of a three-decker captain hearing murmurs of mutiny in the forecastle. The spark must be extinguished, preferably by persuasion but, if this failed, by the majesty of the law. If it were not, who could tell where it might end, and how long it would be before a man came home to find his dinner congealing on the kitchen stove and his slippers unwarmed, while his wife drew up a Bill of Rights in the front parlour? It was something too grotesque to be contemplated by anyone who used a razor. It had about it a horrid abnormality, like a black man commanding white troops in action, or the birth of a child with two heads capable of disputing one with the other and contempt for those who propagated such a proposition was not enough. In the face of further defiance on the part of Mrs. Emmeline Pankhurst and her handsome daughters, the law must act and the doors of Holloway open, offering the missionaries of misrule time to recant, to be forgiven and received back into an ordered society.

*   *   *

This view, crystallised in many a leading article, and expressed in terms of the ironic or the outraged on many a political platform during the period leading up to the radical landslide of 1906, had little effect upon the handful of militants grouped under their W.S.P.U. banner. Indeed, it was soon clear that the vanguard of the move- ment – 'suffragettes' as they were dubbed by some playful male journalist – had hit upon a means of self-advertise- ment that would have doubled the turnover of business- men following a trail blazed by the vendors of Bryant and May Matches, Pears' Soap or Mazawattee Tea.

The bolder the foray on the part of the Pankhursts and their converts, the wider the acreage of print they won for themselves, and the more talking points they provided in first-, second- and third-class compartments of branch trains steaming citywards from the suburbs between seven and eight-thirty a.m. each morning. The progress of the Japanese War, and the toll of the San Francisco and Valparaiso earthquakes, ran poor seconds to the latest outrage of the suffragettes at a bye-election in the provinces or on the streets of the capital and some of the bulletins were all but unbelievable.

Frock-coated statesmen, rising to deliver addresses on matters of moment, like the disestablishment of the Welsh Church, or the growth of the German Navy, had not uttered a dozen words before they were assailed by Furies, old, young and middle-aged, rising from the body of the hall to pose that utterly irrelevant question, "Do you support votes for women, sir?" And as if this was not enough, redoubling their outcry when stewards dragged them from their seats. Nor did it stop at heckling, followed by ejection. Realising that their storming parties were physically unequal to the task of maintaining lodgments in public hall and Corn Exchange, the assailants resorted to a bizarre range of tactics, involving chains and padlocks (with keys secreted where no steward could search for them) bags of soot, bags of flour, the stinkbomb and even banners that unrolled before the statesmen's eyes like the writing on the wall of Belshazzar's palace and bearing much the same message. But in a tongue everyone present could understand.

Soon, as the usage of hall stewards became less chivalrous, and frustrations on their part swept aside the dictates of modesty, glimpses of petticoats and worse were vouchsafed public and press, so that the purists, currently campaigning for the closure of music halls in London, found new targets in the display of undergarments exposed to public view in many a parish and town hall, and sometimes on the pavements outside. But even outrage on this scale did not seem to lessen the determination of Mrs. Pankhurst's converts to make themselves heard, not even when persistent hecklers were down to their well-laced stays. Neither were these unseemly scrimmages confined to public meetings attended by Cabinet Ministers and other notabilities. By the time the year 1906 was drawing to a close the new banditti were roving the streets of the West End, scratching their slogans with diamonds on the windows of blameless tradesmen, marching en masse through the streets of the capital to one or other of their interminable rallies and generally hellraising on a scale that had not been witnessed in London since the week of the Gordon riots.

More and more arrests were made and more and more jubilant martyrs elected to go to gaol rather than pay fines, or give undertakings to return meekly to the seraglio. Most of them, indeed, seemed to glory in an arrest and a ride in the Black Maria, regarding a spell in gaol as a kind of promotion in the ranks of the politically enlightened. And while Fleet Street editors made no bones about where their sympathies rested in this David and Goliath contest, they lost no time in despatching their most experienced reporters and photographers to the scene of the nearest riot or vigil, even when the latter took place within a handcuff-span of Buckingham Palace railings. There came a time when a suffragette riot took precedence, in news value, over coverage of the latest match at Lord's Cricket Ground, and Mrs. Pankhurst and her daughters were thus accorded more space in one week than poor Florence Nightingale had won during her sojourn in the Crimea half-a-century before. National and international topics dwindled to a column, half-a-column and, occasionally, if Mrs. Pankhurst's storm troops had been unusually active or original, to a few inches. Clear across the land her name was heard in bar-parlour and corner shop, during pauses in the musical programmes of suburban soirées and on the terraces of country houses where guests, meeting one another for a few moments between meals and changes of costume, asked one another what the country was coming to when parties of six women proved capable, time and again, of prohibiting free speech and decorating the waistcoats of their opponents with all the ingredients that went into the baking of a Christmas cake. Or, elsewhere in the provinces, where eggs and flour were put to more conventional uses, seeking ammunition in the interior of a master-sweep's hearth-sack.

*   *   *

Adam Swann, watching the world go by and ruminating on these frolics from the vantage point of the Hermitage knoll at 'Tryst', knew his family well enough to make educated guesses at their likely response to Mrs. Pankhurst's campaign. Nowadays he was more domesticated and less informed on what was happening out on the network. Each of his children, passing into maturity, had engaged his mind on one level or another.

Hetty, he would judge, would recoil from Mrs. Pankhurst and her cohorts, seeing them as an admission of failure on the part of women everywhere to bring pressures to bear upon men by methods for which nature had endowed them. Apart from that she had never, in his experience, shown more than a passing interest in politics and would not have bothered to use the vote Mrs. Pankhurst sought to win for her. Politics, in her view, qualified as a male profession, like the Army, the Law and the Church. It was not a fitting occupation for a woman, even a woman luckless enough to journey through life as a spinster. An identical view, he imagined, would be held by his daughter Stella, over at Dewponds, for Stella Fawcett already enjoyed as much independence as Emmeline Pankhurst demanded. Everyone at Dewponds deferred to 'Mother', and he for one had never been fooled by the token deference she paid to that husband of hers, Denzil.

It would be similar, he imagined, in the case of his daughter Joanna, and his youngest daughter, Margaret. Both were essentially feminine, the one relying on her instincts to regulate the balance between herself and that rackety chap she had married, the other endowed with a disposition that would immunise her against the doctrines of women like Emmeline Pankhurst and her valiant daughters. For he thought of them as valiant, remembering the courage and confidence it required to challenge established British practices, particularly those as firmly-based as those at Westminster, so that he saw the campaign as rather pitiful, fearing it could never prevail against such fearful odds. Yet, deep in his heart, he applauded them for their spirit, and even more for their ingenuity. All his life he had hated humbug, especially humbug in high places, and where was humbug more deeply entrenched than among the legislature? Giles, no doubt, would discover this in due course. Until he did, poor wight, let him continue to regard the Mother of Parliaments as the womb of human progress and not a creaking stage, where practised posturing advanced men far more swiftly than originality or virtue. Life had taught Adam Swann many lessons, among them the hopelessness of setting off in search of the Holy Grail ill-equipped and under-capitalised.

His mind continued to probe of the possibilities of Pankhurst alignment within the family. His daughter-in-law, Gisela, would be found among the neutrals. She had never sought equality with men, least of all with George, whom she regarded as the new Galileo, but Lydia, Alex's wife, would regard the campaign with contempt, seeing it as the negation of all the disciplines she had seen practised inside the prisoners' base of a barrack square. He was not so sure about his daughter Helen. Years ago, no doubt, she would have taken Joanna's view, but her experiences in China had changed her in a way that might encourage her to admire the courage and tactics of the W.S.P.U. and their leader. A woman who had shot a man at close range, and in cold blood, would be unlikely to regard the soot-spattering of a Cabinet Minister's waistcoat as a cataclysmic event. Word had reached him that Helen was adjusting to the Irish set and the liveliest activist among the suffragettes would be eclipsed in extravagance by a man like Rory Clarke. As for support on the distaff side of the family, he thought he could count on two – Giles' wife, Romayne, and his adopted daughter, Deborah, now helping her husband, that pleasant chap Jeffs, to run a tinpot newspaper in the west. Both women, he felt, were likely recruits for such a crusade. Romayne because she had always been a rebel of sorts, Deborah because, alone among the Swann womenfolk, she was what he could accept as an educated woman, whose involvement with the underdog went back to the early eighties, when she and W. T. Stead and that tub-thumping evangelist Booth had challenged the white slave traffic here and on the Continent. But musing thus he thought gratefully, 'Thank God I'm old enough to be objective about issues of this sort,' and thankfully turned the page to the Stock Exchange listing.

4

He came far closer than he imagined. At the precise moment he was sunning himself on the terrace of his Hermitage two far-reaching decisions were being made in the family, each involving, more or less directly, Mrs. Pankhurst and her troupe of wildcats. Less than twenty miles away, in a rented flat at the top of Northumberland Avenue, within easy walking distance of Giles Swann's new workshop, man and wife were soul-searching on the subject of his maiden speech in the House. Meantime, some two hundred miles to the west, in the sleepy seaside town where Milton and Deborah Jeffs had lived since quitting the London scene, mail from London was pointing them towards changes that had been in their minds for some time now, ever since they had received a tempting offer for their weekly newspaper from the Harmsworth group, who led the newspaper field in the peninsula and were engaged in adding local weeklies to their empire.

They had been very happy down here, all but out of range of national controversy and engrossed in purely parochial affairs, where they felt their influence was often sufficiently powerful to decide an issue. Both, in their younger days, had worked in Fleet Street, Milton as a feature writer on a range of radical journals, Deborah as one of the first woman journalists in the Street, serving under W. T. Stead. With the prospect of marriage, a vague dissatisfaction had settled on them, reaction in some degree to all the misery and strife they had chronicled, and when Milton proposed to realise every Fleet Street man's secret dream – that of owning and editing his own broadsheet – Deborah had encouraged him to take the plunge.

Since then they had vegetated, or so they thought of it, moving molehills in preference to mountains, with no thought of returning to the London scene until events conspired to make them take a closer look at the probable course of the years left to them. Former friends of

Deborah, drawn into the Pankhurst maelstrom, wrote regularly of the mounting fury of the suffragist campaign, and one of Lester Harmsworth's scouts offered them a handsome profit for the newspaper, enough to enable Jeffs to buy a footing in a much more important journal serving a wider area of population. The coincidence caused the hidden wishes of both of them to surface simultaneously. Milton had said, "It's at least double what I would have asked if I had ever put it on the market. Money is no object to the Harmsworths when they want a thing and a man ought to think twice about refusing a profit of this kind if it falls into his lap. We built this paper up from scratch, remember? It was no more than a local newsheet when we moved in, and if we could do it once we could do it again, before we're too old and too lazy to try." But then he had paused, regarding her thoughtfully, "Only one thing stops me wiring acceptance, Debbie."

"What's that, Milton?"

"You. You and young Deany. We've had a good life down here. And a useful one too, in a modest way. Maybe I oughtn't to quarrel with the kind of luck I've enjoyed ever since I ran into you."

They were well accustomed to talking things over and pooling points of view. There was no paternalism here, for Jeffs' respect for his wife's intelligence dated from the moment he read her articles in the *Pall Mall Gazette* on the sale of fourteen-year-old children to rich old roués. He added, "You've been thinking of a change yourself, haven't you? Ever since the W.S.P.U. began to steal the headlines?"

He was right. She was fifty now, a time for reappraisal, and while she, like him, had found fulfilment in publishing their own journal, she had a sense of the years slipping by at an alarming pace since her son had passed from cot and toddling stage to boyhood. They still called him 'Deany', a diminutive of Houdini, the nickname he had acquired as a particularly active baby who had to be watched throughout his waking hours, for he seemed to be born with a working knowledge of escapology. He was away at school now, her half-brothers' old school on Exmoor, and a change of venue would not affect him much. The flow of letters she had received from former colleagues, inside and outside the Women's Social and Political Union, had stirred her deeply, as had press accounts of the rough-handling the campaigners had received at political meetings. She said, "How long do you suppose Asquith and those other politicians will hold out against the franchise of women, Milton?"

"Indefinitely," he assured her. "Make no mistake about that." And then, shrewdly, "You'd like to play a part in it, wouldn't you? Well, come to that, so would I. They get practically no press support and I see what's happening to them lately as a national disgrace. It's the domestic equivalent to the hammering we gave those poor devils in South Africa. That's what's disturbing about this country. The average Briton, from Prime Minister down to the layabout in the street, honestly thinks of himself as a standard bearer of human rights. But national arrogance, a century of commercial success, suzerainty over a quarter of the world's surface and a navy capable of blowing any rival out of the water, seems to have blinded a majority to aspects of human dignity. Did you know even Hungary has universal franchise?"

"No, I didn't."

"Then say what you have in mind. Irrespective of this Harmsworth offer."

"It's my age partly. With luck I've got around twenty years left to play a part in affairs, to use what talent and experience I've got to alter things, to try and change them for the better. It can't be right to spend them writing about the Withy Brook overflow, and the decaying fabric of our infants' schools in this backwater. Sometimes . . . sometimes I feel an itch to head back to London, to find out things for myself and write about them . where are you off?"

He paused by the door, smiling at her over his shoulder. "To wire Harmsworth," he said. "And just for the record I've had the same itch for a year or more and lately I've been scratching it raw."

5

The problem, similar in so many ways, yet with under-tones more far-reaching concerning each of them, was not so easily resolved by Giles, mulling over his notes in the first-floor flat they had leased from a departing Tory member for a Welsh constituency.

It was conveniently central and they had been lucky to get it, but already both of them were missing the soft, south-west wind over the Rhondda uplands, and the singsong lilt of their constituents. In London, Giles felt, a man could lose his identity if he wasn't careful and his initial reactions to the fulfilment of a dream that had preoccupied him since his early twenties, had been oddly deflating once L.G., and another Welsh Liberal, had introduced him to the House of Commons at that first jubilant assembly, following the February land-slide.

He had always thought of it as a very solemn place governed, of course, by tradition but generating a kind of magisterial impulse that conditioned the mood of the entire country outside. Everything that happened to ordinary people began right here beside the Thames and one was almost tempted to speak in whispers once the portals had been crossed and one found oneself rubbing shoulders with men whose names had been familiar to him since boyhood. But the sense of majesty was soon dissi-pated, perhaps by L.G.'s gentle raillery, and he recalled now that David Lloyd George never had been the least impressed with the place. He had called it crabbed when they met here one afternoon as long ago as spring, 1879, Giles an awed thirteen-year-old, tagging on to a bunch of sightseers, Lloyd George, seventeen and clad in rough country clothes, making his first-ever visit to a building that would dominate his life and destiny.

"It's more of a club, Johnny Peep," he said, "and no club is worthy of stardust. Think of it as a workshop if you can, where policies are hammered out, as upon a bench. Fashioned, refashioned, recast and more often than not rejected after infinite palaver among the journeymen. We get things done, of course, but never in the way we hoped or imagined. We have to compromise one with the other in order to make progress and that's in the nature of things, there being more than six hundred of us, all trying to catch the spotlight."

"I've never known you compromise over anything you regarded as important, L.G.," but Lloyd George had replied, "Well, never in front of an audience, lad. But here? You'd be surprised, shocked even, until you come to understand how essential it is."

There was one issue, Giles had noticed, concerning which most of his closest associates were prepared to compromise upon, and that in the company of men whose policies they had attacked for years while in opposition. No one, excluding that saintly old Scotsman Keir Hardie, seemed disposed to make a party issue out of women's franchise, and it distressed him that this should be so, for he had long since been convinced that it was a vital plank in the efforts of the Liberals to broaden the stage of democracy.

Down in the valleys Romayne had already played a part in forming a local branch of the W.S.P.U. and he had encouraged her, even though the response among the miners' wives had been apathetic. It seemed quite monstrous to him that women as intelligent and socially aware as she or Debbie were denied a voice in the nation's destiny and his misgivings were not dispelled by L.G.'s bland assurances on the subject.

"It's all a question of priorities, Johnny Peep," he reasoned. "It will come, you can depend on that, but in its own good time, when we've dynamited our way through centuries of rubble half-burying the body politic. There are so many issues that I see as vastly more urgent. National insurance, pensions for the old and disabled, reform of the House of Lords, higher education and opportunities for the poor, public ownership of certain national products, a basic minimum wage, the relegation of the very idea of tariffs on to the bonfire, and don't deceive yourself that Free Trade won't be in danger from time to time. Home Rule for Ireland, to shed that pack-load of trouble, all manner of things, many of them linked to the future of your miners and their families. We simply haven't the Parliamentary time and that's a fact, and the tactics of Emmeline Pankhurst aren't doing much to persuade the electorate that women can be trusted with the vote."

"But what else can they do?" Giles had argued. "They've tried lobbying and talking for a generation without gaining an inch. At least they've brought the matter into the open."

"Kaiser Wilhelm is a star turn at doing that but it doesn't make him more credible in the Chancellories of Europe."

He had gone away less than half satisfied, to discuss it all again with Romayne and discovered, as he had expected, that L.G.'s arguments made no impression upon her. Sometimes it struck him that she did not trust the man and this pained him a little, for he still regarded L.G. as the greatest campaigner for reform in the land. She said, "It isn't important what L.G. thinks, Giles. You're a Member of Parliament now. What do *you* think? Honestly and deeply, down in your heart?"

"You know what I think. That all women over thirty ought to have the vote now. And that a Commission should be set up to consider extending it to women over twenty-one. You couldn't get the public to swallow a mouthful that big in one gulp but it could be done in two."

"Would you be prepared to say that in public?"

"Of course I would. I only played it down at the election because L.G. warned me it wasn't wise to raise it until Liberal policy had been decided on the issue."

"And now?"

"There's absolutely no hope that the W.S.P.U. will win enough support in the House to get a bill through the Commons. As for the Lords, why they'd throw it out in ten seconds."

"Then if you believe in it, sincerely and utterly, why not introduce it into your maiden speech?"

He did not answer at once. The possibility had occurred to him but he had shelved it, half agreeing with L.G. that there were so many more important priorities. He said, finally, "I've roughed out my speech. It's devoted almost entirely to the miners' minimum wage. After all, the miners put me here and I owe them the honour of the first salvo."

"Their wives helped and I'm not talking about work in committee rooms and so forth. I mean by keeping their homes and families together, year after year, often under impossible conditions. You owe them a salvo, Giles. Wouldn't it be possible to slip in some reference to a wife's right to have a say in the family's future?"

He looked down at his notes again. "I don't know. I should have to think about it very carefully."

She did not press him further, knowing he was already under some strain concerning the prospect of the speech. His platform confidence, she noticed, varied from shuffling nervousness to a buoyancy where he could dispense with notes altogether and hold an audience for an hour or more. It depended entirely on atmosphere. If he could sense sympathy in the upturned faces he could race away in galloping style, garnishing a theme with all kinds of anecdotes, some from the mountain of books he had scaled, others from personal experiences. But there were times, as now, when the prospect of hostility or indifference could make him sound humdrum or even dull. All the best of his speeches were made in the valleys, where the great majority of his listeners were men whose cause he had espoused as a youth during his first visit to Wales, so that sometimes she thought his father was right when he told her, "Old Giles ought to have settled for the Church. They need people like him, with his kind of innocence and integrity. Politicians can do without it, for politics is a dirty business most of the time. A politician who won't hit below the belt is at a disadvantage."

He came to her briefly the day he was to make his parliamentary debut and said, "Well, I took your advice. I slipped in an oblique reference to the W.S.P.U. campaign."

"Just how oblique, Giles?" she asked.

"I'll read it to you tonight, when it's all behind me. I'd prefer it that way if it's all the same to you. I'm going over there early. I want a word with L.G. before the debate. He's promised me ten minutes before lunch."

"Good luck, Giles," she said, kissing him, glad now that they had agreed she should not avail herself of an opportunity to hear him from the Ladies' Gallery and thinking, 'He'll be more relaxed when he gets back late tonight and I can convince him he wasn't half as bad as he imagined.'

But then, when she slipped out for a walk along the Embankment after their help, old Mrs. Robbins, had come with the shopping and could keep an eye on the children, she had an unlooked-for opportunity to read at least part of his speech, the important part, hours before his return. A *Star* news-vendor was standing opposite Cleopatra's Needle with a contents bill clipped to his board and the legend on the poster read, in handwritten script, '*STIR IN COMMONS – LIBERAL PLEDGES SUPPORT FOR SUFFRAGETTES*' and she fumbled in her purse for the halfpenny, taking the paper across the road to read under one of the globes glowing there beside the plinth.

It was not much of a stir. Whoever scrawled that contents bill must have been desperate for an eye-catching item but it made her start to see the heavy print of the lead-in that began 'Today, in the House of Commons, Mr. Giles Swann, newly-elected Member for Pontnewydd, caused a brief uproar during his maiden speech in support of the second reading of the Minimum Wage Bill . . .' And underneath, a side-heading arrested her eye as it swept down the column, 'Liberal Pledges Support for Labour Motion'.

She folded the paper, aware of a quickening of her pulse and a painful thumping of her heart, and almost ran back across the Embankment and under Charing Cross arch to the flat. She had a near certainty that he would be there, long before he was expected, and in need of her, but when she let herself in and called, "Giles! Are you there, Giles?" only Mrs. Robbins poked her head over the banister and hissed, "Shsh, M'm! I on'y just got the baby orf . . . It's his teething, like I said." She waited a moment to regain command of herself, then mounted the stair slowly, holding the newspaper close to her breast.

*　　*　　*

He managed to buttonhole Lloyd George in one of the corridors after enquiring for him with mounting desperation.

"You did promise me a few minutes, L.G. Run your eye over it, no . . . not the first page, that's along the lines you advised . . . the piece I've written in," and when the Welshman glanced at it, casually at first but then with keen attention, "One of us has to say it, L.G. You think it, but won't make it public. I don't necessarily want your approval, certainly not your official approval. But if you think it's letting you down I'll wait for Keir Hardie's motion."

"You realise what it implies. For you, I mean, and that's all it concerns really, for you'll not win anyone over at this stage. Not even the odd waverer."

"What would it imply. To me?"

"Any chance of patronage. Now and for a long time to

come. No one cares to hear a change in policy so much as hinted at in a maiden speech. They'll forgive dullness, confusion even. But not originality. It doesn't become new boys!"

"You're urging me to take it out?"

"Not necessarily. You know where I stand on the issue, and I was reckoned a firebrand when I first came here. I disappointed them, however. My instinct was to lay low and watch points until I learned my way around."

"And that's your advice to me?"

"If you like, Johnny. Most of them do, you know. What I'm saying is you have to make a deliberate choice between principle and discretion, and that's a choice you must make yourself, without me pointing you one way or the other. What time will you be speaking?"

"Early on. About three-thirty, I was told."

"Well, then, skip the preamble. Take a breath of fresh air in the park and think it over."

He went out into the pale spring sunshine, cutting through Queen Anne's Gate, then across St. James's Gardens to the path circling the lake with its nesting island. The park was all but deserted at this time of day. At the nearer end of the wooden bridge a woman who looked about seventy, probably one of the many professional scrubbers from the Treasury or the Admiralty buildings judging by her cap and sacking apron, was feeding crusts to a small circle of ducks. He stopped to watch, taking in the woman's coarse, reddened hands, swollen finger joints and badly broken nails, and the abstracted look on the craggy features under the crooked peak of the cap. A square of greaseproofed paper that held her lunch or breakfast lay on the seat behind her, and close by a carpet bag, that was almost surely her scrubbing brushes and mopping cloths. His eyes travelled slowly down to the dipping hem of the skirt, noting the broken boots that concealed a fine array of bunions judging by the bulges near the toes. He thought, 'She's probably worked at scrubbing office floors for sixty-odd years and she'll stick it another five. After that it'll be the infirmary at best . . .' but then, his glance moving up again as she chirped "Chick-a-dee, chick-a-dee!" to the swarming ducks, he noticed a ring all but buried in the mottled flesh of her left hand and a burning curiosity to know something of her possessed him. He said, touching his hat, "Good-day. Are these your regulars?"

She turned and looked at him levelly, a hint of mockery in her eyes.

"You could call 'em that. They know me any road. I on'y got to call to 'em. There's a rare lot after it today. That'll be the dripping. They like dripping and I don't alwus 'ave it."

"Bread and dripping. Is that all you bring?"

She looked not so much surprised as mildly outraged. "Lumme, what *else* on their screw?" and she jerked her head towards the offices in the background. He felt in his pocket and took out a half-a-crown, offering it shyly. She looked hard at it and then up at him. "Nice of yer, gov', and I know yer mean right. But we never begged."

"We?"

"Not me, not Thompson. Nor none o' the kids when I was around to fetch 'em one. I'm working and I've got a room. There's plenty who could use that 'arf-crahn sleeping out on the Embankment."

The rebuke, for he accepted it as such, shamed him. He put the coin back in his pocket, saying, "I'm sorry. Is Thompson your husband?"

"Was. Watchman on Grimshaw's buildin' sites for forty-odd years 'til he caught his death, winter before last. Never missed a night until the bronchitis got 'im. Then lay there worrying about it all the time. I told 'em that when I went to collect the half-week's screw they owed 'im."

"How many family have you?"

"On'y two, now. 'Arry's in the army. Middlesex Reg'ment and he'll sign on for another twelve years if he takes my tip. Minnie's married to a streetlighter and they got five kids. I told both of 'em to watch out lars time I saw 'em. God knows how many working days I lorst wi' kids comin' and goin'."

"Coming and going?"

"We buried five. 'Churchyard luck' Thompson called it when they went straight orf, tho' he never said it about 'em when they got parst the first stage."

The incredible hardships of their lives, together with their matchless fortitude, struck him like a blow in the stomach. Her age, and still scrubbing. Thompson, gasping his life away and worrying about his job, as a night-watchman on around twenty-five shillings a week. Seven children, five dead in infancy. He said, "Have you finished work now?"

"Finished?" She scratched a mole on her chin, a gesture of mild surprise. "Gawd no, Mister. I got me offices in Oxford Street now. I knock orf around four an' go 'ome for me tea an' kipper. Rose'll 'ave it all ready."

"Who is Rose?"

"Another White'all scrubber. We share the room fifty-fifty. Whoever's first back puts the kettle on."

"What time did you start work this morning?"

"Five. I do second floor, Adm'lty. Bin doin' it twenty years now."

"Do you mind telling me how much they pay you?"

"Why should I? Regular rate. Tanner an hour."

Big Ben boomed the hour and she wiped her hands on her sacking apron. "I gotter go now, Mister. Nice 'avin' a chat. Alwus someone to chat with in the park."

He handed her her carpet bag and touched his hat and she mocked his gallantry with a jaunty twitch of her cap. He watched her trudge away towards the Mall, her bunions causing her to roll slightly as she put her weight on her heels and the sides of her feet. He thought, 'She's better than ten sermons and fifty blue books. What the devil do the bishops and the economists know or care about the Mrs. Thompsons? Yet they keep the whole lot of us going, the way the miners do. But miners qualify for a vote!' The memory of a recent visit to Henley Regatta returned to him, the river teeming with blazered young bucks displaying their prowess with the sculls, every man jack among them entitled to a say in who ran the country, although few of them would ever do a full day's work in their lives. Certainly not a day beginning before sunrise.

He sat down on the seat where Mrs. Thompson had eaten her dripping sandwiches and reread the paragraph he had shown Lloyd George, hinting at support for Hardie's bill to extend the suffrage to women. It sounded apologetic, an aside in the main purport of the speech that was concerned with the economics of the coalfields. He detached the sheet, took out his pencil, struck it through and wrote, in its place:

And now, at the risk of seeming to introduce an irrelevancy into the argument, I am putting on record, in my first speech to this House, my resolve to fight not merely for a basic minimum wage for the men who dig the nation's coal at the risk of their lives but the right of their wives to join them in having some small say in the nation's affairs, women now classed, like all women in this so-called free society, as second-class citizens, wise enough to raise the nation's children, strong enough to work upwards of fourteen hours a day, but disqualified, for ever it would seem, from a voice in the future of their children, or the regulation of the rewards of that toil. And I do this in my first speech advisedly, for I believe that every Member of this House, rising to his feet to address it for the first time, should avail himself of the privilege of making an unequivocal declaration of his intentions and the fundamental beliefs that were factors in bringing him here. My intention is to battle for universal social justice in this realm. And my fundamental belief is that all adults attaining maturity should participate in the counsels of the nation. The Honourable Member for Merthyr Tydfil is, I understand, preparing a bill to put that right into the statute book. He will have my unquestioning support, as has the bill before us at this moment.

*   *   *

They listened to the earlier part of his speech with a mixture of indifference and lazy tolerance. No more than about a hundred and fifty of them and of those, he would judge, about a third either dozing or preoccupied with thoughts of their own. Very few of the front bench were present but he could see L.G. sitting bolt upright, and paying him the compliment due to a protégé. But then, when he came to the sentence admitting irrelevancy, there was a mild flicker of interest, and it struck him that a few of them might be academically interested in the quality of the maiden speeches, much as sixth formers and cricket colours would bestir themselves to watch the performance of a very junior member of the team brought in as a substitute at the last moment.

The flicker widened. He saw one member nudge his neighbour, so that when he came to the passage dealing with his conception of the duty of a newly-elected member to make a declaration of intent, his real audience had increased to about three score. Lloyd George did not stir. He continued to sit bolt upright, intent on not missing a word.

At the mention of the Honourable Member for Merthyr Tydfil's forthcoming bill, a kind of growl rose from the thinly-packed opposition benches, then spread like a flame to the front bench of the Liberals, where he saw the man next to L.G. turn and gesture, without, however, deflecting the Welshman's attention. When he sat down the response, that began as a growl, increased to a sustained buzz and at least two members were on their feet trying to catch the Speaker's eye. From the area of the House where sat the small knot of Labour members came another sound, not a cheer exactly but a vocal stir that might have been a muted chorus of 'Hear, hear' and 'Bravo'.

The moment passed. Somnolence regained possession of the chamber and he sat down feeling a little foolish yet satisfied, deep within himself, that he had made the gesture . . . Mrs. Thompson's gesture, really, so that his mind returned to her for a moment, scrubbing her way down the worn stairs of some third- or fourth-storey office block in Oxford Street, knuckles gleaming as she tightened her grip on her brush, sacking apron spattered with suds, her dead husband's cap still at a jaunty angle. The thought made him smile.

An usher was plucking his sleeve and handing him a folded slip of paper. He opened it and recognised L.G.'s writing. The scribble ran:

Some might say you've burned your boats, Johnny, and perhaps you have. But I'll refer you to Stevenson – Alan Breck's defence of the roundhouse, remember? 'David, I love you like a brother. And O, man, am I no' a bonny fighter?'

4

Anniversaries and Occasions

THE MOMENT HE OPENED HIS EYES AND, RAISING
himself on his elbow, satisfied himself that Hetty was still
asleep, he hoisted himself carefully out of bed, buckled on
his leg and crossed the room to widen the chink of light
filtering through a gap in the curtains. He stood by the
window gently scratching his chest and noting the promise of another fine day, rare at this time of year. It
seemed to him a good omen for, despite close involvement
with his affections, he was not anticipating his programme
with much pleasure. Strong winter sunshine, of the kind
augured by a clear sky over the Weald and the jocund
glitter of frost points on the hedges, might help to dissi-
pate the glumness a man of his age had every right to feel
at the prospect of lunching two gaolbirds. Especially
when his guests happened to be an adopted daughter and
a daughter-in-law.

Paradoxically (he had always been known to possess
a somewhat eccentric sense of humour) the association of
the word 'gaolbird' with his kith and kin made him grin.
Swann history, so far as he was aware, had no earlier
record of gaolbirds, but he thought it probable, if one
could have searched diligently, that they had existed,
and if this was so it was probable that their offences had
been more serious than a refusal to pay a small fine for
demonstrating on the doorstep of the Prime Minister.
'Might have been looting,' he told himself, massaging his

lower thigh where, on mornings like this, the stump of his leg was tormented by the straps, and the word 'looting' alerted him in the way the word 'gaolbird' had, setting memory bells jingling in the attics of the brain so that he lowered himself on to Hetty's dressing-stool in order to answer them in comfort. He was exploring the nearest attic in a matter of seconds, recovering something that had lain dormant there for a long time. Loot that he himself had acquired fifty years ago this month on a battlefield in India. A ruby necklace of thirty magnificent stones that had, in fact, launched him as a haulier and could therefore be regarded as the original source of all he possessed.

Twenty-nine of the stones had gone their way, some to provide initial capital outlay, others to enrich the Spanish whore his partner Avery had prized until she was murdered by her partner. One remained, set in a ring Henrietta still possessed but only wore on great occasions, although he knew she was attached to it because he had seen her take it from its resting-place in the dressing-table drawer from time to time and contemplate it, remembering, no doubt, an evening over a bivouac fire under the Pennines when he had shown her his loot.

Curiosity stirred in him and after another glance to satisfy himself that she still slept he opened the drawer, foraged in it and drew out the ring, holding it between his finger and thumb in a way that made it take fire in the early morning sun. He thought; 'I wonder if she remembers how I came by it? Or what might have resulted from the discovery that it escaped the clutches of the East India Company by travelling home in the kit of a time-expired lieutenant?' His train of thought ran ahead, all the way down the years to the present moment, eight o'clock on a bright January morning in 1908, when he was debating how to tell her that he had persuaded Giles, and his son-in-law, Milton Jeffs, that it was in both their interests to keep away when the girls were turned out from Holloway.

She had taken it hard at the time. All that publicity,

all those pictures in the papers and the final shattering news that she had a daughter and daughter-in-law serving time in gaol, but he had found it possible to make allowances for her. She had come a very long way in fifty years. Further than him some would say, for she had always valued the respect of neighbours, an aspect of county life that had never bothered him. As to the girls and their offences, he made very little of that. If they cared to sacrifice their dignity shouting and brawling outside that priggish chap's house then good luck to them for it was time somebody pricked the bubble of party complacency. Some of those chaps who had ridden to glory on the Liberal landslide of two years ago already saw themselves as the Lord's Anointed, and all who differed from them as the agents of Baal. He was old enough to understand that politics, especially party politics, were not as clear-cut as that. Even starry-eyed old Giles was beginning to learn this, having been consigned to the wilderness for taking an independent line on women's suffrage.

There remained, however, the placating of Hetty and he wished with all his heart to spare her the embarrassment that would surely follow his announcement that he had told Giles and Milton he would meet Romayne and Deborah and give them the meal they would need after a month on skilly. For there was surely no sense at all in either husband showing up at the gaol gates. Giles would be recognised by the press, and his presence, and relationship to one of the prisoners made public. Milton Jeffs, as a freelance journalist, could not afford personal involvement when the editors he worked for regarded Mrs. Pankhurst and her acolytes as hell-raising harpies, deserving all they got in the way of official correction.

He saw Hetty stir and stretch and crossed over to her side of the bed, the ring concealed in his palm.

"I've got to make an early start," he told her, by way of a preamble, and when she asked where he was going he said, casually, "Over to Holloway. To meet the girls. I promised Giles and Milton I'd deputise for 'em as a welcome committee and I daresay you think I'm a damned old fool to involve myself, but better me than them. Matter of fact I told 'em so when they were here earlier in the week."

She did not protest, as he had expected, but she looked very troubled. "Isn't it their responsibility rather than yours?"

"Yes, I suppose it is. But it won't do Giles any good with his party to have his name linked with Romayne. She went in under her maiden name but the press would start digging if he was seen greeting her outside the gaol. There's bound to be a bit of a stir when they emerge. Wouldn't surprise me if they didn't have a band."

"I'm sure it's quite the silliest thing I've ever heard of," she said, "and I told Deborah so the last time I saw her. All this fuss over a vote! She's a married woman, with a ten-year-old child, and it's high time she knew better!"

He was tempted to remind her of the quarrels they had had over Debbie in the past, notably when the girl was caught up in that *Pall Mall Gazette* scandal about child prostitutes; but decided, instead, on a flank attack. He opened his hand, displaying the ring resting in the palm and at once her eyes widened.

"What are you doing with my dress ring?"

"Remembering," he said.

"Remembering what?"

"How I came by it. Fifty years ago."

"What do you mean by that?"

"It just crossed my mind that I could have served time in prison for taking it, along with those other stones. That or been cashiered at the very least, for I robbed the John Company of around thirteen thousand pounds. We started the business on the proceeds in case you've forgotten. It makes what the girls did small beer, wouldn't you say?"

She took the ring from him and sat up, contemplating it.

"You told me you found it on a battlefield. That isn't stealing, is it?"

"It would have been considered so if I had been caught with it."

"But you fought for it, Adam."

"The girls fought for that month they got. The difference is they believed in what they were fighting for and I never did."

"But you've said over and over again they won't get anywhere with all this uproar."

"That isn't the point, Hetty. It's the fight that's important, and the convictions behind it. That's important all right. It was important to people like Catesby, our Polygon manager, who went to gaol for his share in the industrial riots back in the 'fifties. And to those farm labourers down in Dorset, who were transported for trying to form an agricultural trades union. Everything has to be fought for by somebody. When there's no one around to fight that's the time to watch out, for the men on top will do what they damned well like with all of us. I happen to think Mrs. Pankhurst and her troops are on a wrong tack, strategically that is. There's nothing wrong with what they have in mind and they'll achieve it. In your lifetime, probably." He braced himself. "Listen here, Hetty, will you do something today? To please me rather than them. Will you come up to town with me and *be* there when I meet them? It would mean a lot to them but even more to me."

"Why, Adam?"

"For a variety of reasons but one will do. I'd like your company."

Her expression softened and he knew there was nothing wrong with *his* strategy. "Very well, since you wish it. How long have I got to get ready?"

"I want to be there at noon sharp," he said, "so we'll have to hustle."

* * *

He had promised her a stir, and possibly a band, but she had never expected anything on this scale. It was like mingling with a crowd awaiting the passage of a royal procession or a Lord Mayor's Show, and it was difficult not to be infected by the air of expectancy and excitement among the crowd. She looked about her with lively interest, leaning out of the cab window when he pointed out Mrs. Pankhurst and Mrs. Pethick-Lawrence, whom she instantly recognised from pictures in the newspapers. They did not look like women whose business was public uproar, who encouraged others to smash windows and commit physical assault on members of the Cabinet; more like the women who attended her croquet parties at 'Tryst'. They were neatly dressed in white and each wore a ribbon across the breast, printed with the slogan '*Votes for Women*'. They looked pleased with themselves too, she thought, watching them move among the crowd smiling and shaking hands and when she mentioned this to Adam, he said, "They are pleased. So would I be if the Government gave me a thousand pounds' worth of free publicity."

Then another woman emerged from the ranks of supporters, all of whom were dressed entirely in white as though, for pity's sake, they were on their way to a wedding. The newcomer, young and pretty, wore a kind of apron that draped her from neck to hemline but it wasn't really an apron. It was a placard, advertising a march and mass meeting, with the information, '*The greatest number of free tickets ever issued for a public meeting – You march from Victoria Embankment. Assemble 12.30.*' And above, in heavier type, the obligatory slogan, '*Votes For Women*'.

She had no idea until now that so many people were caught up in the business, having thought of it as the preoccupation of a few intellectuals, women like Debbie, and eccentrics like Romayne, yet it was obvious the movement embraced all classes and all ages. Four girls, carrying a large 'Welcome' banner, were obviously shop girls or housemaids and Henrietta, judging this by the quality of their clothes, wondered how they had found the opportunity to slip away from their work, and what penalties their truancy might involve. Policemen were everywhere, and strangely tolerant, she thought, contenting themselves with keeping the main thoroughfare open.

And then, just as he had warned, a uniformed band arrived to take its position at the head of a procession that was forming, a dozen or more men with trombones and bassoons, and a police sergeant positioned himself in front, as though he was band-master.

Then, across the width of the roadway, there was a stir, rippling outwards like a wave, so that it gusted stragglers back to the kerb. Adam said, briefly, "They're out! But I don't know how we're expected to contact them in this jamboree. Giles and Milton might as well have come after all, for they couldn't be identified in a crowd of this size." He struggled out of the cab, then turned to hand her out, saying to the cabbie, "I'll be going on to the Norfolk Hotel as soon as I pick up my passengers. Can you wait round that corner? I'll make it worth your while."

"I'll do me best, gov'nor," the man said, and began to edge his way along the road away from the gaol gates. And then the band struck up and the procession began to move, Cockney urchins prancing alongside the ranks and indifferent policemen flanking the column of whiteclad women. She said, as they scanned the moving ranks, "It's more like a celebration. Can you spot either of them?"

"No," he said, "and it begins to look as if we've travelled up for nothing," but then, wearing darker clothes that singled them out, the dozen or so martyrs began to pass, and she saw both Debbie and Romayne marching in step some fifty yards behind the band.

They looked wan and tired and their presence there, jostled in a street procession instead of comfortably settled in a cab irritated her, so that she left Adam for a moment, struggling ahead of him and catching Deborah's sleeve and shouting, above the blare of brass, "Your father has a cab! We're taking you to the Norfolk for luncheon."

Debbie turned, looking very surprised but then smiled as she shouted back, "We can't fall out, Auntie! Tell him

we'll catch a cab at Headquarters and meet you there
In half-an-hour or so."

"But how *are* you, for heaven's sake?"

"We're fine But very hungry!" and Romayne, on the
far flank, raised her hand in greeting.

Adam caught her up, very much out of breath.

"Did you get a word with them?"

"They're coming over to the Norfolk in about half-an-
hour. Is that leg bothering you?"

"Like the very devil."

"You're too old for this nonsense and I shall tell them
so!" and she piloted him back to the cab, helping him to
hoist himself inside and giving the driver instructions to
make his way to the Norfolk.

He was badly winded and done up, she noticed, but
he managed to grin, saying, "You know, I believe you're
enjoying this, Hetty!"

"Oh, no I'm not," she snapped, "but it's lucky you
insisted I came along. I really don't know what things
are coming to . . . all these people here to meet a batch
of women just let out of prison. I do wish I could begin
to understand."

"Ask Debbie," he said, "she'll enlighten you, no doubt,"
and he settled back to regain his breath and she saw his
left hand at work massaging the flesh where the straps
chafed his leg.

Suddenly, and for no reason that she could think of, she
wanted to laugh. 'It really is too absurd,' she thought,
'for he's turned eighty and I'm sixty-eight and here we
are driving away from Holloway prison to meet a pair of
hot-heads who refuse to grow up. They were far less
trouble when they were children, for then either Phoebe
or myself were on hand to tell them to mind their manners,
and smack their bottoms when they got too tiresome!
And really he's no better, but there's more excuse for him,
for men never grow up and no woman with her wits about
her eve expects them to!'

But she told herself, none the less, that he was right about her enjoying herself, in an odd sort of way, and she *had* seen Mrs. Pankhurst and Mrs. Pethick-Lawrence in the flesh and that would be something to talk about at her next soirée or garden fête. And it was thinking this that enabled her, in some respects, to come to terms with what she had thought of, until then, as a family scandal. Whatever was going on in the world you could always be sure that somewhere, in some capacity, a Swann or two would be involved in it, and there was comfort, she supposed, to be derived from that. Most women her age had settled for the lace cap and serenity but with a family like hers you could put those things right out of mind. She was feeling almost gay when the cab dropped them at the Norfolk and they went in to freshen up and study the menu against the arrival of the gaolbirds.

It was much later, after the girls (as she still thought of them) had been fed, reclaimed and taken away by their husbands, when they were preparing for bed that looked very inviting when the lamp was lit and the fire made up, that she said, "That ruby necklace you talked about – it isn't the same really, Adam!"

"Tell me the difference?"

"The difference is," she said, "you made sure you weren't caught!" That made him laugh, as she knew it would, and he went on chuckling after the lamp was out and they were abed, watching the shadow play of the flames on the ceiling. It pleased her to score over him in that way once in a while. It proved she wasn't as rooted in the past as it sometimes pleased him to think.

2

She had another opportunity to recant when the spring came round and she was faced with the prospect of marrying the last of her daughters to a man she had not even met until Giles produced him like a rabbit from a conjuror's hat on a sunny morning in early April.

Giles was now accepted as the family ambassador, an

amiable broker for all kinds of delicate missions involving the in-laws and the grandchildren. Everybody took his goodwill and tact for granted, and even the Boer War breach between him and Alex seemed to be healing as evidenced by the fact that both Alex and his wife Lydia were careful not to refer to the embroilment of Debbie and Romayne in that fracas on the doorstep of No. 10 Downing Street.

He excelled himself on this occasion, appearing in the sewing-room during the Easter recess and saying, mysteriously, "I've got someone I'd very much like you to meet, Mamma. It took a lot of persuasion on my part to get him here, poor chap, but he's here now, out there talking to Father. We ran across Father down by the knoll."

She was not immediately aware that he was referring to his prospective brother-in-law, Huw Griffiths, but then his sly smile gave her the hint and she said excitedly, "That miner? Are they *both* here? Is Margaret with you?"

"No," he said, "I thought it might be easier on both of you if you give him a chance to speak for himself. So did Father. I warned him I was bringing Huw a week ago, but don't scold him. I made him promise he wouldn't say a word to you."

"It's . . . it's quite certain, then? The girl has really made up her mind?"

"They want to be married very soon. As soon as can be arranged." Then, "She was worried about your reactions, especially after that 'think again' letter you wrote her. But at least she didn't get married in Wales, and present you with a *fait accompli*. They've been engaged for over a year now, ever since he came out of the pits."

"You're saying he isn't a miner any longer?"

"Look, Mamma, there's nothing degrading about being a miner but it so happens Huw isn't. He's my agent, and we pay him five pounds a week and that's riches in the valley."

"It can't be riches to Margaret. Doesn't she know she's entitled to a share of her grandfather's money?"

"She knows, but she doesn't want a penny of it. Not now and not ever. She says it would destroy Huw's confidence in himself as a provider."

"That's a very silly point of view, isn't it?"

"Not to her. Not to Huw either. They've got a little house near ours at Pontnewydd, and they're perfectly content to leave things as they are. It's their decision."

It surprised her a little to find Huw Griffiths' determination to take this line. Indeed, it elevated him a little in her estimation for at least it proved the man was not the fortune-hunter she had assumed him to be. She said, briefly, "Show him in, Giles. We can't keep him on the doorstep."

"No. Wait a minute, Mamma," he said. "I've got something I'd like to show you first," and he unbuckled the strap of a briefcase he had thrown on the sewing-table, extracting what she recognised as one of Margaret's sketchbooks. "Have a look at these. Particularly the one of Huw Griffiths. He's changed now but I want you to see both versions."

He opened the sketchbook and thumbed through a number of drawings, mining village scenes apparently, for the pen, brush and crayons (Margaret had used all three) portrayed serried rows of narrow little dwellings, looming machinery, dark landscapes studded with debris of one kind or another, and here and there the face of a child that reminded her of Spanish children in a picture by a painter called Murillo that Adam regarded as one of the best in his collection.

"She paints *this* kind of thing down there?"

"All the time. She says it's more exciting than painting woods, fields and flowers, subjects that occupied her before she came to the valley. This is Huw, about the time they first met."

She studied the picture carefully. It showed her a powerfully-built young man sitting on an upturned wash tub in an unkempt garden, and although she knew herself to be no judge at all of paintings or drawings she was not proof against the impact this one made upon her. It was one of humour, frankness and powerful masculinity, all caught, magically to her way of thinking, in the subject's expression, and the set of his shoulders as he turned towards the artist, as though she had called, "This way, Huw! No, not *at* me, over my shoulder! I'm here but you're only half-aware of it and are looking at something to my right."

"This is him? This is Huw?" and when Giles nodded, "Why, it's . . . it's quite splendid! I mean, I always liked her drawings, even when she was a little thing, but this . . . why, it might have been done by a real painter!" and at that he laughed and closed the book, returning it to his briefcase.

"I'm glad you think so for we all do. And now I'll get in the original but treat him gently. He's very shy with the ladies."

'And I don't believe that for a moment,' she thought as Giles went out, closing the door, and her fingers itched to get at the sketchbook again and take another look. She did not, however, remembering her dignity, and the solemnity of the moment, and when Giles returned with the prospective son-in-law in tow she realised that he was shy, despite those merry black eyes and wide smile, one of the widest and warmest, she thought, she had ever seen on a man, especially a man as big and impressive as Huw Griffiths.

It was his size rather than his shyness that impinged on her, however, for she had always thought of Adam as an exceptionally well-made man, and here was someone who could top him by an inch or more and with shoulders a yard wide. Giles said, acting the impresario with just the right amount of light relief, "Well, here he is, Mamma. Your latest son-in-law, and a wild Welshman down to his bootstraps. Don't let her scare you, Huw, boy. She never did me, for you can talk her round in no time if you set about it the right way!"

Henrietta said, blushing, "Hush, Giles, for heaven's sake! You'll have Mr. Griffiths thinking me a perfect dragon! Please sit, Mr. Griffiths, and get the sherry from the cupboard, Giles . . ."

But Adam, it seemed, had anticipated her and came over with decanter and glasses, saying, with a wink in Giles' direction, "I'm sure Huw could do with a drink today, even if everybody in his part of the world pretends to be a teetotaller."

It was surprising after that how effortlessly she adjusted to the situation, a situation that, contemplated in advance, would have promised embarrassment all round. Giles helped, of course, as he always did on these occasions, but Huw Griffiths had begun to shed his awkwardness before his sherry glass was empty and she found herself viewing him as she might have viewed a handsome, well-set-up man forty-five years ago, in other words, as her youngest daughter must have when she first met him, and who could blame her wanting to paint his portrait? Why, it made her feel young and spry again just to be in the same room with him, and she blushed again when she caught Adam's eye and realised, confound the man, that he knew precisely what she was thinking, even if Giles, for all his book learning, did not. She not only approved his figure and bold good looks, she liked his lilting accent and the way his glance softened whenever Margaret was mentioned. All her early prejudice against him crumbled under the assault of his masculinity and she found herself comparing him with the Adam Swann she remembered when she was a bride-in-waiting at Derwentwater all those years ago. The upshot of it all was that Huw was talked into spending the night at 'Tryst', in order that he could make preliminary arrangements for the wedding at Twyforde parish church in early June.

The prospect of another family wedding exhilarated her. She would have thought that she was past the age when this could be so, for it was years now since she had seen one of her sons or daughters married in the old flint church down the road. Stella, her eldest, had been married there as long ago as 1881, and after Stella, Alex. Then Helen and finally, when she was turned thirty, Deborah. George had married abroad, Giles in the city, and Hugo at that fashionable church in Belgravia. Joanna, silly girl, had not had a real wedding at all, just a churching after her runaway match with Jack-o'-Lantern, whereas Helen's second marriage (performed in what Henrietta thought of as a Papist church) took place in Dublin. Now there was only young Edward left and she supposed he would be married wherever his wife happened to live, so she was determined to make the very best of the occasion and spent many happy hours choosing Margaret's gown and her own ensemble.

She wept a little at the ceremony – just for convention's sake – but admitted afterwards that Margaret had proved the prettiest bride of them all, whereas when it came to sons-in-law, Huw Griffiths finished a long way ahead of Denzil Fawcett, poor, dead Rowland Coles and his brother, Jack-o'-Lantern.

The occasion roused romantic echoes that persisted long after the wedding breakfast and excitement of the departure. The renewal of youth, bestowed upon her by the advent of this big, smiling Welshman, remained like a benediction, so that when Adam (surely he must have been subtly aware of her feelings!) mooted the idea of a sentimental journey into the past she could have hugged him, for nothing could have suited her mood more exactly.

It was a brilliant June morning, a day or so after they had all dispersed, that he said, over the breakfast table, "How do you fancy retracing your steps for a week or two, Hetty? It's grand weather, and this place seems as empty as a mausoleum now that every last one of them has moved out. Suppose we do one of our network tours, the way we did those summers after I learned to walk again?"

"Oh, I'd *like* that, Adam!" she said eagerly. "I'd like that very much indeed! We need a change, both of us, and there's nothing to keep us here. But where would we go, exactly?"

"Wherever you like," he said, eyeing her merrily, "the west, for you always liked it down there, and then up north to the Lakes, looking in on Bryn Lovell's boys in the Mountain Square en route. Then up into Scotland if you've a mind to, for it's years since I was there and George tells me Higson and his sons are still scooping up the groats in the Lowlands. I'd like to see just how he goes about it for I always had faith in that young rascal ever since we rescued him from the brute of a sweep in this very room."

It was clear that his mind was working along similar lines and that Margaret's wedding had struck chords in his heart that conjured pleasant melodies out of the past. Like him, she thought of the people he mentioned, not as they were now but as they were in his heyday, when the network was battling for its life in all corners of the land, and he was always hurrying to beleaguered sectors to give aid to his hard-pressed lieutenants. Bryn Lovell's boys must be approaching their thirties now and she knew they were doing well in the Mountain Square, where George had installed them after his reorganisation of the territories. And Jake Higson – she remembered him well, as the one asset salvaged from that frightful shambles on the 'Tryst' hearthrug in the early 'sixties, when Jake's fellow apprentice had been dragged dead from her flue. And since they were travelling north she had other stopping-off places in mind but thought it wiser to say nothing of them now lest he should tease her as a sentimental old biddy, just as if he wasn't as bad in his own special way.

One of the agreeable characteristics of Adam was that, having made a decision, he never lost a single moment implementing it. His holiday proposal had been mooted on Monday. By Wednesday midday they were off, travelling by Southern Railway as far as Salisbury, where they spent a pleasant night with the Rookwoods in what was still called, on the company's maps, the Southern Square.

She had heard a great deal about 'Young' Rookwood, the very first of Adam's Thameside scavengers to make his mark, and looking at the solemn, portly man over his impressively-laid dining table she wondered why, in heaven's name, Swann viceroys still referred to him by that silly name, for she judged him at least twelve years older than Alex, her eldest son, and that would make him fifty-seven. He and Adam talked little but business, booming about here it seemed, with Rookwood's full quota of mechanically-driven vans on the road, but she took a fancy to his gay little wife, another Hetty, and when the men were lingering over their port made so bold as to ask her how she and 'Young' Rookwood had met and married.

"He was our boarder," Mrs. Rookwood told her, "when he first came to these parts as a . . . well, not much more than a boy. Do you know anything about his past, Mrs. Swann?"

"I know he was an orphan, brought into the business as a vanboy by Mr. Keate, our waggonmaster. Keate was always rescuing orphans in those days."

"Ah, the marshal's baton in the Swann knapsack. But there's rather more to it than that. The poor boy spent all his spare time trying to discover who he was, and his failure bothered him so much that he never would have proposed to me if my mother hadn't given him a series of pushes! After that I persuaded him to concentrate on his future rather than his past. I expect your husband will have told you how well he's done down here, and I can tell you he's been a wonderful husband and father."

The story, she thought, had all the hall-marks of a Mudie's Library book, so she asked, "Do *you* ever wonder who he is, Mrs. Rookwood?"

"No," she said, firmly, "I don't and never did! I wouldn't change anything about my life if I had to live it all over again but then . . ." and she looked at her shrewdly, "I don't suppose *you* would, would you, Mrs. Swann?"

"No," said Henrietta, fervently, reflecting what a pleasure it was to meet a woman who was not ashamed to sing her husband's praises in public and to regard him, as Mrs. Rookwood obviously did, as the equal of any man on earth. She had always spoken of Adam in that way but few of her intimates followed suit. Most of them carped at their men as soon as the door was shut on them and she sometimes got the impression they regarded her as very naïve, and fair game for any husband with a trick or two up his sleeve. All the same, she could not readily picture the solemn Rookwood as an ardent lover, although it was abundantly clear that he was an excellent provider, and had she known Mrs. Rookwood better she would have liked to have pursued the subject for curiosity about men in this respect had remained with her since marriage, and so few women would discuss it. Most of them, when they did, gave the impression that a man's demands on his wife, outside the purely domestic sphere, were tiresome and vulgar, and none seemed able to prolong the early excitements of marriage into later life. And yet, as she was ready to admit to herself any time since her wedding day in 1858, it had been of paramount importance to her, converting what might have been a humdrum marriage, of the kind that seemed the norm nowadays, into an adventure more exciting than any to be lived second-hand between the covers of a book. Even now, after all this time, she still felt a stirring under her heart when his arm went round her, or he inclined his weight against her. It would be very interesting to know if she (or he, for that matter) were singular in this respect. She made a mental note to raise the subject with Edith Wickstead again when she next saw her, for Edith's admission that she had once been in love with Adam had broken the barriers of reserve between the two women. They had few secrets from one another.

They moved off the next morning for Exeter and booked

into a hotel in the Cathedral Yard, within three minutes walking distance of the Swann depot in South Street, ruled over by that funny Westcountry character 'Bertie-boy' Bickford, nephew of an even funnier uncle, the late Hamlet Ratcliffe, he who had captured a circus lion, and died hauling a statue of Queen Victoria up the Exe Valley on the eve of the Golden Jubilee.

She had always enjoyed visiting the Westcountry. The lilting names of villages, and the buzz-saw brogue of the locals, fascinated her and she spent a pleasant day with Adam on one of Mr. Bickford's two motor excursion waggons – 'charrybangs' he called them, for some un-explained reason. The 'charrybang', puffing like a grampus at some of the inclines about here, took them all the way to Teignmouth and back in a day, and although she was half choked with dust, and felt as if all her bones had been put in a box and rattled like a set of dice, she enjoyed the experience, her very first aboard one of George's motor-waggons, vehicles she had come to regard as George's private invention, owing nothing to anyone else, alive or dead.

She remembered earlier, smoother rides in four-horse brakes, and when they retired to bed that night she ventured to ask Adam how it was that so many people preferred to be trundled about in this rough and ready manner, when they might so easily have relaxed on a horse brake.

"It's a lot faster for one thing," he said, chuckling, "and almost everybody wants to move faster and further afield these days. I shouldn't quarrel with that, I suppose. I built the business on speed and a point to remember is that those motors of George's are constantly improving in comfort and reliability. Ten years ago that thing we were on today would have broken down a dozen times and as for noise and vibration, well, it was a duckpond sail compared with a ride aboard that first juggernaut he brought home from Austria. In another ten years, I daresay, motors will be bowling along the roads so fast that you'll barely notice their passage. Some of the expensive private motors now can travel at fifty miles an hour, pretty well as fast as a train."

"Well, they won't get my custom," she said, emphatically. "If we do any more excursions on this holiday we'll hire a gig and you can drive, as you used to in the old days."

Bryn Lovell's boys, Enoch and Shad, met them at Newport and took them on to Cardiff, where the Mountain Square depot was now established. All the motor-vehicles about here, they told her, were concentrated in the coal, steel and tinplate areas of the south. They never used them in Central or North Wales, where road surfaces were poor, hauls were mostly agricultural and no one was in a hurry. She had never seen the mountain country of North Wales and persuaded Adam to break the journey north at Chester, hire a trap and make a leisurely circuit of the mountain country where, at a place called Beddgelert, he showed her the spot where Giles met Romayne, 'rescuing' her from a counterfeit drowning. It was the kind of prank one would expect of a minx like Romayne Rycroft-Mostyn and, judging by her recent performance outside No. 10, that had earned her a spell in gaol, she was still untamed, despite years of marriage to a gentle creature like Giles. She said, voicing her thoughts: "Have you ever come close to understanding that girl, Adam?" He said he had not, and neither, he suspected, had Giles, although it was fortunate for him he had been able to channel her nervous energy into politics.

"But doesn't that kind of publicity do him harm?"

He replied, after pondering the question a moment, "No, not in the long run. It would have ruined him a generation ago, but today almost any publicity is good publicity. It's the way the world's going, I'm afraid. Stridency is replacing commonsense. I imagine, in time, Romayne's involvement with the suffragettes will give Giles that extra boost which every public man needs, and Giles more than most, for he's a very modest chap and modesty is a handicap in a politician."

"But you advised both him and Milton to stay clear of that welcome party outside the gaol in January."

"Yes, I did, and you saw for yourself how wrong I was. You can still learn at my age, providing you keep an open mind."

It set her thinking, as did these stirring, age-old vistas about here, about the size of the tapestry they had woven about them in half-a-century of marriage. It was like a piece of embroidery that began life as a child's sampler and grew bigger and bigger until it was an epic scene, embracing every aspect of life. The name 'Swann' now seemed to her as permanent as Snowdon, whose bulk dominated every other mountain about here. They were now drawing near the scene of her first encounter with the real founder of the dynasty, and the place, some miles to the north of it, where she had suggested the device still used on all his vehicles, billheads and in all his newspaper advertisements. It hardened her resolve, when they entered the Polygon area of North Cheshire, to make a pilgrimage to the place where, on a hot July morning in 1858, she and her splendid destiny had merged on a desolate stretch of moorland.

He acceded readily enough. They travelled on to Manchester where her grandson Rudi, second son of George and his Austrian wife, Gisela, was winning his spurs, managing the depot sited at Salford. Here The Polygon's generous quota of petrol-driven waggons were fully extended over flattish terrain, serving both Lancashire's cotton interests and the vast volume of shipping that steamed in and out of Liverpool's docks.

Rudi, liveliest and most winning of George's flock, had always been a great favourite of hers, so that it did not surprise her much when, after handing Adam over to his manager to visit the new Ship Canal docks, he drew her aside and said, shyly for him, "I . . . er . . . I should like to ask your advice on something, Grandmam."

She at once jumped to the conclusion that the handsome young scamp had got into debt, and was seeking a loan, and was therefore dumbfounded when, the moment the office door closed on them, he said breathlessly, "Grandmam . . . I can tell *you*. Nobody down south has an inkling as yet. The fact is . . . I'm . . . well . . . married!"

"*Married!* And your father and mother don't know? *Nobody* knows?"

"Well," – and he gave something between a wink and a grimace – "Evie's parents know, for her father had to give her away. And her brothers and sister know, but nobody in the yard does, not even the foreman. I haven't even told Max, my brother, although I could trust him to keep mum until I'd sorted things out."

"But this is quite ridiculous, Rudi, and you must know it is," she said, severely. "I mean, why all this secrecy? And how did it come about? Your mother would be very upset indeed to think you have married without even telling her. And anyway, why are you telling me now?"

He said, avoiding her eye, "I've got to tell somebody and I knew I could rely on you. As for keeping it secret . . . well, it was all a bit of a rush, and my first responsibility, as I saw it, was to Evie." He looked up, a little desperately, "Can't you *guess* the rest, Grandmam?"

She could guess, and thought herself slow not to have guessed at once. "You mean you *had* to get married?"

"*No!*" He looked quite truculent, his expression reminding her vividly of George when he was thwarted as a child. "I didn't 'have' to get married as they say. We would have married anyway, as soon as I was thoroughly established here. I love Evie. I loved her from the first day I saw her sitting perched on that chair!"

"What chair?"

"That one over there, the high one by the ledger rest. She was a girl clerk, you see, taken on by Bagshawe, our chief clerk, when I was away on a trip. We take girl clerks now, like a lot of firms up here. They're cheaper for one thing, and the best of them are more conscientious than men. Evie's very sharp. She left school at thirteen to go in a mill but she had the sense to go to evening classes and learn book-keeping. You'll like her, Grandmam. She's not just pretty. She's so much, well . . . so much *fun*!"

She thought, only just succeeding in suppressing a smile, 'She sounds it, my lad!' but then the desperate sincerity of the boy touched her and she made a quick mental review of the probable consequences down south, once his secret was out. George, whose gallantries at Rudi's age were still remembered, would probably give the boy a dressing down and forget it, but Gisela, who had been at such pains to adopt English proprieties since she had left the Danube, would be very upset, seeing a marriage of this kind as a blot on the record. She said, "When did you marry, Rudi? And when is the child due?"

"We've been married six months now. The baby is expected any day. We've got a little house out at Timperley, a few miles from here and I'd love you to meet Evie, Grandmam, but maybe you would prefer to wait. I've got a picture of her here. It's a wedding photograph actually. She didn't wear white, of course. Naturally it was very quiet, just her mother, father and sister as witnesses. We managed to arrange it early in the morning."

He fumbled in his jacket pocket and took out a small, studio portrait of a girl with dark hair and merry eyes – George's kind of eyes – that looked out on life with confidence, and an expectation of jokes dredged from the small change of the day. She had, however, a very determined chin, a good figure slightly on the plump side, and her costume, an inexpensive one, was worn with panache.

"Weren't her parents very angry about it?"

He grinned, then wiped the grin from his face.

"Well, no, not really, or not once they understood how things were between us. I like them all. They're a very jolly family. He's a lock keeper on the Canal, and all her sisters and brothers are spinners in Rowton Mill. To be honest I suppose they think Evie's done well for herself but that's only to be expected, isn't it?"

"Yes, I suppose it is, but I hate to think of you hurting your mother's feelings. She thinks a rare lot of you boys. What exactly do you want me to do about it?"

"Break the news, as soon as you get back. Maybe the baby will have arrived by then and if it's a boy mother won't mind so much. She was always on at Max and me to get married and give her some grandchildren. I think she really worried about us staying bachelors so long."

It was true. She knew Gisela well enough to realise that the prospect of growing old without a tribe of grandchildren would not appeal to her, or to George either for that matter. It really was a little odd that, with four children, they had neither sons-in-law nor daughters-in-law for two of Stella's boys were married now, and Alex's daughter, Rose, and Joanna's eldest daughter, Valerie, were engaged to be married this summer. Robert and Richard, respectively eldest and youngest sons of Stella, had so far produced three daughters between them, her first batch of great-grandchildren, but if, as she fervently hoped, Rudi's child was a boy, he would qualify as the first Swann great-grandson, so who cared whether he 'came across the fields' as her old nurse used to say? She said, "I'll do what I can but the very first chance you get bring that girl down to 'Tryst' for I'm sure I'd like to meet her and so would your grandfather. If it is a boy have you decided what to call him?"

"Sam. For Grandfather Rawlinson. After all, he'll be a Lancastrian, and Grandfather Sam did a lot to help my father when he was working to perfect his prototype up here."

She had forgotten that, Sam Rawlinson's part in sponsoring George at a time when he had quarrelled bitterly with his father, and it touched her a little that the boy should want to make this gesture. She had never been close to her father, always having regarded him as a bit of a ruffian, but there was no doubt about it, Sam's strong, mechanical strain was present in the family and his aggressiveness too, when you came to think about it.

"You won't say anything to Grandfather yet?"

"I won't say anything to anyone until I've seen your mother and that can't be for a fortnight or more. We're supposed to be going on to Scotland."

"How do I keep in touch then?"

"Well, tomorrow your grandfather has promised to take me to the place where I grew up, Sedley Mills. Then we shall return to Manchester and catch a train on to Ambleside and stay a day or so at The Glades Hotel before going on to Edinburgh."

She took out her purse and extracted a gold half-sovereign. "The day he's born put this in his hand and close his fingers over it. Then put it away somewhere. It's an old good-luck custom. Adam's father, the old Colonel, did it with all the children, right up to the time he died."

He kissed her, saying, "You're a good sport, Grandmam, and you never seem like a grandmother to me. More like a . . . well . . . like a sister."

It was worth more than half-a-sovereign to get a compliment of that kind.

3

It was surprising how little the vista beyond what she thought of as The Rampart had changed. The Rampart was a string of towns following the course of the great-grandfather of all railways, Stephenson's Manchester-to-Liverpool line over Chat Moss where, for weeks on end they said, Irish navvies had tipped thousands of fascines to form a base under the track. Here town and country met on the northern edge of the Cheshire plain, the vast jumble of mills, shops, warehouses, sidings and cobbled streets, straggling west in what now seemed one huge ugly city and beyond it, to the south, hedgerow land, ploughed furrow, neat black and white farmsteads, and the house where she had grown up, Sam Rawlinson's mock-Gothic lodge, known by millhands in those days, as 'Scab's Castle'.

She had no fond memories of Seddon Moss, the town where her father had made his first fortune, but the moor to the south of it was dear to her and she became very silent and absorbed as the trap rattled over the winding road towards the familiar clump of woodland on the horizon.

He respected her silence, having memories of his own, of a saddlesore young man riding north across the swell of gorse common fifty summers ago and coming upon a scene of riot and arson that turned him back, sick with disgust at the cruelty he had witnessed. Yet something sweet and wholesome had emerged from it, for it was only hours later that he came upon her in a dip beside a shepherd's hut and their life's odyssey, in convoy, had begun right there, weeks before the first Swann waggon, bearing its strange device moved out across Kent in search of customers.

"It was about here, wasn't it, Hetty?"

"No," she said, "a little further on. Just past the Nantwich fork coming this way."

He wouldn't have remembered, or not with that degree of accuracy, but was prepared to trust her judgment. The moment, he guessed, would have even more significance for her. He had taken a long time to evaluate her, some seven years if he was honest with himself. Until then he had been almost entirely absorbed in his work and the terrible demands it had made upon him.

"Here, Adam. Why, you can still see where the hut stood. There, over on the left, just at the foot of the dip."

It was true. An oblong of flattened gorse was marked out by what he could identify as the holes where the posts had been driven in, and he checked the horse and climbed down, helping her to alight and tethering the skewbald to a bush. They moved off the road and stood silently on the patch of open ground, holding hands lightly and seeing themselves, a little ironically in his case, as they had been the morning of the encounter. He said, finally, "Tell you something, Hetty. When I realised you were Sam Rawlinson's daughter I came damned close to leaving you to fend for yourself. The smoke from old Sam's burned-out mill was still on the skyline yonder, and I kept thinking of that boy he had ridden down in the town."

"What stopped you?"

"Oh, a variety of reasons. At least you'd had the sense to run out on him, and you didn't seem much more than a child at the time. Then you coaxed me into a more tolerant humour, thinking Birmingham was a seaport, and that story about deportment."

"I don't recall that."

"You don't? I'll never forget it. Something your governess taught you – 'Never accept a chair from a gentleman until you are satisfied it is no longer warm from his person!' And then again, I hadn't thought about a woman as a woman in more than a year."

"That isn't much of a compliment, is it?"

"A better one than it sounds. Emptying that well at Cawnpore, crammed full of butchered women and children, must have petrified my emotions. You started the thaw."

She wondered how much truth there was in this and how, exactly, she had appealed to him as a woman in that bedraggled green crinoline she was wearing, with her hair uncombed and mud on her face. Hardly at all, she would say, remembering his first embrace beside Derwent-water a few days later, that left her in a turmoil, but had not seemed to make much impression on him. She had worshipped him from the beginning, from the moment he hoisted her on to the rump of his mare and told her to put her arms around his waist, but responsive affection, of the kind that flowered early in their marriage, had not been evident until they were man and wife. Perhaps he was right. Perhaps the horrors of the Sepoy Mutiny had blunted his sensibilities and they had been sharpened, over the ensuing weeks, by physical access to her that had begun in a mood of tolerance and developed in a way that lasted them down the years. She said, "Hold me, Adam. Just for a moment," and he put his arms round her and kissed her gently on the mouth.

They climbed back into the trap and moved on over the crest towards the trees, catching a glimpse of the lodge turrets as they drew near and reining in at a spot where they could see the house through the trees. To her it looked much smaller than she remembered. To him it was one of the ugliest dwellings he had ever seen, a monstrous multiple marriage between domestic Cheshire, mock Tudor, mock Gothic and neo-classical, precisely the kind of monument a vulgarian like old Sam would erect to his brigandage and avarice.

"Great God!" he exclaimed, "no wonder you fled from it!"

"But I didn't, not in that sense, for it seemed a grand house to me. I fled from that awful man Goldthorpe Sam had decided I should marry in exchange for a loading bay area on Goldthorpe's father's land."

"Oh, yes. I'd forgotten the bartered bride angle." And then, with an approving glance, "Nobody would have married you against your will, Hetty. You've far too much spunk."

"I'm not so sure. It was touch and go until you spoke up for me. Come, I've seen all I want to about here. Let's get back to Warrington if we're to catch that train for I wouldn't care to spend a night hereabouts, not even in a shepherd's hut with you on hand. That's another thing I learned from you early on."

"What exactly?"

"To value comfort. I remember you telling me, when I remarked on the trouble you went to make a bivouac weatherproof and cosy, 'Any fool can be cold, wet and miserable.'"

*　　　*　　　*

The Glades Hotel, overlooking Windermere where they had spent their first night together, was still in business, but much larger and more pretentious than it had been half-a-century ago. They dined in the same room, where he had made her half-tipsy on claret and she had suffered agonies of embarrassment wondering how to tell him she was desperate to be excused. 'The miseries we inflict on ourselves at that age,' she thought, smiling as she recalled the relief attending the release of her corset tapes in the ladies' room.

It was still light when they took an after-dinner stroll along the lakeside, with the sun setting over Hawkshead and Coniston Water and the blue peaks of the fells on the far side of the lake. It was surprising, she thought, that they had never retraced their steps here in all this time, for her thoughts, all of them pleasant, had returned here time and again, remembering so much of that stupendous occasion when, or so it had seemed to her at the time, all the secrets of the universe had been revealed to her. And as she thought this she was aware of a rare spurt of rebellion against growing old, reflecting that their relationship had entered a new phase in the last few years, a burned-out phase she supposed, although his touch and nearness still awakened in her echoes of the fearful ecstasy of that splendid time.

The red-jacketed hall porter greeted them in the foyer, holding a buff telegram form, saying, "The telegraph boy arrived with it just after you and the lady went out, sir. There's no prepaid answer but the telegraph office is open until midnight if you want the boots to send a reply."

He took the envelope, drew out the message and read it with an expression of mystification, passing it to her and saying, "Can you make anything of this, Hetty? It's gibberish to me." She took the form and moved nearer the chandelier. The message read, 'SAM DESCENDED ON US TODAY STOP ALL EIGHT POUNDS OF HIM STOP LOVE RUDI' and she realised then that the telegram had been addressed to her and laughed outright, partly at the sauciness of the message, partly at Adam's baffled expression.

"What's the joke? What the devil is the boy driving at? It *is* George's Rudi, I imagine?"

"Oh, it's George's Rudi all right," and she began laughing again, so that he looked quite irritated for a moment and the porter, sensing domestic contention, moved away and pretended to be absorbed in the letter rack beside the receptionist's desk.

"There's no answer," she called across to him, and to Adam, "Come up to our room, Adam, and I'll explain."

His exasperation was really quite comic as she closed the door, laid down the telegram and said, removing her hat and veil, "It's really quite an occasion, Adam. Nothing whatever to scowl about. The arrival of our first great-grandson, no less. That's worth a telegram, isn't it?"

"Great-grandson? But, dammit, woman, the boy's a bachelor!"

"Oh, no, he isn't. He's been married six months or more."

"Six months you say?" He picked up the telegram and re-read it. "How do you know? And why is this addressed to you?"

"Well, it wouldn't have made much sense addressed to you, would it? He confided in me when you were out looking at the new docks. He married his book-keeper, a girl called Eve – I don't know what her maiden name was. I imagine they married a week or so after she discovered she was expecting his child."

"He told *you* that?"

"He had to tell someone, poor lad. They were hoping for a boy and decided on 'Sam', remembering how close Sam and George were in the old days."

He sat down on the bed. "Haven't George and Gisela been told yet?"

"No. They were going to be married anyway as soon as Rudi had settled in as manager of the depot but it seems – well, you know what young men are better than I do. It isn't that kind of marriage, however. They're very much in love and she looks such a pretty, forth-coming sort of girl."

"You've met her?"

"No. He showed me a picture of her."

Humour finally triumphed over his bewilderment and he smiled but then, giving her a steady look of appraisal, "I find that very interesting, Hetty. That a boy in that situation should confide in his grandmother, when he could have made his choice from a whole tribe of uncles, aunts, brothers, sisters and cousins. It establishes something important."

"Only that he needed someone to break the news gently to his mother."

"No, something beyond that. I could have done that for him. So could his father, or Max, his brother or even Giles, whom we all seem to use as a go-between. But he didn't, he went straight to you, and do you know why? Because he sees you as the real power behind the throne, the one person with the broadmindedness and authority to ease him and that girl he's married out of a ticklish corner. I've a notion any one of them would do the same if it came to the pinch, and that means you've kept overall command of 'em. Not as a grandmother but as a person, and it's a credit to you if you think about it. They'd con-fide in me soon enough if it was a business matter but a human problem, that's something different."

His eyes returned to the form again. "Sam, eh? Well, it's fitting, I suppose, for a first great-grandson. Your father would have been tickled. Especially by us getting the news here of all places. Come over here, you witch."

She came and stood before him and his big hands en-closed her tightly corsetted waist, inclining her towards him and then, in a way that was reminiscent of the man she recalled so vividly from the past, his hands slipped over the rim of the corset to pinch her bottom. "You're a very singular woman, Henrietta Rawlinson. I had a lot more sense than I realised when I scooped you off that moor, showed your father the door and brought you here to this hotel, as green a woman as a man ever coveted. By God, I'd give something to be that young again."

"Who wouldn't?"

"You'll always be young and this is proof of it," and he released her, folded the telegram carefully and put it in his pocket. And then, in the last blink of twilight reaching them from the darkening surface of the lake, she saw his eyes light up. "To blazes with trailing further north," he said. "Let's go south again, stop off at Manchester, meet that wife of his and wet the baby's head. After that I'll bow myself out and leave you to introduce Sam Swann to his grandmother."

5

Landmark

THE SWANN TRIBE, TOGETHER WITH THEIR LEAD-
ing henchmen dotted about the country, had many common characteristics, uniformity being the product of the
strain, as far as the family was concerned, added to Adam
Swann's skill in selecting deputies capable of measuring
up to his standards. Every one of them, to some degree,
were dogged and purposeful, not easily turned aside from
the pursuit of what they sought in the way of glory,
rewards and the satisfaction that stemmed from doing a
job well. In addition, almost all of them were capable of a
strenuous effort and an occasional sacrifice demanded by
loyalty to one another and to the firm, for they saw themselves as a unit constantly confronted by rivals and what
Adam referred to as 'the Johnny-Come-Latelys', whose
watchwords were quick profits, with no real regard for the
quality of service rendered. They had in common a
sense of living in the present, that promised endless
possibility, of being members of an élite among their
fellows, especially those (poor devils) who had the misfortune to be born the far side of the English Channel, so
that the pulse of nationalism, quickened by three generations of success, beat strongly in each of them, even in
Giles, who sometimes saw the strident nationalism of the
British as a threat to the harmony of nations. But that
was as far as it went in terms of collectivity, really no more
than a loose but effective alliance of some three thousand

men and a hundred or so women, who respected the past and embraced the present but gave little thought to the future and were therefore not equipped to anticipate the rhythms of destiny.

Adam, the patriarch, had the advantage of all of them, in this respect. He had lived far longer than most of them and the jeopardies of his youth had developed in him a deeper awareness of the wanton twists of fortune. A guarded optimist in most respects he had yet learned, over the years, to live like a boxer squaring up to an opponent of unknown reputation, poised on the balls of his feet and conserving his wind, even when he had an adversary sagging against the ropes. As a soldier and trader over more than six decades of high adventure, entailing so many brushes with sudden death and slow bankruptcy, he understood that it did not profit a man to underestimate the opposition, or over-extend himself, or squander reserves of patience. Someone or something was always lurking behind the hill to exploit any such lapse and he had tried, in his gruff, solitary way, to instil this precept into his children and employees. With very little success, however, for neither the Swanns nor their henchmen had had much personal experience with failure and even Henrietta could look back on the successive crises of the 'sixties with a sense of having met and surmounted them. As for the others, for the children and even the middle-aged among the pashas, not one of them could recall a time when Swann had not been a household word, when there had not been reserves of cash and credit in the bank and, above all, to a time when British citizenship did not carry, as it were, the golden star of precedence over every competitor in the world of commerce.

God knows, Adam sometimes thought, they had grounds for such confidence. Ever since the dawn of the new century, and particularly since the general advance of 1905–1908, family and firm had been riding high. George Swann was now acknowledged the most successful haulier in the country, with over two hundred petrol-driven vehicles on the road and still as many horse-drawn vehicles as his father had fielded in the days when the term 'horse-less carriage' was a carter's gibe. The Swann insignia was now seen in every corner of the country save only the Western Isles, where there was little or no profit in hauling, whereas the overall yield of the firm rose year by year, from fifteen per cent in 1901 to just over thirty per cent in the Swann Jubilee year of 1908. George had achieved his headstart and viceroy investors sometimes asked themselves where their wits had been holidaying in 1904, when he had been voted down by his fellow directors. Now his position was even more secure than his father's had been, for he was reckoned a general who had won not merely Waterloo but the peace that followed it. With his privately owned concern adding to the fleet of Swann-Maxie waggons at the rate of one a week there seemed little prospect of anyone coming abreast of him.

In other fields, seemingly remote from transport, the Swanns had made their mark. Alexander Swann, close confidant of the War Minister and acknowledged expert on small arms, was a force to be reckoned with among the polo-enthusiasts who still thought of Haldane's Territorials as a kind of last-ditch reserve.

Giles Swann, although a little-known back-bencher, cold-shouldered by the patricians of his party, was known to have personal access to two or three powerful men in the Cabinet, notably the Welsh Wizard and the pacifist, John Burns. He was also enlarging his grip on his constituents in the valleys where he was known as that rare breed of politician who could be approached anywhere, anytime, and the prospect of unseating him now was considered remote. Meantime Hugo Swann, war-hero, not only lived on in the after glory of earlier athletic prowess but had won fresh laurels at Netley Military Hospital. He was known as 'Flexer' Swann among staff and patients and there were some, among them the men he treated, who declared there was magic in his hands, a legend that his wife helped to foster among the splendid ones who attended her fêtes and garden parties organised on behalf of ex-servicemen.

Of the Swann girls, two had married men of substance, and even Edward Swann, a solitary young man seldom seen in the metropolis, had a high reputation as a mechanic among manufacturers and exporters in the great Midland swathe marked out on Swann's new maps as The Funnel.

And yet, into the heart and mind of the ageing Adam Swann, head of the tribe, there stole, on this high tide of fortune, a sense of unease as he stumped about his arbours, flowering shrubs and exotic trees on that estate of his sixteen miles south-east of London Stone, and if you had taxed him with it he would have found it very difficult to express in words. It was not that prospects, after so far a run, were due for a change on that account alone, for to accept this would have been admitting to superstition and Adam was the least superstitious of men. Neither did it stem from the stridency of firm and family but from the mood of the tribe as a whole, that had now, seemingly, made a complete recovery from the blight of self-doubt of a few years ago, when sixty thousand farmers had beaten them thrice in a single week. National preoccupation with what he saw as the fairground aspects of the new era might have contributed to his apprehension, for everywhere there was prattle about the garish stucco city they had erected at Shepherd's Bush and were comparing, to the former's advantage, with the Great Exhibition of 1851. And this, he thought, was nonsense, for alone among them he could remember the Great Exhibition, and its air of earnest exploration, whereas now, at this fun parlour they called the White City, the most talked-of exhibit was the giant flip-flap, a joyriding contraption of extraordinary silliness. Then there was the ever-increasing emphasis on outdoor sports, as if German and American competition could be held at bay by an army of cricketers, yachtsmen, prizefighters, jockeys, lady archers and lady tennis champions. Tremendous coverage was given, even in sober journals, to the antics of these tumblers and less and less, or so it seemed to him, to the real business of the nation, so that the British Empire might be going the way of Rome when the approach of the barbarians failed to deflect citizens from gladiatorial conventions in the Coliseum.

The very titles of current successes in West End theatres underlined the pervading frivolity of a nation hitherto dedicated to the pursuit of profit – *The Merry Widow*, *A Waltz Dream*, *The Flag Lieutenant* and *My Mimosa Maid*. Slang was finding its way into the verbal currency of debutantes and top-hatted city gents, as well as that of street urchins. A serious campaign, aimed at extending the franchise to educated women, was treated, by press and public alike, as a lively sideshow running a close second to the White City's flip-flap, so that sometimes he began to equate London – in his day the most industrious city on earth – as a new Vienna, awaiting, indeed sometimes seeming to invite, total eclipse by Berlin and Chicago.

There had been a time, less than twenty years ago, when he would not have wagered a sixpence on the prospects of a successful overseas challenge, but it did not require a dedicated newspaper reader like himself to see Germany and the United States as strong contenders for the title of top dog today. Over on the Continent, he sensed, people still had their noses to the grindstone, whereas over here Bank Holidays, seaside trips, beanos, regattas, day excursions by motor brakes, and all manner of diversions were beginning to rank high on the programme of thirty-shilling-a-week clerks and even, he suspected, collarless artisans, among whom were a thousand or more Swann carters.

He was all for giving the underdog a fair crack of the whip but underdogs ought never to forget that the only road to advancement lay through the portals of application and self-development. Certainly not through the turnstile of the White City or the nearest professional football stadium.

He wondered sometimes how that tough old warrior,

John Catesby, he who had fought so hard and so courageously to establish the Trades Union Congress, would have regarded it. Contemptuously, he would say, remembering The Polygon manager's passionate avowal of the dignity of labour, but there it was – the sons of men whom Catesby had helped to liberate from stupefying labour in mill and factory were now more elevated by news that Britain had won four out of the first five prizes in the International Balloon Race than in improving machinery designed to strike a bargain between boss and hired hand. They did their work – shoddily if some of the new products he had handled lately were their judge – then rushed off to an athletic field somewhere, more often to watch than to play, for the gladiators who drew the largest crowds nowadays were professionals and even village cricket, they told him, was entering a decline.

Glum as they were, however, he kept these thoughts to himself apart from a hint or two to Giles, still struggling towards the Millennium, for it gave him no pleasure to puncture the self-confidence of George, Alex and Edward, and he saw little of the girls now they were all off his hands.

So it was, when George came to him with an invitation to occupy the seat of honour at the forthcoming Jubilee banquet he was planning for late September, he thanked him and accepted, saying, "You'll not want me to make a speech, I hope?" And at that George laughed and said he most surely would be required to speak, for he was down to reply to the toast '*Swann-on-Wheels, 1858–1908*'.

"Who else could do it with your style?" he demanded. "Come to that, who else has survived to challenge the authenticity of all the I-remembers you'll weave into your text?"

"Oh, I daresay a few old crocks will shake the moths out of their festive rig on the promise of free liquor. Not poor old Keate, the original waggonmaster, for he's ninety and anyway he's a teetotaller. But I daresay a few old stagers like Bryn Lovell, Young Rookwood and

Jake Higson, will want to boast about their long-service records. Where are you holding it? At the George Inn?"

No, George told him, it was planned to take place in the largest of the new warehouses, specially decorated for the occasion, and every region was balloting for a deputation of twenty employees, for even the warehouse could not accommodate everyone who would want to come.

"There'll be over three hundred by my reckoning," he added, "and on the same night every region is holding its own celebration dinner. I've allocated a grant of fifty pounds to every depot."

"Wives?"

"A few of them. Would mother be interested, do you suppose?"

"I wouldn't care to be the one who told her she hadn't been invited," and noting George's smile added, "Why do you ask such a question, boy?"

"I don't know . . . maybe because I've always sensed she regarded the network as a rival."

"So she did. But your mother's far too sharp to turn her back on the Other Woman. I found that out when you were a toddler."

It crossed his mind then to wonder how much they knew of Henrietta's achievement when she had hauled the business out of the doldrums that time he lost his leg and was out of action for a year. Little enough, he imagined, for it was all so long ago, and so wildly improbable at the time, a transformation, overnight, of a feckless girl into a merchant princess and it gave him the bare bones of the speech George wanted him to make.

"Send her a card and all the trimmings," he said. "She'd appreciate that, boy."

2

Edith, he recalled, had once seen them as privateersmen, converging on the Thames to plan a string of piratical affrays, but when he reminded her of this, in the

interval when they were milling around before taking
their seats, she smiled and said, "But they've come *en
masse* today, with their private retinues, so I see them a
little differently. As trained bands, converging on the
capital to squeeze the best terms out of the man who
hires them. Or as a company of mercenaries, assembling
under some old brigand like Sir Robert Knollys before
cutting a swathe from Lower Normandy to Gascony."

He liked that and thought about it for a moment as
he watched them exchanging banter round the seating
plan George had fastened to a blackboard near the double
doors. A White Company, well versed in the use of
weapons, and masters of their own tactical skills, yet still
needing the strategical direction of a veteran like George,
a man they had come to trust and admire, forgetting the
occasions when he had led them on unprofitable ventures
and remembering only more recent triumphs in which
every one of them had shared.

They had come here from every corner of the islands,
bringing with them their local prejudices and babel of
dialects but disposed, for once, to set aside old rivalries
and frontier skirmishes for they would see themselves as
meeting on neutral ground.

His eye roved among them, ironically but affectionately,
revisiting their several beats and recalling, over half-a-
century, the men who had planted the Swann banner in
every shire of the four kingdoms. Higson and his band of
Lowlanders and Highlanders, inviting ridicule by appearing in the kilt to which, no doubt, few of them were
entitled. Their leader, Higson, was not among this
minority. Adam recalled him as a rawboned lad of
thirteen, with an accent that placed him no more than
a mile from this spot, but none of the young bucks would
have the temerity to remind him of his origins tonight.
Higson's record was far too impressive. Within two years
of crossing the border he had captured the Lowlands from
the natives. In another year he had consolidated his
gains. And in two years more he had won the Swann

accolade, wresting it from that other gamin, Rookwood, who tonight moved among the upper echelons of celebrants like an exalted Palace flunkey, a cut above everyone save only George and himself, and only marginally below them in Swann seniority.

It was curious, he noted, how the ballot-chosen retainers took their several cues from the regional chieftains. Higson's lot looked like a score of moss troopers embarked on a border raid, whereas the men around Rookwood were a sober, respectable bunch, every man jack of them wearing gloves and evening dress, as though Rookwood had held an inspection on Salisbury Station before setting off for town.

Bertieboy Bickford's westerners were easily distinguished by their brogues and the volume of láughter, a heavy-jowled, redfaced, breezy troupe, who might have been recruited from Dartmoor and Exmoor smallholdings. The Lovell boys had travelled up with a covey of Welshmen, whereas Clint Coles' contingent were Irishmen to a man and gave the impression of having foregathered in advance at the George Inn, down the road, in order to fortify themselves for long speeches. Scottie Quirt was here from the North, with what seemed to Adam an entirely different breed, younger men mostly, many of them still in their twenties, and it struck him that mechanically-propelled vehicles would be unlikely to attract mature men, just as if the general post caused by Stephenson's railways nearly a century ago was being repeated all over again with the phasing out of the horse. Watching them, catching a word or two of their technical jargon, his mind returned for a moment to old coachman Blubb, who had been thrown on the scrapheap by 'that bliddy teakettle', that had reduced professional coachmen to the status of carters.

The elegant Godsall, of the Kentish Triangle, came up to pay his respects to Henrietta and as they exchanged courtesies Adam reflected that Godsall was probably the only bona fide gentleman he had ever enrolled as a manager. Now, they said, he drove about Kent in a big Daimler car, like the one King Edward owned, so that in a sense the ex-guardee was a link between the old cadres and the new.

He managed to have a word with his grandson, Rudi, down from The Polygon and accompanied, he was glad to see, by that saucy little baggage he had married in such a hurry. He said, addressing her, "Well, now, and who's minding my great-grandson tonight?"

"Our Lottie, Grandfather — my youngest sister that is," she replied, pertly enough. "But she wouldn't do it for less than half-a-crown and only then if we gave her permission to have her young man in until Mam comes at suppertime."

"Ah," he said, chuckling, "you Lancastrians are razor sharp when it comes to putting a price on yourselves. They always say Yorkshire folk have the edge on you but I never believed it."

"The difference is," she said, "on our side of the Pennines we don't mind parting with it once we've got it." And he thought approvingly, 'Young Rudi knew what he was about when he picked that lass and so, I'd wager, did she, when she jumped the starter's gun. But they're well matched, somehow, and that's half the battle at their age,' and he turned aside to have a word with Dockett, of Tom Tiddler's Land, one of the very few originals here tonight.

Then someone beat a gong and the company began to sort themselves out but the warehouse was so crowded that it took some time for guests to find their seats. In the hurly-burly he bumped into Young Edward, who looked very spruce in a London-cut evening suit, with a red carnation in his buttonhole and a blue silk colarette, embroidered with the swan insignia. "It's George's idea," Edward said, grinning. "I'm toastmaster, you see," and then, moving to one side, he displayed his partner, the most attractive girl Adam had seen in a very long time.

It was not that she was pretty, in the way most young

girls appeared to him nowadays, especially when they were dressed for an outing, or that her hair was a high, flaxen crown of exceptionally soft texture, or indeed that her eyes, a genuine violet, were veiled in long, curling lashes, so that she reminded him a little of Madame Récamier in David's portraits. She had intelligence as well as good looks in her smooth oval face, and a bloom on her cheeks that made him think of standing in his rose garden contemplating a handful of fallen petals and inhaling their sweetness. He thought, 'My word, she's a stunner! I wonder where he found her . . . ?' but then Edward said, "You've met Gilda, Gov'nor. She's Gilda Wickstead . . ."

"It was a long time ago, when I was in pigtails, Mr. Swann. You came up to the Crescents once or twice when Father was alive but I've been abroad since I left school."

He took her hand, enclosing it in both of his and thinking, 'Now why the devil didn't Edith tell me she brought this lovely creature along . . . ?' but then, his sharp old eye catching the way his son was looking at her, he knew the reason. The boy was obviously much smitten by her and Edith would prefer to leave introductions to him, providing he wanted to make them. He said, "My word, you're quite grown up. I didn't realise . . . we don't, you know, at my age . . . Abroad, you say? Where?" And she said Switzerland, where she had gone to learn French and German and later as a teacher of English at Tours University.

"But she's back for good now," said Edward, with a hint, he thought, of desperation. "We shall have to talk later, Gov'nor. George wants the top table seated. The caterers have been complaining to him that the soup will go cold," and they moved on, the girl inclining her head to him with an enigmatic little smile that encouraged him to whisper to Henrietta, as they took their seats in front of a side table bearing a gigantic cake surmounted by a silver swan, "Young Edward is hooked. Look over there, on the left, that girl in green next but one to Edith!"

He saw her look, frowning with concentration, for he was aware that she was concerned by her youngest son's extended bachelorhood. "It's Edith's girl . . . the one that came along after her boys were grown. She's . . ." but then George was on his feet, and Edward was calling for silence in order that grace could be said, and both of them were caught up in conversations with their neighbours, so that he judged the subject of ending Edward's bachelorhood would not arise until they were back at the hotel and preparing for bed. For that was usually Hetty's time for family inquests, confound it. She never seemed affected by the fatigues of the day.

*   *   *

A sustained clatter of china and cutlery, a nonstop hubbub of talk; the quality of the beef, the hundred and one quips sparked off by the rivers of champagne, ale, Madeira and port. This was a celebration dinner to be remembered and relished as Swann-on-Wheels entered its second half-century. He had never been much of a trencherman – the short commons of youthful campaigns had seen to that – but he had always appreciated good company and a collective sense of achievement and the latter touched him now like a shaft of sunlight, illuminating the long and adventurous road they had travelled together, since he stood on or about this spot (there were no warehouses, as such, in those days) and wished old Blubb, his Kentish manager, good luck on the first Swann Embassy to pass the gates.

So few were present who could share that memory. Keate, the aged waggonmaster could, of course, and Bryn Lovell, about his own age, called out of retirement by the stupendous occasion. Dockett, too, and Morris, formerly of Southern Pickings based on Worcester. And Edith, whose father had once managed Crescent North, plus two of the original yard staff, a smith and a night-watchman. A mere eight out of a company of over three hundred but it didn't matter all that much. There were memories enough to be bandied around and most of them got an airing tonight.

"Do you remember that damned awful winter of 'sixty-five, when we had floods in five southern regions and snow blocks on every road north of Birmingham?" – "Do 'ee mind old 'Amlet vetching that bliddy lion home and getting civic honours from the Mayor of Exeter? Nobody told 'is Worship the poor brute would've rin from a tomcat with a vull set o' teeth . . . !" – "Wass you born, bach, when Bryn Lovell hauled that Shannon pump up a mountain to pump the water out of Pontnewydd pit, then?" – ". . . Seven ton that turret weighed, or so I heard. But George always reckoned it as a shade over six" – ". . . I first smelled smoke when I was coming out of the weighbridge hut and next minute, *woof* – up she goes, and a Clydesdale goes tearing by . . ." Up and down the tables like the exchange of so many brightly coloured balls in a complicated party game that everyone could play, even young Kidbroke, fourteen-year-old van boy, who had drawn a lucky ballot paper in Southern Square, for only last week Kidbroke had been present when a Swann vehicle broke down on a narrow bridge over a Hampshire river and blocked main road traffic for nearly an hour.

And then the cake cutting and the speeches, amusing most of them, and well spiced with anecdotes, but one or two rambling and heard with impatience, so that when it came to his turn he thought, 'I must cut it short . . . They'd sooner flirt and guzzle than listen to me.' But there was complete silence when, in response to Edward's stentorian "Pray silence for Mr. Adam Swann, our Founder," he rose to his feet and put on his reading glasses in the unlikely event he would use his notes.

He thanked them all gravely for honouring himself and the firm and told them a little, just a very little, of what it had felt like to take the gamble he had taken as a rank outsider in the transport stakes of those days. But then, perhaps because he could sense their genuine interest, he warmed to his favourite theme, the marriage of capital and labour that had been his policy ever since he signed on his first two score hands, and that other Swann precept, selecting local men who knew their areas and potential customers for executive positions in most regions between here and the north. He told them something of the tight-rope days, of the first managerial conference a few months before the present managing director was born and how, on that occasion, "we came so close to bankruptcy that Mrs. Swann will tell you those weeks were responsible for the first patches of white on a head where anyone among you tonight would have difficulty in finding a single dark hair." But this reminded him of his original thoughts for a wind-up and he continued, interrupted by a few shouts of 'Hear, hear!', and a cry of 'No politics, please': "We hear a great deal these days, of Women's Rights, and a woman's eligibility to take a responsible part in running the country, so let me conclude by reminding some of you younger folk of a crisis this firm survived, as long ago as 1866, solely on account of the skill and courage of two women, both of them happily in our midst. I refer to my wife, and to Mrs. Tom Wickstead, who encouraged her to take over the personal direction of Swann-on-Wheels when I was abroad, learning to use this tin leg of mine.

"Very few here will remember that challenge, and how it was met, but some will — among them four of the originals, Keate, Dockett, Morris and Lovell, respectively waggon-master and managers of three regions at that time. For the truth is, ladies and gentlemen, I came home from Switzerland in June of that year expecting to have to start all over again but several surprises awaited me. The first was that there was more money in the bank than when I had left. The second was that Miss Wadsworth was no longer Miss Wadsworth but Mrs. Wickstead. And the third — spare Mrs. Swann's blushes — was that I had a three-months-old son I didn't even know about, who grew up to be the Member of Parliament for Pontnewydd in the Mountain Square! So be damned careful, all of you, how you approach the subject of Women's Rights in the future!"

It was probably the most successful joke that he had ever used to terminate one of his speeches and he took advantage of the laughter and applause to sit down and take a sidelong glance at Henrietta, who was indeed blushing, a rare occurrence for her these days. Everybody rose to their feet then and the cheer they gave him could have been heard, indeed *was* heard according to young Harry Hitchens, a vanboy who lived hard by, in Tower Bridge Road.

She whispered, laughing, "Really, Adam, you might have warned me."

"Not on your life. Haven't seen you blush in fifty years."

"Can you wonder, with you for a husband?" she replied. "But I must say they're all very kind, and I'm so glad I came. Do introduce me to that girl Edward's squiring. I'd like to look her over, for it's time he settled down like the rest of them."

But it wasn't that easy in the mêlée that followed, with so many of them passing in and out of the warehouse as they cleared the floor for the dancing that was to follow. He had a brief word with George, congratulating him on the smooth organisation of the dinner, and in tempting so many of them down to London. "Bright idea to have it right here, too," he added. "At a hotel or assembly rooms it wouldn't have been the same somehow. Hello, Milton, my boy, glad you could get here," and he greeted Deborah's husband, the journalist, who asked of George, "Have you told him yet?"

"No," George said, "I haven't had a minute. Tell him yourself and see what he thinks. He likes to pretend he's out of it but that's rigmarole. If we offered him a seat on the board he'd jump at it, wouldn't you, Gov'nor?"

"Don't deceive yourself as to that," Adam said, "I've done my stint. You're not thinking of enlisting Milton, are you?"

"In a way he is," Milton said, "but on a part-time basis," and as George moved away to welcome the five-piece orchestra they had hired, Jeffs said George had offered him a tempting screw to found and run a magazine for circulation within the network.

"Why, that's a perfectly splendid idea," Adam exclaimed. "Who thought of it?"

"Who else but Debbie? I earn a good living but the Street is a young man's life and a three-day week editorial job of that sort would be a wonderful standby. You approve of it, then?"

"Wholeheartedly," Adam said. "What will you call it?"

"We haven't decided. How about *The Swann Bulletin*?"

"Too dull," Adam said, "we've always had a reputation for quirkish titles. How about *The Swann Migrant*?"

Jeffs laughed, saying, "You really are on top of your form tonight, Gov'nor."

Henrietta, he noticed, was surrounded by wives and daughters, and he needed a breath of fresh air, so he slipped out into the yard and stood by the old horse-trough, reviewing a scene bathed in silver moonlight, with the outline of the new buildings stark and clear against the sky and, hard to his left, the slender tower of the belfry that was still the ark of the tabernacle as far as he was concerned.

Moved by an impulse he drifted across to it, aware of stirrings and giggles in the patches of shadow where, no doubt, some of the younger ones were making the most of their opportunities. He went in and tackled the winding stair, needing no light on ground as familiar as this and stumping his way up to the queer, octagonal room at the summit, where the door stood open and moonlight flooded the floor about the narrow casement. And then he stopped, sniffing Turkish tobacco and vaguely aware of a figure standing by the embrasure, looking out on the wide curve of the Thames. He said, jocularly, "Hello there? Who's been sleeping in my bed on this night of nights?"

The figure turned, moving into the moonlight and he saw to his surprise that it was Edith, her mantle thrown over her shoulders and a cigarette in her hand.

"You? Well, I don't know! What drew you up here, I wonder?"

"Memories, mostly. Whenever I thought of you in the old days, and it was every day before I married Tom, it was always here, Adam. Never at 'Tryst', and never out on the network," she said.

"I didn't know you were a smoker."

"Just occasionally, when I want to think. They're Turkish. Will you have one?"

"No, thanks, I'll stick to my cheroots," and he lit one, blowing the smoke up to the cobwebbed rafters as he said, gaily, "Edward introduced me to that girl of yours. She's a rare beauty, Edith. Tom would have been very proud of her."

"Yes, he was," Edith said, "although he didn't have long with her. He died before she put her hair up."

He might have been wrong but he thought he noted a drag in her voice, enough to prompt him to say, "You still miss him terribly, don't you?"

"Yes, I do. I thought it would get a little easier every day but it doesn't. Times like this, when all the survivors get together, are the worst. It wasn't so bad when the boys were at home but they had to move on. I was glad when George gave them a chance to prove their mettle in a busier sector."

"Well, you've got Gilda home now, I hear."

"Gilda isn't the same, Adam."

"How do you mean?"

She turned, drawing thoughtfully on her cigarette. Its aromatic whiff reminded him, momentarily, of the military base at Scutari, where he had spent a month recovering from a wound received in the Sebastopol trenches. "Your boy has proposed to her, Adam."

"He has? Well, I'm delighted to hear it, and Hetty will be too. She has a great deal of respect for you Edith, and I don't have to tell you how pleased I should be to acknowledge a daughter of yours as my own."

"I didn't say she'd accepted him."

"A girl as pretty as Gilda would be sure to keep a man on a string for a month or two."

"There's more than that in it. Gilda . . . well, she's different somehow. Very sure of herself. Too sure, I sometimes think. That's the penalty of over-educating a girl. It would take her a long time to settle down after all her travels abroad, and the kind of people she met and mixed with in France, Switzerland and Italy."

"Well, that's her prerogative. How old is she, exactly?"

"Twenty-two. She's already had half-a-dozen proposals. One was from a French count, I believe." Then, hesitantly, "I don't know Edward very well, Adam, but what I've seen of him I like. He seems a very practical lad, more like George than any of the others."

"He's practical all right. George tells me he's shaping up wonderfully."

"Sensitive? Easily hurt?"

"I couldn't say. No more or less than most lads his age. He's very dedicated to his work. That's all I could say. I didn't have much part in raising them, you recall. Right here was my family, up to the time I retired and by the time I did they had all grown up and most of them had gone."

"Well, I wouldn't like to see a boy of yours hurt or humiliated and I've even gone so far as to tell Gilda as much. If she means to marry him fair enough. If she doesn't I won't have her encouraging him too much."

It surprised him to hear her talking like this, indicating as it did the underlying reason for her presence up here alone, as if doubts concerning her daughter's romance had driven her here, clear away from the noise and high spirits below. He said, "Look here, Edith, don't you concern yourself. Edward's a grown man and must learn to look to himself in matters of this kind. Was that why you came up here? To mull it over in solitude?"

"Partly," she said, "but not altogether. I had a queer

sensation down there tonight, when they were all congratulating one another on the past, present and future prospects of the firm. I can't describe it, exactly, but it wasn't altogether removed from – well – a sense of foreboding. So silly on an occasion like this."

"Not so silly," he said. "I've had a niggle or two under my own ribs just lately. Not about the firm, however, about the country generally."

"Tell me."

"I can't, or not precisely. It's old age, I daresay, and the rate of change I see about me. But the fact is, as I see it, we're too damned confident, the whole boiling of us. We've all had a wonderful run for our money, had it all our own way for too long. As a trading nation, I mean. I thought we would slow down and take stock when we got that drubbing from the Boers a few years since but we didn't. The minute we had 'em on the run we were the same arrogant, overweening tribe of chest-beaters. It never seems to occur to anyone that the Continental and American competition is getting tougher every day. There's a lot I don't like about the international scene for that matter. These constant confrontations between Russia, Austria, Germany and France, and our politicians' tendency to stick our nose in, instead of minding their own till and exploiting the tremendous potential in the dominions and colonies. The Continent's business isn't our business, and I never did trust the French any further than you could throw the Arc de Triomphe!"

He had succeeded in cheering her up anyway for she laughed, saying, "You don't change a bit, Adam. And I'm glad, and so is everyone down there. Come, I've not had more than a word with Henrietta, and if anyone finds us up here in the dark the old rumours will start circulating on the Swann grapevine."

"Not," he said, mournfully, "at my age. At yours, maybe, for you don't look more than forty in moonlight," and he took her hand and led her across the threshold and down the stairs into the brightly-lit yard, thinking as he did of a time she came up here with some tomfool notion of emigrating to Australia simply because she believed herself hopelessly in love with him. 'But that was before she met Tom,' he thought. 'After that I might not have existed,' and it prompted him to ask her, as they crossed the yard to the warehouse, whether she had ever told Gilda and the boys about Tom Wickstead's past as a man who had once walked abroad with a revolver strapped to his wrist. "Never," she said. "What purpose would it have served? Besides, he never was a bad 'un in that sense, not even before I met him. He was only hitting back at a society that had stamped on him and his. His father was transported for twelve years for stealing a piece of cloth to make clothes for his mother and sisters. His mother died in the workhouse at thirty-five and his eldest sister went on the streets, for it was a case of that or starve. Incidentally, he named Gilda for her. It's ironic how the wheel turns full circle, don't you think?"

He had no time to answer for, seeing them, half-a-dozen people converged on them, but he thought about it at intervals all the evening and later when Henrietta said, as they undressed, "I had a talk with that girl of Edith's. She seems terribly brainy – Deborah's sort of braininess. I do hope Edward hasn't bitten off more than he can chew."

He replied, a little grumpily, "If he has he can spit it out. The same as we all have to from time to time. Turn out the light, woman. I'm dog-tired and you ought to be."

And then, as she climbed into bed and settled herself, he forgot Gilda and Edith too, his mind basking a little in the splendour and fulfilment of the Jubilee, and all it represented in terms of personal and collective endeavour. As to the nation, he supposed it was like Edward, mature enough to absorb any shocks and disappointments that lay ahead and equipped to ride them out, the way he had done since he came to this city to prise up a few of those golden paving-stones they were always talking about in the shires.

PART FIVE

Journey into Chaos

I

Win One, Lose One

IN THE LONG AFTERGLOW OF HER LIFE, WHEN
warmth had stolen back into her bones, when she had adjusted, more comfortably than most women who had
worn crinolines, to short skirts, sounding brass and the
rootlessness of the post-war era, Henrietta Swann would
challenge those who claimed that the old world died in
August, 1914. Her memory calendar was at odds with
those of her contemporaries, showing a discrepancy of
some five years, and there was a logical reason for this.
For Henrietta the onrush of the terminal sickness of the
age began as early as the summer of 1909, when the first
of a string of domestic catastrophes occurred, shattering
her serenity and undermining her abiding faith in her
destiny. And after that, in quick succession, came a long
run of crises demanding more and ever more of her impressive stocks of resilience, and resource – and all this
at a time of life when one could reasonably look for repose.
For she had then entered upon her seventieth year and
was ready, if only occasionally, to sit back and assume the
role of an interested spectator.

It was not to be, however, and perhaps the scurviest
trick fate played upon her at that time was to open the
year with a discharge of Swann rockets designed to light
up the achievements of the dynasty, enabling her to look
back into the past and forward into the future with a
grandiloquence that Adam had always found comic,

particularly after she passed her sixtieth birthday and he came to see her as equating, on county level, with Victoria in that photograph showing her surrounded by a swarm of dutiful, popeyed relations, the least of them a duke.

The family firework display began on New Year's Day when the newspapers carried reports, some of them flatteringly detailed, of sovereign recognition of Hugo Swann, Layer on of Hands. The bombshell was not entirely unexpected. His wife, Lady Sybil, had been over at 'Tryst' in late autumn, dropping mysterious hints on the subject but neither Adam nor Henrietta, or indeed anyone else outside Lady Sybil's exclusive charity circle, had regarded them as pointers to the fact that Hugo, least promising of all the Swann boys, would be the first to attain the rank of knighthood, and even when she saw it in print Henrietta wondered, a little fearfully, if there had not been an embarrassing mix-up somewhere and Hugo's name had emerged from the hat in error.

For it seemed preposterous to think of dear, bumbling Hugo, one-time athlete, sometime war hero, latterly, she gathered, a kind of doctor's auxiliary at a hospital, as *Sir* Hugo Swann. She had never been one to minimise the achievements of any of her brood. Indeed, it had crossed her mind many times during the last thirty years that her husband's contribution to commerce should have earned him an official accolade of some kind. But Hugo, even in his heyday, when he sometimes brought home two trophies a week, had never figured in her dynastic daydreams. There was no reason why he should when he faced such formidable competition on the part of his brothers, three of them well advanced upon their careers and winning mention, from time to time, in the national press. Alex had earned his first headline as long ago as 1879, when he sent home an account of that battle with the Zulus at a place with an unpronounceable name. George had fought his way to the forefront on four wheels and carried, or so it seemed to her, the whole country with him, for she never saw a motor-bus or a motor-car nowadays without reminding herself that the very first of them, so far as she was aware, had arrived in England with George's baggage when he landed with his Austrian bride in 1885. As for Giles, his present place in the high counsels of the nation could have been predicted when he was a boy of thirteen, reading his way through his father's library at the rate of one tome a day. Even Edward, they said, nine years younger than Hugo, was considered a gifted engineer and currently a Swann viceroy in one of the network's most lucrative sectors. Was it to be wondered at that she had overlooked Hugo, a man who walked with a white stick and was followed about by an ex-rough-riding sergeant who barked like a collie every time his master had need of him?

Yet there it was – Sir Hugo Swann, honoured, it seemed, for his work among the human wreckage of that awful war in South Africa, the war that everybody had thought so splendid at the time but which was now dismissed as a faraway squabble that had been settled, in the way of all these colonial squabbles, by Earl Roberts' tact, Lord Kitchener's scowl and promises of good behaviour all round.

Even Adam, so rarely surprised these days, had been stunned by the news yet not so much as not to quarrel with the rumour that the honour was the result of canvassing behind the scenes on the part of Lady Sybil. He said when this story was relayed to him, "Once in a while, every hundred years or so, those honours brokers reward someone deserving by accident. Go down to Netley and watch him at work on patients. I did just that, admittedly out of curiosity, and I came away humbled. I'm not a religious man but I believe in some miracles. One has to when one hears a blind man preach a sermon through his fingertips."

He did not say this to her but his comments were repeated to Henrietta by Debbie's husband Milton. Neither did she take it up with him later, sensing that she would not comprehend any clarification he condescended to make and also (he was oddly touchy in some areas) that questioning on the subject would embarrass him. She was prepared, as always, to take his word on matters that baffled her and assumed, from then on, that Hugo's endowments, unlike those of his splendid brothers, had been hidden from her by an inscrutable Providence.

Adam's verdict was only part of the truth. Lady Sybil had, indeed, been tireless on Hugo's behalf, but his selection from a swarm of probables was really another kind of miracle, brought about by a flash of inspiration in the minds of what Adam called the honours brokers and what others called the Faceless Ones; an inspiration, lighting up the imagination of men rarely responsive to romantic impulses and national moods. Men who, for the most part, were guided by motives far too complex to be comprehended by the man in the market-place, who might regard Hugo Swann's services to the nation as more deserving than, say, the transfer of a small part of a large fortune to areas where its arrival would make the maximum noise.

But circumstances, on this unique occasion, combined to answer Lady Sybil's prayers. When the list of candidates for New Year's honours were being considered it was apparent, even to the Faceless Ones, that to elevate them en bloc would be to give substance to recent murmurs that knighthoods had ceased to be earned with anything but hard cash, discreetly distributed, later 'discovered' by the press. Thus it was that Hugo came to be seen as a kind of minority candidate, isolated among a swarm of contenders whose prospects, on the face of it, were infinitely brighter, almost as though the adjudicators had reasoned: 'As God is our witness, his claims upon us barely exist. He was once acclaimed by the great unwashed as a pot-hunter. He was careless enough to lose his sight in a conflict that is now regarded as a national blunder. He has since buried himself alive in an infirmary without so much as an M.D. to explain his presence there.

He has no influence anywhere, has never contributed a pennypiece to either great political party and his nod in anyone's direction would count for nothing in the way of preferment. But stay! We are overlooking the obvious! Sporting laurels, sacrifice on the field of battle and political anonymity are the very ingredients capable of producing a compound capable of exploding the myth that our rewards are bought and sold.'

So it was that Hugo's name went forth and Lady Sybil, bringing the news to him, was taxed to convince him that it was deserved.

"*Me? Knighted?* But it's quite absurd, Sybil! What have I ever done to get knighted?" he asked her, quite amazed.

"Hugo, dear," she said, taking his hand, "it's for what you've done right *here*."

"Here? In Netley? A bit of massaging?"

"Yes, dear, for . . . a bit of massaging. *They* see it as important."

She realised she could never hope to make him understand that and did not try. She had watched him expand day by day, coming to terms with his disability in a way that a man learns to adapt to the customs of a strange country and create, within himself, a sense of belonging. He had learned to dispense with eyes, not so much because his other senses had enlarged themselves but because, through his bones, sinews and nerve ends, he had regained his old ascendancy over competitors in the field.

"I couldn't accept, Sybil," he said. "The fellows here would see it as swank."

"That isn't so, Hugo dear. You *must* take it. There's a very good reason why you should."

"What reason?"

"Because it signifies official acceptance of the work you are doing here. I don't mean personally, but in the wider sense, of men like you helping and encouraging one another, of establishing the value of expert massage inside the medical profession, of proving that a man without sight can play a useful part in society. That's why I insist you accept, Hugo."

It was, of course, a shoal of red herrings. She did not give a button about the abstract aspects that tripped so glibly from her tongue but she understood the regenerated Hugo Swann well enough to realise that these were the likeliest means of overcoming his essential humility and she was right. He sat thinking a moment, hands resting on his enormous thighs, and presently he said, "Would it help to persuade them to set up that training centre I suggested? Would it convince some of those stick-in-the-mud army surgeons that a masseur and an osteopath isn't necessarily a quack?"

"I think it would."

"Very well, then. I'll accept."

"Thank you, Hugo. I knew you'd be sensible," and she was glad she could safely indulge herself in a smile of triumph and went her way rejoicing. For although she was glad for him she was even more relieved for herself, seeing the recognition she had won for him as the last and most impressive of the string of penances laid upon her for her share in encompassing his fate. She had no way of knowing that his enlargement since he had been caught up in rehabilitation work had been brought about by an almost parallel process, that his successes here had in themselves been acts of atonement for taking the life of a child on a ridge thousands of miles from Southampton Water. It was some time since he had been troubled by the dream that had returned to him time and again over the years, a dream of looking down on the face of an enemy in a slouch hat who lay flat on his back staring sightlessly at the sky and then, although manifestly a dead face, transformed its features into those of a child he had never seen, his own seven-year-old son.

2

The second rocket soared a month or so later when Edward, coming into the hall at a run, announced that Gilda Wickstead had at last capitulated and agreed to marry him at Easter.

The news, long expected but unaccountably delayed, delighted Henrietta, so much so that she found she could forgive the stupid girl for keeping everybody on tenterhooks for the better part of six months. It was a relief to see the youngest of her sons released from the private purgatory to which that Wickstead girl had consigned him, and there had been times, over the last few months, when she could have shaken his beloved until her teeth rattled, notwithstanding her sincere regard for Edward's mother-in-law elect.

Time and again she had tried to coax from Edith the source of her own and her handsome daughter's reservations on the match but no important information had been forthcoming. Edith hinted that the girl had been spoiled, first by her father, then by her brothers, that she wasn't ready for marriage, that she might not be content to vegetate in the English provinces after so much acclaim in foreign cities, and even that Gilda might have ambitions of her own that did not include marriage. It was this hint that alarmed Henrietta, for she had a suspicion that Edith, known to be sympathetic to the Pankhurst hell-raisers, was hinting that Gilda was a suffragette, as if two martyrs in one family wasn't enough to get on with. But Edith, challenged on this point, smiled and shook her head.

"A militant? Our Gilda? No, you can put that aside, Henrietta. If Gilda campaigns it will be for Gilda."

It was strange and rather chilling, Henrietta thought, that a mother could talk that way about her daughter, almost as though she neither liked nor trusted her. Gilda was exasperating, certainly, and probably more experienced mashers than Edward had succumbed to her undeniable charms, but she wasn't unlikeable, or even particularly vain. Reluctantly, for Henrietta was very fond of Edith, she put it down to maternal jealousy, of the kind she herself had sometimes felt (although never admitted to) for Helen and Joanna, when they were young, slim and pretty, and licensed by a tolerant father to play fast and loose with a troop of young gallants in a way that would never had been allowed a generation before.

But then, just when Henrietta was beginning to resign herself to having a bachelor son at the tail of the family, everything sorted itself out and she was plunged into preparations for what she thought of as the last of the first generation weddings, and grandchildren's weddings were not the same, for you hadn't the fun and the bother of helping to stage them. Henrietta always put as much effort into her sons' weddings as those of her daughters. It was a wonderful excuse to try out the very latest fashions seen in one or other of the dozens of costumiers' catalogues that found their way into 'Tryst' at all seasons of the year.

Her pleasure might have been muted had she known the background of Gilda Wickstead's hesitation, aired during a rare, serious discussion between mother and daughter a day or so before Edward came pounding into the house with news of his reprieve.

Edith had not enjoyed watching the son of her oldest and dearest friends waiting on her doorstep. Like Henrietta she would have preferred to take some positive action calculated to hasten a climax. Nothing would have given her greater satisfaction than seeing Gilda marry into the Swann family but all her life, as regional manager, as wife and as mother, Edith Wickstead had been excessively irritated by ditherers.

Just as Henrietta would have liked to have shaken a decision out of Gilda, Edith was sometimes tempted to apply a spur to Edward. Ordinarily, and she had got to know him very well during his managership of her old territory, he was a very practical young man but her daughter's presence seemed to reduce him to the status of a minor flunkey privileged to serve royalty. And this, she had long since decided, was quite the wrong approach to make to a girl of Gilda's temperament. She would have liked to have said to him, "Look, Edward, for everybody's sake, but mostly your own and hers, tell the girl to make up her mind on the spot. You've a great deal to offer, and all she is bringing to you are looks that won't last her a lifetime! If she turns you down then go out and find somebody who will make you a better wife, lad. If she accepts then in heaven's name assert yourself. A man who doesn't won't get far with our Gilda!"

In the event it was Gilda who herself raised the matter, admitting that 'she was fond of Edward but that was as far as it went'.

"Then it's not far enough," Edith said tartly. "Your commonsense should tell you that, girl!"

And Gilda replied, with one of her superior smiles that made Edith regret yet again Tom's insistence, before he died, that she should receive the best education they could afford, "On the contrary, Mamma, it's my commonsense that urges me to marry Edward as soon as maybe. Before he goes off the boil, that is, for I'm not likely to get a better offer here or abroad. I surely don't have to tell you the Swanns are better off than anyone else we know."

The cynicism implicit in the girl's reasoning was so much at odds with Edith's character that she came close to boxing her ears but restrained herself, saying, "That's no way at all for a girl your age to talk, Gilda! Either you care for the boy or you don't, and money, given enough to be housed, fed and clothed, should have little to do with it!" She saw her daughter's eyes widen.

She said, wonderingly, "You really *believe* that, don't you? But then, you're a romantic, and I'm not, so we aren't likely to agree about it, are we? Was Papa penniless when you married him?"

Not simply poor, Edith reflected, remembering how, in effect, she had had to do the proposing, but a man with a police record, who had served time in broad arrows and had been planning an act of theft when serving as one of her waggoners. Suddenly it occurred to her that here was an occasion when part of the truth about Tom Wickstead, so carefully hidden from the children over the years, might have a beneficial effect upon his daughter. She said, quietly, "He was not merely poor. He had seen the inside of a gaol and was busy hauling himself up by his bootstraps!"

She had expected that the information, regretted as soon as it was out, would have shocked the girl half out of her wits. All it produced was a shrug of Gilda's pretty shoulders. She said, "Oh, that isn't new to me, Mamma. Papa told me how you met and what he had been only a month or so before he died."

"He told *you*! *All three* of you?"

"No, just me. I was named for his sister Gilda, wasn't I? The one who went on the streets while he was in prison."

"He told you that ... everything? About his father being transported, about his mother dying in the workhouse?"

"Yes."

"But why? I mean, what possible motive did he have? And for not telling me that you knew? Did you pass it on to the boys?"

"I didn't pass it on to anyone. He made me swear I wouldn't but in any case it isn't the kind of thing one would boast about, is it? I thought about it, however. I thought about it for years, all the time I was away from home and you needn't worry, I'm not ashamed of it. It taught me more about life than I ever learned from books."

"What did it teach you? What specific thing, Gilda?"

The girl looked at her levelly. "It taught me that the very worst thing that can happen to anyone is to be poor. That's why I've finally decided to marry Edward Swann."

So there it was, and sitting, because suddenly she felt a little dizzy, Edith groped for the key that opened a door on so much about Gilda she had never understood. Her ability to detach herself from her surroundings. The tight control she had over her emotions. Her unusual reliance on her own judgments, so unlike the boys who had always, to some extent, leaned on her when they were growing up and going out into the world. In her presence now she felt deflated and oddly helpless, and yet, behind her confusion, there was a glimmer of hope that out of this they might find a bridge to a better understanding. She said, finally, "You do what you think best, Gilda. In a way I suppose I've misjudged you. I loved your father to distraction but I can't help thinking it wasn't very wise of him to confide in you without consulting me first. He probably had a good reason, or what he thought was a good reason. You were always more important to him than the boys. Maybe he saw you as that sister of his, born all over again with a better chance. If you'll take my advice you won't tell Edward. His mother and father know but they can be trusted. All there is left to say is if you do marry Edward do your very best to make him happy and to have the kind of marriage I had, and Edward's father and mother have had all these years. It's the only thing worth having in the end."

She got up and walked upstairs to her room. Unaccountably, and for the first time in thirty years, she wanted to weep. To weep for Tom and his sister Gilda. For all the wretchedness and deprivation they had suffered under a social system that valued goods and money high above human beings. Perhaps Gilda had it right after all. Perhaps the only ultimate sin was poverty.

2

The Swann firework display continued, at intervals, all through spring and summer to a time when the first shades of gold were beginning to show on the curling edges of the 'Tryst' chestnuts and the early south-westerlies – 'Sussex skies' Adam called them – came probing over the county border, reminding him that it was time to get his apples in and give his ornamental lake its annual dredging.

Edward's wedding, staged, to Henrietta's delight, in Twyforde Church rather than in faraway Northamptonshire, was behind them now and everybody had stopped teasing Hugo by prefixing his name with 'Sir', a family joke that bewildered Hugo's punctilious soldier-servant, whose chest expanded an extra inch every time he looked at his master nowadays, giving substance to Adam's remark that the sergeant was the most outrageous snob in the country.

One golden September morning Henrietta put on her shawl and carried the post down to the terrace of the lake, where Adam was superintending the drainage, a task that needed considerable care if the sluices were not to jam and his paddocks flood. He looked like a ruffled old heron standing there in his rubber thigh boots, issuing gruff directions to the gardeners, and when she called to him he waded out and joined her on his stone seat fronting the water, a seat that had once formed part of the original embellishment of 'Tryst' in the sixteenth century and had been rescued from a potting shed behind the stables.

"The mail looked important," she said. "Here is your quarterly report, one from Alex, who has gone over to Ireland, and one from Margaret, addressed to you for some reason."

He opened Margaret's letter first because he could see she was curious about it and drew out a cheque bearing his own signature, together with a letter and a photograph of the latest addition to the Griffiths family, a fat and very jolly-looking baby sitting on the obligatory bearskin rug.

He said, passing her the photograph and pocketing the cheque, "I won't get any peace until I explain. They can't be well off, so I sent her twenty pounds for her birthday. She's returned it, as she has returned other cheques I've sent her. I suppose it's time I took the hint and stopped playing fairy godfather. That husband of hers seems to have a surfeit of Celtic pride. She says they are several pounds a week better off now, for Giles made over his M.P.'s salary to Huw as his agent down there."

"I didn't know they paid Members of Parliament!"

"They've just started to, and I don't care to think what might come of it. They're a shifty enough lot as they are. Pay 'em for going there and we'll have some real black-guards scrambling for the cash. However, it doesn't sur-prise me. About Giles, I mean. He'll see it as a way of helping them and pretending it's a rise. I daresay that prickly young Welshman will swallow that."

His attitude to his in-laws often amused her. Ever since Joanna had run off with Clinton Coles in the middle of the night Adam had referred to him as Jack-o'-Lantern. Helen's first husband had been 'That pill-rolling Bible spouter'. Now the handsome Huw Griffiths was 'That prickly Welshman'. He was a little gentler with his daughters-in-law; George's wife, Gisela, was generally 'That nice gel', and Romayne 'The flighty one'. Alex's wife, Lydia, was still 'The Colonel's daughter', Hugo's wife, 'The Prima Donna'.

So far he had made but one jocular reference to Ed-ward's wife, commenting on the astonishing self-possession she exhibited at the wedding in April. He named her 'The Ice Maiden'.

Alex had interesting news. He had been sent to Ire-land, he told them, by Lord Haldane, Secretary for War, to make a survey of territorial recruiting prospects over there if and when the Irish Home Rule Bill was approved by Lords and Commons. When Henrietta, like so many others baffled by what successive generations of politicians referred to as 'the Irish Question', demanded to know whether Ireland would become an entirely separate country if the Irish at last had their way, he said: "Not for defence. Haldane is far too sharp for that. There will always be some of our chaps over there, if only to keep an eye on Paddy."

She left him then, to mull over the latest news from the

network and he unwrapped the latest copy of *The Migrant*, for Deborah's husband, Milton, had used the name he jokingly suggested when the quarterly journal had been launched.

It was, he decided, a thoroughly workmanlike broadsheet, well-edited, well-printed and full of interest to anyone like himself. He read, among other things, that George had just commissioned his four-hundredth motorvan and sent it out to earn its bread in The Polygon. There was also a quarterly report by the Managing Director and he went through it word by word, telling himself that affable old George sounded oddly pompous when he committed himself to paper. He mused, tucking *The Migrant* into his boot, 'He's got a right to feel smug, I suppose . . . He was a big jump ahead of all of 'em twenty years ago, when nobody, least of all me, believed in that snorting great engine he brought home from the Danube. But it won't do for him to go on thinking nobody can ever catch him up. There's always an outsider with a new trick up his sleeve, and there always will be. If there wasn't commerce would be desperately dull and he'd be the first to realise it with all that energy . . . Besides, it's clear enough now that everyone is latching on to the potential of commercial motoring and his presence out there in front is a challenge to 'em . . .'

He gave some final instructions to the head gardener and turned to make his way up to the house for lunch, looking round him with pride of a kind he had never experienced beside the Thames, for up there someone was always around to disturb his sense of order whereas here, now that his estate had matured with its imported trees and shrubs, he could keep strict control on the landscape and intended to do so, as long as he lived. What would happen to it then he could only guess. The only one of his sons who had inherited his taste was Giles, and he doubted whether Giles would ever be tempted to turn his back on his lame ducks and become a country gentleman.

He was wondering, idly, what kind of instruction he could insert into a codicil to his will concerning the future care of 'Tryst' and its treasures when he saw Henrietta emerge from the house and make her way, very swiftly for her these days, across the forecourt, turning her head this way and that as though she was looking for him. The moment she saw him she broke into a little trot and he called, "What's the hurry, woman? I'm coming . . ." but then his sharp eye caught the glint of tears in her eyes and he hastened his step, saying, "What is it, Hetty? What's upset you so suddenly?"

She said, breathlessly, "Wanted to catch you . . . tell you before you saw her . . . Edith's here . . . She's got news . . . dreadful news . . ." and she broke off with a sob, tears running parallel courses down her cheeks.

"One of her boys . . . ?"

"No, no . . . it's Gilda. Gilda and Edward. Edward came to her yesterday . . . Gilda's gone."

"Gone? Gone where?"

"He doesn't know. She just . . . well, left, in the middle of the night. They had a tiff, nothing at all so he said, and when she didn't appear at breakfast he went to her room and found that her bed hadn't been slept in."

His immediate reaction was one of profound irritation that something as trivial as this, a tiff between newlyweds, should provoke such an emotional response in her but then his impatience transferred itself to his son and daughter-in-law. Surely they were old enough to know that young marrieds who occupied separate beds in separate rooms could expect to quarrel and say things to one another that they would afterwards regret.

"I don't know what Edith can be thinking of to come posting down from Northamptonshire on this kind of excuse," he growled. "As for you, Hetty, there's no sense at all in you upsetting yourself over something of this nature. How long have they had to get used to one another? Three months? Four? They have a quarrel and she decides to teach him a lesson by going home to mother.

How many times would you have gone at her time of life if you had a mother to run to. Or if you hadn't been reasonably certain I'd tan your backside when I came for you."

"I don't think you understand," she said, "for it isn't like that at all. Gilda didn't go to Edith's and Edward traced her as far as Dover. She's gone abroad and from the note she left it's quite clear she intends to stay there! Let Edith explain . . . I . . . I just wanted to warn you that she seems to regard it as her fault, and that's non-sense . . ."

He thought, savagely, 'What the devil is the matter with everybody? Am I the only one about who isn't going senile? Hetty getting hysterical over a farce like this, and Edith, as sane as any woman I know, blaming herself for having a feather-brained daughter . . .' And suddenly that vague sense of unease that had been prowling about under his ribs for a long time now found an outlet, driving the sparkle from the morning. He said, gruffly, "I'll have a word with her, but this won't amount to anything, take it from me," and he stumped on ahead, mounting the portico steps two at a time.

3

A sense of deep, personal failure had attended Edward from the very beginning, from the first moment they were alone after the hurly-burly of the wedding reception, the plaudits and the send-off of trailing the usual assortment of threadbare slippers and old boots. And it was the more oppressive because he had no previous experience of personal failure and would have found it very difficult to put into words, even to old George, in whose shadow he had stood ever since he could remember. For until then he had been concerned with tangible things, with nuts, bolts, gradients, time schedules, metal stress, trade potential and profit margins, inanimates that responded to patience and logic, whereas Gilda, the prize that had fallen to him so unaccountably, and after so long a siege, did not respond to approaches that had solved his problems as an engineer, a regional manager and master of his trade.

In the first few weeks of their life together he tried variants of all the methods that had served him so well in the past. Flattery, bribery and a careful study of the opposition's defences; aggression, compromise, the storming salesman approach, favoured by George, and even craftiness, but all in vain. He had won her on paper and lost her in practice. Her very passivity was her strength and his weakness. His experience with women was no more and no less than that of most young husbands, but he had a conviction that an accomplished masher would have retired baffled from the single room she had insisted upon occupying as one of the articles of her surrender. Yet this is not to say she had denied him access to her on any occasion. She betrayed no sign of fear, shame or even embarrassment that he had expected when she was obliged to share his bed during their touring honeymoon into the west.

In the first weeks of married life in their new Birmingham home, surrounded by the highly-trained staff he had enrolled for her, she spent the time he was absent in reading, walking and writing letters acknowledging their array of wedding gifts. When they were together, on excursions about the city, dining or merely sitting by the fireside, she performed all her domestic functions faultlessly, acceding to his every wish save the one that began to obsess him. All he was to be granted, it seemed, was her presence. A beautiful slave, obedient to his every caprice but enjoying, by some feat of legerdemain, far more freedom and personal privacy than was available to her owner.

Turned back upon himself by her stillness and chilled by her impersonal acknowledgment of his affection, he began to change in a way that his intimates were not slow to observe. He had always been an amiable young man, unruffled by minor setbacks of the kind that came the way of every regional manager in the course of a working day. Now he became strangely intractable, given to gruff replies and short, explosive bursts of temper. And at the same time his methodical approach to problems involving consultation with senior subordinates and customers became casual and off-hand as he took to spending much of his time closeted in his office, leaving all but the major decisions to deputies.

That was before the weekly letters from Paris began to arrive for her, the first of which merely excited his curiosity, so that when he asked who had written it she passed it to him and he ran his eye down the page, discovering that it was written in French and turned at once to the final page to look at the signature.

"Who is this 'Clothilde'?"

"A friend."

The reply was typical of her replies to all his questions, polite but yielding nothing.

"What kind of friend?"

"We shared rooms."

"Where?"

"At Tours, when I was teaching English at the University. Her name is Clothilde Bernard."

"How old is she?"

"About my age."

"What does she write about?"

"Mutual acquaintances. Shall I translate?"

"No, no, it doesn't matter, I didn't mean to pry."

"You are not prying."

He forgot the incident almost at once but recalled it when, almost as regular as a Swann hardware haul to Coventry, identical-looking letters arrived, always from Paris, always on a Wednesday and always, presumably, from Clothilde Bernard, so that his curiosity concerning them became so intense that, taking advantage of her temporary absence one day, he opened her bureau and counted them.

There were twelve, all looking alike save the most

recent delivery, a bulkier package containing photographs. He took them out and found they were not the ordinary amateur photographs he had expected but professional pictures, depicting what looked like some kind of entertainment, a melodrama presumably, for they depicted dramatic confrontations between a young, spade-bearded man wearing evening dress, and a young woman in a ballet costume. The little ballerina, it would appear, was being victimised in some way, for the man in the pictured numbered 'one' was threatening her, arm upraised. In the picture numbered 'eight' she lay dead at his feet and he was being arrested by gendarmes, a revolver in his hand. He made nothing of these but a ninth picture interested him. It was a still of a young actor in the costume of the eighteenth-century and he looked very elegant and self-assured. It was signed 'Etienne' and below, in handwriting so full of flourishes that it defied analysis, was some kind of greeting.

He returned the photographs thoughtfully, wondering at her preoccupation with this kind of frivolity for over here she had given no indication of an interest in theatricals. But curiosity nagged at him so persistently that, when a thirteenth letter arrived, he asked outright what subject it was that Clothilde found so much to write about. She answered, quietly, "As I explained, what goes on at the universities. She is now at the Sorbonne, teaching drama. Upstairs I have some photographs of her work. Would you care to see them?"

"Yes, I would. Very much."

She got up from the table and glided away, moving as noiselessly as she invariably did, and a moment later she was back with the photographs he had already seen. He made a pretence of looking at them and asked, "Who is Etienne?"

"Clothilde's brother."

"Another university tutor?"

"No, a professional actor. There he is playing Monsieur Beaucaire."

"What has he written under the picture?"

"*Souvent femme varie — Bien fol est qui s'y fie.*"

"What does that mean?"

"Woman often changes; he is a big fool who trusts her."

"Was the picture meant for you?"

"Of course."

"You knew him that well?"

"We were friends."

"Is he implying you broke a promise to him?"

"Perhaps."

"No, not 'perhaps'. Surely this is a direct reference to you getting married."

"He made no proposal of marriage to me."

It did not tell him much but enough, once he had left for the Swann Bull Ring depot, to disturb him deeply so that he began to ask himself if she had been as frigidly unresponsive with Bernard as she had been with him since he led her to the altar. His wits were very woolly these days and he realised that, without further elucidation, he could make no real attempt to gauge the relationship that existed between her and this actor fellow.

As the days passed, however, the shadow of Etienne Bernard, and the childlike trust he had reposed in her, began to gnaw at him until uncertainty became unbearable. A week later he went to her room with the intention of reopening the subject and persuading her, if that was possible, to tell him more.

It had been customary, until then, for him to tell her when he would come to her after she had retired but on this occasion he said nothing and did not even knock when he entered her room, discovering her seated at the dressing-table in a silk shift, engaged in brushing her lovely, corn-coloured hair. The sight of her, so bewitching and vulnerable, disarmed him and he moved over to stand behind her, taking the brush and applying it in imitation of her own sweeping strokes. She made no protest and he remarked no change in her expression as he watched the reflection in the mirror but then, bending low, he kissed the nape of her neck, saying, "I've been a bear lately, Gilda. I don't mind admitting that I was jealous."

"Jealous of whom?"

"That actor chap, Bernard, the one who sent you those pictures. It's foolish, I know, for whatever he meant to you or you to him is of no consequence now. How could it be. It was before we met."

She said nothing, so he went on. "Do you mind if I stay?"

"If you wish it, Edward."

Her voice was so impersonal that it stirred in him a kind of fury. "If I wish it? Good God, of course I wish it! We're man and wife, aren't we? If I had my way we'd share a bed every night!"

"But that was agreed, Edward."

"I know it was agreed but I never imagined it would be like this, living together under the same roof but behaving as if we hardly knew one another. It's the craziest thing I ever heard of and no man I know would put up with it."

At least he had made some small impression on her. Her face flushed and for a moment it seemed as if she would match his anger, but then, with a shrug, she stood up and when she turned her features expressed the familiar and dreaded blankness of all the other occasions he had come here as a supplicant. She said, "I will go to bed. Come back if you wish. The door will be ajar," and lifting her nightdress from the eiderdown where her maid had laid it she shrugged herself out of the flimsy shift and raised her arms to replace it with the linen gown.

It was the smooth ripple of her breasts that stimulated him to a degree that nothing else could have done. He saw it, swift and infinitely sensuous, as the lifting of a curtain in everything about her that he had coveted, won and was now so infamously denied. He said, huskily, "Wait, Gilda!" and reached out, taking the nightgown from her and tossing it aside, then seizing her and crushing her against him with such impetuous force that she cried out involuntarily as her flesh came into contact with his clothes. Half distinguishable words, fierce but caressing, accompanied the kisses he rained on her face and shoulders and then, gathering her up, he hooked the open door with his foot and carried her across the landing to his own room. Once here, momentarily undecided how to dispose of his prize, he paused and set her down, turning his back on her for a moment to slam the door and turn the key in the lock.

The click of the tongue slipping home had a curious effect on him, proclaiming perhaps his unexpected victory over her reservations and his own apparent mastery of the situation. He said, gruffly, "Like it or not you'll stay here tonight," and began to pull off his clothes, tossing them in a heap on the floor.

She said, still very quietly, "No, Edward, not this way. I had your promise," but the sight of her standing there stark naked and proposing terms for a conditional surrender increased his sense of outrage. He found he was able to look at her in a way that had never been possible before, objectively and impersonally rather than the summit of all he had ever hoped for from women. His eyes took in every part of her, not sensually, as in her room a moment ago, but coolly and almost mockingly. He went on undressing but less hurriedly, retrieving his jacket and waistcoat from the floor, putting them over a chair and saying, as he sat to remove his boots, "Sometimes I can't imagine why you married me. Since you have, I've rights to exercise whenever I choose."

She remained perfectly calm, a fact that secretly astonished him in the circumstances.

"I've never denied you access."

"Aye, but always on your terms."

"On terms we agreed."

"I renounce them."

He had got as far as removing his trousers and she had him at a disadvantage. Her movement was like the spring of a cat. Before he could regain his balance she was at the door, had turned the lock and laid her hand on the door knob.

He caught her before she could pull it open, seizing her round the waist and dragging her back into the centre of the room where she writhed from his grasp and made as though to try again but he shot out a hand and caught her by the ankle so that she fell flat on her face, a flailing arm coming into sharp contact with the fender.

Her fall, and the metallic clang of displaced fire-irons, brought him up short so that he paused, suddenly aware of the farcical element in the quarrel, she sprawled naked on the carpet, he half entangled in his trousers.

"You aren't hurt, are you?"

She rose to her knees, her left hand holding her wrist where it had struck the metal. She looked so childish and pitiful that shame invaded him. The light of the bedside lamp fell on her back and her crouching attitude, with her hair touching the carpet, suggested the pose of a wounded animal.

"Gilda, it doesn't have to *be* like this! I'm sorry I treated you that way but in God's name try and understand how I feel. I love you and want you. Why can't we be like any other married couple? In God's name, why not?"

She rose slowly to her feet, still massaging her wrist.

"Let me see your arm."

She turned facing him and her eyes were blank.

"Do what you have to and let me go back to my room," and she began to walk slowly towards the bed.

Anger ebbed from him. Submission, on these terms, wasn't worth exacting. Sullenly he unlocked the door and threw it open.

"I'm damned if I'll beg, not even from you – wait, you can't go like that," and he stepped out, crossed the landing and entered her room, retrieving her nightgown and returning with it. She took it wordlessly and slipped it over her head. Then she went out, closing the door.

*　　*　　*

The moment he was certain she was not in the house he forced himself to think logically, rummaging in his mind for possible refuges at her disposal. He could think of none other than her mother's house in Northampton, so he went out breakfastless and summoned a cab to take him to the station, with every intention of boarding the first available train for Peterborough, and some half-formed plan of confronting her in Edith's presence. He did not know what her mother would make of it. He did not know what anybody would make of it. Their quarrel, seen in retrospect, was pointless and childish and while he had sacrificed his dignity she, in her mysterious way, had succeeded in rescuing hers. He was like a fugitive with the hounds on his heels, brought up short against a twenty-foot wall, and had no alternative now but to face the consequences of the ridiculous episode, already, no doubt, the subject of gossip among servants, who would know that she had fled during the night and that he had gone in pursuit without so much as a cup of coffee.

It was while he was standing in front of the departures board trying, with all his might, to focus his mind on the train schedules displayed there, that Garside accosted him, touching his cap and saying, "It's gone down, sir. I managed to get it on the workmen's train just after six," and Edward turned, wrinkling his brow and staring at the deputy stationmaster as if he had been a stranger and not a man with whom he had had scores of consultations concerning the despatch of freight since he came to the district as manager.

"What's that you say?"

"Madam's trunk, sir. The three-fifteen was on the point of leaving . . . matter of fact, I shouldn't have let her pass the barrier, but she was clearly in a great hurry to catch it. I got her on and put her trunk on the next train, as promised. It'll catch her up with that express label on it. Her cross-Channel doesn't leave until just after nine, sir."

His brain, completely fogged at Garside's initial approach, began to clear a little so that he was able to make some kind of sense out of the man's remarks. Gilda had come down here in the small hours with a trunk but had been unable to catch the three-fifteen save by jumping aboard when it was moving off on the whistle. To do this, she had been obliged to abandon the trunk and shout instructions for its forwarding to the obliging Garside, who had obviously recognised her and gone out of his way to help, probably because he regarded Swann-on-Wheels as one of the city's most important patrons of his railway. It was Garside's reference to the cross-Channel packet that baffled him. He said, carefully, "Is that three-fifteen a through train to the coast?"

"Yes, sir, though there's a longish wait at Victoria. Long enough for Mrs. Swann to get breakfast, I daresay."

"Thank you, Garside." He reached into his trouser pocket and drew out a half-crown.

"That isn't necessary, sir."

"Take it, man."

Garside took it with another salute. "Glad to help, Mr. Swann. The ladies will cut it fine, sir."

He went off and Edward, passing a hand over his unshaven chin, sat on a platform seat and made a tremendous effort to think clearly and purposefully. It was no use going after her. By the time he got to Dover (he remembered now that the early morning train from Manchester connected to Dover) she would be in France. It was no use trailing over to her mother's either or not yet, not until he had had time to think up some plausible story for Gilda's absence. As to the future, he had no wish whatever to explore that. The best course he could take now was to get himself shaved, make some kind of pretence to eat breakfast, and stop the news of her flight being broadcast to tradesmen who might well be numbered among Swann's regular customers. If that happened, the depot would get to hear about it within hours and the thought of moving among the clerks and waggoners as a newly-married husband, whose wife had fled from him in the middle of the night, was not to be contemplated.

He went out of the station, called a cab and drove home, telling the housekeeper that Mrs. Swann had been summoned away on urgent family business and that he had been to the station to send on her luggage. He had no means of knowing whether or not she believed him but she was a discreet woman and he could rely on her to relay the information, for what it was worth, to the other servants. She said, "The breakfast is cold, sir. Shall I get cook to send up some more?" and he said no, for he planned to follow Mrs. Swann after a visit to the depot, and would make do with coffee and eat on the train. He then dismissed her and went upstairs to shave, finding that he had to use extra care with his cut-throat for his hand was unsteady. He packed an overnight bag and came down again in ten minutes to drink a single cup of coffee. Then saying no more to anyone, he went out and walked the distance to the station. The depot could await a wire explaining his absence. In the meantime, the need to confide in someone was imperative and he could think of no one but his mother-in-law, Edith Wickstead.

2

Incident in Whitehall

HE WAS NOT ILL, OR NOT OF A SICKNESS THAT COULD
be diagnosed and cured, yet those who remembered
Edward Swann in the days of his apprenticeship, and his
surge into the Westcountry with his brother George when
the two of them had raised the eyebrows of every transporter in the country, began to think of him as a sick man
for both his appearance and character had undergone
dramatic changes in the last few weeks.

He had always been a ruddy-faced, well-set-up young
man, quiet and deliberate in manner. Not too talkative,
perhaps, but friendly enough, and a very good man to
have beside you, behind you, or even over you in a crisis.
He was more equable than George and more approach-
able than his father, someone who would always listen,
who had time to spare for the lowliest employee in the
sector, a gaffer, moreover, who was reckoned a first-class
mediator in a local dispute and almost as good as his
brother Giles at pacifying irate customers. Now there was
hardly a trace of those characteristics that had played such
a part in enabling this sector of the network to adjust to
the 1905 realignment of frontiers and reshuffle of executives after the switch to powered transport. Moody and
unpredictable, he slouched through his daily schedule like
a sullen schoolboy harassed by an imposition, ranging off
to the nearest public-house as soon as the yard shut down,
not to royster, it was rumoured, but to sit in a corner

drinking and snarling at anyone who offered to share his company.

The direct cause of the vast change in him soon got about, despite his mumbled stories of his young wife being on an extended trip abroad. "Completing her studies," as one senior clerk said to another when the subject was raised in The Funnel's counting-house, and his companion had winked solemnly as he said, "Studies in what, I wonder?"

It could not have been housewifery, for the Swann house at Edgbaston was closed and coming up for auction, its staff dismissed and its new furniture in store at the Bull Ring warehouse. When this proved to be more than a loading-yard rumour, and the young gaffer had taken to biting heads off in every direction, clerks, drivers, mechanics, waggoners and even customers shared the view that someone should take Edward in hand before the sector slipped to the bottom rung of the Swann ladder, to rub along with regions where the horse and cart predominated. Opinion was divided as to who that someone should be. One Barnes, a summarily dismissed loader at the yard, was heard to exclaim that it should be that flighty young wife of his, after she had been dragged home by the hair, given a hiding and put to work at milking the bile out of the gaffer. The senior clerk was more restrained. He let it be known that brother George should be informed of how things stood and summoned to give the region an old-fashioned going over. Older men said the Old Gaffer would have sorted it out in a trice, for he had always been partial to sacking from the top whenever things went awry in a particular region. None of these speculators were aware that George had already been called in and been told to mind his own damned business, that no one this side of the Channel knew where the flighty young wife could be located, that old Adam himself had made little or no headway with the boy and that Edith Wickstead (still 'Gaffer Wadsworth' to the oldest hands about the place) had twice waylaid her son-in-law and urged him to put her daughter out of heart and mind before his life went sour on him.

Edith came as near as anyone to making a breach in Edward Swann's glowering defences when she said, with her Yorkshire forthrightness: "The girl's not worth a glass of cold gin, lad, and I would have told you that before you married if there had been the slightest prospect of you heeding me. She was hopelessly spoiled from babyhood and had her own way in everything until her father died. By then it was far too late to get it into her head that she wasn't somebody very special, destined to become a great actress or a king's trollop."

It was the word 'actress' that made Edward look up and he at once demanded to know if Gilda had always had an ambition to go on the stage.

"It was one of her grander fancies and the most persistent of them. She appeared in school plays, and had a good deal of amateur experience abroad, I believe. But everyone knows that kind of life needs real talent and far more stamina than she possesses, drat her. I thought she had put aside all thoughts of it when she married. For security," Edith added, "she even had the gall to tell me that!"

Edward said, in a low voice, "She never pretended she was in love with me. She was honest in that respect. But I got the impression she preferred me to any other man she had met. I didn't know about that chap Bernard until later."

Edith had been on the point of interrupting and telling him, with some notion of shock therapy in mind, that what Gilda had preferred was not Edward Swann but Edward Swann's prospects, including his share in his grandfather's fortune but his mention of Bernard checked her.

"I never heard of anyone of that name. Who is he? And how do you come to know about him?"

He told her the story of the flow of letters from Bernard's sister, and the little he had learned from Gilda of the man who sent the inscribed photograph. "It was brooding about him that sparked off that silly row," he said. "I got it into my head that he had been her lover in France but I don't think so now. Since you mention her being obsessed with the stage other things seem to fit."

"What kind of things?"

"The kind of books she read, for one thing. Plays they were, mostly, by Shakespeare and so forth. And French writers too . . . especially a chap called Molly something."

"Molière?"

"Yes, that was it. She used to read him aloud when I wasn't around, or so the housekeeper told me. She was always dressing up, too. She'd spend hours up in her room, messing about with costumes of one sort or another. Not real clothes, you understand, but well – fancy dresses. As a matter of fact, I thought it odd that she left most of her own clothes behind and took all those costumes away with her in that trunk. Could it be that she was still set on being an actress?"

"I would have thought so once but not lately. There's no security on the stage and she's sharp enough to know that."

"But if she thought she was good enough – I mean, to become someone like Ellen Terry, wouldn't she have decided that money would come with success?"

"It's possible, but listen here, lad, I didn't hunt you down for the purpose of discussing my daughter's castles in the air but to persuade you to get a hold of yourself. You tell me you've had no success with your enquiries in France and I certainly haven't a notion where she is or what she's about. Neither do I care as things are, but your father and mother are my oldest friends and I feel badly enough about this to go to work on you. Sooner or later, if she doesn't turn up, you'll be well advised to get shot of her on grounds of desertion. It might take a long time but you're young enough to live through it. And for another thing, why don't you buckle to, and drown your misery in work instead of drink? That road is no way out, not your way at all events. I'd offer you a home with me but it's too far from your depot. Suppose you rent a house locally and I come over and run it for you?"

He shook his head. "It's kind of you, Edith, but I need time . . . time to ride it out, and either find her or forget her. It's not just . . . well . . . losing Gilda. God knows that's bad enough, and there isn't an hour when I don't think of her and want her. It's looking such a damned fool, knowing everyone at the yard and out on the network and in the business men's clubs about here sees me as someone who married a girl as pretty as Gilda, showed her off everywhere I went, then woke up one morning to find she'd ditched me like an old pair of boots."

He paused frowning. She said nothing so he went on, "I don't have to tell you the name of Swann stands for something up here. The Gov'nor and George saw to that. How will people think of us now, I wonder? Or me particularly? A man who couldn't even stop his own wife walking out on him after five months of marriage?"

"Most people won't think of it at all, lad. Most people have forgotten it already. Or would do if you'd let them."

"But how am *I* supposed to think and feel in these kind of circumstances? I mean, what does everyone expect me to do? Dance a jig in the Bull Ring?"

"I imagine people who count expect you to write her off like a bad debt. One that costs far more to collect than it's worth, and it's her mother who is telling you this. Those letters you mentioned. Did you try the address on them?"

"I'm not that much steeped in liquor," he said, with a touch of his newly acquired asperity. "I wired and wrote five times, and when the letters came back I hired a man to go over there and check on the place. The woman who wrote to her had gone, leaving no forwarding address."

"And the universities? At Tours and in Paris?"

"He went there too. They couldn't help, or maybe they didn't choose to."

"Well, at least promise me one thing. Keep in touch, and come over for the weekend whenever you feel like it. Maybe you won't but it's better than going home to 'Tryst', and a lot better than drooping about by yourself with your head in a tankard."

*   *   *

A few days after his conversation with Edith he turned a corner and came headlong into collision with the realities his mother-in-law had urged him to face.

It came about in a curious way, when he found himself in the New Street area one Saturday afternoon, with more than two hours to wait before George's train arrived. He had been surprised when George had wired saying that he was coming up for the weekend. He knew that his brother was heavily engaged with what promised to be an important development in powered transport, although it was one that, so far as Edward could determine, was unlikely to profit private enterprise. George, it was whispered, had at last talked his brother Alex into arranging a test-haul, made under the auspices of the Automobile Association, of a battalion of Guards from Aldershot to Hastings in a variety of motors, and Edward could only suppose that George saw advantages in the publicity. He did not know that Edith had written to his brother the day she had left Birmingham, urging the Managing Director to look to his crumbling defences in The Funnel.

Time, now that Edward had lost all interest in work, hung tediously on his hands. He spent most of Saturday morning in a public-house, had lunched there on bread and cheese and finally drifted down to the station where, checking George's wire, he noted that he could not arrive until around four in the afternoon. It was now two o'clock, and his fuddled head, and the sour taste on his tongue, disinclined him to return to the bar. It was then, only a few steps from the station entrance, that he saw the bill-boards outside the Biograph Theatre.

He had heard, in a general way, about these biograph entertainments, moving pictures depicting news and fictional tales flashed on a screen in a darkened auditorium, but he had never had the time or inclination to visit one. Grudgingly he examined the advertisements outside the narrow little hall, wedged between a warehouse and a shop, a display of garish posters proclaiming the new wonder of the age and hung in a frame, under the canopy, photographs of the kind of entertainment promised within. It was some sort of desert epic, featuring Arab sheiks and camels, and away in the back of his mind he connected them with those pictures Gilda had been sent from France. The similarity caused him to take a closer look and he isolated a picture about six inches square, showing a fierce-looking Bedouin photographed in the act of thrashing a prostrate woman with his whip.

Like the pictures in Gilda's letters it had about it the trappings of improbable melodrama. The gestures of the victim, hands raised, eyes wide with appeal, dress disordered, revived memories of the entertainment he and his brothers had once derived from a magic lantern, and he was on the point of moving on when something in the woman's face checked him so that he looked again, peering very closely at the blurred image, then wrinkling his forehead with disbelief.

The woman on the ground reminded him vividly of Gilda. She had Gilda's wealth of hair and Gilda's smooth, oval face. She had Gilda's petite figure, too, and he thought, 'It's almost surely a fancy . . . I'm beginning to have hallucinations . . .' But he paid his money and went in none the less, groping his way to a seat facing a blank screen centred by a small, circular light. Then the hall went even darker and somewhere towards the front a piano began to tinkle as a series of flickering images trooped on to the screen. Isolated here in the dark he forgot his miseries, his lifelong interest in technology absorbing him as he witnessed a moving photographic record of a steeplechase in which the horses seemed to cross the screen powered by clockwork mechanism and all the stewards and sightseers had the same jerky gait and gestures, even when they raised and lowered their straw hats. A mild sense of wonder invaded him, that it was possible to make pictures move in this way, and he began to enjoy the intimacy of the place as he watched first some French Army manoeuvres, then a seaside scene and finally a swift tour of the Earl's Court and Anglo-French Exhibition.

The round-up of news pictures was followed by a display of conjuring and then some mimed comedy in which an actor fell into a pond, and, having emerged, pranced about on the bank shaking his fist and mouthing oaths at mocking witnesses. Then the screen went blank for a moment and after an appreciable pause projected a frame announcing the main attraction, subtitled in English, *The Terror of the Desert*.

It was, Edward soon decided, a very silly story, concerning what seemed to be an expedition into the Sahara, attended by a caravan of camels and horsemen, and led by a wildly gesticulating young man who spent most of his time spurring up and down the line of march mouthing directions at his underlings. Once, when the face of the leader was grossly enlarged, it had about it the same hint of familiarity but again he dismissed this as fancy or coincidence. It was only when, after the travellers had encamped at an oasis, and the horseman entered his tent, that he sat up with a jolt that almost projected him from his seat. The woman rising from a silken couch was either Gilda or Gilda's double. He identified her not only by face and figure but even more surely by her mannerisms and that gliding walk of hers.

It was an extraordinary sensation sitting there watching a shadow play involving the woman he had loved to distraction, since the moment he met her at Edith Wickstead's home nearly two years ago. It was as though he was dreaming an exceptionally vivid dream, in which were incorporated elements of amazement, a deep yearning and the wildest kind of farce, far more improbable than the scene in his room the night she left home. But then, before he could determine whether or not he was in the grip of some self-induced deception of the senses, the action of the epic changed and the oasis was attacked by a horde of Arab horsemen, who succeeded in scattering the expedition and abducting Gilda, who was carried away on the saddlebow of a bearded chieftain, whose eyes rolled like those of a man in the grip of an epileptic fit.

There followed a short series of scenes, more or less connected, showing the chieftain's impetuous siege of his prize and her ultimate consignment to the harem where, in the presence of half-a-dozen fat, inscrutable-looking women, she alternately raised her hands to heaven and collapsed sobbing on a couch. This orgy of despair lasted, perhaps, five minutes, before the Arab chieftain arrived with the obvious intention of thrashing his captive into submission but hardly had he begun the work when the gesticulating horseman turned up again, firing endless volleys of shots from his revolver and accounting, so far as Edward could judge, for rather more than half the population of the town. The chieftain went down as he tried to escape with the struggling Gilda, after which the cameras played on a fond reunion scene, with Gilda fluttering her eyelids as if they had been automatically-operated blinds, and the gallant pistoleer kneeling on one knee and running a scale of kisses up and down her arm.

Before he could emerge from his daze of incredulity the screen went blank and the lights came on and everybody around him got up and went out into the daylight. He had no power in his legs to follow them but sat there with his lips parted, gazing up at the blank screen, until a man in a rusty-looking frockcoat touched him on the shoulder and said, civilly, "Nex' show five o'clock, sir. Rich, weren't it?"

Edward hauled himself to his feet and said, "That . . . that actor and actress, do you know them?"

The man looked almost as astonished as he felt and

replied, "Lor' no, sir, I don't *know* 'em. I mean, 'ow would I? It's a French reel, rented for publick exhibition . . ." but then, "Wait a minnit tho', I got the contrac', 'aven't I? I'll 'ave a squint if you can 'old on a jiffy. Alwus 'as the names o' the leading actors on the contrac'." He pottered off into his little office under the balcony where the projectionist was housed, emerging again with a document that resembled a conveyance. "Now let's see. *Terror o' the Desert*. Made in Paris, like I said, tho' I dunno how they managed for sand and what-not. They get up to all kinds o' tricks over there, same as the Yanks. Made by a cove called Jules Lamont, wi' – here you are, sir, – Monsewer Bernard Villon an' Mamerselle Fantine Grenadier. I remember we've rented several wi' the same team and the customers like 'em, judging by the takings."

"That picture you have in the foyer . . . the one of the two of them, could I buy it?"

"*Buy* it?" The man scratched his head. "Well, I dunno. I don' see why not, seeing this is Sat'dy, and we got to send this lot on to Mr. Hamilton's Picksherdrome at Wolver'ampton tomorrer. But they woulden miss one display picsher. What do you say to 'alf-a-dollar, sir?"

Edward gave him half-a-crown and they went into the foyer together where the manager removed the picture from its frame and handed it over. Edward walked blinking into the daylight and down to the station hall, noting that it wanted but twenty minutes for George's train to arrive.

He sat on the seat he had occupied the morning of her flight and studied the picture anew. It was like Gilda and yet it was not. The delicate moulding of her features were disguised under what might have been a thick coating of actor's greasepaint and distorted, to some extent, by her simulated expression of terror or loathing. She looked a little like a doll conceived by some malevolent scarer of children and yet one knew, at a glance, that she was play-acting and that the agonised look was a pretence and a poor one at that. He thought, dully, 'It's her right enough and she exchanged me for this . . . this mummery . . . She threw over the name Swann, and even the name given her by her parents, for one that goes along with this kind of nonsense . . .' Suddenly he was persuaded that it was not love for Bernard or anyone else that had urged her to decamp with that trunkful of theatrical clothes but the allure of seeing herself in this kind of role, a shadow on a screen, to be gaped at by strangers in places like that seedy little hall he had just quitted. It seemed incredible to him someone sane could make such a choice but in a way, at some distance below incredulity, it fitted her personality, for it was really no more than a gross extension of the self-deception she had been practising ever since he had known her and almost certainly, if Edith was to be believed, since her childhood. The yearning to be 'someone special' had milked her of all her natural feelings and responses, of the capacity to love and be loved, of obligations to anyone other than herself and this, in a round-about way, accounted for her woodenness towards a man she had married.

Painfully and vaguely repugnant memories of their brief association returned to him like clumsy fingers probing a wound. Gilda accepting a gift. Gilda at meals. Gilda, with her lovely hair spread on a pillow and her body beneath his, but always with that blankness behind her eyes, as if, at the very moment of coition, she was transforming him into the person of that prancing horseman or eye-rolling sheik. Or perhaps not even that. Perhaps she was visualising herself drooping about a stage tent dressed as an Arab houri, wooed and whipped by other shadows. But always as a person uninvolved in life as it was lived by everybody but 'special people', always pretending to situations in which she was never required to be involved emotionally and as he thought this a kind of shudder passed through him.

The sensation was like the quenching of an unbearable thirst, rich, satisfying and uplifting, so that his memory revived for him a story old Phoebe Fraser, nanny to all the Swanns, had once read him and his sister Margaret, a story called *Pilgrim's Progress* that had promised to be dull because it was holy but had proved surprisingly absorbing and adventurous as the hero, Christian, journeyed to the Celestial City. He remembered with surprising clarity how Christian had ascended the Hill of Difficulty with his burden and struggled upward to the cross where the burden fell away, tumbling down, down and out of sight and leaving the pilgrim untrammelled for the road ahead. Sitting here, with the hissing din of the station in his ears, he could identify with Christian at that very moment, a man miraculously freed of a weight so intolerable that it clouded his mind to the business of the day.

Deliberately, and with a kind of dedicated joy, he tore the picture into small pieces and let them fall on to the platform. Then he glanced up to see George's train sliding in and George's face scanning the platform, and he grinned. It wasn't often anyone saw old George looking bothered.

*   *   *

The brothers had always been close. Closer than any of the others save, possibly, Joanna and Helen, so that it did not surprise him much when George understood the intricacies of the story so readily. He said, as they sat over a pint in Edward's favourite snuggery, "I don't know . . . marriage is always a bran-tub to a man who is interested in his job. I was damned lucky, considering, remembering the gambles I took before I fetched up with Gisela. I've played the fool since, come to that, and might have again if I'd ever found time. Work, that's the best tonic in the long run." And then, giving his brother a shrewd look, "You're pretty much behindhand from all I hear. Maybe I can suggest a short cut or two. Or would you prefer some other distraction? A music-hall, maybe?"

"I'd like to go down to the yard, providing you'd come

along. God alone knows what's got buried in those in-trays," and for the third or fourth time since he had met George at the station he raised his left arm and scratched himself vigorously. "As if I hadn't got enough on my plate," he said, ruefully, "I caught a flea in that sleazy little theatre!" George, predictably, threw back his head and laughed and Edward joined him. It was his first laugh in a very long time.

It was coming up to midnight when they returned to the hotel after six hours spent unravelling the muddle that had accumulated since the day Gilda had left. He was very tired but pleasantly so, a different kind of tiredness from that induced by liquor and by his long self-pitying walks through city and suburban streets. He felt very sleepy and far closer to George than he had ever felt, judging himself extraordinarily lucky that his brother's visit had coincided with the moment of revelation. He said, thoughtfully, "Do you see any future in that moving-picture business, George? I mean, will it ever amount to more than a showman's stunt?"

George replied, "Oh yes, there's money in it now, and there'll be a lot more as time goes on. Those biograph theatres are mushrooming in the London suburbs but I wouldn't invest in it, although I've been urged to by several claiming to be in the know."

"Why not then?"

"I suppose because I never did derive pleasure from play-acting of any kind. Our sort can't, and I can tell you why. We're too curious to go behind the scenes and find out what goes on. And then there's the folk associated with theatricals. They're crazy, nearly all of 'em. I mean, who the devil can begin to understand what makes a fine-looking woman like your missus spend her life prancing around pretending to be somebody else?"

He stretched his legs, enlarging on his theme. "I re-member once when the Gov'nor took us all to our first pantomime at the Lyceum. It was before you were born, I imagine. Old Alex, Stella, me and young Giles. Must have been somewhere around Christmas 'seventy-four or five. 'Jack and the Beanstalk' it was, and all the others were nearly sick with excitement. I wasn't. The show itself left me cold but I remember puzzling all the way home how the hell I could make a beanstalk grow in front of an audience and still keep 'em guessing. I worked out that it must be by a system of ropes and pulleys, high up behind the proscenium arch. It's odd how different people can be inside one family. You're the only one I've ever really understood. I suppose that's why I caught on about how you felt in that picturedrome, weighing that woman's worth against the network." He sat thinking a moment. "Shall I tell you something else? When he was your age the Gov'nor had trouble with mother but he was luckier than you. Or more ruthless, maybe. He nursed her round to his way of thinking. Maybe, given time, you could do the same."

"I'll tell *you* something," Edward said. "I wouldn't bother to try. I'm over it, George, and through with it. She can go to the devil for all I care," and he broke off, stifling a yawn.

"Go and sleep it off, lad. I'll have a nightcap and follow on. We'll have another crack at that backlog tomorrow. Our way of going to church!"

Edward left him in the lounge and George was still there, puffing on his cigar, when he heard himself being paged by a boy in a pillbox hat. He called, "Hi, my name's Swann. Who's asking for me at this time of night?"

The boy said, "I don't know, sir. The night porter has the message if you'll ask at the desk."

He lounged over to the desk, thinking, "The Gov'nor once told me the network was a seven-day-a-week, twenty-four-hour-a-day job, and he was right." Having identified himself at the reception desk he was shunted on to the hall porter who said, "It's a telephone message, sir. It came in about ten o'clock. The lady asked if you would ring this number, no matter how late it was."

He took the slip with some disquiet, assuming it must be Gisela in some kind of fix, for she was chary of pursuing him on his frequent lunges up and down the country. But then he saw that it wasn't his own number but one of the inner London exchanges, and tipped the porter to call while he went over and retrieved the second half of his whisky and soda.

He recognised the voice as that of Milton Jeffs, his brother-in-law, and was at once alerted by the strained undertones in Milton's voice as he said, "*George?* Thank God! Debbie wants to speak to you. Something urgent . . . bad news, I'm afraid. She found out where you were from Gisela and badly wants advice. Wait, she's here now." Deborah came on the line saying, "Something bad has happened, George. It's Romayne. She's been seriously hurt in a suffragette demonstration outside Parliament this afternoon."

"Is that all you know?"

"She was knocked down and ridden over by a van."

"Is she with you?"

"No, no, she's in Westminster Hospital. George . . . she isn't expected to live."

He could tell by the catch in her voice that she was fighting very hard to control herself. He said, bracing himself, "Take it easy, Debbie. Take your time. Tell me how I can help."

"I don't know . . . I've been at my wits' end trying to trace Giles. He's away in his constituency on account of that trouble they're having in the mines and nobody seems to have heard of the telephone down there. I've wired his home, of course, and Huw Griffiths, but there would have been an answer by now if they had been anywhere in the Pontnewydd area. I felt so helpless and I have to get back to the hospital right away. I dare not tell the old folk so I rang Gisela and she told me where you were. We've got to find Giles and bring him home as soon as possible."

"The Welsh police could help . . ." but she cut in,

sharply, "No, not the police! Not even in these circumstances," and he guessed that the police had been involved in what had occurred outside the Houses of Parliament that day. He said, quickly, "I'll find him. I'll hire a car and drive down. That's by far the quickest, for it's Sunday now and God knows how long we might be getting there by train. I'll find him and bring him back. By tomorrow afternoon at the latest."

"Thank you, George. I'd be very grateful. There's at least a chance that way."

"She's that badly hurt?"

"A fractured skull, so the surgeon said. She's not regained consciousness."

"Leave it to me. Go straight back to the hospital. And Debbie . . . !"

"Yes?"

"Don't even try to notify the old people. They can't do anything to help, or not yet, and remember the Gov'nor is over eighty."

"Very well, George. I'll be here if I'm not at the hospital. They might not let me stay . . . there may be no point in staying anyway. You'd handle Giles better than any of us."

"Not better than you, Debbie. But I'd waste time coming to pick you up."

He replaced the receiver and stood thinking, holding the full import of her message at bay while he grappled with the practical aspects of a night journey by road to Wales. They could get a powerful motor somewhere. Edward would know where, and it would take them the better part of the night to reach the valleys. If they were lucky, and found Giles, they could refuel at the Cardiff depot and make a dash for London. But even if they encountered fair weather, unlikely at this time of year, they would be lucky to reach London before dusk. For a moment he toyed with the idea of going over Debbie's head and trying his luck with the Cardiff police but thought better of it. Giles was probably a marked man in that part of Wales, torn by strikes and political dissension. His wife, with gaol sentences behind her, and the current one hanging over her head under the 'Cat and Mouse' Act, whereby suffragettes on hunger strikes were released and re-arrested, was not likely to engage much official sympathy. It was better, in the circumstances, to rely on Edward's local contacts and his own ingenuity.

He knocked on Edward's door and, getting no answer, went in, finding his brother heavily asleep. He would have preferred to leave him sleeping and shift for himself but that wasn't possible. He needed Edward's local knowledge if he was to get hold of motor transport at this time of night.

He shook his brother awake. "Sorry, old son, but I'm off my own patch and badly need your help. Who do you know around here who would be likely to lend or hire us a Daimler, or some motor with that kind of performance?"

Edward said, rubbing his eyes, "Grayson, the big brewer, has a Panhard. He's an old customer. So is Sir Alec Gratwick, the draper. He runs one of those new Silver Ghosts. It's a corker. But what's happened? What do you want with a car?"

"I'll tell you later. How friendly are you with Grayson?"

"Not very. I know Sir Alec rather better."

"He's in politics, isn't he?"

"Yes. He'll be the next mayor."

"Liberal or Tory?"

"Liberal. Rabid. He stood for a local Parliamentary seat last election."

"Then he's our man. Would your association with him stand for rousting him out and asking a favour of this kind?"

"If it was important. He's a good sort and has been on our books since the Gov'nor's day."

"Then take me to him and leave me to do the explaining. I'll tell you as we go along."

2

The demonstration had the makings of a fiasco from the outset. The opposition in Trafalgar Square had been exceptionally noisy and abusive, and even Christabel Pankhurst, Mrs. Pankhurst's daughter, had been unable to get a hearing. It came on to drizzle as they formed up at the top of Whitehall, flanked, as always, by police, mounted and afoot, but the police seemed to be in a neutral mood today, trudging along with bored expressions and fulfilling their invidious role as a shield against the rowdiest elements of the crowd, who followed the line of march closely, eddying from pavements to carriageway and sometimes getting close enough to jostle.

Before they had passed the Horse Guards Romayne realised how mistaken she had been in parading and volunteering to carry a banner. She badly needed rest. Three days out of Holloway, following eight on a hunger strike, wasn't a long enough interval to recuperate, much less to march, and the banner, heavy with rain, was a terrible burden. At the House, when Christabel was due to speak again, she would have to surrender it to someone but in the meantime she thought she could manage, providing there were no mêlées. In the course of their shuffling progress to a point level with Downing Street she had a chance to look about her, peering closely at the cavorting bully-boys and asking herself yet again what it was that made them care enough to turn out on a rainy Saturday afternoon in order to abuse a few hundred women waging a lopsided war on a Government that called itself 'Liberal' and had proved, against all predictions, more implacable than its predecessors up to the landslide in 1906. It could not be fear, that she supposed accounted for most of the world's cruelty. Or envy, that accounted for the rest. It was probably no more than a mild revolt against the boredom and pinchpenny economy of their own lives, for most of the men in the crowd looked like mechanics or labourers, cloth-capped in the main and half-tipsy probably, seeing that it was payday for the majority.

The street sign 'Downing Street' reminded her of earlier, happier days of the crusade, when she and Debbie had earned their first arrest and spent their first fortnight in Holloway. That was getting on for five years ago now and she had been inside three times since then and twice subjected to forcible feeding before someone thought up that diabolical 'Cat and Mouse' scheme, a method of prolonging the agony capable of converting a dedicated campaigner into a morose fanatic. She had not reached that point yet but she was nearing it, her entire being rebelling against the demands made upon her physical resources over the last few months; and again she thought of her stupid rejection of the offer to go down to Lynmouth, where the W.S.P.U. ran a rest home for released hunger-strikers. In her present condition she wasn't much use to the cause, dragged down by this terrible yearning for sleep and stillness, for the predictability of a humdrum day in her own home, with the children and Giles if he could spare time to comfort and counsel her.

He would have counselled her now, no doubt, and extricated her from this untidy scrimmage, hailing a cab probably, and cheering her with news of progress on other fronts, but he had been away in Wales when she emerged, unexpectedly, on the eighth day of her twenty-eight day sentence, and she realised that he had troubles enough of his own, with the valleys in revolt, a lockout at the mines, and money to be raised for families who were pawning bedclothes in mid-winter to fortify their bellies against another week without wages.

She envied him his inner serenity, his ability, acquired little by little over the embattled years, to absorb the trials and tribulations of so many, allotting each its proper place in a scale of priorities. She envied him his resilience too, and the dynamo of nervous energy that enabled him to move through a working day that would have prostrated more robust men. He had the knack, that so few of the militants seemed to acquire, of isolating injustices like microbes under glass and studying each objectively before deciding how to deal with it. But when the moment came there was never a time when his coolness deserted him and he was tempted to abandon one plan in favour of another promising more spectacular results, a very common failing among crusaders.

Someone in the crowd threw an egg that struck the banner pole just above her head and spattered the shoulders of the woman in the rank ahead. The procession halted for a moment, closing up from behind and while she waited, resting the butt of the pole on the road, the remaining traces of the egg slipped down the pole and over her fingers, sliming them and making the pole difficult to grasp. The yearning for sleep made her senses reel and the shouts of the crowd, apparently blocking the march ahead and being broken up by mounted police, merged into a long, incessant roar so that she thought, distractedly; 'I'm going to faint and I mustn't faint here in full view of these louts. I must find Debbie and tell her to take my place for a spell, but how can I do that without abandoning this greasy pole . . . ?' And then, as though boosted from the direction of Trafalgar Square by a strong wind, the ranks behind her began pushing forward and the woman ahead remained stationary so that the section in which she was marshalled split and spilled sideways on to the pavement, the column losing cohesion as the banner was torn from her grasp. A bellowing policeman cantered past and she dodged to one side, brushing a lamp-standard with her shoulder. Behind it, leering at her like a centaur, was a fat middle-aged man with beery breath and heavy blue jowls singing snatches of the music-hall song, 'Ta-ra-ra-boom-de-ay', and beating out the time with his furled umbrella.

Then a fresh thrust from behind flung her forward into his outstretched arms and the whiff of his breath was so pungent and putrid that she retched and all the time he kept chanting, 'Ta-ra-ra-*BOOM*-de-ay!', even when he lost balance and they rolled together in the gutter.

When she rose to her knees he had disappeared in a swirl of legs and she crouched there close against the lamp-standard, shaking her head to and fro and her unpinned hair fell across her eyes and the sour smell of her own vomit reminded her of the cell in Holloway, where the little Scots doctor, with desperate patience trying to insert the feeding tube between her clenched teeth, kept repeating, "Awa', lassie! Dinnae mak' me do it . . Dinna *mak'* me . . . ." she lost all sense of time and place and became isolated from the chaos all about her.

The two-horse van appeared out of nowhere, running wild and free it seemed, so that she half rose to her feet and tried to ward off the goring butt of its shaft with both hands. It bore down on her inexorably, however, and she had an impression of being lifted as upon a wave and tossed the full width of the pavement. And after that the sustained roar of breakers on a rockbound coast dinned in her ears and Giles' sunburned face peered down at her from the bridge arching the river Gladwyn near their old home in Caernarvonshire.

He looked so much younger than of late. No more than a youth and he had a pack on his back that he jettisoned to climb down to where she stood waist deep in the shallow water. She was aware of the terrible importance of touching his hand and this she succeeded in doing, but only just, so that she had to scrabble with her toes to reach the level of the road. But when she got there it wasn't a road, only that long, bare dormitory of the emporium in the north where she had once lived the life of a shopgirl drudge. And then the scene changed again and they were in the bedroom of their little stone house on the side of the hill at Pontnewydd, where their life began all over again in a spirit of tender camaraderie that was startlingly new in their marriage. And suddenly she felt glad and free and at peace with the world, smiling and enfolding him, pressing him close and assuring him over and over that this would be different for both of them and that here, in this drab little room with its faded wallpaper, she would conceive his child. The sound of the breakers assailed her again then, louder and terribly insistent, so that she held him with all her strength and presently a wave broke over them both completely submerging them. But when it receded she still had him close against her breast.

3

They got him there just as dusk was creeping up river and the lights of the Embankment were winking like a vast necklace lit by a moving candle against a background of murk. They were all three chilled to the bone, despite heavy coats and mufflers and both George and Edward tried hard to persuade him to get a hot drink inside him before he went in but he shook his head.

"No, George. Go on home and take Edward with you. You've done enough for me, and I'll never forget it," so they left him and drove the borrowed Silver Ghost over the bridge and down Whitehall to the Strand. George said, glumly, "By God, I need a stiff one. Let's stop at the Savoy and give her a chance to cool off."

*　　　*　　　*

Giles went in to the lobby and here Deborah claimed him, breaking away from a nurse and saying, fervently, "Thank God you're here! She's been conscious but only for a moment . . . long enough to ask . . ." She piloted him into a waiting-room being vacated by the last of the Sunday visitors and heavy with the scent of chrysanthemums.

"Is there any chance at all, Debbie?"

She lowered her glance so he went on, with surprising calmness, "You were on the march? You must have seen what happened?"

"Not really, I was away up at the front. The mob surged on to the road and cut the column in half. Romayne was further back, carrying a banner. Sit down a minute. You'll be able to see her but you have to know, you have to understand first."

He sat on a long wooden bench, drawing off his gloves, and slowly chafing his numbed hands. "I was at Tonypandy. They're in a bad way down there."

"We're all in a bad way," she said, bitterly. "What makes us think we're unique as a nation, when things like this keep on happening? Romayne was a fighter, Giles. She could have taken the rest-cure in Devon, with all the others who were turned loose, but when she heard Christabel needed backing for the rally she insisted on coming along. Don't blame yourself for not being here. This is a war on so many fronts."

She told him how the march had attracted the usual horde of layabouts, all looking for a wet Saturday afternoon's diversion. "It's the papers I blame. They keep whipping them on like a lot of foxhounds. The police were fair – they did what they could but there wasn't nearly enough of them. They broke up the procession opposite Downing Street and the van that knocked her down was a Black Maria, moving in to pick up the rowdies."

"How bad are her injuries, Debbie?"

"Spinal, and a suspected fractured skull. But they're not absolutely sure yet."

A young doctor approached and conducted them wordlessly through a maze of corridors to a ward containing about forty beds. There were screens around most of them, so that he assumed the patients here were all on the danger list. Nurses swished to and fro, absorbed in their own business. Lights burned low and from all around rose a low, persistent murmur of distracted protest. He thought, 'It can't be right for people to die without privacy. These places need looking to, like every other institution in the damned country . . . if she holds on I'll get her out of here somehow . . .' And then a sister, distinguished by her dark blue overall and small coif, came up and said, "She's conscious intermittently, Mr. Swann, but don't stay more than a moment. Don't talk either and only one of you, please."

Her head was swathed in bandages and she lay very still, her long, shapely hands spread on the coverlet in what he saw as a gesture of resignation. He lifted one of them and stood holding it and presently there was a slight break in the rhythm of her heavy breathing and she stirred, her eyes opening, closing, then opening again. He forced himself to smile and something in the refraction of her pupils, and a slight pucker about the lips, indicated that she was half aware of him. His heart thumped painfully against his ribs as he saw, or thought he saw, her trying to frame words.

"Don't talk. I'm here now, it's Giles, dearest."

The eyelids fluttered again and the tip of her tongue emerged to moisten her lips. He took a damp flannel from the bedside locker and drew it gently across the mouth and cheekbones. She looked surprisingly young, he thought, about half his own age, and her skin, emphasised by prison pallor, was smooth as wax. He remembered he had always been aware of the texture of her skin, ever since that first impulsive kiss she had given him when, as eighteen-year-olds, they had met under the looming bulk of the mountain at Beddgelert. He reckoned up the interval, a span of something over twenty-five years, but it did not seem so long. More like twenty-five months, a summer's morning a year or two ago and yet, in that space of time, her personality had undergone a dramatic change. In those early days she wouldn't have given a damn about women's suffrage, miners' pay or anything else save how to get her own way in everything. He wondered what agency had transformed her to that extent, from a spoiled millionaire's brat into a dedicated freedom fighter, willing to sacrifice all she had won from life for deeply-held ideals involved with justice and equity among people of both sexes and all classes. It could not have been his own influence on a personality that had once been as self-centred as that of her father and as feckless as a child, and his mind went back to that curious withdrawal of hers before they were married, when she had fled her father's home and found work in a draper's shop for a few shillings a week, eating the kind of food they fed paupers at workhouses. He wondered if, for all his love of her, and for all his book browsing, he had ever come near to understanding the impulses and aspirations of the brain behind that smooth, white brow. In a way, she was like a woman who had taken the vow and never gone back on it, and he wondered if the sense of dedication that had swept both of them down the years into this murmuring ward would re-occur in either of her boys. He doubted it. More likely it was unique, welling from some Celtic blend of fervour and mysticism in the genes of Cambrian ancestors.

Her eyes were open now and the tapering fingers tightened their grip on the ball of his thumb. He whispered, "Romayne? Romayne, darling?" The slow, painful smile confirmed his belief that she was conscious. She made a distinct sound then and he bent very low over the pillow, without releasing her hand. She tried again and this time he could just identify the word, a single syllable that, in the present context, seemed strange and very moving. It was only part of a word really, 'Pont . . .', the Welsh word for 'bridge', but it had a message for him. She had been trying to say 'Pontnewydd', the name of his constituency, and it seemed to him that in the confused labyrinth of her lacerated brain, she had all but found her way back to the point in their lives where they had discovered fulfilment, both personal and public. For that was the word that had signposted them here to this parting.

Her head lolled sideways, just as the sister reappeared in the aperture of the screens. She lifted the wrist, stood poised for a moment, then looked across at him, shaking her head. She said, very quietly, "I'm so sorry, Mr. Swann." And then, "I knew her, knew you both. Will you come down again now? I'd like to have a word with you if I may. Mrs. Jeffs has left. She's been here almost continuously, ever since they brought Mrs. Swann in, but I persuaded her to go home. She needs food and rest."

He followed her down to the cheerless waiting-room, wondering vaguely what she could have to say to him, and when they had passed inside she closed the door and stood with her back to it, looking vaguely embarrassed.

"The porter is bringing some tea. He won't be a moment. You've had a terrible shock and a long hard drive from Wales."

"Mrs. Jeffs told you?"

"She didn't have to. We've all three met, you see. Just the once."

He forced his mind away from the memory of the angled, bandaged head upstairs, trying to identify the woman who stood watching him, her back to the door. She was Welsh. He could assure himself of that much by her accent, and she looked Welsh too, one of the blonde, less full-faced Celts one met occasionally in the valleys but more often in the north, about L.G.'s stamping-ground.

"You're from my constituency?"

"Near it. From Swansea. But you couldn't possibly remember me. It was so long ago. I was the cause of a . . . a disagreement between you and your wife in a London shop. You weren't married then, I believe."

"I'm sorry?"

"Don't be. It's of no consequence, or not to you, Mr. Swann. It's just that . . . well, it crossed my mind that it might cheer you a little to know. I was a millinery counter assistant in a shop in Oxford Street, and you and Mrs. Swann came in late at night to buy a hat in the window. I was tired and refused to serve her. Afterwards I fainted and you hustled her out. I never forgot about it because it was the turning point in my life. I suppose that was why I followed your career so closely, and Mrs. Swann's too, after she became so involved in the W.S.P.U. It's terrible for you that this has happened but it might help people to realise . . ."

She stopped, giving him time to absorb the astonishing completeness of the pattern involving three lives, perhaps many more. He remembered her now, a tall girl with blonde hair, who had been goaded to mutiny by Romayne's petulant insistence on getting a hat out of the window at past eleven o'clock at night after the girl had been on her feet for fifteen hours; the intervention of an outraged floorwalker and the girl, probably appalled by her outburst, fainting behind the counter. It was the night he broke off their engagement, seeing no kind of future in their association, but he had been wrong. The incident must have made an even greater impression on Romayne, for it was that which prompted her flight and enrolment in the ranks of the hard-driven. Indeed, her involvement in causes of all kinds had dated from that very moment. It seemed very strange and wonderful that this woman should be present to witness her sacrificing her life for yet another cause. He said at last, "How do you mean – a turning point?"

"I was sacked, without a character. It meant leaving the drapery trade. I took up nursing. I needed that push and Mrs. Swann did me a good turn because that wasn't any sort of life and this . . . ? Well, you'll understand – one feels useful, needed, more able to help. The way you help people."

"I wish she could have known."

"It was hopeless from the start, Mr. Swann. We did everything we could."

"I'm sure you did. What is your name, Sister?"

"Powell. I'm a senior ward sister, studying for my finals. I hope to get a matron's post somewhere in a year or so. In Wales, perhaps. There's plenty of need for trained nurses in that part of the country." She paused, turning to open the door in response to a knock. A porter came in with a tray of tea and she took it and dismissed him.

"It is very kind of you, Miss Powell."

"Nonsense. You can't leave yet. There'll be papers to sign in the office."

She poured his tea and handed it to him. It was scalding and strong and he sipped it gratefully. She said, hesitantly, "I wonder . . . would it seem impertinent . . . would you mind telling me why your wife became a militant? Was it because of your work as an M.P.?"

"No. She was involved in a variety of other lost causes long before I won the Pontnewydd seat. One of them was the pay and conditions of shop assistants. It began on account of you, on account of that silly business about the hat," and he told her of the sequel to the incident and how, a year after they had parted, he had traced her to a draper's sweat shop in the north.

"Doesn't it strike you as a kind of . . . well, a design of some sort? As though it was a plan, involving all of us?"

"Yes," he said, "very much so. That's why I wish my wife could have known."

"I'll get those papers. Please help yourself to some more tea."

"Thank you."

She went out, her starched skirts rustling like dry leaves underfoot and he sat hunched, his fingertips seeking warmth from the cup. There was, as she said, 'some kind of design', but what kind, and leading where, was more than he could say. He would have to think about it. Sometime when he felt less tired and drained and hopeless.

* * *

The day after the funeral he accepted his father's shy offer to take advantage of the frosty sunshine and walk through the woods to the plateau overlooking Denzil Fawcett's rough pasture at Dewponds. It was a walk they had often taken and one he seldom failed to appreciate for up here, in his father's genial company, they had discussed, over the years, every topic from hymns to haulage and poetry to poverty.

Adam said, as they emerged from the beech grove, "I'm glad you rejected that showy funeral they were planning to give her. Wouldn't have suited her nor you. Not your way of going about things."

Christabel Pankhurst had come to him with plans for a big W.S.P.U. turnout, but he had politely declined the offer, accepting only the magnificent wreath the movement sent her for the grave at Twyforde Churchyard. The cause was very dear to him. But not dear enough to encourage him to use Romayne's broken body as an advertisement.

They buried her a few plots away from his Grandfather Swann's grave. It was where he would wish to lie himself, a swallow's swoop from this corner of the Weald where he and all the other Swanns had been born and reared. It was the first Swann funeral in thirty years.

He said, bitterly, "I'm with them, body and soul, and have been, from the very beginning. I see it as the most important social issue of our time."

"It's important, I grant you."

"But not vitally so? Well, it shouldn't be difficult for you to see why it is to me. Enough to consider crossing the floor and joining up with the Labour Party. They're fully committed to Women's Suffrage. Our people are digging their heels in deeper every day."

Adam looked at him shrewdly. "You're saying you could quit the Liberal Party and still hold on to Pontnewydd?"

"Not at first, maybe. Eventually, I'd win it back."

"In the meantime you'd be prepared to split the vote and let a Tory in?"

"What does it matter, Tory or Liberal? A majority in both parties still regard women as serfs and demand passive acceptance of bed and bondage. How can you work alongside men of that kind? What do their clamours for reform amount to when they're made exclusively on behalf of the male half of the population?"

"Don't do it, old son."

"They've got some good men in that minority party. They go a lot further than we're prepared to go. Not just about this, about other issues."

"Ah, yes, I daresay and maybe that's why I'm doubtful. Not concerning their intentions but their hustle. I've read all their speeches and some of their pamphlets and they mean well enough. But there's something awry somewhere."

"Can you explain, Father?"

The climb through the last part of the woods had winded Adam. He found a convenient five-barred gate to lean upon and looked eastward towards the heart of the Weald and the sea.

"No, just an instinct. A prejudice, even."

"A prejudice against what?"

"Not against anything. A prejudice in favour of something. Of going about reform in the way the English radical always has, a nibble at a time."

"Does that mean that, deep down, you're with Asquith, that you don't feel the women should have the vote yet?"

"No, no . . . I'd give it 'em, but it's only a part of what wants doing and what will be done if we're not led astray by the grab-alls, the blowhards, and the peacocks."

"But this is a personal business for me now."

"So it is, but you're holding a long line, boy. Plan for a general advance. Don't spend yourself storming a single redoubt. The strongpoint will be over-run anyway in a general offensive."

Giles said, gloomily, "Power changes parties as well as individuals. I've seen it happening, ever since 1906. We aren't the same men as we were in opposition all that time."

"*You* are."

He turned aside from the gate and seated himself on a convenient log. "Tell you something else, my boy. I've been watching you ever since you were in short trousers. I've lived a long time, and kept my eyes open most of the time. There's Alex's lot, George's lot, and your lot. The Army, Trade and Politics. All three of you have had to contend with stupidity, greed, excessive caution, complacency and so on, and you've all worked out your own ways of tackling 'em. I like your way best. The quiet way. And so, in the main, does the country. Our people aren't fools. They soon learn to sort out the men they can trust and the men they can't. Takes 'em time but they learn and the difference between you and your friend Lloyd George is a case in point. You decide issues from conviction. His starting point will always be personal preferment. Folk find that out in the end. Go back to your miners and get on with your job. That's my advice for what it's worth. Well, I've had my breather. Let's get on before it clouds over."

They walked together across the winding heath path, in companionable silence for the most part, but when they reached the briar-sown track down to the curve of the river, where it rejoined the 'Tryst' boundary, Giles said: "What did you mean, precisely. 'Unless we're sidetracked by grab-alls, peacocks and blowhards'?"

"I was looking well ahead. You can do that objectively at my age. I can't say I am reassured by what I see, for civilisation as a whole or for us in particular. Forty . . . thirty years ago the twentieth century seemed a golden age but it's like most things we mistake for gold at a distance. When you touch it it's pinchbeck. Things seemed to be getting better all the time. Machines were going to give everybody more leisure. Poverty was going to go the way of feudalism. Universal education was going to work wonders. You must have heard it all in your line of business?"

"Things have got better, haven't they?"

"In some respects. We still resort to eighteenth-century diplomacy in our chancelleries. And then think of the scramble for Africa, and this naval arms race between us and Germany. I sometimes wonder where it will lead us all. Down the Gadarene slope if we don't look sharp. Mind, we've always had to contend with the gluttons. I once knew a merchant in The Polygon who boasted of running his business on boys and old men. He sacked the boys the day they finished their apprenticeship and paid the old-stagers half the current rate, since it was that or the workhouse. You can legislate against that kind of thing nowadays but you can't frame laws against secret treaties made by the idiots who find reassurance in music-hall ditties written on red, white and blue scores. Those are the jokers who worry me the most and the sickness is spreading fast. It started here, back about the time you were born, and it's taken hold in Potsdam, Paris and even Washington. All over the West people who should know better think money and prestige are the touchstones. They aren't and you've only got to read the history books to prove it."

"What are the touchstones, Father?"

The old man knitted his brows. "Ah, now you're asking. Respect for human dignity, maybe, and for Donne's dictum – 'Each man's death diminishes me.' Mercifully there's still evidence of that here." He paused as they drew level with the river, low for this season of the year and fringed with frosted brushwood sparkling like a long row of Christmas trees. "As for your loss, try and regard her as the French view the loss of Alsace-Lorraine – 'Speak of it never, think of it always.'"

Giles reached out and touched his father's arm. "A walk with you is the best tonic I know, Father."

"Glad somebody thinks so. If you can serve any purpose at my age one shouldn't complain."

"You're good for a long time yet, Father."

"A year or so, given mild winters," and in his bones he believed it, for at eighty-two he had less aches and pains to bother him than many men twenty years his junior.

He would not have believed, however, that he would live to see yet another royal funeral.

3

The Last Rally

IT WAS THE FINAL RALLY. SURELY THE LAST HE would live to see and perhaps, who knew? the last occasion when a constellation of kings, princes and grand dukes, garnished, gilded, splendidly mounted and serenely untroubled in their Godgiven right to occupy the centre of the world's stage, would use the passing of one of their number as an occasion to catch up on family gossip and practise a little harmless skulduggery on one another once the royal corpse was decently below ground at Frogmore.

There was no logical reason why he should view it in this cryptic manner, or none save that slight stir of uneasiness somewhere near the bottom of his rib cage, the pulse he had sometimes referred to as 'the little feller in here' when expressing undefined doubts about a project. This was no cause, however, for foregoing the occasion to celebrate (for that was how Henrietta regarded it) his own longevity and go posting up to town to bribe or bully one or other of his old cronies to find him a place on a balcony or a window overlooking the funeral march.

He saw it as a rally of the privileged, most of them stemming, in one way or another, from the loins of that gloomy German chap Albert. 'The stud house of Europe', Napoleon had called the House of Coburg. For here they were, a whole shoal of them, in their frogged tunics, glittering orders and absurd headgear, assembled to pay homage to a corpulent man whom some thought of as a peacemaker and others a mere womaniser, but whose death that summer had caught everyone off balance. For these days a monarch was not reckoned old at sixty-nine. After all, the fellow's mother had reigned almost as long and even his great-grandfather, Farmer George, had made eighty-plus.

Yet there it was. He was gone, and his bright new halo with him, and Adam could find cause to regret him, for, just as he had grown to dislike his tetchy old mother, he had come to respect her roystering son for the dignity and despatch he brought to his job when he was summoned after such a long and frustrating wait in the wings.

He did not know whether most people had had time to adjust to his style, so different from Victoria's, with its opening of social doors, and the application of shrewd personal judgment in foreign affairs, sound but not showy. At least, the foreigners respected him in a way they had never respected his mother. Somehow he had taken the measure of them, especially of his nephew Wilhelm, with his fierce upturned moustaches and loud-mouthed braggadocio. He had brought to his job the dignity that had been lacking for nearly three centuries, since the time Elizabeth rallied the nation at Tilbury.

Mainly, of course, they were here to show off their plumes but he suspected there was another reason for their assembly. Deep down the more responsible of them were genuinely worried by his abrupt departure from their midst. He was, in essence, a kind of stabiliser in the chancelleries, a factor that had to be reckoned with in small matters and great, and it was no time for the vacuum to be filled by that unassuming Prince George, whose experience, outside the navy or a pheasant shoot, was very limited.

It might well be, of course, that he too would surprise the cleverdicks. He was known to be an amiable man, anxious to play out his life on a low key. Most of them, no doubt, would hope that he would continue in this way, enabling time for their personal plans to mature, but with a Coburg one could rarely take such things for granted. Nobody had rated Albert very high when he married Victoria two generations ago yet he had succeeded in surprising most people, just as Edward, his scrapegrace son, had only a few years back.

Meantime they composed their expressions and marched a dutiful slow-step, eyeing one another with a certain caution.

* * *

They did these things superbly well, did the English, he thought, his mind returning to Victoria's funeral in 1901, and her glittering Jubilees of '87 and '97. Weather as good as this, of course, was sure to increase the demand on vantage points, so he went up to town the day before and was in position before the procession set out from the palace at nine sharp. Yet even he, used to such spectacles, had not anticipated a show on this scale, with eight kings and a royal duke, riding three by three, followed by five heirs-apparent, forty imperial or royal highnesses, seven queens, and ambassadors from every country on the map.

They had talked about Queen's weather at the Jubilee but here was King's weather, with the sun riding high in a cloudless sky, temperatures soaring into the seventies, and not even the lightest breeze to ruffle the white plumes of Kaiser Wilhelm's field-marshal's hat as he reined back slightly to give Cousin George the precedence demanded by protocol. He was worth a look, this plunging grandson of the old queen, who was reported to have said of Britain, "I am proud to call this place home . . ." But it didn't seem to stop him reviling it when he was in one of his 'encirclement' moods. They said he had a withered arm but if it was true it didn't show. His right hand held the marshal's baton, his left the reins of the docile grey he was riding and, as at his grandmother's funeral, he seemed to be on his very best behaviour, although even a mild-mannered man might have been forgiven irritability under all that sweaty clobber he was wearing.

The leading trio passed, the new King, Wilhelm and the dead monarch's only surviving brother, the Duke of Connaught, and in their wake the kings of Denmark and the Hellenes, brothers of the widow, flanked by her nephew, Haakon of Norway, and after them Alphonso of Spain, Manuel of Portugal and a mourner wearing a silk turban whom he had some difficulty in recognising as Ferdinand of Bulgaria.

He thought, cynically, 'Well, they carry themselves well enough, I suppose, but they're always getting bombed or shot at. And that chap Ferdinand has to bolster himself by calling himself "Czar" and buying Byzantine jewellery from a theatrical costumier . . .'

His sharp eye roved beyond to the next trio, Franz Ferdinand, heir to old Franz Joseph's ramshackle empire, God help him; Yussuf, heir to the Sultan's Turkey; and a tall, less showy man who seemed to Adam to sit his horse as an expert. He recognised him as Albert, King of the Belgians, and thought: 'He's the only one among 'em embarrassed by all this and wishing to God he was anywhere else . . .' His scrutiny returned to the corpulent Franz Ferdinand, who had replaced Prince Rudolf, after the poor bemused devil shot himself and his mistress in a hunting lodge, and placed such a fearful strain upon Habsburg flunkeys to explain how it happened. And an equal strain on the credibility of the journalists, obliged to select one of a dozen contradictory theories.

The great thing about an occasion like this was that it gave a man an opportunity to ponder the infinite variations in the pattern of the Continental carpet as it unrolled, little by little, year by year. Not by everybody, of course, but by the privileged like himself, who kept pace

with events, who had lived a long, long time, and who was endowed with a selective memory. There wasn't one of these gilded popinjays concerning whom he could not have told a story or two they would have preferred forgotten and it gave him a feeling of thankfulness that he had been able to pick his own way through life, unfettered by protocol and tradition, responsible to himself, his family and his work force certainly, but to no one else alive. And as he thought this there came to him a conviction that he was watching a cavalcade out of a dead century, mounted in an era long before that of universal male suffrage, and the rise of the new commercial aristocracy, the twin nineteenth-century forces that had made these people as obsolete as dodos.

Japan was represented by the brother of the Emperor; Russia by the Grand Duke Michael; Italy by the Duke of Aosta (what fancy handles they attached to these royal jugs!); then came Carl of Sweden, Henry of Holland, any number of Balkan nabobs and in their wake a flock of grand dukes, petty princelings and top-hatted civilians from the world's republics. His old friend, Lord Roberts, was there, as always upon these occasions, together with as colourful a display of military detachments as he had ever seen assembled in line of march – Coldstreamers, Gordon Highlanders, Household Cavalry, lancers, dragoons and hussars of every crack Continental regiment, and even a handful of gold-epauletted admirals. And between these and the swarm of British office-holders, all in their traditional best bibs and tuckers, a typically British touch – the dead man's charger, that had never once been called upon to charge, followed by his wire-haired terrier, 'Caesar' led by an academic-looking chap in a college gown.

It was all very splendid, a little too splendid for anyone like himself, who had walked by night among the London destitute, reflecting sometimes upon the strange idiosyncrasies of a race that valued its dogs and horses above most of its children, and spent far more on the dead than

the living. For this was really no more than a dazzling reflection of an East End coster's funeral, paid for by the indigent widow out of her twopenny-a-week insurance policy. People were the slaves of their tribal rituals.

*   *   *

The heat was beginning to distress him so he made his way through the crowds to the Strand and thence to his hotel where he took a tepid bath and, after that, a light luncheon and a refreshing afternoon nap. By twilight he was back at 'Tryst' and Henrietta, perhaps remembering earlier homecomings, came down the yard steps when the coachman (he had never let George talk him into selling his carriage bays and replacing them by a motor) was giving the horses a rub down. She led the way across the hall and into the dining-room where it was dark and cool and he regaled her over supper with a detailed account of the procession, noting that even here, in deference to the servants he supposed, she had tied a black crepe bow on the sleeve of her blouse.

"King George, what kind of man is he, Adam?" she asked. "I don't recall much about him. It was always his brother, the one who died, who was going to be king."

"George? He's all for a quiet life and I hope he gets it. But I doubt it very much after a close look at the poor chap's relations," he replied.

"You mean they'll make trouble for him? But how could they? I mean, after all, he's King of England now."

"King of Britain, my dear. I'm always afraid you'll say that in front of old Phoebe Fraser, who went to such frightful pains to get it straight with the children."

"Well, Britain then. Are you referring to that silly man, the Kaiser?"

"Him among others," Adam said.

"Oh, he's just a braggart," she said. "The King will

soon put him in his place. And as for all those others
you were telling me about, well, they wouldn't care to
pick a quarrel with us, any one of them."

"No," he said, stifling a yawn, "I don't suppose they
would, Hetty. I'm quite worn out. It was so devilishly
hot in town. Shall we make an early night of it?", and
he rose, foregoing his final cheroot of the day and the
stroll in the forecourt he enjoyed at this season of the year.

But sleep, perversely, evaded him and he woke up
soon after midnight and slipping on his dressing-gown
went downstairs and let himself out of the tall windows
opening on to the balustraded terrace he had built along
the front of the house during his renovations twenty years
ago.

The front of the house was bathed in moonlight and
between the lilac clumps, at the head of the drive, he
could see as far as The Hermitage beyond his artificial
lake. It was very quiet out here, and reassuring too in an
odd sort of way, for the presence of the old house behind
him, and the broad, down-sloping vista studded with
imported trees now growing to an impressive height and
looking as if they belonged here, gave him a sense of
permanence and stability. 'I shall hate leaving it,' he
thought, 'not the network and the family so much, for
the one is in safe hands with George and Edward, and the
other will manage. But this . . . these coppices and fields
and flowering shrubs that smell of England all the year
round . . .' As his mind returned to that gun-carriage
and the empty saddle of the royal horse . . . 'How much
longer can *I* expect? I've already overstayed my welcome
by several years but, by gum, I've had a wonderful
innings and ought not to resent making way for others.
If only they'll learn to value it – this corner of an old
landscape, and the way of life that goes with it – peace,
order and progression . . .'

He looked up at the sky, searching for familiar stars
and it occurred to him for a moment to contemplate
the infinite, something he rarely did. *Was* there anything

to follow? Did it matter one way or the other? He had never had any deep convictions about it and felt no special need of them now that his time was running out.

He extinguished his cheroot in a flower urn trailing geraniums and went in, closing the windows. A few minutes later he was back in bed and drifting off to sleep, his arm resting across the generous hip of his wife, who stirred slightly and murmured something unintelligible.

4

Snowslide

THE SHOCK OF THE BAD 1911 MIDSUMMER FIGURES
had them reeling. Not even the older and least venture-
some men in the network had experienced a slide of this
length and steepness. They were all aware that they
were passing through a bad patch after the relaunch of
six years ago, but the consolidated bi-annual returns,
privately circulated among them, converted speculation
into furious self-questioning.

No region was altogether exempt from the dip although
some, mostly rural territories, seemed to be holding their
own better than others. The overall drop in turnover was
slight but that only made the January to June profit
margin look more preposterous than ever. For the hard
facts were profits had fallen to a miserly five and a quarter
per cent, compared with eight and a half in the preceding
six months, and sixteen per cent in the corresponding
period last year.

George did what everybody expected him to do,
calling for regional reports and convening an extraordinary general meeting for the second week in July.

The favourite excuse, of course, went under the
heading of 'a general business recession'. It had a com-
forting vagueness and could be laid to the door of German
competition, plus the unsettled atmosphere overseas.
After that, a close second, came the old whipping boy,
the weather, for the winter had been long and wet,

particularly in the north and west, and as recently as February some of the busiest regions had had a third of their vehicles in the repair shops. Higson, in the far north, for instance, thought he could be forgiven a falling-off in his rural areas, where the snow falls had been heavy and his quota of motor-vehicles seldom penetrated, but it seemed odd that Bertieboy Bickford, whom all of them thought of as a yokel, came close to finishing top of the regional poll, an almost inconceivable circumstance in these days, for the Western Wedge was jocularly referred to as 'the turnip patch' and Bickford, operating in the Western peninsula, must have had his fill of sloughed roads and flooded valleys.

The cancer seemed to be located mainly in the flattish, densely-populated areas, where lorries had all but super-seded the horse, and industry was still expanding; regions like The Polygon, The Funnel and the Scottish Lowlands. It was on the figures from these regions that George con-centrated during his two-day exile in Adam's tower, whither he retired as soon as he had ridden out the initial shock.

At first, with regionalised bleats spread the whole length of the trestle tables he had rigged up, he could discern no real pattern in the slump, nothing to show why the blight should have struck so savagely and so quickly. At last he began to see that it was high time he made some sweeping reassessments, not only of national transport trends and Swann-on-Wheels as an enterprise operating within those trends, but also of himself, a man of forty-seven, hitherto of cool judgment and with nearly thirty years' experience under his belt.

*   *   *

George had always seen himself as a pioneer, in advance of other pioneers, a man ready to look ahead, so that he had succeeded in pulling something out of the hat well in advance of his viceroys, even the few gamblers out along the network. His tenacity and unswerving belief in himself had gained for them all that impressive start over every competitor in the field. But he supposed now that that start had been altogether too impressive, encouraging him to sit back and live off his fat, and it soon became obvious to him that he had lost his place in the vanguard.

The evidence of these unpleasant conclusions were everywhere, but particularly telling in his newspaper cutting file where he found evidence of advances that would have put a cutting edge on his curiosity a few years back. There were those London 'H' type 'buses, now operated by the London and General Omnibus Company as far as Hampstead. There was news that the last L.G.O.C. horse 'bus was due for retirement in early autumn this year, and the same company's spectacular success in the private hire field, where even councils composed of men who had never ridden in a motor were commissioning 'bus excursions for schoolchildren. There was Morris's amazing advances down at Oxford, and Austin's breakthrough with his baby car, that had somehow caught the imagination of a public unimpressed by the impossibly expensive, carriage-built vehicles of ten years ago. But beyond all this there was the flood of new, high-performance foreign cars on the roads, the Renaults and Unics, the Napiers, the Charrons and the Panhards, pouring from continental workshops where, he suspected, commercial vehicles, capable of outpacing and outhauling the best of Scottie Quirt's Swann-Maxies, were already over their teething troubles and promising formidable haulage competition in the near future. Indeed, it seemed that the very name 'Swann-Maxie' had an old-fashioned ring about it, like last year's slang, so that he gave a thought to that other and infinitely more adventurous form of transport, the staggering advances made in the conquest of the air over the last two or three years.

There was no commercial future in air transport, or

none that he could discern. A machine that was still unsafe for a man was unlikely, in the foreseeable future, to enter the haulage field. Yet George Swann, his mind conditioned to evolving patterns of transport over three decades, could sense the impact aeroplanes were beginning to make on a public that had for so long regarded the motor as a rich man's toy. The public mood was changing, year by year, and month by month, ever since Blériot made his cross-Channel flight in the summer of 1909, and that human dynamo Northcliffe (quick as a fairground barker to spot a crowd-collector) had initiated his air races. Even ballooning was now no longer regarded as a happy-go-lucky way of breaking one's neck. The Germans were reported to be making impressive progress with airships, led by that dedicated aeronaut, Count Ferdinand Zeppelin. And here perhaps air haulage was at least a possibility.

Swann-on-Wheels, once accepted by every transport man in the country as first in the field, was no longer 'in the frame' as the bookmakers said. Was even in danger of slipping to fourth or fifth place in the national table.

What was to be done about it? How could the plunging downward trend in Swann's graph be halted, levelled off, and encouraged to rise? Or what common factor could be isolated as the arch villain and placed squarely in the dock? He had often been baffled, but never this baffled. He turned back to his viceroys' reports, beginning with the Eastern Region facing the North Sea, and ending with the turnip patch, where Bertieboy Bickford, with his assortment of outmoded men-o'-war, frigates and pinnaces was still holding his own.

It was pondering this – Bertieboy's curious immunity from the slump – that suggested an answer. Not the whole answer, certainly, but a hint that there must be a common factor in the falling off in orders and the sharp drop in profits. Bertieboy, largely concerned with bread and butter hauls over rural routes, and fobbed off with teams and vehicles that were already obsolete in the north and midlands, none the less enjoyed a built-in advantage over all his rivals with the single exception of Clint Coles, operating on the far side of the Irish Sea. He had, so far as George could discover, no serious competition. Some seventy per cent of his customers (a cross-check with accounts established this) were either farmers or merchants marketing agricultural goods of one sort or another, and there was something else that seemed, against all probability, to be operating in Bickford's favour, something that was not difficult to assess if you knew his beat as well as George knew it. Bickford's territory was served by a very poor road system, that had changed surprisingly little from the coaching days. The gradients thereabouts were fearsome. Indeed, it was for this very reason that few Swann-Maxies were seen in the peninsula, and these two factors had to have an important bearing on the exemption of the Western Wedge from the general depression.

He turned back to the detailed reports from The Polygon, The Funnel and the Scottish Lowlands and suddenly the general pattern of the dilemma emerged. *In areas where the ground was favourable to the motor, where distances between cities were short, where potential customers were thick on the ground, the amateur was emerging as a successful challenger to the professional.*

Not individually, of course. Nobody running a fleet of transport vehicles, powered or horse-drawn, had cause to lose an hour's sleep over the odd Johnny-Come-Lately who built or bought a single motor-vehicle and advertised himself as a haulier of goods. These people had always existed, even in his father's day, and they had never succeeded in making a dent in the Swann economy. But that, possibly, was because there were so few of them and most of them were locally based, operating no more than a few miles from the waggon sheds where they kept their decrepit carts and stabled their ageing beasts. A glance at his brother Edward's report convinced him that this was no longer the case. In the Birmingham–Wolverhampton area alone Edward had listed thirty-seven

one-man operators, and according to his son Rudi, up in
The Polygon, an almost identical swarm of parasites was
skimming the cream from the house-removal trade.

Spurred on by a sensation of discovery he did a rapid
cast of the number of one- or two-vehicle operators in
these three regions alone and the total frightened him.
Country, seaside and beauty-spot excursion promoters –
in several regions summer excursions had yielded a rich
harvest for Swann-on-Wheels since they were introduced
a generation ago – together with prominent local tradesmen involved in every kind of traffic from haberdashery
to undertaking, there were no fewer than six hundred and
eight competitors in three of Swann's busiest regions!

*   *   *

His sense of humour returned to him as he thought, with
a grin:

> *'Each bug has a lesser bug upon his back to bite him*
> *And that flea has a lesser flea, and so ad infinitum . . .'*

and the tag prompted him to do yet another sum, this
time concerned with the number of firms and factories in
the Metropolitan area known to field their own motor
transport. The result was equally daunting. In the Home
Counties, according to the latest check, seventy-four
former customers had, within the last two years, announced that from here on they were equipped to do their
own haulage.

Here it was then, the elusive common factor that he
sought. Lesser bugs proliferating across the country plus
a new breed of merchant who had seen the light that
George had seen beside the Danube twenty-five years
ago and were using it to find a way towards cutting transport costs.

He went over to the window, propping his elbows on
the stone sill and looking out on the view that had always
offered his father a challenge, the broad brown curve of

the Thames below London Bridge, with its steady flow of river traffic down to the forest of shipping at the docks. He had his conundrum and he had to solve it, before he got bogged down in the slough of generalities that would emerge from the meeting in two days' time. He thought, 'I can't solve it here. I've studied those reports until my eyes ache and those chaps out there are each concerned with their own patch. It isn't fair to expect them to see the picture as a whole. That's *my* job and, by God, it's time I tackled it.' The line of thought suggested another. He reflected, 'At the Gov'nor's age a man is entitled to live on his memories but I'm not much more than half his age. Somewhere in the 'seventies, when he was the right side of fifty, he must have faced a dozen challenges equivalent to this one. I'll take a walk and get the smell of this damned slum out of my nostrils,' and he flung himself out and down the narrow staircase to the yard, then towards the bridge, thick with horse and motor traffic.

His steps led him via Cannon Street to the top of Ludgate Hill, then down past the Old Bailey and Snow Hill in the direction of Smithfield Market. It was a long time since he had passed this way on foot but in the days of his heir-apparency, more than twenty years before, he was often on the prowl hereabout, drumming up new contracts among the wholesalers, hoteliers and restaurateurs who frequented the great meat market from first light.

He had never been much of a walker, doing most of his thinking in cabs or suburban trains once he was clear of the yard, but it was soon apparent to him why his instinct had chosen this particular route through the city's most congested area on a hot July morning with the promise, by noon, of another scorching day. He was checking, half-consciously, the city's traffic patterns, comparing the flow up and down these streets with the groundswell in the same location in his youth, and soon found confirmation about the general drift towards the use of powered vehicles. In the old days these streets were choked with hansoms, four-wheeler growlers, flat drays and high-slung waggons, some of them bearing the Swann insignia, all moving at a snail's pace through a complex of thoroughfares laid out in London's reconstruction after the Great Fire of 1666, when the city's population was no more than a seventh of today's. Now, although there were still a few cabs to be seen, and more than half the moving commercial vehicles were horse-drawn, the motor was very much in evidence and he recognised at least a dozen different makes in his progress between St. Paul's and the Holborn Viaduct. Squat, hooting taxi-cabs nosed their way through all but stationary lines of two-horse drays and vans, and even the horses seemed to have adjusted to their blare and rattle. He remembered a shoal of urchin crossing-sweepers here, darting between traffic blocks in peril of their lives, but now a single old scarecrow represented the ancient calling. The noise had a different note too, a more strident, less musical orchestra, punctuated by intermittent toots of the bulb horn and the squeal of brakes, whereas the acrid smell of crushed manure, although still evident, was moderated by the fumes of exhaust and the smell of dust spiralling from the rubber-tyred wheels of the newcomers.

A small tribe of street arabs, mounted on what seemed, at first glance, a string of soapboxes, debouched from Snow Hill at a rattling good pace and sent him skipping into the gutter, clutching his straw hat and bringing him into contact with an iron lamp-standard. He turned to curse at them as they slowed to a stop but then, screwing up his eyes against the fierce sunlight, he checked himself, for it seemed to him there was something very novel about the six-wheeled conveyance that had come close to upsetting him.

It was more than an urchin's soapbox, of the kind one saw in every city and suburban street where youngsters were at play. To begin with, it was non-rigid, its steering apparatus housed on what looked like a small, elevated raft on which the steersman sat on a biscuit box nailed to the main structure. Behind him, carrying a total of four passengers, three girls and a boy, was the carriage itself, two linked fish-crates, with the glitter of scales still on their boards and he noticed also the astonishing lock the design of trolley gave the steersman. Using his right foot as a means of propulsion, he brought the whole thing round in a tight circle as he shouted in high, nasal Cockney, "Everybody aht! 'Arry, Floss, 'Arriet – look sharp, an' stand by ter tow her up for the nex' trip!"

Three of the tiny passengers scrambled out. The fourth, a little girl about five, sat hugging her knees and crooning with glee as the older boy added, "Orl right, leave Ada be. She don't weigh nothing," and he seized the looped cord fastened to his steering box preparatory to hauling his trolley up the incline.

George sauntered over, saying, "Hold on there – just a minute, boy. You've got a nippy little runabout there. How'd you come by it?"

The older boy, who wore a cloth cap with the peak at the back, said, with that mixture of amiability and insolence only met with on the streets of the capital, "Well, I didn't nick it, gov. Ast the kids if you like. Knocked 'er up I did, lars night." And then, with a craftsman's pride in his work, "She ain't bad, is she? Turns in 'arf 'er length and seats the 'ole bleedin' fambly. Get aht of it, kid, and let the gent 'ave a proper squint at 'er."

The sole remaining passenger climbed out and joined her brothers and sisters as George, bending low over the steering platform, peered between biscuit box and foremost fish crate to observe that the front axle was part of a perambulator, with its original wheels bolted to the chassis. He moved along its length and inspected the coupling, a length of steel wire running through a pair of sizeable staples and then turned to the engineer, saying, "She's first rate. Best I've even seen and I'm in the trade. Where did you get the idea for that steering-gear?" He had been on the point of saying 'articulation' but realised that the word would mean nothing to the boy who had clearly arrived at a means of improving the lock by the application of commonsense.

"Well, I 'ad the pram chassy and I thought I'd try it on for a change. There's five of us, see, and Mum won't let me aht if I don't take the bleedin' tribe. My ole 'bus woulden take no more'n three an' you coulden turn 'er on the pavement." He gave George a long, speculative look and added, half-mockingly, "You wanner try 'er, gov? You c'n take over for a tanner."

George Swann was probably the only middle-aged man in London who would have accepted such an offer. He said, chuckling, "Why not? Can you leave the girls with your brother for a minute?"

"I c'n lose the four of 'em fer a tanner," the boy said, and with a brief, authoritative nod at his brother and sisters he began lugging his trolley up the slope to a point where the pavement levelled out.

It was a very narrow side street, free of traffic for the moment and almost clear of pedestrians. The few that were there were obviously Londoners to a man and acclimatised to eccentrics, for they gave George no more than a glance when he seated himself behind the driver and went shooting down the hill at the pace of a fast-trotting horse.

They had almost reached the waiting children and were slowing down appreciably when George shouted, "Bring her round – full circle!" and the boy did, leaning heavily to his right as the linked soapboxes swung the full width of the pavement and stopped. He said, warmly, "My word, she's a corker!" and then, extricating himself, "What's your name, boy?"

" 'Ere, what's the catch? No names no pack drill my Dad alwus says."

"All right, no names. What'll you take for her as she stands?"

"You got kids? You wanter buy it?"

"I've got kids and I'll buy if you'll deliver. How about five bob, and an extra shilling for delivery?"

The boy now looked more suspicious than ever but then, having tried and failed to guess his patron's motives, he grinned and said, "You're 'avin' me on, ain't yer?"

But George rummaged in his trouser pockets and brought out two half-crowns and a shilling. "I'm not having anybody on. Here's the money . . ." Then it occurred to him that so original a boy deserved an explanation and added, "Do you know Swann-on-Wheels, the hauliers?"

" 'Course I do. Everybody does, don't they?"

"Do you know Swann's depot, in Tooley Street?"

"You bet."

"Well, my name is Swann and I deal in everything on wheels. Here's your money and you've given me an idea worth more than six shillings. I'll go to ten if you'll have that soapbox in my yard inside the hour. Now will you tell me your name?"

" 'Ardcastle," the boy said, pocketing the silver, "but I still don' know what you're at, gov."

"I'll tell you, Mr. Hardcastle." But then, to George's mild distress, the smallest of the boy's sisters began to blubber, and was at once joined by the girl he had addressed as Ada who wailed, "But it ain't yours to sell, Arty, it b'longs to all of us, don't it, 'Arriet?" And the eldest girl said, in an aggrieved tone, "We helped yer make her, didden we? We did, didden we?"

"Yerse, yer did," said Arty, with unexpected mildness, "but I c'n start knocking up another the minnit we get 'ome. The back 'arf o' that pram's still in the yard, ain't it? Besides, you c'n 'ave a tanner all rahnd if you'll give me an 'and over the bridge. Then yer can buy enough gob-stoppers to make yerselves bleedin' well sick, so 'old yer row, will yer?" He turned back to George, "Ten bob it is, then? You coming wiv us?"

"Er . . . no," said George, wrenched from a speculation of a network served by a fleet of Arty Hardcastles, "I'm going ahead by cab to make sure you aren't turned away at the yard gate, but before I go, and in case we miss one another, would you mind telling me when you leave school?"

"In a fortnight, thank Gawd."

"Got a job lined up?"

"Sort've. My Dad's a porter at Smiffield. Reckons he c'n get me taken on as an errand boy with 'Enson's, 'is firm."

"How much will that pay?"

" 'Arf a crahn a week. Couple o' bob more in tips maybe. Depends on me rahnd. West End's all right, 'otels especially, but the 'olesalers is stingy. I know, see, I done a bit o' delivering before school summer-time."

"Well," George said, "I can pay you twice that and you can start on a suburban round where some of my vanboys make ten shillings a week in tips alone if they look lively. Here's my card. Show it to the Tooley Street weighbridge clerk but don't part with it. Give it to your father and get him to bring you along first week of the holidays."

The boy took the card and examined it carefully. Then putting his fingers in his mouth he produced the most earsplitting whistle George had ever heard. A taxi-cab, bowling along the Old Bailey, braked hard and George said, "Thank you, Arty," and walked towards the cab.

*   *   *

Unlike his father, George was not, and had never been, a man of quick decisions. In this respect at least they were complete opposites for, whereas Adam would, almost invariably, act upon instinct, George would contemplate each factor in any problem and then form a pattern in his brain. Once formed it was seldom subjected to adjustment.

It was so in this case. The pattern had been all but complete when he was nearly overset by Arty Hardcastle and his articulated soapbox in Snow Hill, but he had been unaware of it. The final piece in the jigsaw was missing and without it the pattern was not applicable. Now it was, however. Arty, turning that tight circle on the pavement with his full load of passengers still safety seated, had struck the spark that had fired George's train of ideas, for it occurred to him on the instant that here was the real answer to all that niggling local competition and that formidable drift of trade away from wholesalers and manufacturers converted to the notion of owning their own transport and saving costs.

The answer had two parts. One was concerned with manoeuvrability, afforded by the housing of vehicular power forward in a compact unit with independent steering; the other was a matter of stowage involving linked vehicles in the form of trailers. Together, he decided, they could revolutionise one's entire concept of road haulage, for so far the mulish rigidity of a vehicle, driven in streets designed solely for horse traffic, had applied severe limits on the size of the following container, it being impossible to employ a motor over a certain length in the sharp turns and angles met with in the old towns and congested cities of every region in the network. An articulated vehicle, based on Arty Hardcastle's precept, promised far greater mobility and more mobility meant more overall length allowing twice as much stowage. And this, in turn, meant cheaper hauls over long and short distances.

It did not take him long to evolve a detailed plan – a few hours at the sketchboard, a ten-hour session with Scottie Quirt (summoned by telephone from his Manchester workshop) and finally a long discussion with Withers, the chief accountancy clerk, roughing out an approximate estimate of the initial outlay partial conversion required. His sole remaining concern was to convince the viceroys, summoned to discuss the crisis, each of them, he suspected, in a suitably chastened mood.

Swann-on-Wheels had never concerned itself much with records, that is to say, with data that might prove invaluable to a historian of the firm in the distant future.

It had never once occurred to Adam, or indeed to George, that developments over the years, and changes in policy generally, would be likely to concern anyone but themselves and their current work forces. For both, in their time, had been men of the present and the future, apart from what it was likely to yield in increased turnover, could be left to itself. Thus George Swann had worked, year by year, developing the commercial motor. In the accumulation of day books and minute books and old ledgers stored in the depository adjoining the new counting-house, one could have found any amount of data concerned with the day-to-day running of the firm but very little relating to the inspirations, doubts and arguments of individual members of the firm. There were, in that small depository, maps by the score marking regional frontiers old and new, ledgers in which diligent searchers could have discovered the ratio of profit and turnover in every part of Britain, details of the rewards of men who administered and operated them and careful records of expenditure on plant and rolling stock, from the day Adam Swann sent his first three-horse waggon into rural Kent with old coachman Blubb on the box. But the real heart and bones of the enterprise were not to be found in these day-by-day recordings, not even in the master minute book, started by the head clerk Tybalt, in December, 1863, when Adam first summoned his managers to help him surmount his first major crisis. Decisions were there but not the manner in which decisions were arrived at or the pressures that lay behind those decisions.

And yet, once in a while, a researcher of the future might have come across a nugget of gold among all this dross. Such a find lay in the laconic entry towards the end of the twenty-odd pages recording the business of the extraordinary general meeting of July 12th, 1911. It ran:

Resolved, by sixteen votes to three, no abstentions. That the sum of £50,000 should be set aside for the conversion of twenty motor vehicles to articulated lorries based on the accompanying sketches, a maximum of half this sum to be earmarked for the assembly of three new vehicles and subsequent research thereon. This total to be reviewed at the January conference, 1912."

There was no mention of Arty Hardcastle's soapbox and why should there be? The production of a child's soapbox, assembled from a discarded perambulator, a biscuit box and two fish crates taken by stealth from Billingsgate Market, had no place in the deliberations of some score of serious-minded transport men, each and every one of them worried by a sharp falling off of profits. And, in any case, when George laughingly displayed the soapbox to some of his colleagues as they trooped out into the yard at the conclusion of their discussions, the clerk whose job it had been to take shorthand notes of their deliberations was already on his way home to his young wife and baby in Clapham. He did not hear George say, to a puzzled group of executives, that included his own son Rudi and two of his nephews raised on a Kentish farm: "Take a good look at her, gentlemen. She cost me ten shillings. She's just cost you fifty thousand!"

2

Most of the third generation Swanns (they now numbered around a score) had a favourite uncle and had a poll been taken among them it is probable that Lieutenant-Colonel Alexander Swann, veteran of Isandlwana, Rorke's Drift, Tel-el-Kebir and various other engagements featuring thin red lines and slaughtered savages, would have emerged the winner. After Alex, no doubt, would have come Uncle Hugo (also performer of a deed that won the Empire, once winner of an entire roomful of athletic trophies and now *Sir* Hugo) but Giles, a mere politician, would have come third; a poor third, notwithstanding the fact that he was a playful, soft-spoken man.

Edward, who was not much older than some of the elder grandchildren, qualified as a courtesy uncle.

Uncle George, despite his jocularity and generosity at Christmas-time, was not a contender for the title. Perhaps, on account of his high spirits, the younger Swanns saw him as one of themselves, but there was one at least who did not, who entertained for him a respect approaching reverence. This was Martin, second son of Denzil and Stella Fawcett of Dewponds Farm and his regard for his Uncle George had nothing to do with Christmas stockings or birthday tips. It was based on his easy familiarity with a real live giant and dated from a summer afternoon around about 1890, when Martin, then aged about eight, had been invited into the old stable block at 'Tryst' to watch the Giant Maximilien, who lived there.

Martin had never forgotten that enchanting afternoon and in a way it had dictated the course of his life. For, alone among the Swann grandchildren, he came to share George's affection for the great shining monster, with its brassy lungs and blue breath, seeing it not as an ogre (and a very noisy, smelly and dangerous one at that!) but as the bondsman of his Uncle George, who told Martin that he had found him far across the sea, had since taken care of him, fed him with oil and given him a home in the tile-hung outhouses on the eastern side of the stable-yard.

Martin, soon a very regular visitor, thus grew to love both Maximilien and his master, seeing them as interdependent on one another. For he discovered, as time went by, that Uncle George came out here to commune with his servant at all hours of the day and night, giving as his explanation that Maximilien was a restless, thirsty fellow, who needed a great deal of exercise to prevent his joints getting rusty and that Uncle George, having found him scared and lonely in a strange country, was now obliged to keep him in good fettle against the day (not long now, Uncle George prophesied) when Maximilien would travel at a speed faster than any horse in the world could gallop.

For three years, until he was turned eleven, Martin did not believe this part of the story. He had never seen Maximilien actually move, that is to say, to step down from his wooden blocks, pass the stable door and cross the outside yard. He always looked as if he was about to do this but he never did, contenting himself with a kind of stationary dance that involved rapid movements of all his vitals and a steady spinning of his two immense rear wheels that sometimes turned at such a speed that the giant began to gasp and puff his blue breath into every corner of the stable. He was far too big, anyway, to pass the door, and while George assured him that he could take Maximilien to pieces and put him together again, Martin did not believe this either, having long since decided that the stable must have been built around him the day he arrived.

In the meantime, however, it was fascinating to stand here and watch Uncle George tend the brute, touching a knob here, pulling a lever there, applying his oil can to various joints in the giant's armour and sometimes polishing him with rags and leathers. Martin said, one day, "You're *jolly* kind to him, Uncle George, I mean, considering he doesn't *do* anything," and George had said, "Ah, but he will, as soon as he's ready and I give him the nod. You see, Martin, he's promised to make my fortune one day. Mine and your Auntie Gisela's, so naturally I have to keep him fit and good-tempered."

Martin accepted this as a reasonable explanation of his uncle's cheerful servitude but he could never have said at what point in his boyhood the brassy-throated Maximilien transformed himself from fairy-tale figure to fact of life. It must have been somewhere around the day he came over here, when he was thirteen, to find the stable doors swinging free and both Uncle George and the monster gone, the latter never to be seen around these parts again.

His grandmother told him what had happened.

Uncle George, she said, had taken the Maximilien away to Manchester, to show him to *her* father, and Martin's great-grandfather, Sam Rawlinson. It was more than a year later when Martin saw George again and asked him if this was true and he said it was, and that Maximilien had kept all his promises in the north and had even persuaded Grandfather Swann of his merits.

From then on a warm relationship developed between uncle and nephew, beginning with the admission that Maximilien was not a stray monster but a mechanically-propelled vehicle, and Martin's confession that he had known this for some time but had never liked to admit it in case he was forbidden the stable. He also added, with a grin, that he had earned several thrashings from his mother for coming here, for his mother, in common with all the womenfolk about the estate, regarded George's engine as a potential child killer.

It was some years after that that Martin was dramatically rescued from the never-ending chores of his father's farm and sent up to Manchester himself, there to work in Uncle George's engine shed, where any number of stream-lined Maximiliens were assembled and sent out to work on the roads.

The translation, from Kentish countryside to a clamorous northcountry workshop proved to be the most exhilarating experience of his life and while Uncle George's manager, the taciturn Mr. Quirt, was a heavy task-master, given to sudden outbursts of temper, he came to enjoy every moment he spent on the benches in the company of his brother John and about a dozen other apprentices.

John Fawcett, unfortunately, did not last the course and emerge as a journeyman mechanic. In his second year up north he developed asthma and was ordered south again, there to find open-air work in Swann's Maidstone depot, for Dewponds was not sufficiently prosperous to support three families, Stella's eldest son, Robert, having married and moved into the farm's tied cottage.

In the meantime, Martin, learning something new about the internal combustion engine and heavy coach-building each day, qualified as Scottie Quirt's favourite assistant, a fact that seemed to please George for every time he came up here – it was generally at least once a month – he called for Martin's progress reports and, having studied them, demanded of Scottie whether or not (family favouritism on one side) Martin could be given further responsibilities as head of the draughtsmen's section.

It was not often that Scottie paid anyone a compliment. His northern dourness compelled him to qualify any praise he doled out, or at least to preface it with a warning such as, "Ye'll no' get bigheaded aboot it!" Or, "When you've been at the trade as long as me ye'll have reason to ask yourself . . ." On this occasion, however, he was more forthright.

"The laddie's the best ye've sent me, there's nae doot aboot that! He doesna give a hoot how long I keep him at it when we're pushed and, by God, George Swann, ye've been pushing us hard lately, hae ye not? Aye, gi'e that lad a year at the drawing board and see what he comes up with."

"And after that?"

"Och, maybe he'll tak' on where I leave off, for the fact is I canna teach that boy any more."

It was the first time in their long and strenuous association that George had ever heard Scottie concede technical equality with anyone.

So Martin Fawcett went into the drawing office, emerging, from time to time, with some very practical blueprints aimed at various modifications, and it was to him, more than to anyone else, that Quirt turned when George presented them with a seemingly impossible challenge – the almost overnight conversion of a small fleet of Mark IV Swann-Maxies to articulated steering, with an engine thrust capable of providing the power to haul two loads in one. This, plus an edict to design and build three articulated trailer vehicles from scratch and do it all by the turn of the year, now less than six months ahead.

Scottie had argued vehemently that it could not be done, not even if they signed on a dozen extra mechanics and worked double shift. "Ye'll hae to choose between one or the other," he declared, "for ye canna hae both, man, in that span of time. Do you no' ken the size o' the task in these quarters, when there's no room to swing a cat?"

George conceded him the point regarding space. For a long time now the present quarters in Macclesfield had been badly overcrowded and the assortment of tin-roofed sheds in the yard outside had not kept pace with regional demands for more vehicles and faster repairs. He said, briefly, "Then we'll separate the projects. You stay here, and get ahead with the conversions, and Martin can build the prototypes in premises I'll rent for him in Leeds. You'd join me in backing him for the job, wouldn't you, Scottie?"

"Aye," said Scottie, judiciously, "I'd back any lad I'd trained. But yon more than most."

3

It was wonderful watching it grow. It was marvellous to watch it move, stage by stage, from a sheaf of sketches, blotched by oily thumb-prints to blue-print, and thence to the foundry, factory bench and carpenter's shed. But best of all was to contemplate it in the white glow of the unshaded lights after all the others had shed their overalls and gone home, to sense its assumption of a corporate personality from mere hunks of tortured metal and baulks of timber, so that it was no longer an artefact but a thing of sensibility and temperament, that needed to be tamed and schooled by someone who had created it from a thousand and one components.

Time ceased to exist for him. In some ways, indeed,

time telescoped, so that he was sometimes a child again standing beside the flailing, hissing Maximilien in the 'Tryst' stables, sometimes a journeyman mechanic working on his first real assignment, and sometimes the kinsman of men like Gottlieb Daimler and the Wright brothers, or Blériot and Captain Cody, whose pioneer flying feats over English shires had captured every headline in Fleet Street.

This thing had moods. Occasionally winsome and more often fractious moods. There were days when it was sluggish and inert, and others when it was wooden-limbed, like a sulky child being dressed for Sunday for an unwanted outing. There were times when it seemed to resist a stage in its assembly, so that it seemed like a huge, fractured pipe men were trying to reduce to its original pattern. When this happened Martin's landlady saw nothing of him for days together, for he would stay on the job all night, snatching a few hours' sleep on a bagged-out mattress in the drawing office and living on fish and chips and cocoa brewed on a burner.

But gradually it took on shape and form and a kind of looming grace, reaching almost from one end of the shop to the other, preening itself under its three coats of green and gold paint with the Swann emblem etched in black on the sides of the trailer. Then he would prowl around it, contemplating its immensity and the ponderous thrust that lay dormant under its downsloping bonnet, and he would picture himself driving it over the most punishing roads of England dragging a load that no Swann vehicle had ever hauled across a regional frontier in the fifty-three-year history of the enterprise.

Uncle George came north once a fortnight now, praising his tirelessness and ingenuity, and sometimes bringing messages from his Kentish homestead. In October, when they were well forward he commissioned Martin's chief lieutenant to begin work on the second giant and in early November, having been assured that Mark I would be ready to run by mid-December, he told his nephew that four regional viceroys were quarrelling furiously over the honour of putting the first articulated trailer van on the roads and he had been obliged to draw lots between his son Rudi in The Polygon, his brother Edward in The Funnel, Higson in the Scottish Lowlands and Rookwood in the Southern Square.

Word came, a day or so later, that Rudi had emerged winner so that the vehicle's trial run, exclusive of routine road testing, would constitute its delivery, entailing a short but stiffish haul over the Pennine ridge to the Salford Depot, a mile or so west of the cotton capital.

Work was all but complete by then and Martin left the finishing touches to the three apprentices and the painter, retiring to his littered office, that reeked of a hundred fish and chip suppers, to plan his route, George having told him that he had succeeded in persuading Scottie Quirt to delegate the honour of the first journey to the man who most deserved it. He paid Martin another compliment, the biggest compliment anyone had ever paid or was ever likely to, when he said, with a grin, "Have you thought up a name for her? We've christened every other vehicle in service, from pinnaces to frigates to Goliaths, so she'll have to have a name of some sort."

Martin said he hadn't thought about naming her although the team who had worked on her over the five months period of assembly had called her by a variety of names, all of them unprintable. George said, seriously, "Well, I'll always think of her as a 'Fawcett', so you'd better do the same from now on. And to make it official get a couple of nameplates stamped out and screwed to the radiator and trailer tailboard." He hurried off then to catch the London train for he could see Martin blushing through his rash of freckles and after the shed had closed down for the night Martin stayed on until nearly midnight, stamping out the name, first in letters four inches high but afterwards, afraid of seeming to put on side, reducing them to three.

* * *

The run was scheduled for December 13th and Quirt advised travelling empty. "If she jibs at some of those inclines at least we can get her off the road and send someone by motor-cycle to gie you a hand," he said. "Loaded she'll need towage and a brace o' waggons to offload." Martin thought the precaution unnecessary. She wouldn't jib at any incline and as for descents, there was no metalled slope on the west side of the Pennines that he feared, with his rim block brakes, revolutionary contracting transmission footbrake and equally novel handbrake controlling internal-expanding units on the rearward wheels of the forward section. There was a further feature Scottie seemed to have overlooked, the speeded up interchangeability of the enlarged driving sprockets, enabling the gear ratio to be altered to match laden or unladen running and varying road conditions. Up or down dale Martin Fawcett had no doubts at all about his four-ton Fawcett holding the road. He would have wagered all he possessed on this even before the road tests buttressed his faith in the giant.

On the day before he set out a bulky package arrived for him and was delivered to his lodgings. It turned out to be a handsome present from Uncle George, a heavy leather coat with stylish crossover fastenings, a vizored cap to match, leather gauntlets and a pair of aviator's goggles. There was a note attached in George's handwriting, reading, " 'Rich not gaudy, for the apparel oft proclaims the man!' Good luck. Uncle George and all at H.Q."

He was glad then the spanking new kit had not been sent to the sheds for he could never have waited to see himself in it and the result, reflected in the mirror of his landlady's wardrobe door, did not disappoint him. Cody and Blériot would have envied him the rigout; he looked more like an aviator than an engineer.

He rolled her out into the yard and backed her round facing the double gates ready for a flying start in the morning. She handled even more easily than he had hoped, as light on the steering as a Swann-Maxie with less than a third of her cubic capacity but there was no mistaking the chant of her three-cylinder engines. They sang of power and conquest, of even coasting along high plateaux and swift, controlled descents into the valleys. They spoke to him of capacity hauls of over two hundred miles a day, spilling goods into the four corners of the land with a speed and profusion that a fleet of his grandfather's waggons could not have achieved. They made the latest model from the Macclesfield sheds seem as obsolete as a Roman chariot and a seat on these leather driving-box cushions was a throne, elevating him to the status of king among road travellers. He climbed down and went round to the bonnet, glancing covertly at the shining letters of the newly-affixed nameplate, a just reward for all the hours of toil that had preceded this moment of triumph. He said to an acolyte, unable to restrain his exuberance, "My stars, but she's a beauty! She's the most beautiful thing I've ever imagined! And this time tomorrow, from here to Salford, she'll pull in the crowds wherever she rides!"

The man to whom he spoke, one Dyson, a carpenter who had bent and fitted her hood poles, was to remember this remark. Especially when his daughter brought him his illustrated paper towards the end of his lie-in the following Sunday morning.

His route was a double compromise.

By the shortest distance, and probing for low gradients and good, metalled roads, he could have knocked miles off his journey and as much as three hours off his time schedule, but he had to reckon on the near certainty of traffic congestion in the complex manufacturing centres stretching eastwards and southwards from Bradford through Halifax to Huddersfield and Oldham. He knew this ground well. Only by night, or on a Sunday, was it free of heavy haulage, up here mostly horsedrawn, and there was no certainty of an easy passage of any of the West Riding towns in mid-week. On the other hand, a more northerly and circuitous route up the valley of the Aire, bearing west by Haworth, then south via Hebden Bridge and Rochdale, presented serious hazards at the time of year. Most of the road ran over high, windswept upland, with the virtual certainty of ice on some gradients. There was, however, a third alternative, the compromise within a compromise, a more tortuous approach over the lower landmass enclosing the Aire gap, heading north-west for Keighley and beyond it to Cross Hill, where the road branched north to Skipton and south-west for Colne and the eastern frontier of the cotton belt. Thus, of the three alternatives, two offered virtual freedom from traffic and of these two the Keighley–Colne route promised the easier climb, although adding more than thirty miles to the journey.

It was this approach he finally chose, stowing two extra drums of fuel in the trailer, for he had no experience on which to base his probable petrol consumption. His own guess was that it would be nearly double that of the heaviest Swann-Maxie on the roads, particularly over the spine of England, but he was in no particular hurry and a series of long climbs and the twenty-mile drop into Lancashire might provide him with the answers to some of the many questions both George and Scottie Quirt would be sure to put at the inquest. And a searching inquest, with two other prototypes in the making, was vital, with a prospect of saving weeks of trial and error when fed back to the Leeds mechanics. It might also be generally useful to Scottie's men in the Macclesfield yard, for every six months or so modifications were adapted to the standard vehicle and not all of them came (by fair means or foul) from the brochures and workshops of competitors. Perhaps half were derived from personal experience within the network, sedulously circulated to the regions in the columns of *The Migrant*.

The morning was bright, clear and cold, with the thermometer hovering a couple of degrees over freezing point in the city, so that his hoped-for early start was delayed. There had been a sharp frost in the night and he decided to wait for the morning sun to get to work on the ice patches. The wind, coming from the west, was very fresh, altogether an exhilarating morning to begin an odyssey, and he set out about ten-thirty, heading west-south-west through Shipley and Bingley, well north of the Bradford suburbs and finding the road surprisingly open.

He was right about the Fawcett attracting attention. Errand boys whistled with surprise as he rumbled past and he saw one jot down the name of the vehicle in a notebook. He thought, smiling, 'That'll fox him for sure. Nobody but Uncle George and me, and the Leeds mechanics, have ever heard of the name applied to a motor.'

He made very good time, averaging around twenty miles an hour, and before starting the climb to Cross Hill and the Skipton junction he pulled in at a tavern and ordered a ham sandwich and a cup of coffee, occupying himself while the coffee was brewing by stamping about the yard and swinging his arms to restore circulation to his fingertips. The leather coat and gauntlets were a boon but it was still cold up on that high box. Only his feet were warmed by the engine and the coffee was so good that, after a reassuring glance at his watch, he ordered a second cup.

The sky had clouded over as he gained height and the wind freshened, veering to the north-east. There were still patches of ice here and there but he travelled most of this section in second gear, driving with excessive caution. The trailer was inclined to snake a little when he built up speed and his mind was occupied, as he went along, with ways of how this problem could be tackled satisfactorily. Probably by adjustments to the coupling, he thought, as the crossroads came into view a mile beyond the village of Steeton.

From here on it was almost all downslope, a stretch of about eight miles into Colne and the prospect of flatter ground from then on, together with the near cer-tainty of heavy traffic, slow-moving in these narrow,

Lancashire streets, after he reached Nelson and Burnley and turned south for Rochdale.

He pulled in to the side of the road at the summit and fed ten gallons of fuel into the tank, using his tin funnel with a filter but impeded somewhat by the ever freshening wind that whipped the hood of cabin and trailer causing them to exclaim like sails and spraying a fine rain of fuel over his gauntlets and the engine cowling. He rolled the cask back and up the plank slide to the trailer tailboard, thinking that it might have been wiser to bring along an apprentice to do the chores, but not seriously, for this was an experience he did not care to share with anyone, not even with Uncle George or Scottie Quirt, whose brains had contributed far more than his to the creation of the monster. There were parts of it, however, that were indubitably his, so that the name was not really undeserved. He looked westward down the long, straight stretch of road he was to travel and thought: 'Longest route notwithstanding, I've made rattling good time. At this rate I'll be in Salford by late afternoon, and Cousin Rudi and I can celebrate with a pint and a dish of Lancashire hotpot!'

Then he was off again, tackling the decline at about twenty-two miles an hour but changing down when he saw the long squiggle of ice crossing the road diagonally from south to north where a streamlet had frozen during the night. He had not expected ice this side of the Pennines. Almost always the eastern side was the colder but it must be the wind blowing in from the North Atlantic.

He felt the skid and heard the distant toot of the horn at the same instant. A hunting horn it was from somewhere on the fell away to the left and a second later, as he was steering into the skid on the shoulder of the hill, he saw the hunt streaming diagonally across his front, a straggle of about twenty riders less than a hundred yards behind the pack and clearly in full cry, for they were pounding over the frosted turf at a cracking rate, the huntsman out ahead, horn to his lips.

The spectacle did not distract him. He was too good an engineer for that but he wasted a split second gauging their probable line and trying to judge where, precisely, they would cross the road bounded by low stone walls, no obstacle to experienced horsemen and certainly none to the scrambling pack that went at it in a bunch and were all over the road in a matter of seconds.

He had to brake harder then and out of the corner of his eye he saw the leading horsemen pulling on their reins and one or two of them cavorting parallel with him as the horses, baulking more at the Fawcett than the wall, swung left on a downslope. It was then that he went into the real skid, a long, skittering slide left, right and left again, and he had a moment to be afraid; not for himself but for the Fawcett, for it flashed across his mind that this would be a ridiculous way to conclude his odyssey, broadside on against a loose stone wall on the eastern slopes of the Pennines.

The landscape lost coherence for him then, at the moment of the first impact. He was hunched over the steering column, wrestling with the heavy vehicle as with a Mastodon and it was not answering to any of the directions transmitted through his hands and feet. It was like an elephant that had run wild, lashing out with its immense hindquarters and grinding everything in its path. The hunt foamed up on the far side of the wall and about a dozen laggards among the pack were still spewed over the highway, running it seemed in all directions, as though to escape the thundering passage of the vehicle, now almost broadside on with its trailer ricocheting from the base of the wall but always, impelled by its own weight and anchored apex, returning for more punishment.

Then, as though the whole world was turning topsy-turvey, he lost all sense of direction as the cabin heeled over, was checked by the pull of the trailer, half-recovered its upright position and finally somersaulted twice, ending up on its nearside wedged between the two walls and piled in the form of a barricade across the full width of the road.

He had a sense of being picked up by the heels and shaken, a vanquished rat in the jaws of a terrier, and experienced a single spasm of fear as he saw, all about him, a soft orange glow and smelled the reek of blazing fuel. His last conscious thought was of that unstowed reserve drum in the trailer, surely the main contributory factor to this holocaust, and his lips framed the word, "Fool *fool*!" as he remembered that he was the man who had placed it there, without so much as a brace or a piece of rope to hold it in position against a contingency like this.

5

Stella

GEORGE HEARD THE FULL TRUTH BY TELEPHONE
from Rudi, who had received it from the police at Colne
who, in turn, had got it from the infirmary surgeon
examining the charred bundle they brought in for him to
certify as dead.

By then Rudi was in Colne himself having rushed there
by motor-cycle, arriving, chilled to the bone, about dusk,
when a team of corporation men were still trying, without
much success, to clear the road six miles to the east. Rudi
telephoned before notifying Scottie Quirt and the Macclesfield depot. Shocked half out of his mind he still realised
it was his responsibility as Polygon viceroy, and com-
missioner of the new trailer, to pass the information to
Headquarters and ask for instructions.

He could sense his father's numbed horror over the
two-hundred-mile gap between them, and when George
remained silent for something approaching half a minute,
he said, urgently: "You did get it, sir? You . . . you heard
everything?"

George replied, in a voice that seemed to come from the
other side of the world, "Yes, Rudi, I heard. It's awful
. . . frightful . . ." but then, rallying a little, "You're at
Colne? Then go out to the scene of the accident. Talk to
the police, to anyone who was early on the scene. To the
master of that damned hunt if you can find him. Get all
the information you can. Every scrap, you understand?"

"Yes, sir. I'll stay on overnight."

"Arrange to stay indefinitely and I'll join you for the inquest. I'll get someone to stand in for you at the depot. Meantime I've got to tell his mother and father."

"Can't someone else do it? The police? Grand-father, perhaps?"

"No, son, it'll have to be me, for I was the one who took him from that farm. Stay on the job, there's a good lad. And thank you for letting me know so quickly. Don't bother with Scottie, I'll see he's notified from H.Q."

"Right, Father. Goodbye."

"Goodbye, son. Leave word where you're staying with the Colne police."

He rehooked the receiver and sat motionless, forcing himself to assemble the factors fed him by Rudi into some kind of sequence. A head-on collision with a hunt in full cry on a Pennine slope. A pile-up, with that immense weight bearing down on the buckled cabin and the man inside it. The first puff of flames, a soft explosion, then an inferno, far too fierce to permit hope of rescue, even if the nearest horsemen could have got to him in time. He remembered the last time he had seen Martin, only a few days ago, and told himself how splendidly the boy was coming along, and what an asset he would be to the network in the years ahead. Now he was not a person at all, just a blackened corpse lying in a corporation mor-tuary two hundred miles to the north, awaiting a string of coroners, solicitors, witnesses and jurymen to pronounce upon the circumstances of his death. And after that, he supposed, a coffin would trail south, containing all that remained of Martin Fawcett, one-time farmhand, lately someone of infinite promise and charm.

He drew a jotting pad towards him and wrote a few instructions for the head clerk, calling a vanboy and telling him to deliver the note to the counting house at once. The network viceroys at least would have to know in advance; they would never forgive him if they learned it from the newspapers. And thinking of newspapers he rang for

Jeffs, his editor, who came close to breaking down when he heard the news and said, in answer to George's query: "Fleet Street will get on to something of that kind very quickly. Local correspondents will wire in stories by tonight but there won't be any, most likely, in a place the size of Colne. Probably staff men will go over from Manchester, certainly one on behalf of the Northcliffe press. He'll feature this as his front page tomorrow."

"As soon as that?"

"Almost surely, George." He looked at him steadily. "It means Stella and Denzil will have to know tonight, doesn't it? Would you like Debbie and me to drive over with you?"

"No, this is something I've got to cope with alone. Thank you all the same, Milt. Go on home and arrange for Debbie to go down to 'Tryst' and tell the old folks in the morning. There's no need for them to know yet. The London papers don't get there until around eleven o'clock. Tell Debbie I'll be there by then."

He dragged himself up and across the yard from his ground-floor office block near the weighbridge to the spot where his Daimler was parked. The mechanic in charge was polishing the windshield. George said, gruffly, "Leave that, Rigby. Is there enough petrol in the tank to take me down to 'Tryst'?"

"It's half full, sir. I checked a minute since."

He got in and waited for the man to swing the starting handle. Then, tuning the engine, he drove slowly through the main gates and headed south into the thick of the Old Kent Road traffic. The Daimler's oil lamps battled with a low swirl of river mist as he nosed his way carefully into the southbound stream.

He had one meagre slice of luck. Bumping down the length of unsurfaced track from river to farmyard he saw the wink of a lantern in the byre on his right and pulled up, opening and closing the door softly and treading over frozen ruts to the byre. Denzil was inside, anxiously watching one of his Guernseys. The shed reeked of warm, country smells, touched with a whiff of disinfectant. His brother-in-law looked up as he entered, his broad, red face expressing surprise as he said, "George? You here, this time o' night? Stella never said   "

"Where is she, Denzil?"

"In the kitchen. I've only come out to look before locking up." He nodded at the cow beyond the rail. "She's through it but we had a worrysome hour or two. Vet was here twice since she started, around noon. Twin heifers. Alwus look for trouble with a pair. Still, she'll do now, I think. Take a look at 'em," and George peered beyond the lantern ray to see the mild-eyed Guernsey munching at her rack, one calf at her udders, another curled at her feet in the straw. He said, with a rush, "Listen, Denzil, I'd sooner break it to you here   . alone. Martin was . . was killed today, up in the Pennines . ."

"Killed? Marty!" His head came up so sharply that George heard the cricking sound of his neck. "How?"

"He was driving one of the new vans from Leeds and skidded on an icy road trying to avoid a hunt. He was dead before they got him out. Rudi telephoned from a place called Colne."

He watched the farmer ride out the shock. His weather-beaten face first drained itself of colour and then a heavy flush returned to his pendulous cheeks as he raised a hand and rasped the palm across a day's stubble.

"My boy? Dead, you say?"

George nodded and stood waiting. The only sounds that broke the stillness of the byre was the lisping suck of the calf and the champ of its mother at the rack. Presently Denzil said, "When did it happen, George?" George said he wasn't sure but it was probably early afternoon. The van Martin was driving was brand new, one that he assembled himself and partially designed on his own drawing-board. He added, "He was keen, Denzil. The keenest lad we ever had in the machine shops. It's a frightful thing to have happened, the first man we ever lost on a motor run. I don't know much about the circumstances except that there was a fire . . ."

"A fire? On the road you mean?"

"The vehicle caught fire but Martin was almost certainly dead when the flames reached him, or so Rudi says."

Denzil was staring at him aghast and he knew why. Within yards of where they were standing Denzil's own father had died in a fire, trying to save his cattle when the farm was gutted. That was before he married Stella, something like thirty years ago. Stella had told him how, on that occasion, Denzil had carried his father's body to an outhouse down the approach lane and afterwards she had watched over him all night while he slept on sacks in ɑ shed behind the piggeries.

"We'd best go in now and tell his mother, Denzil."

"Nay, I coulden do that."

"You don't have to, I will . . ."

"*No!*" The farmer shot out his huge hand and caught George by the wrist. "Let me think on it a minute . . . Burned up, you say? . . . I can't tell her that. She's alwus been afraid o' fire, ever since we lost Dewponds that time. Every time she smells smoke she makes me go out an' do the rounds. No, I dassn't tell her that, not yet any road."

George could hear his breath wheezing but soon, rather sooner than he expected, his brother-in-law recovered some sort of grip upon himself. He said, finally, "You wait on. Wait in the yard. I'll go in and break it, best I can. It'll be better comin' from me, seein' she was always dead against them boys goin' up there in the first place. Wait on 'till I come."

He plodded slowly out of the byre, closing the door and moving across the beam thrown by the Daimler's lights towards the kitchen. He went in and George saw his shadow move against the muslin curtains of the big, low-beamed room.

It was a room, he recalled, that his sister had helped Denzil to rebuild when she was a girl of about twenty, slowly emerging from the shock of that disastrous first marriage to a vicious wastrel over the Sussex border. He understood then why she had opposed the exodus of her boys from this farm and this plodding way of life. Everything that was real and important to her was right here, in this flowering corner of Kent and everything beyond it, even 'Tryst', where she had been born, was alien and charged with menace. She had renounced home and family the night of that fire, identifying herself body and soul with that lumping great chap, Fawcett. Why and how nobody had ever discovered. Not even his mother who had done all she could to encourage the unlikely match.

About five minutes passed. The sweat on his forehead and under his arms struck cold and he shivered, making the effort of his life to resist the temptation to leap into the motor, reverse madly up the lane to the river road, and drive off into the night. Presently Denzil came out and called, not to him but to someone working in a milking shed on the far side of the yard. Robert, Denzil's eldest son, emerged, shouting irritably, "What's to do now? I'm milking. Charley's gone and I said I'd finish!" But his father called again, sharply this time, and Robert stumped across the cobbles to join him and they stood talking for a moment in the doorway before Robert went in and Denzil came across to the byre. He said, "Woulden it be better if you left it? If you just drove off, and come back in the morning?"

"No, it wouldn't, Denzil. The papers might be full of it in the morning and even if you keep them from her busybodies from the village are sure to come posting up here falling over themselves to tell her the gory details. No, no, I don't want that, and neither do you if you think about it."

"Ah, come on in, then, but don't say more'n you have to for she's taken it bad. She's taken it real bad, George."

She was in her customary place at the head of the long oak table, as though about to preside over supper. She sat bolt upright and her plump round face was perfectly blank, almost as though she was asleep with her eyes open. She gave no sign when he moved around and took a seat close to her, furthest from the fire. He took her hand, coarsened by years of farm work, and held it tightly. It had always been difficult to equate her with the elegant sister he remembered in the days when they were all growing up together at 'Tryst' and she was reckoned the belle of the county and the best horsewoman for miles around. The Stella of those days had died before she was twenty and this heavy, practical, unsmiling woman had taken her place. He said, brokenly, "I'm sorry, Stella . sorry," but could say no more, lowering his head so that he was only half aware of her sudden, incredibly swift movement up and away from the table. He only realised that the hand he had been clasping had been whipped away, as from the fangs of a snake. He heard Denzil and Robert cry out together and a combined rush of boots on the slate floor. There was a sudden flash and a shattering report, blinding and deafening him and then, as his chin came up, he saw Stella struggling with her husband and son, the latter with one hand on the gun forcing the barrel towards the floor. Then, very suddenly, she went limp, her knees buckling as she pitched forward and would have fallen had not both men grabbed her, Robert throwing the twelve-bore to the floor. The kitchen was half full of smoke and the reek of gunpowder made him cough and splutter. Robert said, breathlessly, "Leave her, Dad. I'll see to her. I'll carry her up. Fetch Dolly fer Chrissake! For Chrissake run an' fetch Dolly!"

George subsided on the bench, the noise of the shot still singing in his ears and through a haze of smoke he saw Robert lift his mother as though she was a slip of a girl and move ponderously towards the stairs. He was unable to help him. There was no power in his legs. The big kitchen clock ticked on and a Welsh collie, that had scampered for cover when the shot was fired, emerged cautiously from beneath the table and arranged himself carefully beside him, slowly wagging his bush of a tail.

Dolly, Robert's brawny wife, hurried in and went straight upstairs. Then Denzil returned, wordlessly picking up the gun and breaking it open. "T'other barrel weren't loaded," he said. "That must be young Dick. On'y Dick's vool enough to leave a loaded gun about the place."

"Did she mean to kill me? Or was it to scare me out of the house?"

"God knows. She had the gun on you any road, and if Bob hadn't been mighty quick . ." He ran his hand over his stubble again, making a sound like a hand-saw. "It's all on account of what the boys did, I reckon, leaving here to work on those motors of yours. She's never been the same. She never got used to it and alwus blamed you for it. She told me just now you killed him, same as you shot him but she didn't mean it, not really."

"How do you feel about it, Denzil?"

"Not the way she does. It was what they wanted, or young Marty wanted any road. We had letters from him saying so and his brother woulden come back to a farm, not now."

"That's how it was, Denzil. I'd like you to believe that. I'd like you to try and make Stella understand that. Martin was a born engineer and was first-class at his job, right from the start. He wouldn't have been happy doing anything else. Do you think you could convince her of that?"

"No, I don't, but I'll try, once she gets over the shock."

"There'll be an inquest. I'm going up for it. Would you or Robert like to come?"

Denzil shook his head. "No, neither of us. We're busy here, dawn to dusk. You can't leave livestock same as you can motors. Besides, what purpose would it serve, seein' the boy's dead?"

He sat down heavily as Robert came clumping down. "Dolly'll stay with her while I take the mare and ride for Doctor Fowler. Maybe he'll come, or maybe he'll give us something to quieten her. Meantime you'd best take a gill, Dad. You, too, Uncle George." He went over to a cupboard in the big dresser and took out a bottle and two cups, pouring into the cups and adding water from the iron kettle beside the hearth. "I'll be back in less than an hour, providing he don't keep me waitin'."

His father raised his head. "Watch out for ice on that footbridge. Don't try and ride over, get off and lead. We've had trouble enough for one night."

"I'll mind the ice. You drink up. You, too, Uncle George."

He went out, a big, strong, very capable man, ideal to have around in a crisis. Something about his gait reminded George vividly of the Adam he remembered from childhood. He thought wretchedly, 'They've all got more Swann than Fawcett about 'em. That must be because Stella's the dominant partner . . .' Slowly he reached out for the liquor and lifted it to his lips. It was sloe gin judging by the taste, and well matured. The cloying stuff warmed his belly and soothed his throat, still irritated by the whiff of gunpowder. The big clock, inevitable as doom, ticked on. The collie's tail maintained its steady, friendly whisk. He said, finally, "We'd best keep this to ourselves – the gunshot I mean. It could lead to her being put away somewhere. The old folks must never hear about it. I can't face them right now. Debbie is going to cope with telling them in the morning . . ." He heaved himself up, "I'll keep you informed, Denzil. And be sure the newspapers are kept from her. Come to that I wouldn't read them myself if I were you. They'll play it up, if I know 'em."

He felt drained and useless. All his striving since he had recoiled from that June balance sheet had amounted to this, a favourite nephew burned to a cinder. His own sister trying to blow his head off with a twelve-bore. He went out, reversed the Daimler down the lane and straightened her out on the river road. He let in the clutch and drove off into the frosty night.

2

Down the years, good and bad, the Swanns had demonstrated that they could ride out the buffets. Hugo's blindness. Stella's disastrous first marriage. The death of Giles' wife in a street riot. These sombre events had been absorbed into the mainstream of life. Not forgotten, of course, but shelved, like bills that were inconvenient to pay on demand, and never featuring in the conversational traffic of a family as large and gregarious as the Swanns of 'Tryst'

So it might have been with the death of Martin Fawcett, and that despite the furore in the press, had the boy's mother been seen to mourn the boy with dignity, to divorce the tragic incident from her long-standing grudge against George concerning the nature of his work and his involvement with George's concerns rather than his father's. But the shattering report of that gunshot seemed to have released tensions within her that no one suspected were there, least of all her easygoing husband, and her big, capable son, known about Dewponds as Young Master. Her physical prostration lasted no more than forty-eight hours, and in the days that followed, at least to the farmhands and villagers, she seemed to potter about her chores much as usual, but those close to her could not fail to note an abrupt change in her manner and a marked increase in her taciturnity that had passed for matter-of-factness since she had renounced the role of county belle for that of farm wife on a three-hundred-acre holding.

She was not seen at the funeral in Twyforde Churchyard a few days after the tragedy but then no women were present inside the family. There was no occasion for display when, at the very moment of interment, the leader writer of *The Times*, and his opposite number in Northcliffe's *Mail*, were at war with one another on the vexed question of heavy road traffic, the one declaring that the appearance on the nation's highways of motorised giants represented a menace that almost justified re-introduction of the Red Flag Act; the other holding that an occasional mishap of this kind was a small price to pay for the dramatic spurt Britain's motor engineers had achieved since that idiotic piece of legislation had been repealed, enabling the country to regain its lost lead over Continental competitors.

George watched the controversy from the touchlines, resisting, on the advice of the editor of the Swann broadsheet, the temptation to contribute a letter pointing out that the accident could never have occurred had the master and hunt servants involved shown a little commonsense, or made an allowance for Martin's difficulties in braking a heavy vehicle on an icy gradient.

He growled, when he ran his eye over the spate of letters from the hunting shires. "Here's proof, if we wanted it, that the English value the life of an animal at twice that of a man earning his living. If Martin had run clear through that damned pack, and killed a dozen or more, you would have heard baying from Channel to Border. As it is, seeing the kid sacrificed his life for them, they vent their spleen on the vehicle! In the name of God, what do they imagine keeps the nation fed? Trade, or the entrails of foxes?"

But Milton Jeffs said, quietly, "Let it ride, George. No one can stop the motor now. There was the same uproar when the railways carved up the fox-hunting country. Ask Adam if you want confirmation of that."

He was sometimes tempted, indeed, to consult his father on the current turn of affairs, and more particularly on his own inclinations as regards further development of the Fawcett trailer but he held back. The old people had taken a series of hard knocks lately, what with Romayne's death, and the moonlight flit of young Edward's giddy wife, and at their age they would lack the resilience for which both had been noted in the past. So he kept clear of 'Tryst', waiting for the press controversy to die down and be replaced by another, the public hazard

of low-flying aeroplanes over cities. But the unease at
Dewponds persisted, as he learned from Debbie who was
often over there, trying to coax Stella out of the doldrums.
She said, early in the new year, "Poor Denzil's worried
half out of his wits. He says she's so tetchy he hardly dares
open his mouth and they both seem to be sleeping badly.
Did you know Stella was abnormally scared of fire?"

"Not until the night I was there. Denzil told me then.
He said she has him up going the rounds every time she
smells a bonfire. It's understandable, I suppose, seeing
that Dewponds once was burned to the ground, and old
Fawcett lost his life in the outbreak."

"Well, it's gone beyond that according to him. He tells
me she has him out of bed as often as three times a night
and when he's hard to rouse she goes on the prowl
herself. I got the doctor in again and he prescribed for her
but Denzil says no one can lead Stella to medicine. Most
of it goes down the sink according to him." She paused,
regarding him sympathetically. "There's another thing,
too. She knows the full circumstances of Martin's death.
One of the farmhands blurted it out and was sacked for his
pains. How do you feel about calling in and asking Giles
to talk to her?"

It was an old Swann nostrum. When the medical profession had had its fling they usually sent for Giles, the
family wiseacre. He had a knack of coaxing secrets from
closed minds and finding unsuspected paths out of an
impasse, but he had no luck as regards Stella. After an
unresponsive hour with her he told Denzil: "I can't reach
her. Not yet, anyway, for I daresay that doctor's right.
The shock came at a bad time for her, when most women
of her age are finding it difficult to cope. However, I'll
prescribe for you if you'll heed me."

He looked shrewdly at his brother-in-law, not liking his
haggard features and the sag in his belted belly. He had
lost, at a guess, upwards of twenty pounds in the last few
months, and it was obvious that interrupted sleep was
taking its toll. "Get her into a nursing home for a month

or so and I'm not talking about an asylum. It's more of a retreat, a place I know at Broadstairs. They just sit about and are cosseted during convalescence. It's expensive but she can afford it. She's never touched that money of Grandfather Sam's, has she?"

He admitted this was true. There had been times, Denzil said, when they could have used her private capital, but he had never asked her for it, not even during the severe agricultural depression of the 'nineties.

"Why not, Denzil?"

"I had my reasons. She come to me when she was in bad trouble. I never dreamed she would but she did, forsaking your lot for this, and a hard and toilsome life mostly. I wanted her. By God, I wanted her, ever since I was a boy, but I never wanted her father's money, or her grandfather's, come to that. We've made do and rubbed along happily enough until now and we'll come through this I daresay, without packing her off anywhere."

He looked around the yard. "She rebuilt this place with her own hands. You woulden know about that, being no more'n a boy at the time but she did, or the pair of us did. Laid every beam, every brick and every tile. You take her from here and she'll get worse instead of better."

"I'm not thinking so much of her. You put in a fourteen-hour day and you need your sleep, man."

"Aye, I do," Denzil said, "but there are times when a man must go short of it and this is one of them. She's been a wonderful wife to me and a fine mother to the boys. What sort of man would I be to pack her off to some kind of hospital at the first sign of trouble? She never had a day's illness in her life until now."

"But this is a different illness, Denzil, a mental illness. Temporary almost surely, but something you can't expect to handle alone. Why don't you think about it?"

"I'll think on it," Denzil said, but Giles knew he would not. Brood, possibly, but not think, for he was not equipped for that kind of thinking, any more than was the village practitioner who brought her bottles of medicine from time to time. Giles said nothing of what was uppermost in his mind, that brief murderous attack that he had dragged from George the last time they discussed Stella's plight. Among them all, however, he came nearer to understanding his sister's dependence on this three hundred acres tucked in a fold of the Weald. It had saved her reason once, a long time ago, and perhaps it could do so again. Spring was on the doorstep, the busiest season of the year for people living off the land. It was possible, indeed likely to his way of thinking, that the demands of a lifetime, grafted on to the very bones of their existence, would reassert themselves as soon as the longer days came round. Hard routine work, as he knew by bitter experience, was the only real anodyne. Providing one had faith in what one was about.

*   *   *

They had entered into a conspiracy to keep it from the old people, soft-pedalling whenever the subject arose and one or other of them paid a call at 'Tryst'. When Henrietta asked a direct question they would reply with half-truths. Stella was slow to shake off her depression and reassert herself as mistress about the place. Denzil had taken it more philosophically, helped no doubt, by the confidence he reposed in his first-born, Robert, and that cheerful village girl Robert had married a year ago. Dolly, they added, was expecting her first child in early spring and the presence of a grandson or granddaughter about the farm would prove a compensatory factor – it often did, in these cases, Debbie argued, wondering how much a man as shrewd as Adam was taken in by this kind of prattle.

Debbie had less misgivings as regards Henrietta. Martin, gone from these parts several years now, had never been as close to her as most of the grandchildren, boys like his brother Robert, the first of them, or Gisela's tribe.

who had grown up down at the old millhouse at the foot of the drive. Or perhaps she reserved her deepest sympathy for George, whose habitual grin was rarely seen these days.

But Deborah was in error as regards the impact Martin's tragic death had made upon the woman she had long ago accepted as a mother. Henrietta had never learned to ride the buffets fate had in store for everyone. For so long a stretch, all through her young and middle years, she had walked in sunlight and had come to expect it as the right of the circumspect. True, Hugo's blindness, and a son-in-law's violent death in distant China, might have counselled wariness in these matters but these sombre occurrences, sad as they were to contemplate, had taken place far across the sea and Henrietta's world was local and enclosed.

The death of young Martin was something else. She saw it not only as a shocking waste of a young life but as a kind of culmination to the swarm of tribulations that had beset the family of late, an unlooked-for plague at her time of life. They had begun with that shameful abdication of Edward's wife, a blow not only to his pride but to hers, for it seemed monstrous that any girl should seek to exchange a lifetime as a Swann vicereine, in Henrietta's eyes the most envied future available to a woman, for a career as an actress. Then followed the death of a daughter-in-law in a vulgar street riot and while Henrietta could not help but feel this was a likely outcome of trespassing on male preserves, she was not insensitive to the misery it inflicted upon the most sensitive of the brood, even though she had long abandoned any attempt to understand what went on in the overstocked head of a genius. For that is how she had thought of Giles since he was a child.

Hard on the heels of all this came news that the firm was going through a very bad patch and in a way this information disturbed Henrietta more profoundly than the wounds inflicted on Edward or Giles, for these were of a personal nature. Adam's admission that Swann-on-

Wheels was in rough water was like a hint that the British Empire itself was in jeopardy, or that the Bank of England was expected to close its doors in a week or so. In a way it cast doubts upon Adam Swann's infallibility and this struck at the very roots of her faith in the stability of life. It was symptomatic too of all she witnessed, and more that she sensed, about the times, so different, so very different from those of her middle years, after Adam had been miraculously restored to her and his affairs had been seen to prosper to a degree that put him alongside enterprises like Pears' soap, Lipton's and all the other businesses she saw advertised on hoardings and public transport.

The signposts of change were there for all to see. Nicely-brought-up girls had taken to marching about the streets with banners. Divorces in high places no longer proscribed the departure of parties concerned to Boulogne. And half the families she knew had exchanged carriage and pair for a variant of George's nine-day-wonder that had once been confined to the stable block but had now, it appeared, spawned a thousand and one children, encouraging folk to swarm here, there and everywhere like itinerant salesmen. There was no sense, so far as she could see, in any of it.

And then, as if to confirm her worst fears on this particular issue, they came to her with news that Stella's boy, Martin, had been crushed to death by one of these monsters. Both crushed and burned she understood, although she was at pains not to enquire into the details and it was clear then that the family was undergoing a series of plagues, like the affliction visited upon the Egyptians in Exodus, and that this was a hint that even a dynasty as firmly-based as hers was mortal and that the troubles besetting them were designed, perhaps, to chasten her pride.

She even took to attending church more regularly, and tried hard to persuade Adam to do the same. In this she failed, but having, as it were, renewed her nodding acquaintance with God, she set herself to relearn the habit of prayer as a possible means of warding off further disasters.

It was not easy after all this time, a lifetime of worshipping Adam rather than the nightshirted Jehovah of her girlhood. He seemed so remote and, just lately, so implacable, and phrases to address Him were hard to find if one was looking for anything more than the public approach set out in the Book of Common Prayer. She would have liked to have consulted Adam on her route (after all, he was recognised as Britain's most famous router) but she knew, instinctively, that he could not help her much as regards the best way to propitiate the Almighty. He had never been a churchgoer and she suspected that he had no real belief in survival after death or, for that matter, in the existence of a divine plan and even this, contemplated in the abstract, was strange, for he was certainly what she thought of as a *good* man, and a good Christian, too. Always, ever since the day she had met him up on that moor, he had concerned himself with the troubles and deprivations of the poor, as recommended so insistently in the gospels, but that did not seem to help. What she needed now was a guide along once familiar roads where, unfortunately, the Swann-on-Wheels insignia counted for little.

She could not bring herself to consult the rector, who occasionally came to dinner at 'Tryst'. She had always thought of him and his predecessors as semi-dependants and social inferiors, men who would look to her and hers for help in their routine labours about the parish. What she required, she felt, was an ecclesiastical equivalent of Adam, say an archbishop or, at least, a bishop, and the bishop of her diocese had never been to dinner. Now that she came to think about it he had not even attended one of her At Homes, croquet parties or garden fêtes.

There seemed no reason, however, why this should not be remedied and she broached the subject to Adam when she was drawing up an invitation list for a dinner party she was planning for her birthday. His response was irreverent. All he said was, "Why the bishop? What's he done to deserve it? I can't ever recall having set eyes on the chap, though from all I hear he'll probably take you up on the invitation. He's a rare gad-about, I'm told, and a good judge of wine." And then, with a twinkle, "If he accepts let me know well in advance. I'll look out something special for him, for I wouldn't like him to spread it around that our cellar wasn't one of the best in the diocese."

But then, before she could think of a way of coaxing a qualified spiritual comforter into the house, disturbing hints reached her that Stella was making very heavy weather of things and behaving very oddly on that farm of hers a mile up the river. She took it for granted that Stella's eccentricities could be attributed to the meno-pause and not, as Debbie was inclined to think, delayed shock regarding poor Martin's death in the north and there were grounds for this supposition. From all she knew of her daughter, particularly since she had shaken loose of that scoundrel she had married in such a hurry, Stella was not a person to let a misfortune like this disturb the rhythm of her life for long. What temperament she had possessed as a girl she had shed, like her social background, the minute she married that lumping farmer's son, Denzil Fawcett. Since then, somewhat to Henrietta's dismay, she had identified herself with the yeoman class and was now, Henrietta would have said, the least imaginative of all the Swanns and as practical as, say, George or Edward. On Henrietta's occasional visits to Dewponds she had seen her as the undisputed mistress of the place, with a sharp tongue for everyone, male or female, who did not measure up to her standards of efficiency. But nobody there, least of all Denzil, would regard this as unnatural. Denzil had never recovered from the shock of having acquired her as a wife, where the Swann bossiness had clearly asserted itself as soon as Stella had learned the rudiments of husbandry. For more than a quarter of a century now Stella's word had been Holy Writ on Fawcett acres, and

it was therefore disquieting to hear that her recent behaviour was the subject of gossip among local chaw-
bacons and Twyforde villagers. For it was through these
freely available sources that Henrietta learned more of
what was happening at Dewponds than anyone suspected.
Stella had, it seemed, abdicated authority over the staff
and spoke very little, even to Denzil or Robert, her eldest
son. In the daytime, Henrietta learned, she kept to her
room or chimney corner, leaving the preparation of meals
to a slut of a girl she employed, but by night, or so it was
rumoured, she more than made up for her withdrawal.
Sometimes as many as five times between lock-up and
dawn she made her rounds of the homestead and farm
buildings, obsessed by the fear of a second disastrous fire at
Dewponds, and here again Henrietta would have liked
very much to have consulted Adam on what was best for
the girl. She was restrained, however, by Adam's own
preoccupation of late, and this was yet another source of
disquiet, causing her to wonder if his age was not beginning to tell on him at last, despite his apparent fitness for
a man about to enter his eighty-fifth year.

He gave no outward sign of senility and his step, notwithstanding an artificial leg, was as brisk as a boy's.
His eyes were clear too, clear enough to read small print
without spectacles, and his last spell of illness was so long
ago that she had forgotten its nature. And yet, when she
thought hard about it, there *was* something different
about him, a hint or two, no more than that, of his
daughter's opting-out of affairs other than those relayed
to him second-hand in his newspapers and journals. He
enjoyed his solitary walks about the estate and his contemplation of the pictures, furniture and valuable china
he had assembled over the years. He liked his books too,
and whenever the weather was bad could always be found
in the library, absorbed in one or other of the hundreds of
leather-bound tomes they had inherited from the previous
tenants of the house. Meantime she had no complaint at
all regarding his temper. He was invariably kind and soft-

spoken in his dealings with her yet she could not but feel, since about the time their recent spate of troubles had begun, that she had lost touch with him, that they had moved appreciably further apart than the era when he had been disposed to demonstrate his approval of her in a very practical way.

It occurred to her more than once when she was lying beside him in the great Conyer bed (her recent anxieties had revived her old trouble of insomnia) that here, possibly, was a reason for his new-found stillness. Perhaps a man's need of a mate and a good deal of his appreciation of life, disappeared when his senses were no longer capable of being stirred by a woman and this was more likely to be true in the case of a man with a mind as well-stocked as his for it might well enable him to find all the stimulus he needed in the contemplation of abstracts that had never interested her very much. But she could do no more than guess at something as complex as this and even the bishop, if she finally lured him to 'Tryst', could hardly be consulted on a subject so personal and delicate.

Thoughts such as these, deeply nostalgic and tinged with sadness, were drifting across her mind like cloud wisps in the small hours of the first day of spring, when the wind, gusting in from the south-east and circling the wooded spur behind the house, had banished all prospect of sleep and given her a couple of hours to pass before she could slip from the room and brew herself an early dish of tea in the kitchen. He had been reading until very late and had not come to bed until long after she had retired but he was sleeping soundly now and in the first glimmer of dawn she turned and looked at him, wondering how a man with so much behind him, and so brief a span ahead, could relax so completely.

He did not look more than about seventy, with his clear skin and firm, slightly aquiline features. His hair, although snow white now, had never receded and his teeth, surprisingly, were as preserved as those of a man in his thirties. She thought, pettishly, 'It's not fair   the way some men stop themselves ageing, just as if they were empowered to slam the door on time . . . No woman can do that, or not once she has lost her shape child-bearing and is running to fat, and her hair has thinned and turned grey . . .' But then, chiding herself for taking advantage of his repose to find fault with him, she forced herself to remember the good times she had had with him right here, in this vast bed, the bed that he always declared had been used as a mating couch for that old pirate Conyer and his haughty-looking wife, for whom he had named this house more than three centuries ago. And they had been good, too, those gay, rollicking hours when she was in her early twenties and he was in his mid-thirties, and but recently embarked upon his glorious adventure.

She had always thought of this room and particularly of this bed as a refuge from the family and the external pressures of his life and hers, and in those days he had taken such a delight in her and all she had to offer, which was really no more than he had taught when he had married an eighteen-year-old goose as green as grass, totally ignorant of what men wanted most from a wife. And remembering this she took heart a little, reminding herself of the astonishing durability of his satisfaction in her, for he had never once wandered off in search of fresh pasture. There had always been the network to hold him and after the network her own supple body, and the two had sufficed to keep him to her and hers over a span of more than fifty years.

She supposed she could give herself some credit for that and, indeed, for surviving this long as his partner. Almost all the women she had known in her youth and middle-age were dead or widowed, and here they were, in comparatively good health, getting on for fifty-four years after their first encounter on a heath a few miles north of her father's house . . .

She was wide awake now and could see through the chink in the curtains that it was all but light outside. There was no prospect of dropping off again so she eased herself cautiously from bed and slipped into her favourite bedgown, a silk one emblazoned with gold and silver dragons that he had bought for her from a tea importer years ago.

She would try her luck at tip-toeing downstairs and making that much-needed dish of tea without disturbing him and, testing each old floorboard before putting weight on it, she got as far as the door before he stirred, heaving himself over and shouldering her share of the bedclothes but not waking, or not so far as she could determine, for his breathing at once became regular again and she was able to lift the latch and slip into the corridor, leaving the door ajar rather than risk another rattle.

It was much lighter in the kitchen, with its uncurtained east-facing window and it took her no more than a minute to bring the water in the iron kettle to the boil and lay herself a tray. The big, solemnly-ticking clock told her it was coming up to six and in the brief interval she allowed for the tea to brew she stirred up the fire, for the kitchen, opening directly on to the stableyard, was full of draughts. It was then, in the act of stabbing at the smouldering log with a poker, that she heard the step outside and at once, without a split second's pause for rationalisation, she was gripped by panic.

It was not unreasoning panic either. Her memory, travelling backwards at the speed of light, reminded her of an almost identical situation, a little tableau set out in this same high-ceilinged room at approximately the same hour of day, in which there were two principals; herself and Denzil Fawcett from Dewponds.

He was 'Young' Denzil then, a lad of around twenty, who had walked here through wind and rain with news that he had come upon her daughter Stella drenched through and hysterical after her mad flight from the Moncton-Prices over the county border and now she knew, with horrid certainty, that the scrape on the gravel outside was a variant of those same circumstances, betokening yet another period of wretchedness.

She was so sure of this that certainty robbed her of any surprise she might have experienced when she crossed the room, drew the bolt and threw open the door. It was not Denzil who was climbing the short flight of steps from the yard, however, but Denzil's son, Robert, the eldest of her many grandchildren.

She said, without preamble, "Something's wrong, isn't it? Badly wrong! Come in and speak quietly. The maids will be up and about in less than an hour."

He came in, leaving a trail of mud on the slated floor, saying, "I wouldn't have said anything to anyone but you or Grandpa . . . I would have made some excuse. But seeing you're up and about . . ." And then, looking wildly distracted, he broke off.

"What is it, Robert? What's happened?"

"It's mother. She's wandered off again. God knows where this time, for father's no idea how long she's been gone. We've searched the buildings and the fields on both sides of the river but there's no sign, or wasn't when I left."

"When was that?"

"Under half-an-hour ago . . . Dad's scared, Gran . . . She wasn't wearing her dressing gown and she usually does, or so he says, when she's on the prowl. She'll be chilled through time we find her, and God knows who might run across her meantime. I thought I'd make sure she wasn't here before I got everyone out looking and talking about it."

He sat down and gave her a despairing look, the kind of look his father had given her all those years ago when he came scratching on the door on an even gustier morning with news that Stella had run away from her husband and was being dried, fed and cared for over at Dewponds.

"Was it that silly notion of fire again, Robert?" and he nodded, adding, more to himself than to her, "It can't go on . . . Father's fair done up after weeks of it, and damn it, I'm not much better, as you can see, what with everything to see to. But he won't hear of . . . of sending her away anywhere. The doctor says it'll pass, given time, but I keep remembering that place Uncle Giles thinks she should go."

"What place is that?"

"A kind of special hospital. At Broadstairs, I think. A swanky place, that charges a lot. But like Uncle Giles says, what does the money matter? We can't watch her twenty-four hours a day. Not Father, not me, nor Dolly either with her expecting any minute."

She wanted very much to comfort him. She wanted most desperately to give him aid and advice, to command the situation in the way she had when his father made an almost identical appeal to her years before he was born. But she had lost the knack of command somehow and neither words nor plan suggested themselves. She could only sit there chafing her hands, reflecting that, on Robert's testimony alone, it would soon be post-office gossip in the village and every farm kitchen for miles around, that Stella Fawcett had lost her wits and taken to wandering the country-side in her nightdress, and that there was talk of 'putting her away somewhere'.

She said, finally, "How long, Robert . . ? I mean . . when did it begin? Seriously, I mean?"

He replied, glumly, "Ever since she heard. Ever since they told her about Marty and she took that shot at Uncle George."

A wide variety of rumours had reached her via local gossip but the most alarming of them had not included this.

"*Shot* at him? Stella shot at *George*?"

He looked badly bothered for a moment but then he shrugged. "We all decided not to tell you but I can't see as it matters now. You would have found out sooner or later."

"Tell me. Tell me exactly what happened."

He told her and when he had done she bowed her head. She felt so weak and sick that she could hardly answer him when he said, rising, "Look, I'd best get back. Maybe you could send the groom and gardeners over to help look."

She managed to say, in a whisper, "No, don't go! Not until your grandfather hears . . . he'll decide who is to know and who isn't . . . I can't, I can't even think straight just now," and she dragged herself out of the kitchen and up the stairs, wondering if she had the resolution to rouse Adam and tell him that his daughter had lost her wits and was a danger to herself and everyone about her.

Standing there, her hand on the door latch, she thought, 'The last time this happened he was away. I had to cope with it quite alone and I did, very successfully. Where on earth has all my courage gone?' and she went in to find him in the act of strapping on his leg.

"Get dressed," he said, shortly. "Get something on and leave this to me."

"You heard?"

"Enough."

"Robert wants some of the servants to go over and help search."

"Robert can want. I'll deal with it."

"But Adam, it's terrible . . . terrible . . ."

"It could be worse."

"Shall I get Phoebe to tell Chivers to harness the trap?"

"No trap. I'll ride over."

She thought, 'I envied him repose an hour ago . . . now it's his coolness and courage . . . At eighty-four he's still got more than any man alive!' She dragged herself across to the dressing-table and sat staring at the forlorn reflection in the mirror.

As he was struggling with his riding boots she said, "What can you do anyway, at your age?"

"Whatever has to be done, Hetty."

*   *   *

There was still no trace of her when he rode into the farmyard. Denzil was there, looking like a man dragged from a deep sleep. He stood rubbing his eyes as Adam said, stormily, "Why in God's name didn't you or George tell me about that shooting incident? Hadn't I the right to know?"

"George wanted to keep it from you. It didn't seem all that terrible at the time, just a flare up of . . . well . . . temper and a spite against George. She never wanted the boys to leave the farm and work on those motors and she was right, I reckon. But I sided with George. It seemed the best thing for them at the time."

"Never mind that, tell me exactly what happened last night."

"Nothing particular. She was restless, same as usual, and I must have dropped off, I was that worn out. I woke up about five and found her gone. I went down and looked around but when she wasn't in the house . . . when I realised she was in her nightdress and nothing else, I roused Robert and Dolly. Robert got the two hands to search the farm buildings but there was no sign of her, apart from that one footmark."

"What footmark?"

"The one in the cow pat down by the bridge. It don't mean she crossed the bridge, does it? I mean, she might ha' turned aside and gone along the tow path. Charlie and William are looking there now."

He said, dismounting, "See to the horse. I'll take a look myself."

He went behind the barns and across the short stretch of pasture to the footbridge. The wind had dropped and the sky was overcast, promising a spatter of rain. At the approach of the bridge only a few yards on the farm side of the first plank, he found the tell-tale cow pat. It carried the clear imprint of a naked foot but he could find no subsequent footprints in the hard-packed slope leading down to the river. The water was fairly high, running three feet or so below the level of the bridge. During several wet springs in the past he had known the bridge covered and old Fawcett, Denzil's father, had often had trouble with flooding about here. He went back up the bank to the bridge and began to cross it, testing the handrail on either side as he went. The middle section was looser than the approach sections, a single two-by-four batten, nailed to stout posts sunk into the river bed. He leaned hard against it, and felt it give a little, then harder still, steadying himself by the upright until the rusty nails yielded and the rail nearest the farm sprang loose, one end of the section holding it in place but leaving a gap over the deepest section of the river. He went on over to a downsloping field where there was a couple of hen-houses, abandoned now for Robert had moved the nest boxes nearer the farm. There was a lot of litter about here, broken planks, a sheet or two of corrugated iron, and a pile of mouldering straw raked together as though for a bonfire. He stood there looking down at it for several minutes, his heavy brows drawn together in thought. Then, with a glance over his shoulder, he took out some matches, stooped and set the straw alight. It blazed up for a moment before subsiding into a spiral of yellow, pungent smoke. He went back across the bridge and met Charlie and William, the two farmhands, returning from their unavailing search of the tow path.

"A section of that handrail is loose. Take a look at it. I'll tell Mr. Fawcett myself."

The men looked startled but Charlie moved swiftly to the bridge and he saw him jigging the loose section. William said, "There's smoke over there, zir . . . there by the old hen-houses," and Adam said, "I know, but I've looked there. Who made a bonfire there yesterday?"

"Nobody so far as I know, sir. Master Robert was pulling down the shed but didn't get to finishing the job. You can ask him yourself, sir."

"I will. Take Charlie and try the southern reach as far as the stone bridge where the road passes over."

"Yes, Mr. Swann."

He went back to the yard where Robert was standing talking to his father. "I've sent the two hands downstream as far as the road bridge. I'm going back now and I'll get my own men to search downstream towards the islet beyond 'Tryst'." Then, looking hard at them, "If she's found, leave Dolly with her and come straight over. Come in any case if she isn't found before noon."

He led his horse over to the mounting block and heaved himself into the saddle. They watched him ride away at a slow trot and Denzil said, in a low voice, "I know what he's thinking. He's sure she's in the river but I'm not letting myself think that. Not yet, any road."

*   *   *

They found her close to the spot he had anticipated, where the river made an ox-bow opposite the little islet that Henrietta always referred to as Shallott. The stream here was shallow, running over what had been a ford and still was in summer. Roots and branches, washing downstream, had piled up to form a dam and she was lying near the far bank in about two feet of water, half-concealed by a curtain of trailing briars.

Boxall, the groom, brought her ashore and laid her under the screen of willows that lined the bank. Her passage down the river had not disfigured her in any way. In her sodden nightgown, and with her tawny hair streaming loose, she looked like one of those women in a pre-Raphaelite painting. Expressionless and make-believe, as though she had never been anything more than a painter's model. Looking down at her, after they had freed her hair of twigs and bracken fronds, there came to him, with the poignant sadness of a blackbird's song in mid-winter, the memory of a little girl toddling beside him to the summit of the wooded spur behind the house forty-odd years ago and the sound of her voice trying to say the word 'foxglove' when he pointed to a clump and told her they were his favourite wildflowers. He said, "Go back, the pair of you, and fetch the dogcart. I'll stay here and watch. And you can tell Phoebe Fraser to break the news to Mrs. Swann. Don't be longer than you can help, although you'll have to go the long way round. That dog cart is too wide for the bridge." And then, as they shuffled off, "One other thing, apart from telling Phoebe. Keep it to yourselves, you understand? If anyone asks I'm still looking."

They went off at a fast walk and he sat down on a drift log, his mind conjuring with the kind of questions a coroner would be likely to ask. He thought, savagely, 'They'll need priming, every one of 'em, and there's not much time before the tongues start to wag. George will be here by dusk and George will see it my way. As for the others, they'll damned well do as they're told and say what I tell 'em to say!' It was very quiet and still here at this hour of the day. A few birds rustled in the thicket about the dam and the stream sang as it rippled round the breast of the islet. He thought of his father, who often came here to paint in watercolours, and wondered if the riverside scene would ever hold anything but dismal memories for any of them in the future.

6

The Strategist

WHEN ALL THREE OF THEM WERE PRESENT, quietly awaiting his pleasure, he had second thoughts about Hetty and said, addressing George, "I'll fetch your mother. I don't care whether she's equal to it or not. She'll have to know what we're about," and he clumped out into the hall before George, Denzil or Robert could protest. Henrietta was in the sewing-room, hunched over the fire, an untasted cup of tea on the table beside her. He said, "You'd better join us, Hetty. There's something you have to know, along with the others. It won't take long. Then we'll talk things over among ourselves. Just you, me and George, for Denzil and Robert will want to get back and make their arrangements."

She rose and followed him back into the drawing-room, taking a seat George offered her by the hearth and pulling her shawl close about her shoulders. George stood with his back to the fire. Denzil and Robert sat close together near the window as though poised to flee his silent wrath.

He said, clearing his throat, "There are things you have to know and I don't want a word of this mentioned outside this room. I'll have my say and after that it's up to you to pick holes in it. However, as I see it and with ordinary luck there shouldn't be any trouble, for the fact is, fair means or foul, I mean to squeeze a clear verdict of accidental death out of that coroner and I can only do it with your backing. You don't have to worry about that doctor. He'll know precisely what's in my mind and I think I can rely on him. First of all let me deal with that broken handrail on the bridge."

Robert spoke up, a hint of truculence in his voice. "That rail wasn't broken yesterday. I was over there several times during the day and I'd have noticed."

"Noticed it was loose?"

"I didn't look at it that closely."

"Well, your man will bear me out. One end was swinging free." He glared at them. "I made damn sure it was before I sent him to look at it."

"You pushed it? Pushed it hard?"

"Hard enough to make a gap. And while we're at it you might as well know it was me who relit that straw beside the hen-house."

He heard Denzil hiss. Robert was staring hard at the floor. There was silence in the room until George shuffled and Adam, swinging round on him, said, addressing him as though he was a child, "Don't fidget! Get glasses and pour Denzil and Robert a stiff tot of whisky. I'll take brandy, so will your mother. Help yourself if you care to join us."

George did as he was ordered. The heavy silence continued, broken only by the chink of decanter on glasses. Robert took the drink gratefully but he had to push the glass into his father's hand. He said, at length, "I was working on that hen-house most of yesterday. I piled the rotten straw but I don't recall setting a match to it. I was going to but I thought of mother and I left it."

"I'm not asking you to say you lit it. You'd had fires there before by the look of the ground. Nobody is likely to press the point if you say there was a bonfire stacked from straw out of the roosts. I'll say it was smouldering. On oath, if necessary."

George said, hoarsely, "You'll have to be more explicit, Gov'nor. Robert and I are getting your meaning but I don't think Denzil is, are you, Denzil?"

Denzil looked up as if seeing them for the first time. He took a gulp of his whisky and said, "She walked into the river. That footprint proved as much, didn't it?"

"Not one of us is in a position to prove anything one way or the other. All I'm aiming to do is to stack the evidence in favour of an accident. If there's reasonable assumption of that, seeing who we are, the coroner and jury will go our way. She's your wife, Denzil, and your mother, Robert, but before that she was my daughter and I'm damned if I'll have her branded as a suicide." He paused momentarily, glaring round the circle. "I'll say more. I'll never forgive any one of you who mentions that shooting incident. If that comes out there's no other verdict they could return, so bear it in mind, all three of you."

"They aren't likely to call George as a witness," Robert said. "Why should they?"

"They might. On account of the big fire at Swann's yard."

"Great God, Mr. Swann," Denzil burst out, "that was years ago! What's your fire got to do with my Stella drowning herself in the river?"

"Who knows whether it had to do with it? Who knows whether she didn't get started on this line long before that, the time of the Dewponds fire? Three fires, two of them fatal. Her father-in-law dead in one, her son in another. And in between half her father's property goes up in flames. Wouldn't that give a sick woman in shock a morbid fear of fire? Wouldn't it give coroner and jury good grounds for thinking so? That's all I need and I mean to get it. You'd best be clear on that, all of you, for if necessary I'll fight for it in open court."

The force of his personality held them in thrall. They were silenced by his vehemence and again there was a long silence in the room as he glared at each of them in turn.

"Well? I'm asking for holes in the theory. If you see any now is your chance to point them out before somebody else does."

The whisky seemed to have steadied Robert. He said, setting down his glass, "Neither Charlie nor William noticed that loose handrail. It's true they hadn't crossed over today but Charlie particularly was surprised and said as much. He was across there yesterday, carrying new planks and taking back the old ones I prised loose for him."

"Would a man with his arms full of planks notice a thing like that?"

"No, but neither Charlie nor William will be called, will they?"

"Not if I can help it. I've already given a list of witnesses who could help to the constable and their names weren't on it. I'll give evidence myself of finding her, and of seeing that rail and that smouldering bonfire. Denzil will have to tell them how he missed her and searched the farm buildings. No more than that so far as I can judge, save to bear out the doctor's testimony."

George said, "What will that testimony be?"

"That depends on him."

"Not really. If you've dropped this number of hints you will have gone further, just that much further. You saw him when he certified death. What did you say to him?"

"What would you expect in the circumstances? I primed him, much as I'm priming you."

"But it isn't the same, Gov'nor. He's not in the family."

"In a way he is. In a way the coroner is, and the locals on the jury will be. Prejudiced in our favour that is, so where's a conflict of evidence to come from? Only the collie that followed her down to the river knows what really happened."

There was another pause. Then Denzil said, pleadingly, "Tell it your way, Mr. Swann. Tell it the way you want it told and talked about afterwards."

"Is that necessary?"

"I have to hear it. Hearing it maybe I can believe it. Now, and for the rest of my days."

"Very well, Denzil." The querulous note had gone from his voice. He sipped his brandy and set aside his glass, moving over until he was close enough to lay his hand on his son-in-law's shoulder.

"Listen, my boy, and listen carefully. None of us know and none of us will ever know but this is how it *could* have been. There's no secret about how Stella felt as regards fire. I daresay it was how your mother felt until the day she died after watching your father die trying to save his cattle all those years ago. Or how *I* felt, watching my lifework go out in smoke beside the Thames. Or how George feels, come to that, when he thinks on young Martin in that wretched trailer up in the Pennines. There's nothing strange about that. It's how any of us feel deep down about something that threatens anything near and dear to us. Besides, she was in the change of life. The doctor will testify to that. Under that kind of stress, multiplied a hundred times maybe by Martin's death, fear of fire dominated her thoughts, night and day. That's real enough, for it kept you and Robert and Dolly on the jump ever since the night George broke the news to you. But this time there was a fire of sorts, a glow from a dying bonfire across the river, and the river was running high. She went over to take a look and put too much weight on that rail. There's a strong current midstream when the river is high. Strong enough to carry her two miles downstream. Why do we have to assume it was anything but an accident? If it didn't happen that way it happened some other way, brought about by factors we'll never know. Not us nor anybody else. Finish your drink, Denzil, and go on home. Take two of those pills the doctor left for Stella. They didn't help her but I daresay they'll ensure you a night's rest."

He went back to the fireplace and picked up his glass. When nobody moved he went on, "There's only one thing more I'd like to say and doubtless Hetty will join me in saying it. It has nothing to do with today's wretched business, or the misery you've had to face in the last few

weeks. It counts for much more than that, son, and as I
say, it comes from all of us here, but especially from me
and her mother. You've been a good husband to her
from the beginning. All this time, ever since you helped
her through that other piece of foolishness, Stella has had a
good life and a full one. Try and bear that in mind. It
doesn't come everybody's way and the fact that it came
hers, after such a bad start, was your doing. No one else's,
just yours, do you hear?"

They went out then and George walked with them into
the yard where their trap was waiting, lamps glowing in
the light swirl of mist closing down from the spur above.
He watched Robert help his father into the passenger
seat and climb up himself, gathering the reins. Then, after
the little rig had clattered through the arch and passed
round the rhododendron clump at the head of the drive,
he walked slowly back, hands deep in his pockets. The
Gov'nor had given them their rations, plenty enough to get
on with for the time being. But he had a queer certainty
that his own were still awaiting him inside the house.

*　　　*　　　*

They were much as he had left them, his mother seated
by the fire draped in her shawl, her face puffed under the
eyes, her cheeks flushed by the brandy he had forced on
her. But he noticed that the old man held himself poker-
straight and thought, meeting his steady glance, 'By God,
but he's a hard man to follow! How can any of us *feel*
a gaffer so long as he's around?' Adam said, with the
merest trace of anxiety in his voice, "They won't let us
down, will they?" and he said no, they wouldn't. Robert
had got the message and would rehearse his father carefully in what to say and what not to say in the witness
box. Adam said, "Right, then, now I can move on to you
and your mother. Not about what's said in public, or
gossiped around concerning your sister, but about things
in general. It's time somebody spoke up and as long as I'm

around I'll not shirk the job, not even tonight. Help yourself to another drink if you want one."

"I don't need another drink, Gov'nor."

"Well then, sit, for this will take time," and George sat. "It's about drift. Drift and muddle and woolly-mindedness generally. I've held my tongue until now, hoping one or other of you would take the initiative, but you haven't. Not you, nor Edward, nor Alex, who must have noticed what was happening to us since we ran into this string of setbacks. I don't count Giles. He has enough on his plate without worrying overmuch about us. You were ready to push on with that articulated trailer and I've not heard a word about it since young Martin was killed on the prototype. Have you shelved it?"

"Not shelved, exactly. We halted production on the other two."

"Was that a Board decision or yours?"

"It was mine."

"Then it underlines everything I've been thinking. Tell me something else. That new vehicle was going to put the old firm back on its feet, wasn't it?"

"It would have done that."

"How? In a few words, that your mother can understand."

"Well, articulated vehicles can operate where we're meeting our stiffest competition – in congested towns designed for horse traffic, for it's there that one-man operators are hauling our goods in driblets. Apart from that, a trailer would more than double the weight of haul per vehicle. Only that way could we check the drift of big firms to organise their own haulage fleets. We could deliver faster and far cheaper."

"It's much as I thought. But after Martin was killed you didn't push on?"

"No."

"I've never heard such damned nonsense! That isn't what I'd look for in a son of mine." His disgust created in him a need for further stimulation. He went over to the decanter and poured himself another brandy. "See here, it all adds up to what I feared. You're all losing your nerve and looking over your shoulders and it won't do, d'ye hear? Why should we expect nothing but fair winds? The best of us run into squalls from time to time but that's no damned reason for putting back into port, like a lot of frightened amateurs. We're *not* amateurs! We're the toughest and most experienced professionals in the game, and I thought I'd lived long enough to establish that beyond doubt. Do you think *I* never had self-doubts? I did, time and again, but I never let 'em make a nincompoop out of me. What's scared us so badly? Lay it out for yourself, clause by clause. Edward's flighty wife makes a fool of him so he takes to the bottle and let's his region go to the devil. Oh, I know he's over it now, but my information is he still spends too much time in pubs instead of casting round for a wench to give him something better to think of in his off-duty hours. Clause two: your sister-in-law gets herself killed in a street fracas, but that's her business not yours and certainly not Swann's, as a firm earning its bread and salt in the open market. Clause three: we have a big drop in profits and you hit on a way to turn the tide, but the first sign of danger and difficulty you run for cover and keep your head down, hoping the trouble will go away of its own accord. That boy Martin was a casualty but you can't expect to come through everything, every hazard, unscathed, the way you did when you stole a march over everyone by mechanisation, and it ought not to have led us here, sitting round like a lot of undertaker's mutes feeling so damned sorry for ourselves that instead of fighting back we cry into our beer. With commonsense, and a bold front, it could have been avoided. On your part and Denzil's. On Giles' and Deborah's too, if either of 'em had had the damned sense to come to me and give me the facts."

Henrietta spoke up, the first word she had uttered since Adam steered her into the room. "They were trying to save us worry, Adam. You're eighty-four   "

288

He made a savage gesture with his free hand. "What the devil's my age got to do with it? I can still think clearer than any of you! I'm proving it now and I'll prove it at the inquest tomorrow. Stella was sick and sickness needs treatment. I can't say whether she could have recovered or not but that isn't the point. My complaint is that every one of you, saving Giles maybe, let your personal problems make fools of you and that talk of sparing me grief is no more than a face-saver."

Avoiding his eye, Henrietta said, in a whisper, "They meant well . . . What else could they have done?"

His jaw shot out. "I'll tell you since you ask, Hetty. George here, and Denzil and Edward and Deborah, and Alex, too, as head of the family. They could have put their heads together and evolved something practical instead of hushing it up and going at it piecemeal. That's what a firm and family is, or should be. But I blame you most of all, George, for you were the most like me in a rough and tumble. At least, I always thought so. I'm not so sure now. Well," he drained his glass, "it's not too late. At your age your mother and I had our share of setbacks but we turned things in our favour and you can if you put your mind to it." He stopped for a moment, looking baffled, as though he had mislaid the thread of his argument and was too disturbed to hunt for it but the check was temporary and George, sensing this, said nothing. The fire rustled. Outside the wind got up again and went to probing the tops of the avenue limes, seeking its familiar passage through to the chimneys that had resisted its siege for three and a half centuries. Hearing it at work George thought, 'He's like this house . . . rooted and braced, for all his eighty-four years. Who would suppose he had just dragged his own daughter from the water and was waiting to hear her death pronounced upon by outsiders? The worst affront you could offer him would be pity.'

He said, at length, "That's not all, is it, Gov'nor?"

"No, though I'm speaking out because somebody has to and there's only one excuse for your muddle-headedness to my way of thinking. It's the times, the way the whole damned lot of you are going about things lately. Not just here but clear across the world. You're all sleep-walking and if you don't prick yourselves awake you're in for a God Almighty tumble. For here we are, with everything to make a new world and a new society, but all people with money in their pockets are concerned with is a month at the seaside, the next country house-party, Fanny's coming-out dress, a search for gentility and soft living generally Even the international apparatus we rely on to keep the garden-party going is as antiquated as feudalism and not nearly so efficient, and this attitude has a nasty habit of spreading down, to the city clerk, whose main ambition nowadays is to hoist himself another niche up the social scale. Not that there's anything wrong with that – as a spur, for it's what makes the world go round. What's wrong is the way he goes about it. Not by hard work, clear thinking, self-education and self-reliance, but by putting on airs, currying favour with the fellow above him, and learning how to talk with a plum in his mouth. It's all a sham and I hate shams wherever I find 'em. I hate backsliders too, so if you'll take a tip from me, George, you'll go out of here and do some hard thinking and hard planning, the way you used to before you had things too easy. And you can pass that on for what it's worth once we've got tomorrow's business behind us." He turned his back, spreading his hands to the fire as though signifying by this gesture that he had finished.

George turned to his mother. "Could I telephone Gisela and say I'll be staying overnight and going home after the inquest?"

"Of course. We'd be glad. Find Phoebe and tell her to air the bed in the big guest-room."

"I'd sooner have my old room. Is that possible? Without too much trouble?"

"Of course it's possible. Tell her to get a girl to make up

the bed and put a bottle in." She glanced at the clock. "They won't have all gone to bed yet."

"I'll see to it then, don't you stir."

He went out without another word and they heard him climbing the back stairs that led to Phoebe's quarters in the east wing.

She said, "You hit him too hard, Adam."

"I had to. I got through to him. That's what matters."

"Haven't you anything saved up for me?"

He seemed to her to relax a little.

"Certainly no broadside, Hetty."

"Ah, but something?"

"Advice. It can wait until this wretched business is behind us."

"That isn't necessary." She chose her words carefully. "I was wondering . . . would it be possible for me to . . . to come with you tomorrow?"

"To the inquest? You could face that?"

"I'd prefer it to waiting here alone and hearing a second-hand account. George isn't the only one who has been waiting for things to go away of their own accord."

He looked at her tenderly, feeling a pity for her that he had been unable to feel for Denzil, or even for Stella lying under the poplars with her hair enmeshed in the flotsam of the river.

"It's different for you, Hetty. Nothing I said applied to you. When you were young and spry you faced up to things better than any woman I know."

"You're not young, Adam, and you still don't shrink from them. Not even from something as bad as this."

"I'm a very obstinate old cuss."

"I don't think it is a question of age. I was thinking back, when Robert came to us to say she was missing — back to that time of Stella's other trouble with the Moncton-Prices. You were hundreds of miles away then but I managed."

She could have reminded him of other occasions, many of them, when she had faced trouble squarely and alone, and made decisions most women of her acquaintance would have shirked making. The fire had died in her now and deep down she could isolate the agent that had extinguished it. It was not age but pride, and a very counterfeit pride indeed compared with his. Flabby, overweening pride, that most people would call conceit.

She said, "Part of what you said to George applied to me. For years now I've thought of myself not only as privileged but deservedly so. Bad things just didn't come my way. Not because I was lucky but because I was sharp. Well, it isn't so, and I see that well enough now. If the others must have a share in what happened to Stella I'm not blameless. I should have visited her more and found out for myself how things stood. The reason I didn't would be hard for you to understand."

"Tell me if you want to."

"The truth is I lost patience with her long ago, ever since she sold out to the Fawcetts to the degree she did and let herself go. As a woman, I mean. I was never able to see it for what it was, a rejection of all she had thought of, up to that time, as the strictures and conventions of her own class, or that it was a natural result of what happened to her as a young bride."

"That isn't true, Hetty. Damn it, you steadied her up by young Fawcett. Do you imagine I didn't know you handed her to him on a platter?"

"Not for her sake, for my own. I would have married her off to a tinker if necessary. Later on, when I realised she didn't give a button for her waistline, or the clothes she wore, or even the way she came to speak, I think I began to despise her. It never once occurred to me that she really grew to love that farm and what it stood for, or that in her own way she loved Denzil as much as he loved her and coming to his level was the best way of showing it. Well, it's too late to alter that now, except to be kind to the boy, and do what I can to nurse him through the next year or so. God knows, I mean to do that." She got up, discarding her shawl. "I'll see Phoebe about George's room. Will you be long?"

"No, not long."

He caught her hand as she passed him and pressed it to his lips. There was no point in trying to eradicate her sense of guilt now but he would set about the job shortly, just as soon as the page was turned on tomorrow. And after that somehow, by some means, direct or devious, they would fight their way through to a peaceful close.

2

She thought of him then as performing the office of the Dutch boy in that old story about the hole in the dyke. A man more resolute and steadfast than any man in the world, self-dedicated to the task of averting a catastrophe, and although she was emotionally involved in every word they were saying, and aware of the covert glances they stole at her from time to time, she had eyes only for him and no more than a cognisance of the others who followed one another into the witness-box, or those who sat mute, listening to the dismal tale.

She had never previously attended an inquest and the formality of the phraseology startled her. It had an archaic touch, like something out of Magna Carta – " . . . Touching the death of Stella Fawcett . . " "draw near and give your attendance . . ." as though they had been staging a pageant instead of establishing, if it could ever be established, how the first child she had borne came to disappear in the middle of the night and reappear as a corpse two miles down the river.

She followed the drift of each witness. The long-faced doctor, who told of his examination of the body, then of his visits to Dewponds for the purpose of treating a woman in shock. The pills and potions he had prescribed. His professional opinion of the deceased's state of mind between the date of his first call in December and the twenty-first day of March. He had treated her for insomnia. He did not consider the 'deceased' as ill or not in the accepted sense of the word. Under stress, certainly, but not ill.

She could not get used to hearing Stella described as 'the deceased', as though everyone was under an obligation not to speak her name aloud, and she wondered if this oddly impersonal term bothered Denzil too, or whether he was too bewildered and shocked to relate it to the woman he had worshipped since he was a boy. They got little enough out of him anyway, so that she wondered if George was right about Robert rehearsing him in what he had to say. He told them that his wife had been 'upset' by news of her son's death and that all their married life she had had a very real fear of fire. Pressed gently by the coroner he admitted that this fear was based on the fact that Dewponds had been burned to the ground and that the fear increased when she learned that fire had played a major part in the fatal accident last December. He identified the body taken from the river as that of his wife. He had last seen her when he went up to bed on the night of the twentieth.

The coroner, whom she recognised as a local solicitor whose wife, a rather twittery creature, had attended her garden parties, was very considerate and seemed genuinely touched by Denzil's distraught manner. He said, gently, "You searched for her personally when you discovered her missing, Mr. Fawcett?"

Denzil replied, in a scarcely audible voice, "Aye, I looked around. I didn't think much to it. She'd often get up and poke around after lock-up."

"You never heard her threaten to take her life?"

"Take her life?" He seemed outraged. "Lord no, sir, she never once said anything o' that sort." And then, "She never said much about anything save the work on the farm. Not lately, that is."

She glanced across at Adam, awaiting his turn to enter

the box, and now wedged between Robert and George, legs crossed, arms tidily folded. He gave no sign that Denzil was on dangerous ground and unlike herself, was clearly indifferent to the glances of jurymen and those standing at the back of the hall although he must have known almost everyone of them by name. In a curious way, even when sitting there, he dominated the proceedings, much as he had dominated her life for more than fifty years. He had a presence everyone else lacked and she wondered if he had always had it, even as a boy, or whether it was something that had settled upon him about the time he made history in the Crimea and India shortly before he met her, and later developed to a degree that empowered him to set all those wheels in motion across the country.

Surprisingly, to her at least, George was called, and she compared father and son, seeing them alike and yet curiously unlike, for George, although in full command of himself, lacked his father's air of authority, his ease of manner and natural amiability showing through even here. The evidence he gave was brief. He told of bringing news of her son's death to his sister in December and the manner in which she had received it but no one could have guessed, from his reasoned tone and calm expression, that he had come within an ace of violent death himself on that occasion and the reflection turned Henrietta's thoughts to the hatred Stella must have felt for him at that moment. *Was* she mad? Were they all hard at work trying to conceal the fact and, if so, was such deception wrong under the circumstances? Perhaps so. The solemnity of the proceedings, here in this stuffy parish hall, had made its impact on her and the flutter of uncertainty about the propriety of their concerted suppression of the facts inclined her to glance back at Adam as though for reassurance. His expression was as unchanged as his posture. He might have been listening to an Act of Parliament being read aloud, or a prose recital at one of her winter soirées, so that she thought, chillingly: 'Would he look like that if they were discussing my death?' and she bowed her head for, at that moment, he seemed as remote as the God she had tried to approach in her prayers just lately.

She caught the last few words of George's evidence, something about the big fire at the yard at that time, and saw him leave the stand, to be replaced by his nephew Robert. Robert, poor lad, was clearly under strain and she knew why. He was a truthful, literal soul and it was upon him that the burden of sworn fiction would lie most heavily. Even the voicing of a half-truth, if that curious story about the fence and the bonfire qualified as such, would not come easily to him.

They asked him the same question as they had asked his father, had his mother ever threatened to take her own life and he answered in the negative emphatically and with a certain defiance. He then told of his search of the buildings and assumption, planted by a footprint, that his mother had gone down to the bridge, some little distance from the farm. Could he give any reason why a woman haunted by a fear of fire should have gone in that direction? She saw Adam's head come up sharply as he turned his dour gaze on his grandson; Robert said, carefully, "Yes, sir, there was a reason, to my mind at least. We had been burning straw on the far bank near an old hen-house. Maybe the wind had whipped up the bonfire."

It made a disproportionate impact, producing a low sustained buzz from the body of the court and she saw, out of the corner of her eye, Adam's features relax to resume their former impassivity. She saw the coroner's next question as the crux of the whole enquiry. The constable, in earlier evidence, had mentioned a loose rail in the bridge. Was the witness aware of such a rail and if so when? She could sense the expectancy of everyone present to his answer and at length it came, as if dragged from him. "One of my men pointed it out to me that same morning. I hadn't noticed it before. The rail was four to five years old and the bridge often gets flooded. Maybe the nails holding it to the upright were rusted."

"Thank you, Mr. Fawcett. Call Adam Swann."

It seemed so silly, so ritualistic to say that, with Adam no more than five yards away, and a surge of impatience passed through her. Let Stella be buried, quickly and decently, like everybody else who died. What business was it of strangers or acquaintances to pursue enquiries into her state of mind, her obsession, her very movements up to the moment of her death? But the moment passed as Adam straightened himself and clumped up to the stand, his artificial leg echoing on the bare boards and, now elevated some two feet above floor level, his dominance was even more profound so that she saw him as a kind of Moses passing judgment on Aaron's calf-worshippers. It comforted her enormously just to contemplate him, a man older in years than anyone in the court but secure, utterly so, in his authority, and replying to polite questions in a way that implied they were not merely irrelevant but vaguely impudent.

"You are the father of the deceased?"

"I am."

"You were leading the party that recovered her body from the river?"

"I was."

"You visited the farm early on the day of her death?"

"I did."

His steadiness affected even the coroner. "Er . . . could you tell the court anything you noticed on that occasion relative to this enquiry?"

"I noticed a loose rail on the parapet of the footbridge. One end was secure, the furthermost end. The near end was loose. Slight pressure on it produced a gap measuring about a foot. It was at a point over the deepest section of the stream."

There was no hint of irresolution here. He was stating plain, incontrovertible fact and she knew they would believe him in every particular. It was impossible not to believe him. It was as though he was telling an assembly of attentive children that the world was round, that the sun rose in the east and set in the west, that two and two made four and it was profitless to imply that it could ever be otherwise.

"You drew the attention of others to that rail?"

"I did. But before that I crossed over and went down to the half-dismantled hen-house mentioned by the previous witnesses. There was a smouldering bonfire of damp straw. No flame, just smoke."

"Thank you, Mr. Swann. As regards finding the deceased – I am sorry to have to distress you – but it is necessary I establish precisely where and how the body of the deceased was recovered."

"You cannot help distressing me. In company with my groom and gardener I recovered my daughter's body from a pool formed by flotsam just above the ox-bow, about a mile below 'Tryst'. It was on my land. We brought her to the bank and I waited while my employees went back to the house for a vehicle. It was about three p.m. on the same day."

"Thank you, Mr. Swann. I don't think it necessary to ask you any further questions. Neither, I think, will it be necessary to call further witnesses."

He stepped down, still impassive, still holding himself erect, and resumed his seat between son and grandson. There was a moment's silence, broken only by the soft riffle of the coroner's papers and an apologetic clearing of throats. He said, at length, "The facts in this tragic case would seem to be clear. This unfortunate woman, not in the best of health, and dogged, it seems, by a fear of fire, left her bed in the small hours of March the twenty-first and seemingly began to cross the footbridge between Dewponds Farm and her husband's land on the west bank. What happened precisely cannot be known but the existence of a loose handrail, and a smouldering bonfire beyond, would seem consistent with the fact that she was on her way to investigate and slipped or fell into the river. If the jury wishes to retire to consider the facts as given by witnesses they may do so now."

Abel Treloar, a carpenter at Twyforde, rose slowly from his seat at the central table. "We don't wish to retire, sir." He paused, momentarily and glanced round at his silent colleagues. Nobody spoke. Nobody met his gaze. "We find that the poor lady died as a result of an unfortunate accident, sir."

He sat down very abruptly after two brief nods from the coroner and Henrietta could find it in her to be sorry for him. She had known Abel since his apprenticeship days and both he and his late father had often been to 'Tryst' to do patching. Almost surely he recalled Stella as a toddler and even then he would have addressed her as 'miss' or 'missie'. It would have been very surprising, she thought, if he had prolonged his speech, or had come to any other conclusion, and it occurred to her that Adam, the strategist, had taken his presence as foreman, or somebody very like him, into his calculations. She heard the coroner say, in the same subdued voice, "Then I find the deceased died from drowning as the result of an accidental fall into the water in the early hours of March the twenty-first, and return a verdict, based on the evidence that has been put to me, of 'Accidental death'. It only remains for me to express my deepest sympathy with the bereaved family in these tragic and entirely unforeseen circumstances . . ."

It was over and she watched Adam rise stiffly to his feet, his left hand massaging that part of his thigh where the straps of his harness chafed the flesh. It was a very familiar gesture, dating back to the day he had been restored to her, miraculously or so it still seemed, after that shambles at Staplehurst. It served to banish the curious sense of his remoteness and impersonality that had persisted through the enquiry. He came over to her and said, in a low voice, "Let's go home, Hetty. George is bringing the motor round," and took her arm. She was surprised then to feel his fingers trembling and for some reason the tremulous touch reminded her of Denzil standing a few yards away, listening to the halting condolences of Abel Treloar and some of the other jurymen. She said, suddenly, "We must take Denzil back to 'Tryst'. I want him near us until after the funeral, Adam," and he said, "As you please," and beckoned to his son-in-law. She thought, 'It hasn't been as easy for him as I imagined. It only looked that way, so that maybe, in the days ahead, he'll need to lean on me a little.'

7

Interception

I T WAS BETTER, FAR BETTER THAN HENRIETTA HAD hoped when she made her resolve at the termination of the inquest.

After the funeral he seemed to her, although not to others less close to him, to sag. It was then that she found herself able, in some small degree, to feed back to him a little of the fortitude they had borrowed from him after they came to her with news of a drowned daughter.

There was no possibility of restricting the funeral to a private ceremony, of the kind that had been achieved when Romayne was buried here three years ago, for here was a local tragedy and Stella, child, girl and farmwife, had been very well known in the rural community. Her funeral would have attracted a large assembly of un-official mourners had she died a natural death so that no one was surprised to find the little church full to over-flowing.

They followed, these unofficial ones, at a discreet dis-tance, when the cortège procession wound its way past the yews to the extreme south-east corner of the churchyard which the Swann clan had appropriated to itself. Hen-rietta, glancing aside from the committal, sensed their silent sympathy and realised a good deal of it was for the Fawcetts, who had farmed here for centuries. The Swanns had been here a mere fifty-two years, reckoned almost nothing in the mind of a rooted rural community. She thought, 'I wonder if any of them remember the circumstances of her birth, the first evening her father and I set eyes on "Tryst"? For had it not been for that I doubt if we would have ever bought a place so far from that slum of his beside the Thames . . .' But then her mind, seeking a less melancholy pivot, returned to a warm evening in April, 1860, when a carriage horse called Dancer ran away with their carriage and upset them against the stone pillars of the drive, thereby bringing on her labour.

She was able to draw some small comfort from the solidarity of the Swann clan. All save Alex and his wife were present, Lydia having wired to say he was on active duty in the far west of Ireland and found it impossible to get leave of absence and travel over in time. But Joanna had come, bless her, although such a poor sailor, apologising for Clinton's absence. One of the younger children had been down with scarlet fever, she said, and Clint was due, that same day, to fetch her home from the isolation hospital. She caught Joanna looking intently at her father as the sexton's team withdrew the bands from the grave and thought, 'She's probably thinking this will knock years off his life but she doesn't really know him. None of them do, save me. Not even George.' It was later that week, when Adam, seeking consolation in the spring glory of his flowering shrubs, was away from the house, that she had occasion to put a rather different interpretation on Joanna's searching scrutiny of him at the graveside.

Joanna had been prevailed upon to stay over for a few days after news came that her daughter Mary was convalescing satisfactorily. It was seldom now that 'Tryst' saw much of her or her younger sister, Helen. Both, it seemed, were fully occupied with their social life in and around the Irish capital and the journey, by sea and land, was long and tedious. She looked well enough, Henrietta thought, but preoccupied for Joanna, least complicated of the brood, so that she was not much surprised when Jo, having established that Adam was clear of the house, said,

"Could we have a chat, Mother? About something . . . well, bothersome. I'd appreciate your advice. Before I approach Papa, that is."

Henrietta said, guardedly, "How bothersome?"

"Bothersome enough. I badly need advice."

"About Clinton?"

"No, nothing to do with Clint this time." A fleeting smile lit up her plump, pretty face for an instant so that Henrietta guessed her daughter was remembering another time, twenty-three years behind them now, when she had sought, willy-nilly, counsel from her mother concerning her pregnancy before the stage-managed elopement that had earned Clinton his family nickname. "It's about Helen."

"She's well . . . happy?"

"She's well. I never saw her looking better in my life. Happy? I couldn't say really, although she must be to go to the lengths she did to look after that rascal she married."

"Just what do you mean by that, Jo? I thought you and Rory got along very well."

"We did. I always thought him a bit extravagant but most of the Irish are. And he certainly transformed Helen after her terrible time in China. But now – well, I daresay you know how things are in Ireland since they passed the Home Rule Bill."

She didn't know, not really. Politics had never interested her and just lately, with blows raining down on them from all directions, she had not been disposed to give a rap for Irish squabbles. They were not new to anyone of her generation. All her life Ireland had been in a turmoil over one thing or another. She said, "What leisure have I had just lately to worry about Ireland's troubles? Haven't I enough of my own to go on with?"

Joanna looked uncomfortable and said, "Oh, well, I'll not worry you. I'll have a word with Papa before I go back."

"You'll do no such thing, or not if it's something likely

to upset him. Good heavens, child, he's had his fill of worry recently."

"Yes," Joanna said, knitting her brows, "I see that well enough. But this . . . well, I'm not sure it should wait. He might even want to know."

"Let me be the judge of that."

Joanna seemed to weigh this in her mind before she said, reluctantly, "Very well, I will, providing you'll give me your solemn word to tell nobody but him, no matter what. Will you give me that promise?" She smiled again, adding gently, "You aren't all that good at keeping secrets, Mother."

"I can keep certain secrets," Henrietta said, grimly, and led the way into her sewing-room, carefully shutting the door.

*   *   *

It was Mary's restlessness that accounted for Joanna's inability to drop off to sleep that particular night. The doctor had not been summoned then and the girl's flushed face and temperature had been put down to a feverish cold, so that Joanna, finding at one o'clock in the morning that sleep was likely to evade her, slipped out of bed and stole along the corridor past Alex's room to take another look at her daughter before going downstairs and brewing herself some tea.

There was no other reason for her to be abroad for she was usually an excellent sleeper and the evening, apart from some slight anxiety regarding her youngest child, had been a pleasantly convivial one. Both Alex and Helen were guests in the house and it was some time now since she had had such an opportunity for a family gossip. She saw Helen frequently, whenever her sister drove into the city, sometimes with Rory, now that he had lost his parliamentary seat, but more often with her maid in order to do some shopping. Alex, however, was a much rarer visitor and the day she heard he was in Belfast she telephoned the mess, suggesting he spent the weekend with them. He agreed readily, promising to be there on Friday evening and stay until Sunday. It happened their conversation coincided with one of Helen's half-day visits to Dublin and Joanna, meeting her for an hour, and telling her that Alex was due down for the weekend, suggested that she and Rory might like to come over again on the Saturday for lunch. She was surprised when Helen looked doubtful and said, "I'd like to, for I haven't seen Alex in a long time. But I should have to consult Rory first."

"About having lunch here? With your own brother?"

"Yes. Rory's funny that way. Maybe he has guests and he hates to entertain in my absence. Suppose I telephone tonight and let you know?" and that was how it was left.

Helen rang through late that same evening, just as they were going up to bed, saying that she would not only like to come to lunch but asking to stay over for the night if that was convenient. Rory, it seemed, was due to speak at a political meeting in Tipperary and would be away from home. She added, after a long pause, "Will Lydia be with Alex?"

Joanna told her not. Lydia accompanied Alex on all his longer tours abroad but had not come to Ireland for Alex, she gathered, was not here on a regular tour of duty but on some special assignment to do with his territorials. "He'll only be in Ireland about three weeks," she added. "Then he goes back to London to prepare for another tour in Malta or Cyprus, I forget which . . . But I'm sure he'll be pleased to see you. It's a pity Rory can't join us."

It was not, she reflected, all that regrettable. On the few occasions they had met, she noticed that Rory Clarke, who came as close to embodying the traditional elements of the stage Irishman as anyone she knew, and Colonel Swann, the dedicated, humourless professional soldier, had very little in common, either as relatives or acquaintances. For herself she was sorry Lydia would not be present, for Lydia had a mellowing effect upon stuffy old

Alex but it would be pleasant, she thought, for the three of them and Clinton to have a cosy little dinner party at home, with the odd man out in Tipperary. She put Alex in the best guest-room and Helen in the old nursery on the other side of the house, a comfortable enough billet for the one night, and Helen duly arrived by train about midday on Saturday and was met by the family Belsize and driven back to the house for luncheon.

The two sisters and brother had little in common beyond memories of 'Tryst', in the days before either of the girls were married. Alex was six years Joanna's senior and nine years older than Helen, and they had seen very little of him in their girlhood, when he was away campaigning in various parts of Africa and India. Sometimes he had been absent for years at a stretch.

Alex seemed to get along very well with Clinton, however, and the two men talked animatedly over the political aspects of impending Home Rule, with particular regard as to how it was likely to be received in Ulster. Joanna would have thought this political talk would have bored Helen but this was far from being so, indeed, Helen seemed better informed on the subject than either of them. She remarked also a subtle change in her sister of late, wondering why it had escaped her during recent meetings. She was tense and animated and talked incessantly of Ireland's prospects of settling down once Home Rule, now in the process of becoming law, was a fact, so that Joanna thought, ruefully, 'Time was when she was only interested in clothes, bicycling, tennis and beaux, but some of Rowley's terrible earnestness must have rubbed off on her after all. She's beginning to sound like a regular bluestocking . . .' And then, watching her sister closely, 'One thing is for sure – she doesn't know that husband of hers, despite all the billing and cooing they do whenever I see them together. She obviously takes his political claptrap seriously. It sounds as if they talk Irish politics in bed . . ' But then, being Joanna, she chided herself for uncharitable thoughts, for the truth was that Rory

Clarke had undoubtedly been the saving of Helen a few years back.

All the same, in view of the way Irish politics dominated the occasion, and the time Alex took answering the complicated questions Helen put to him, it proved a dull weekend for her as hostess, particularly as Mary, her youngest, had come home from school complaining of a headache, and had been hustled to bed with a temperature before dinner.

They all went upstairs at about half-past eleven and Clint, who had drunk more than his nightly quota of port, Madeira and brandy, was snoring in a matter of minutes. Joanna heard the clock at the far end of the crescent strike midnight, then all the quarters through to one-fifteen before she got up without disturbing him, slipped into a gown, and went along the corridor to look in on Mary.

Her eleven-year-old was asleep but very flushed, she thought, telling herself she must call Doctor Connolly in first thing in the morning and leave Clint to drive Helen and Alex to the station to catch their trains.

She had moved over to the window with the object of raising the sash an inch or two, when her attention was caught by a motionless vehicle parked almost opposite, close against the gardens. There was no cab rank there and at first she thought it must be a private conveyance awaiting a passenger higher up the crescent. But then, as she turned away, a vague familiarity with this particular cab made her take a closer look.

It was drawn by two horses, the hindquarters of which were revealed in the circle of light thrown by the street lamp but the cab itself was in shadow. She thought, wonderingly, 'But it can't be! For what on earth would Rory's fancy equipage be doing out there at one-thirty in the morning? If Rory had driven it there he would have knocked, and if he hadn't why had Helen come to Dublin by train, when the coachman could have driven her here as usual?'

Without precisely knowing why the very presence of the motionless vehicle disturbed her, the more so as there did not appear to be a driver in attendance and the fact that the curtains of the interior were closely drawn. It almost surely *was* Rory's cab, for she had always thought of it as one of her brother-in-law's stage properties, a low-slung, extremely elegant little carriage, shaped like a shell, with gilt mountings now reflecting gleams of lamplight. It was usually drawn by a pair of matched bays, fast-movers but superbly trained by Rory himself. The horses, unfortunately, were in so much shadow that she could not be absolutely sure, but if Rory's cab had been copied by one of the fashionable Dubliners it was curious that the owner should station it almost opposite the house in the middle of the night.

She stood there a moment longer, coming to no conclusion, but then her ear detected the scrape of a foot on the back stairs, hard left of her daughter's room, and she moved over to the door, watching through a chink the section of corridor opposite the all-night gas jet that illuminated this side of the first storey. If it was not one of the servants she could only suppose the person climbing the stairs, and very cautiously by the sound of it, could only be Rory, although how he had gained entry into the house without knocking she could not imagine.

It was not Rory's shadowy figure that came into view, however, but Helen's, moving a step at a time and without benefit of candle, and Joanna was so surprised that she came close to hailing her but checked herself. She followed her out, however, as soon as Helen had passed beyond the gas jet and watched her progress as far as the next circle of light thrown by the outside lamp through the landing window opposite the guest-room occupied by Alex. And here, to Joanna's increased bewilderment, Helen stopped, hand on the door-knob, head on one side as though listening intently

It flashed through Joanna's mind that her sister was sleep-walking and the memory returned to her of a woman teetering on the edge of nervous collapse, whom she had encouraged to climb into bed with Clint when they were at 'Tryst' shortly after Helen's return from Peking. And yet, there was no real indication of sleep-walking here. Indeed, her sister's carriage and movements were those of a person thoroughly alerted to her surroundings. And then, while Joanna still watched, Helen turned the knob and slipped inside, leaving Alex's door ajar.

She was not out of sight for more than twenty seconds, hardly time enough for Joanna to come to terms with the fact that she was not dreaming herself, and when she emerged, recrossing the shaft of light adjoining the main landing, Joanna saw that she was holding something flat and bulky close against her breast.

The strangeness of what she had witnessed, a sister prowling about the house like a burglar, seemingly for the purpose of purloining her brother's luggage, did not register on Joanna at first. She told herself, standing there with one hand gripping the edge of the door, that there had to be some innocent explanation of what she had seen and again the thought that Helen was acting under some mysterious pressure returned so that she thought, desperately, 'I can't challenge her here, right outside Alex's door, and within earshot of Mary . . . she might scream or struggle and that would rouse the servants as well as Alex and the child . . . And yet, I can't leave it there, without finding what she's taken from Alex's room and why . . .' But then Helen herself decided her next move by passing round the wide curve of the stairhead to descend by the main staircase and this served to increase the mystery, for her own quarters, in the old nursery, lay in the east wing of the house approached by the corridor matching this one. Whatever purpose Helen had in mind it was clearly not to take her spoil back to her own room and realising this her sister's eccentric behaviour made a connection with the presence of that motionless cabriolet outside.

She knew then, with a small spurt of relief arising from decision, precisely what she must do. If Helen had some notion of leaving the house, and passing whatever she had stolen to the driver of that cab in the crescent, she must be headed off and this was still possible, providing she moved quickly and quietly. The back stairs led directly to the kitchen quarters at the rear of the house and these were partly on ground-floor level occupying a semi-basement area, with one door opening on the tradesmen's alleyway and another into the enclosed yard bounded by high brick walls. Access to this part of the house – already, or so it would appear – visited by Helen that night, was direct by the back stairs but indirect by the front hall to which Helen was now descending. Moving quickly Joanna passed into the corridor and hurried down the stairs as far as the green baize doors, double doors here to prevent cooking smells rising to the bedrooms. She passed one and put her hand on the other, holding it open an inch or so, to give her a clear view of the kitchen.

She was just in time. Steps, less cautious now, approached from the servery and the door opposite opened, revealing Helen holding what looked like a small leather portmanteau fastened with a brass lock in addition to straps. There was a light in the kitchen and she could see her clearly. In the old days Joanna had always been known as 'the pretty one' for Helen's complexion was sallow, and her eyes were deepset, emphasising high cheekbones, but seeing her now, with her dark hair streaming, and a flush of excitement on her cheeks, she looked, Joanna thought, beautiful. She stood framed in the aperture for a moment before gliding into the room, putting the case on the scrubbed table and emitting a kind of sigh that enlarged itself into a startled gasp as Joanna flung open the second door and stepped through it.

For a moment they stood regarding one another and then Helen's expression crumpled so that she suddenly looked like a child, caught in an act of mischief. "You've been following me?"

"Why not? This is my house and I've a right to know what you're about taking things from Alex's room," and she laid a hand on the case, anticipating Helen's swift movement towards it. There was a silence. She could see her sister's breast heaving under her ruffled nightgown and loosely-tied robe. Helen said, slumping down in a chair, "What's the use? How could you possibly understand?"

"I understood last time."

"That was different."

"And this, whatever it is, concerns Rory Clarke, and all those fancy ruffians he consorts with? Well, I realised you were committed to him, but not to this extent, not to the extent of raiding your brother's room in the middle of the night. It *is* Rory's cabriolet outside? And he's waiting, waiting for you to hand him this, whatever it is."

"He doesn't intend stealing it. We aren't pickpockets."

"Great God!" Joanna burst out, "how can you do this? Creeping about the house and taking things from the luggage of a guest in someone else's home? What on earth has Rory done to you to make you so much as think of behaving in this way? Keep it, copy it or look at it, what does it matter in Heaven's name?"

"As I say, you know nothing about these things. Nobody English does, not even people like Clint, who have lived and worked here all this time."

"You're English, aren't you?"

"Not any longer."

Joanna sat down facing her. She kept both her hands on the case and noticed that they were trembling. "Then tell me. Tell me if you can. What's in this case that makes a thief out of you?"

Helen looked across at her, very levelly. "A list of the military depots he's visiting, with inventories of the arms and ammunition held in each of them. I said I'd get it for Rory to look at, no more than that I swear. Then I was to return it and Alex wouldn't have known a thing about it. No one could have held him responsible for the information in there getting to us for no one would have known how we came by it."

"'Us'! 'We'! You talk as if you were fighting some kind of war and Alex was the enemy."

"We are fighting a war, or will be the moment the British implement the Home Rule Bill. Doesn't it mean anything at all to you that those people up north are buying guns from Germany and drilling openly in the streets? With encouragement from Parliament and the army? Haven't the Irish the right to know what's going on, when more than half the senior officers at the Curragh sympathise with the Protestants in Ulster and won't even try and stop them when they start a civil war?"

"No, it doesn't matter to me. All I know is I can't ever ask you into my house again. That matters terribly, to me if not to you!" She took a deep breath. The kitchen was large but it felt unbearably close tonight. "I saw you on the back stairs before you went to Alex's room. That means you were down here earlier so you'd best tell me why, before I rouse Alex and Clint. And I'll do that I swear, unless you tell me exactly what you had in mind. Well?"

"Don't do that, Jo."

"You're saying Rory and his friends are prepared to do violence to get at these papers?"

"I'm not saying anything of the kind. All I want you to understand is *why* I took it, what it could mean in terms of other people's blood. I did come downstairs earlier, to unbolt the back door for Rory won't stir from the cab until I give the signal."

"What signal?"

"What does it matter what signal? I can't give it now. You've spoiled everything by interfering."

"*Interfering?* Wouldn't anyone in my position interfere in these circumstances?"

She was some time answering. Finally she said, in a low voice, "Yes, I suppose they would, Jo. In your circumstances, that is." She turned away, her expression infinitely troubled. "You've always been good to me. I hate hurting you, and I realise how it must look to you but . . . this . . . it means everything to me, just everything, you understand?"

"No, I don't, Helen. You tell me if you can."

"It proves I'm *with* them, don't you see? It would make all the difference to my life. And nobody need ever know. Alex is asleep and I could give you my word of honour that case will be back in his room in less than an hour."

Joanna jumped up, tucking the case firmly under her arm. "It'll be back in five minutes. And no one, least of all Rory, is coming into this house to pry. I'll make sure of that," and she went into the scullery and reshot the top and bottom bolts on the door leading to the alley. "Now you can make whatever signals you please, for I shan't leave you until you're dressed, packed and out of the house."

"You won't do this one thing for me?"

"Of course I won't! Not for your sake, for Rory's or for the king of the Cannibal Islands!" She glanced up at the kitchen clock, noting it wanted a couple of minutes to two. "I'll give you fifteen minutes to leave. After that, if you haven't gone, I'll wake Alex and tell him what you've done and why. I'm not leaving you down here either, to open that door again and use my kitchen as . . . as a plotters' den. Get up and get dressed. I mean to see you upstairs and out of the house."

They went through the hall and up the main staircase, turning down the corridor to the old nursery. She stood wordlessly by the door and watched Helen dress and it was as if a terrible weight was pressing on her breast. In ten minutes they were back in the hall and she pulled the lobby curtains aside and looked out. The cab was still there. She said, "Draw the bolt and turn the key. You can let yourself out," and at that Helen turned and she was surprised, and a little startled, to see tears streaming down her face.

"We've been close a long time, Jo."

"All our lives. You think this is easy for me?"

"No, no, it can't be, but you still don't understand. Rory's committee, especially since he lost his seat and joined the staff . . . well . . . they didn't trust him before. They don't trust any of Redmond's men. But they trust him now. Him but not me. Because I'm English."

"Dear God, it can't be all that important, Helen! It just can't!"

"To stand well with Sinn Fein? No, that isn't important. Not on its own it isn't. But can't you understand, Jo, it's all I've got to offer Rory. I'm years older than him, and I've never had your looks. And I can't give him children. It's too late for that."

She had a glimpse then of the hidden pressures at work in the relationship of this ill-matched pair; one a man consumed by his own conceit, his mind lost in the fog of Celtic legend and the real and fancied injustices practised upon these people, the other a woman whose entire being was centred on a younger man's flattery and probably unable to think straight once he laid hands upon her.

She said, "I understand in a way but it doesn't make any difference, Helen. You must see that, besotted as you are with that man. From here on we've no choice, have we? You go your way, I'll go mine," and she moved past her to withdraw the bolts of the front door. And then, as the night air struck chill on her, she remembered something else that might be important.

"I'm returning that case. You'll have to tell me where it was in Alex's room. It wouldn't do for him to find it had been moved in the night."

"You won't tell him then?"

"I don't know. It's something I'll have to think about."

"It was on his chair. He isn't very careful for a man with his responsibilities."

Was it the vaguest of threats? Or a last-minute warning? Did it mean that, from here on, Alex was a marked man as long as he moved unescorted about Ireland? Joanna didn't know. Suddenly she was too tired and too depressed to think about it. Instead she watched her sister descend the steps and stand hesitating under the street lamp. Opposite the cab door opened and somebody got out but she did not wait to identify him.

2

Back at 'Tryst', Henrietta's first reaction was of intense relief that she had prevailed upon Joanna to tell her, without piling this additional load on Adam's shoulders. It was enough, as she had found to her cost of late, to put a bold face on one's own troubles without meddling in the affairs of factions, sects and nations. Her spirits lifted for she recognised, in her interception of Joanna's tale of woe, an opportunity of service, a way leading back to the summit she had occupied in her youth when, by common consent, Adam had confined himself to his business and she to hers, that of steering the family through the crosscurrents of the years.

She said, unequivocally, "Don't mention a word of this to your father. You'll not so much as hint at it, is that clear?"

Joanna, looking pained and puzzled, said, "But surely I have to, don't I? I mean, suppose Helen or Rory come here on a visit? And suppose that visit coincides with one from Alex and Lydia?"

"I'll deal with that if it arises but I'll not have your father worried, you understand? It was right of you to tell me, and right of you to act as you did. But this is as far as it goes, do you hear?"

"And Alex?"

"There's no point in saying anything to him either. You know that in your heart, Jo."

She paused, recalling an earlier family quarrel that had never really healed, one between Alex and Giles in connection with that awful war, and the misery that had emerged from it for Hugo. What would be served by widening the family breach to include Alex and his sister,

315

who were unlikely to meet again for years? Ireland, confound it, could look to itself. For her part, having lost a grandson, a daughter-in-law and a daughter in swift succession, she was concerned with what remained. Nothing else mattered. She said, "Listen Jo, Alex and Lydia are sailing for India in a week or two. I was sorry when I heard but I'm right glad now. Let it pass. Leave it where it is." And then, dejectedly, "You and Helen – I suppose you'll keep yourselves to yourselves from now on?"

"How else could it be?"

"No other way. But it's sad just the same. And very stupid, too, if you think about it. Meddling in men's affairs is always dangerous. What did it bring Romayne but a messy death? What purpose does it serve any of us in the end?" She mused a moment, aware that Joanna was watching her intently. "A woman should have more than enough to absorb her, especially if she has children to rear."

"Helen has no children."

"No, and more's the pity, for if she had she wouldn't have made such a fool of herself. Think yourself fortunate, Jo. Go back to yours and forget this happened. That's my advice, and that's what I want for all of us."

"Is that all you have to say, Mama?"

"Almost all." She got up and went over to the fireplace, lifting a photograph framed in silver from its pride of place above the hearth. Adam wasn't overfond of a display of family photographs – 'sentimental clutter' he called them, much preferring to decorate his walls with oils and water-colours acquired in his forays up and down the country, some of them worth a penny or two, or so he claimed. She took his word for it, but this group photograph meant a lot to her. It was a silver wedding photograph, taken on the lawn in September, 1883, and they were all there, every last one of them, together with the three senior in-laws, Denzil, Lydia and Gisela, and the first brace of grandchildren, Robert and Martin Fawcett. Sixteen all told, less than half the Swann muster today.

She studied the group, forgetting Joanna was still there. Jo and Helen were sitting crosslegged in the foreground, sixteen and thirteen respectively and very conscious, judging by the exceptional solemnity of their expression, of the great occasion. She said, passing the picture to her daughter, "It doesn't seem long ago, does it? But three of that group are dead, and now Helen is dead to you. That makes four. Providing you wish it so, that is."

"Are you really saying I should pretend to myself it never happened?"

"I don't know. It's for you to decide. You and Helen, as you get older, and fewer of you are left who remember how it was at 'Tryst' when this picture was taken. I can't tell either of you what to do or what not to do at your age, with homes and husbands of your own. Apart from sparing your father more worry, that is, and I'm in no doubt about that. But I can tell you something I've learned here in all these years. The family is the only thing worth a row of beans in the end and that's about the only thing in life I learned in advance of your father. I'll tell you something else. When I was a girl, I thought the only sons worth having were soldiers. I don't think so any more. No woman does once she's gone to the trouble of bearing children, and, what's a great deal more tiresome, raising them until they can stand on their own feet. You think hard about that. Helen and you were as good as twins once. Well, I'd value that high above a piece of foolishness hatched up by men, for men never grow up anyway, or not in the way women do." She took the photograph back and rehung it, glancing as she did at the mantelshelf clock. "Go and find your father. Tell him luncheon will be ready in about twenty minutes. He has to be coaxed to eat just now."

* * *

As soon as Joanna had left she went over to her bureau beside the window, taking out her address book and leafing through it until she came to the 'C's. She could rarely remember these outlandish Irish addresses and even when she did she couldn't spell them without a copy. When she came on Helen's address she put a marker in the book and sat thinking, grateful for a brief interval of solitude. But presently, having watched Joanna pass beyond the lilac clump and cross the area of lawn where it sloped down to the lake, she took up her pen and began to write, continuing to do so until she had filled one sheet and half another.

The words came easily, for somehow the act of writing restored to her some measure of the authority she had once wielded but had lost since the brood had grown up and gone about their own affairs.

My dear Helen,

Thank you for your letter about Stella and for the lovely wreath that arrived in time. We did not expect you to travel over at such short notice and by now you will have received the newspaper I sent, explaining everything, or everything that matters.

You might like to know your father was wonderful throughout it all. Without him I can't imagine how Denzil and I would have managed, but he feels it as much as either of us, and so does George, who regards himself as responsible for what happened. But this letter isn't about Stella. What happened to her, all the sadness and waste of it, is behind us now and can't be altered, one way or the other. That doesn't apply to you and Jo, however, and I've told her so a moment since, together with advice – that I mean to see she takes – to never breathe a word of it to her father or Alex. That way, given time, you can both pretend it didn't happen. You can do that with most things if you've a mind to, for I have and still do where there's no other way out. And there isn't for you and Jo, or not as I see it. But even supposing either or both of you can't or won't, this is to say that *I* mean to, because that way, if you ever want to come back here, with or without Rory, there's nothing to stop you, and why should there be? This is still home for all of you and as long as your father and I are alive I mean it to stay so.

She signed and sealed it and put it in her tray among a dozen others, each acknowledging wreaths and messages of sympathy. It was the only letter there, she reflected, that really said anything.

To Adam and Joanna, slowly climbing the drive in sunshine that was exceptionally strong for the time of the year, the luncheon summons seemed very sonorous, almost like a judgment.

8

As From a Pinnacle

IN THE TWO YEARS LEFT OF THE OLD WORLD, AND
what some (half-forgetting that Teddy had been replaced
by the blameless George) would call 'The Edwardian
Afternoon', Adam watched as from a pinnacle, armoured
against the byblows of fate and able, to some extent, to
disassociate himself from all but the process of growing
old and that detached curiosity about men and their
affairs that had made him the oracle others thought
him.

He was like a veteran general, with countless battles
behind him, who was yet peripherally caught up in the
current war and in receipt, from time to time, of scribbled
despatches brought him from afar. And having, as it
were, studied their content he would listen gravely, or
sympathetically, or half-humorously, to what the messen-
gers had to say and then prophesy, so that they went away
stimulated, or sobered, or mildly fortified by his wisdom.

In the late spring, summer and early autumn months
he could usually be found out of doors, pottering about
his Hermitage museum, or seated on a log in one of the
patches of wild wood that varied the pattern of his planted
areas, or on one of the stone seats or balustrades that em-
bellished his demesne. But when the rains came and the
winds went whooping over the Weald, he retired to his
study fireside, browsing among his books.

He was here, one day, when Deborah called for consolation as regards her old and trusted mentor, W. T. Stead, lost on the *Titanic* and last seen, so survivors said, absorbed in a book as the great liner, symbol of all the new technologies, poised for her final plunge, making nonsense of the claims that she was unsinkable.

"Her sinking seems to me symbolic of all I've observed over the last few years," he said, shaking his head. "Of my generation, too, I suppose, tho' to a lesser extent. For my lot were improvisers, whereas those who came after us – like George – relied on sums worked out in the office instead of in the market-place. Sad that Stead had to be sacrificed to their pride, however. The old warrior deserved better. Reading a book, you say? Well, that was in character, I suppose. He had a high opinion of you once. What did he think about you and the suffragettes?"

Deborah replied that he didn't really approve, for Stead's violence was always confined to words and edited words at that. "But he was a bonnie fighter," she added, "and I'll always remember him as that."

"Me too." And there returned to him, over an interval of thirty years, the memory of a distraught man awaiting him in his turret at the time of the *Pall Mall Gazette*'s strident campaign on behalf of child prostitutes, served up to satyrs for five pounds a hymen, a man he had been ultimately to champion.

"Well," he said, by way of valediction, "Stead won most of his battles, so maybe the pen does have the edge on the sword."

She knew then that he was debating with himself the old imponderable. Did the end ever justify the means? Or did the end get grotesquely distorted by the means, in their case assaults on the person of the Prime Minister, on the Lossiemouth golf links, the slashing of the Rokeby Venus in the National Gallery, a bomb in the house of the Chancellor of the Exchequer, another against the walls of Holloway Prison and the militants' Calvary. She had pondered this herself many times, waiting, pinched with hunger, to be released under the Cat and Mouse Act but had never arrived at any irrevocable decision. Yet she knew that he had and tried to coax it from him.

"You're wavering, Uncle Adam. You've probably decided we're our own worst enemies."

"No, no, not that, for no one can say you didn't give the pen a fair trial," he replied, smiling. "Why, I was reading your pamphlets forty years ago. Aye, and averting my eyes from the first knickerbocker suit too! It's just that sometimes I wonder if Britain is the best place for you. In France you would have been home and dry long ago, riot being the staple diet over there."

"But that isn't why they hate us, is it?"

"No, it isn't," and his eyes twinkled for a moment.

"Why then?"

"Because you deny what's meat and drink to the politician. Patronage. He can't get along without that. But tell your friends not to despair, my dear. The moment the Government of the day finds it convenient to pat your heads instead of kicking your backsides, you'll get your vote."

He had one of his rare visions then, of a time when every pair of hands, white and gloved, red and calloused, would be needed at the pumps, and out of it, no doubt (providing the ship of state did not follow the *Titanic*), might come universal suffrage, so effortlessly perhaps that even Mrs. Pankhurst would be caught on the hop. But he said nothing of this to her, for he knew that she, and that clever husband of hers, and George, and all the rest of them, did not believe in his Armageddon.

*   *   *

One of his most regular visitors these days was George. A George, he was glad to note, who had recovered most of his natural ebullience once he was satisfied he had stolen yet another march over his competitors by shunting his Swann-Maxie fleet into regions where they could do the kind of work Swann's one-horse pinnaces had once done, leaving the heavy hauls to his latest nine-day won-

der, the articulated trailer, an improvement on the prototype that had cost Martin his life on a Pennine slope.

There were far less Clydesdales and Cleveland Bays on
the Swann roster nowadays, and horse-drawn transport
was now confined to local runs, or over routes where, even
yet, motor-vehicles jibbed at the terrain.

A visit from George was usually an ego-booster to the
prophet on the pinnacle. For a long time now he had been
aware that his advice was no longer sought out of deference but as insurance, in premiums George had been more
than willing to pay since the night he rehearsed them in
the parts they were to play at Stella's inquest. You could
say that for George, he thought, and it was one reason why
he backed him to stay out in front.

Just as Debbie kept him up to the minute on what was
happening in the suffragette sector, and Giles briefed him
on the national issues, so George kept him abreast on the
latest trends in transport.

Their relationship had deepened and broadened appreciably since Stella's death. The partnership had steadied
of late, not only because George had evaluated his shrewd-
ness and steadfastness but because Adam had at last adjusted to the stupendous changes in the transport scene
since the arrival of the self-propelled vehicle. George saw
himself as a master of tactics but when it came to strategy
he was always ready to defer to a man who carried in his
head a large-scale map of Britain, and indices of all the
products that kept the country in the forefront of the
world's trading nations.

*   *   *

It was different again with the younger children, whom
he saw less frequently, or with one or other of his many
grandchildren, who saw him as a kind of eccentric sage,
excessively tolerant in most areas but obstinate and
adamant in others and sometimes giving advice of a kind
they did not comprehend at the time.

It was this way with his daughter Helen, devilishly wary, he thought, when he quizzed her on Southern Ireland's response to Carson's bloodcurdling threats from Ulster. When she told him the Catholic South was recruiting to raise a force capable of confronting the Orangemen, he said, "Will you carry a message from me back to that husband of yours, my dear? Tell him to leave the sealing of this business to the British. I speak as a Home Ruler from Gladstone's day and that bill is law. Only one thing can stop you going your own way now and I'll tell you what it would be – if you people jump the gun *ahead* of Ulster and put yourselves in the dock!"

She was still digesting this when he added, with a smile, "You can remind Rory Clarke of something else. Tell him that your mother's mother was as Irish as the shamrock, and landed penniless in Liverpool ahead of the potato famine. So you've really no call to feel an exile over there."

In truth she had forgotten and it made her thoughtful during the remainder of her stay. It went some way to explain, perhaps, her identification with the Irish and her tendency, since her second marriage, to look at history through Irish eyes, and she said to him, on the last day of her visit, "You're as English as anyone I know. What made you back Home Rule all those years ago? You never set eyes on your mother-in-law, or so Mamma tells me."

"No, I never did, but I served in Ireland in the 'fifties, a year or so after the 'Great Hunger' as they call it, and I understood their grievances. It didn't take me all that long to realise the English had been asking for this how-de-do for seven centuries. Bad as things were they weren't peculiar to Ireland and the Irish. You're looking at a man old enough to recall seeing men transported for poaching and petty theft. Not all were from County Cork and County Mayo. Some were from Hampshire, Dorset and right here where we're sitting."

*　　　*　　　*

Giles called less often, spending an occasional weekend at 'Tryst' between his parliamentary chores in Westminster and Wales. Adam felt great sympathy for a man who, at the age of forty, had been robbed not only of the woman he loved but also his faith in British democratic traditions. There was no more talk of Giles joining the Labour Party, however (although the presence of Keir Hardie as his constituency neighbour at Merthyr Tydfil was a permanent temptation) but he was disenchanted with the conformity of the Liberals. He said, when they were discussing Women's Suffrage one day, "Do you remember what Abe Lincoln said on the practice of slave-owning before the Civil War out there – about it being impossible for a nation to remain half-free and half-slave? Well, that's how I've come to feel about us. For as long as we deny women the vote how can we prattle on about the home of the free, Father?" When Adam said he should use the analogy in a speech in the House, he replied, with a smile, "Oh, I plan to. The next time we get a debate on the issue. And don't think I begrudge the chances of preferment I've given up by identifying myself with the suffragettes. I owe that much and more to Romayne, wouldn't you say?"

Adam said, gently, "You still miss her, don't you?"

Giles nodded. "The only relief I get from the permanent ache is in the valleys, doing what little I can for the people who sent me to London."

"Well, you can warm your hands there, boy," Adam told him. "Personal local representation is the only justification for your profession and from what I hear and read most of 'em up there forget as soon as they've counted the votes." And then, taking a chance, "Have you ever thought of marrying again, my boy?"

"Oh, I've thought of it," Giles said, and then, perking up somewhat, "I might even surprise you and mother one of these days."

And before very long he did, confounding them utterly, by turning up, uninvited, with a very pleasantly disposed but rather sad-looking woman of what Henrietta described as 'a sensible age'. Giles introduced her as Sister Gwyneth Powell, presently on the staff of Westminster Hospital, whose home was close to his headquarters at Pontnewydd.

Long before he told them how they had met on the night of Romayne's death (he withheld the story of Miss Powell's part, years ago, in that flare-up over a hat in an Oxford Street store) they had wholeheartedly approved of her, although neither Giles nor Gwyneth hinted at anything more than friendship and mutual political sympathies. Even so, when the carriage taking them back to Bromley Station was out of sight, Henrietta said, "Well, Adam?" And there was no mistaking the matchmaking gleam in her eye.

"I'd put it at odds on. In less than a twelve-month, m'dear." And then, "When will I learn to mind my own business? I advised him to remarry the last time he was over. If it goes off at half-cock I'll feel responsible."

"She seems very steady and sensible," Henrietta said, disregarding him, "for my part he could go further and fare worse."

2

He had his silent visitors too, what he called his Grace and Favour tenants whom he encountered pottering about his terraces and coppices, or taking a breather up on the wooded spur, or when he was immersed in his newspapers on the knoll behind the Hermitage museum.

There was the pair of nuthatches, rare in these parts, who nested in the bole of an elm and were, he would have said, the least demanding of his charges, for their neighbours, an army of tits, were forever swooping on the bird tables he had set up hereabouts, squabbling among themselves for the fat he hung there and the split maize he spread upon the ground. Every kind of tit – great tits, with their neat black skullcaps, blue tits by the dozen and an occasional crested tit or marsh tit, though only once did he catch a glimpse of the long-tailed variety. There were finches, too, a swarm of them, but one particular chaffinch, who seemed to him not only extraordinarily long-lived but unusually perceptive, for he ignored the largesse on the tables and always made a personal approach for crumbs of cheese Adam balanced on his boot. He told Giles – the only one among his children who shared his tolerance for this army of blackmailers – that Joe, the chaffinch, not only knew the whole range of cheeses but could distinguish between his sound and his artificial leg, distrusting the latter's stability, for if, by chance, he put cheese on his left boot, Joe would execute a furious little dance about his feet, waiting for it to fall. But if he placed it on his sound leg he would hop right up and eat it on the spot, waiting until Adam spread his hand with more cheese, when he would perch on his thumb.

Giles, smiling at this recital, said, "It's queer, I always thought of you as a city man. You seemed to belong in that slum beside the Thames in my younger days and I can remember you jeering at city merchants who turned themselves into squires the moment they made their pile. At what point in your life did Wordsworthia set in?"

"Around the time of that yard fire, I imagine. I was seventy then, late in the day but not too late. I saw everything I'd slaved for for over forty years go up in smoke in two hours and it struck me then, for the first time, I think, that everything but land, and what thrives on it free and wild, is a short-term credit, likely to be called in any time. I begrudged every day I spent there after that."

Just beyond the plank verandah of The Hermitage was a buddleia and on hot days he would move out there to watch the butterflies skirmishing round every blossom. Red Admirals, Peacocks, Tortoiseshells, Commas, and his firm favourites, the local Chalkhill Blues, all making a Donnybrook Fair of the bush. He sometimes watched them for thirty minutes at a stretch. But the birds and the butterflies, with the single exception of Joe, the cheese connoisseur, took him very much for granted, whereas his

warier tenants did not, regulating their comings and go-
ings by the degree of solitude he enjoyed.

There was the old grey badger, whose set was inherited
from a line of ancestors stretching back to a time when
this part of the Weald formed the western margin of the
Rhine estuary. He was a suspicious old codger and it
took Adam months to win his confidence, but once this
was achieved Old Blubb (his grizzled, flattish head and
wary looks reminded Adam vividly of Blubb, the ex-
coachee who managed the Kentish Triangle in the 'sixties)
took him very much on trust when he poked around looking for fresh bracken for his set. On the spur behind the
house there were other familiars, an old dog fox that had
learned the hunt never drew this near the house and rarely
ventured off limits. Adam would watch him upwind,
'loping along like a Pathan scout', Adam observed, and
wearing a self-satisfied grin on his return from a successful
hunting foray and he thought, as he watched, 'I'll wager
he's led every local pack about here a dance or two in his
day, but they'll never catch him now. He's like me, a
born survivor.'

Down on the banks of the stream that he had diverted
from the river to keep his lily-ponds filled, he often saw
otters, voles, herons and the comical long-tailed field mice
who seemed to live mainly on insects they found on the
wild irises, although Adam knew their winter stores of
food were treasure houses of berries, nuts, peas and grain.

It was watching these tenants of his, over a period of
months and years, that went some way towards adjusting
his views about the world outside, for he reasoned – 'They
manage their affairs much better than we do. Stick to
their own patch and never kill, save for food. Whereas,
look at us. We've been roaming and pillaging ever since
we came out of the trees and it'll bring us down in the
end.'

And then, when the evenings grew shorter, he would
take to going into the house, and paid visits to his in-
animate friends. Here, too, he had his favourites, some of

them under glass and never handled save by himself or a fellow connoisseur. There were many examples of the English and Irish glass blowers' art, opaque glasses with twist stems, baluster stem glasses with a royal monogram, a pair of magnificent Jacobite goblets, engraved with the image of the two Pretenders and a flagon showing the Stuart rose with six petals.

He was less zealous of his silver-ware, extending to Henrietta and Phoebe Fraser the privilege of keeping the pieces bright, but the maids were forbidden to handle his china after one dropped a Derby comport and made the mistake of trying to excuse herself by saying, "I was in that of a rare hurry, sir." He was usually very tolerant with the servants, but Rachel, the culprit on this occasion, got a tongue-lashing. "If the man who had made the comport had been in that of a hurry," he roared, "you wouldn't have had the privilege of laying your hands on a piece of craftsmanship made by people who took their work seriously! From now on *I'll* do the china dusting in this house, and that's an order!"

It was one of his very rare flashes of temper for usually the mere contemplation of his treasures brought him serenity. He loved to ponder the moulded decoration in the form of mermaids and festoons on his George I salt cellars, the fan and chrysanthemum motifs on his early Worcester glazes, his choice pieces of Nantgarw, Pinxton, Coalport and Rockingham, but above all some of his late eighteenth-century English furniture, pier tables, pole-screens, rosewood veneered tables inlaid with brass, japanned corner cabinets, the Torricellian barometer in the hall and his magnificent breakfront bookcase, veneered with curled mahogany, measuring nine feet, two and a half inches by twelve feet five inches and holding nothing but calf-bound books, the earliest an atlas, dating from the sixteenth-century, the latest a first edition of *Gulliver's Travels*.

He could tell how and when he had acquired each piece; by cajolery, by hard bargaining and sometimes (for he was a shrewd and a not altogether scrupulous collector) by pretending to do a customer a favour by relieving him of something he regarded as inherited junk. There was very little in the house that was made outside Britain. "We're the finest craftsmen in the world," he would claim, adding with a characteristic touch of cynicism, "At least, we were, before chaps like George got it into their heads that everything had to be done at the double!" And when George reminded him that he, too, in his heyday, had advertised the speed of his deliveries in the press, he said, "So I did, but I had more sense than to treat a consignment of Worcester china as if I was hauling a load of turnips. Look at our insurance files if you want proof of it. No, no, I reckoned one claim a month was excessive and proof of bad bedding-down or sloppy off-loading."

If there was one part of his collection that afforded him more contemplative satisfaction than another it was his picture gallery, where, he would claim, "There isn't a canvas that won't treble in value before you boys trundle me up to that churchyard yonder, some that haven't done so already for that matter."

If he was prejudiced in favour of English silversmiths, English and Irish glass-blowers and English cabinet makers, he was more catholic in his taste for paintings. Up here, along the wainscotted walls of the east and west galleries, or concentrated in the big drawing-room where there was a north light, he had several Dutch masters, including a Van Huysum, two Fragonards, a Claude and a Cranach, besides a selection of English landscape artists, among them a Constable that he had bought at an auction – "Held on a day when a timely blizzard kept everyone with a longer purse away from the auction mart!" He took great pleasure in his English landscapes for they reminded him of his forays up and down the shires since his first prospecting trip on horseback, in 1858. In addition to Constable, artists like Crome, Cotman, Richard Wilson and Bonnington were well represented, reproducing the four seasons and most areas of the country, and when some of his more pernickety visitors expressed regret that he had never been able to get his hands on the work of one or more of the greats, a Leonardo, a Rembrandt or a Velasquez, he would protest, "But, damn it, I didn't haul goods across Italy or Holland or Spain! I made my living right *there*, in *that* narrow country lane, dragging a ton of goods over *that* very hill, or fording *that* particular river and often in *that* kind of weather!"

It was a strange kind of conceit but they left him to it. After all, he was a very old man and could be forgiven his eccentricities.

9

Upon St. Vitus's Day

ON THE TWENTY-FIFTH OF JUNE, 1914, A THICK-set, middle-aged man wearing the uniform of a general of the Austro-Hungarian Army, set out on the first engagement of a three-day assignment in the province of Bosnia, in south-east Europe.

Plumed, girdled, fiercely moustached and over-bemedalled, he accompanied his wife, Sophie, in a drive from the small spa of Ilidze into the capital, Serajevo. His approach was greeted with respectful acclaim on the part of the mixed population of Serbs, Croats and Turks, and the Serbo-Croat shout of '*Zivio!*' betokened his welcome. But that was no more than his due as heir apparent to the Austro-Hungarian throne.

In the local bazaar, where he and Sophie did a little shopping, the crowds were so thick that his entourage had to clear a path for the visitors, but one man, a narrow-face, slightly-built nineteen-year-old did not shout '*Zivio!*' He was too absorbed taking stock of the couple he was to shoot dead three days hence, on Saint Vitus's Day, June 28th, a Serbian national holiday.

The movements of these three people, the Archduke Ferdinand, his morganatic wife, Sophie and their slayer, Gavrilo Princip, over the next seventy-two hours were to have a direct impact upon the lives of every man, woman and child in Europe; to some extent, every man, woman and child then living on the planet, and succeeding generations; to a time long after the hauling firm of Swann-on-Wheels had been forgotten. Because of them, because of their momentary impulses and trivial decisions within this short span of time, ten million Europeans were to die violent deaths within the next four years. Double that number were to live out their lives as chronic or partial invalids. Empires would dissolve, national frontiers would undergo drastic changes and crowned monarchs would become hunted fugitives. Yet neither of these two men, momentarily within touching distance of one another, were aware of more than a tiny fraction of those whose lives were cut short by their encounter. Their encounter that day, or their ultimate confrontation three days later.

* * *

The ensuing two days were spent by the Archduke witnessing the manoeuvres of twenty-two thousand troops in the mountain country near the capital; by Princip, the assassin, in brooding, conferring with fellow assassins and visiting, for the purpose of renewing an oath, the grave of a dead revolutionary called Zerajic, buried in that portion of the Serajevo churchyard reserved for criminals and suicides.

At the conclusion of the army manoeuvres the Archduke, well-pleased, wrote, "I had been convinced that I would find nothing but the best and my expectations were fully confirmed by the outstanding performances of all officers and men." On the same day, Princip, together with two fellow conspirators, wrote a postcard to a common friend living in Switzerland but what they wrote is not recorded.

* * *

Far away to the south-east, in Punjab mountain scenery more dramatic than the Bosnian crags, Alexander Swann's occupations during these corresponding days of June had something in common with these men.

Seven thousand feet up in the foothills of the Himalayas, breathing an atmosphere rarefied not only by the mountain air but by the social graces and taboos of the British Raj, Lieutenant-Colonel Alexander Swann had occasion both to brood and to write, as he studied the reports of a batch of young officers undergoing a course of instruction in a climate that their fellow subalterns, sweating it out on the plains, would have envied. For Simla, the summer residence of the Viceroy, was, by European standards, the most civilised and salubrious town in the sub-continent of India at that time. A visiting artist had written of it, "Everything here is so English . . . one would fancy oneself in Margate."

Unfortunately, however, Alex was too dedicated a man to enjoy the mountain air, or anything Simla had to offer in the way of social amusements. Never much of a mixer, he was currently engaged on work that distressed him, both as a highly-specialised professional soldier and as a rationalist. For he too, in a sense, had been engaged in reviewing and his conclusions were less euphoric than those of Franz Ferdinand in faraway Bosnia. The field work of the candidates, he decided, had been sloppy in the extreme, but if possible that sloppiness was exceeded by their written work. Putting them together he was hard put to it to find a single student eligible for a recommendation to a staff college.

This was bad enough, out of a course of twenty-four. What was worse was the underlying reason for the overall poor quality. The young men selected were either favourites, with some kind of backstairs influence, or regimental failures, the kind of men a busy colonel would not miss for a month or so, and one reason or the other accounted for their presence here. Otherwise it was very unlikely that they would have been detached for the course in the first place. In addition nearly all the candidates were cavalrymen.

Take Willoughby-Nairn, for instance, typical of the kind of subaltern Alex had encountered all over the Empire during the last thirty years. Twenty-three, the younger son of a guardee and an Admiral's daughter; educated Eton; gazetted to a smart regiment on passing Sandhurst at his third attempt. Cherubic-looking, easy-mannered, a great favourite with the ladies, the winner of innumerable polo cups and pig-sticking trophies but running slightly to fat, despite so much outdoor exercise. A proven toper in the mess. Much given to skylarking. Supremely satisfied with his own modest attainments and his future. As a soldier in the field recklessly brave, no doubt; as a leader of men worthless; as a trainer of soldiers worse than useless.

His pen hovered over Lieutenant Willoughby-Nairn's character summary at the foot of page three of his report and he would have given a month's pay to write a truthful assessment of this arrogant young puppy, who embodied all that he most detested in the service. But by now he knew his limitations, both as a small-arms fanatic and as the son of a tradesman. He wrote, "In my view this officer is not temperamentally suited for staff work," and left it at that.

He said rather more in his daily letter to Lydia, for his wife was his emotional safety valve on all these occasions. Of the class in general he wrote: "God help those led by these men in any scrape with a modernised army. Their sole hope of survival would be the elimination of their platoon commander in the first brush and his replacement by a time-serving N.C.O. I use the word 'platoon' rather than 'squadron' advisedly. What nobody here seems to realise is that, in a war with any disciplined force, every man jack among them would serve as an infantryman. I warned my class of that one day last week. Those who were awake looked at me as if I had uttered a blasphemy, as indeed I had in their view . . ."

An overbold monkey, one of the many he had heard thrumming on the iron roof over his head all the afternoon, made a quick grab through the open window at a bowl of fruit on the ledge and suffered for Lieutenant

Willoughby-Nairn's shortcomings. Seizing the first opportunity to release his inner tensions Alexander Swann, square peg in a round hole, smashed his fist down on the intruder, clipping the end of his tail. The monkey fled, screaming with rage. Alex picked up his pen and resumed writing.

The incident afforded him no more than temporary relief. Soon, shuffling his reports, he rose and made his way through a labyrinth of corridors to the Mall outside, threading his way down the winding road towards the barracks. Past block after block of some of the ugliest administrative buildings in the world, monstrosities raised on girders held together with stanchions and roofed with corrugated iron. Architectural eyesores that had been described as 'pyramids of disused tramcars'. Past the premises of military tailors, past estate agents, a bank, two provision merchants, a very English-looking church, Peliti's Restaurant (where you could learn who was cuckolding whom), and as he went rubbing shoulders with Pathans, Sikhs and Tibetans, with strolling Europeans, civil and military, and a string of panting rickshaw drivers. He had eyes for nothing and nobody. The accumulated weight of his misgivings bore on him like a heavy burden. A few high-ranking officers had been impressed by his reiterated pleas for increased fire-power. Had it been otherwise, he would not have been here, marking the test papers of the Willoughby-Nairns, but he knew, and they knew, that his sponsors, men of Haldane's and Roberts' calibre, would not be confronting the enemy if and when the challenge came. That would fall to the Willoughby-Nairns, mostly to men half his age, who thought of him, most of them, as a prig and a bore.

It was the price, he supposed, of having seen so many men needlessly sacrificed in a dozen campaigns; that, plus the misfortune of being born of a practical mother and an imaginative father and of having inherited their commonsense, but not their humour.

He went on past the trim houses of the Little Tin Gods,

with their Sikh guards and their regimented rows of lupins, on down the Mall in the general direction of the vice-regal palace. His steps led him instinctively towards the range, silent at this hour of the day when parades were over and Europeans took their ease.

The armoury was housed in a long shed, a hundred yards beyond the guardhouse. He acknowledged the salute of the sentries and passed inside, pausing to glance through the barred window of the building and seeing there something that mildly surprised him, at least enough to penetrate the gloom that had tormented him since he sat down to mark those test-papers. A shirt-sleeved lance-corporal was at the bench, coiling belts of heavy machine-gun ammunition and something reverential in the youngster's movements arrested him. The gun, dismantled, lay on the bench but the lance-corporal was wholly absorbed, coiling the belts like a bride-to-be winding ribbons. Alex went inside and the young soldier – Alex judged him to be no more than twenty at the most – sprang to attention, his arms held stiffly by his sides, thumbs in line with the seams of his breeches.

"Are you the armoury guard detail?"

"No, *sir*!"

"What are you doing here? Are you on duty in the guardhouse?"

"No, *sir*!"

"Did you strip that Vickers?"

"Yessir."

"You were given authority?"

"Sergeant of the guard. *Sir*."

The young man seemed petrified in the presence of a lieutenant-colonel. He held himself poker straight and when he spoke his lips moved like those of a ventriloquist's dummy.

"All right, lance-corporal. Stand at ease."

The man relaxed, muscle by muscle. It was like watching someone thaw.

"You're interested in the heavy-machine-gun?"

"Yessir."

"But not a qualified machine-gunner?"

"No, sir."

"Then who taught you to strip a gun?"

"No one, sir . . . I . . . I watched . . . watched it being done during the course, sir."

"Then you must recognise me as the instructor?"

"Yessir."

"What are your duties on the range?"

"Setting up targets, sir."

"But you have never actually handled a gun until now?"

"No, sir."

"Could you reassemble it?"

"I believe so, sir."

"Do it then."

He took a seat on the end of the bench, watching the lance-corporal's expression. His body was at ease, or nearly so, but his features were still frozen into a blankness bordering on that of an imbecile. Yet gradually, as his hands closed over the dismantled pieces of shining metal, the expression changed, the hard, staring look softening to one of dreamy absorption. The oil-stained fingers, long and supple, moving very rapidly but with infinite precision. The only sound in the hut was the soft click of metal as the gun took shape. Alex glanced down at his watch, then at the man's hands, then at his watch again. The operation occupied one minute, fifteen seconds. He said, "What's your name, lance-corporal?"

"Hunter, sir."

"How long have you been out, Hunter?"

"Two months, sir."

"Where do you live in England?"

"Kent, sir."

"What part of Kent?"

"A place called Hildenborough, sir."

"Then you probably know my father's home, 'Tryst', near Twyforde?"

"Yessir." There was a pause. "I used to deliver telegrams there, sir. Before I enlisted."

It was an odd coincidence. He must sometimes have seen the boy, pushing his red bicycle up the steep drive from the old mill-house, for telegrams from the Tonbridge office were constantly arriving at 'Tryst', especially in the years before his father had installed a telephone.

He sat pondering a moment, Lance-Corporal Hunter having stepped back a pace and resumed his at-ease posture, head up, legs astride, hands clasped behind his back.

"Automatic weapons fascinate you, Hunter?"

"Yessir."

"Since when? You never saw one during your recruits' training."

"Since I was a kid . . . a child, sir. I once watched a demonstration at a tattoo."

"Where was that?"

"At Hythe, sir."

"You have applied for transfer to a machine-gun section?"

"Yessir. But there's a long waiting-list, sir."

"Are you sure of that, Hunter?"

"So I was told, sir. Sergeant Topham, sir."

"Strip that gun down again."

The young soldier leaped forward, his hands seeming to tear the segments apart but he laid each of them down on the bench with infinite care. The operation was completed in under the minute.

"I'll recommend you personally, Hunter."

The lance-corporal's jaw dropped an inch, but then, his reflexes reminding him that this was disrespectful, it snapped shut again.

"Thank you, *sir*."

"Where is your sergeant now?"

"In the guardhouse, sir."

"Thank you, Hunter. Expect to begin training tomorrow after first parade. I shall be here. I'll arrange your course of instruction myself. Now reassemble the gun."

"Sir!"

He did not wait to see it done but went out without a backward glance, his step appreciably lighter. The weight had lifted from his brow and he thought, making his way over the scrupulously-swept asphalt towards the guardhouse, 'What the devil does it matter if the Willough-by-Nairns of this world go to their graves without learning the difference between a lance and a Vickers machine-gun? Providing, in places like there, here and on home stations, there are waiting-lists of Lance-Corporal Hunters?'

*   *   *

On Saturday, June 27th, the heir to the Austro-Hungarian throne and his wife, Sophie, presided over a formal banquet served in the dining-room of the hotel at Ilidze.

The night was warm. Windows were thrown open. Outside on the lawn the band of the Serajevo garrison played Schumann's 'Traumerei', a phantasy on 'La Bohème', a Léhar medley and the obligatory 'Blue Danube'. The guests ate soufflé, lamb, fillet of beef, roast goose and fruit. They drank French wines, the local Mostar and Hungarian Tokay. Towards midnight, Franz Ferdinand remarked he was glad his Bosnian visit was almost over, and someone suggested that the brief visit to the capital scheduled for the following day should be cancelled and the archducal couple should make an immediate return home. Then, being persuaded that Serajevo dignitaries would be hurt and disappointed by the cancellation, a decision was reached to adhere to the original schedule. The hands of the dining-room clock moved up to midnight. The day of St. Vitus had begun.

2

That same night, at round about the same hour as the Archduke's dinner guests were doing justice to their roast goose, Edward Swann was eating a less exotic but appetising home-cooked meal in the dining-room of his mother-in-law, Edith Wickstead, near Peterborough, Northamptonshire. He had company but it was not Edith's and although unaware of it at the time Edward too had a surprise immediately ahead of him. For he, too, in a very small way, was the target of a conspiracy.

Although outwardly himself again, encouraging his brother George's colourful comment that "He's blown his nose, dusted himself off and emerged the same good old go-steady-think-twice Edward again," he had been changed inwardly by his wife's desertion and in a way that even George, his mentor over many years, was unqualified to judge. The real trouble with Edward was that he had absorbed, one could say, a quadruple dose of ancestral practicality. From his French grandmother, Monique d'Auberon, daughter of a Gascon pastrycook, he had inherited the same strain of hard commonsense that ran so richly in the veins of his father and mother and had been present, in full measure, in the blood of his maternal grandparents, one a Lancastrian millhand who had made two fortunes, the other an Irish peasant, whose commonsense told her she should seek her pot of gold in Liverpool rather than County Kerry.

The same strain, to a degree, ran in all the Swanns but with nothing like the same urgency, and whereas it stood him in very good stead as an engineer, and a man of business, it made it almost impossible for the same man to rationalise his wife's dream of becoming a celluloid goddess.

For a brief spell, after watching, openmouthed, Gilda's eye-rolling and cavorting on the flickering screen of that little picture-house in Birmingham, he had been comforted by the acknowledgment that he had made the biggest mistake of his life by falling in love with her. He was not in love with her any longer.

This was how things stood with him when Betsy Battersby was unleashed upon him for Betsy, it could be said, was the price Edith Wickstead paid to get her conscience out of pawn, a brawny, cheerful, uncomplicated Yorkshire lass, her favourite among a tribe of nieces and great-nieces left behind in the North Riding when she moved south to take over the old Crescent territory in the 'sixties. Edith, missing her own family when the boys grew up and Gilda went abroad, grew to like Betsy's undemanding company, particularly when Tom was out about his business, and after Tom's death she became a frequent visitor, giving her great-aunt a hand with the house chores so that Edward, also a frequent visitor, came to think of her as a family hanger-on, midway between a domestic help and a house guest. While under the spell of Gilda, however, he never saw her for what she was, a well set-up girl in her mid-twenties, that is to say, some ten years his junior. She had flaming red hair, light blue eyes that always looked pleasurably surprised, regular if slightly heavy features, a generous mouth, much given to laughter, and an excellent figure that Edith always thought of in Adam's terms as 'promising', recalling that neither he nor Tom had cared for wraiths, much in vogue during their courting years. Tom, she remembered, had always admitted that 'he liked plenty to catch hold of' and Betsy Battersby certainly came into this category of women.

The idea of deploying her against Edward, however, as a kind of consolation prize for the manner in which a real slut, her own daughter, had served the poor boy, did not occur to Edith until she had had an opportunity to make a full assessment of the harm Gilda had inflicted on him and this she was only able to assess by instinct, after Edward's response to the first letter from America.

It arrived out of the blue, about two years after Gilda's flight to France, telling a tale that the truant might have borrowed from the Arabian Nights. Her films, it seems, had been seen in America and an agent had negotiated a contract enabling her to travel all the way to California to make a costume film about the French Revolution. This, so Gilda reported, had led to other films and a better contract, so that she was now in receipt of the equivalent of a hundred English pounds a month, with the promise of much more to come. She had changed her name again and was now known as 'Gilda de la Rey'.

Reflecting that there was surely substance in the adage that the wicked prospered like the green bay tree, and remembering also that she had always been inclined to doubt the validity of that contradictory saw about virtue being its own reward, Edith read the final page. It scouted a proposition that, as they were unlikely to meet again, Edward should supply grounds for a divorce and was set down, Edith thought, as though this was the bestowal of a royal and gracious favour upon an unworthy subject.

She took the only course open to her, telegraphing Edward to visit her and discuss the matter and was not surprised when he growled, after scanning the relevant page, "Let her whistle for her divorce. I'm over it now and I'm damned if I'll make it public. Just don't answer the letter, Edith."

She said, gently, "That's precisely how I felt about it at first, but then it occurred to me you might be cutting off your nose to spite your face. Divorces, nowadays, aren't the end of the world, as they were in my day, and this would be undefended and wouldn't create much stir. Anyway, look at it from another standpoint. You might want to get married again some time."

"When that happens you can certify me," he said. "Don't answer it, Edith. Hasn't she caused both of us enough grief?"

She said, carefully, "I know you're over it, Edward. I know also that you must ask yourself sometimes why and how you came to fall in love with a girl as heartless and self-centred as that. I'm glad Tom didn't live to see the way she turned out. However, be honest with yourself. You've got red blood in your veins and you're only in your mid-thirties. What do you propose to do about women for the rest of your life?"

He said, without meeting her glance, "I don't need women in that sense. If I did I could buy one."

"But that's not you, is it?"

"How do you mean 'not me'? Look here, Edith, you were gaffer of a region here and must have seen most things. You know that men who want a frolic can get one, providing they've got money in their pockets."

"I know that, yes. But it wouldn't be your way and you've probably found that out for yourself."

He was silent, so she said, with a sigh, "Very well. I won't answer it. But if she writes again I'll re-address the letter to you and you can decide for yourself whether or not you read it."

He left her in an ill-humour and she suspected he was going to drown his sorrows. In spite of what the family were saying about him it was clear to her that he still had some to drown. But then, within minutes of his departure, her spirits lifted, for Betsy arrived with luggage and asked if she could stay a week or so.

"It makes a rare change," she announced, "for down here it's free and easy, and back home I'm faced with a choice of playing nursemaid to other folks' babies or filling my time with chapel activities. That's the two alternatives open to old maids in my part of the world."

"I'll never think of you as an old maid, Betsy," said Edith and Betsy replied, cheerfully, "No more will I until I'm the wrong side of forty. It was hot and dusty in the train. Can I pop up and have a bath before supper?"

She was calling from the top of the stairs in five minutes. "Auntie Edith! There's no more than a sliver of soap in the dish. Can you throw me a cake?" and Edith, getting a new tablet, took it to the stairhead where Betsy was standing naked on the landing.

It was her nakedness that fired Edith's imagination.

Somehow it had never previously occurred to her how comely Betsy might look without clothes that were usually home-sewn and out of fashion. With her flaming red hair reaching as far as her broad buttocks, her high bust set off by a waist that looked two inches narrower than it did when she was dressed, she looked like a Viking's bride and she thought, with a mild rush of excitement, 'By God, if young Edward could see Betsy now it would do more to put that stupid wench of mine out of mind than any amount of soothing talk on my part. Or tumbling with whores, for that matter . . .' But all she said was, "Here's your soap, Betsy. And over supper remind me that I've a proposition to put to you."

"What kind of proposition?"

"We'll see, shall we?"

*　　*　　*

On Saturday, the 27th of June, about the time the archducal guests assembled in the Ilidze Hotel, Edward Swann appeared at his mother-in-law's door in response to an invitation for a weekend stay.

He was met by Betsy, who said that Auntie Edith was visiting a sick friend a mile or two nearer Peterborough, and wouldn't be back until after dinner

"She asked me to cook for you and it's almost ready. Give me your grip and I'll take it up while you treat yourself to some sherry." And without waiting for his response she grabbed his bag and tripped upstairs where he heard her humming a snatch from the music-hall song, 'Won't You Come Home, Bill Bailey?'

In the dining-room a meal was laid for three. There was, he noticed, a bottle of champagne in the ice-bucket and he thought, 'What's Edith celebrating, I wonder? She doesn't generally run to champagne. Maybe it's her birthday.' He said to Betsy as she reappeared, "Is it Edith's birthday, Betsy?" and Betsy said it was not but it happened to be hers.

"I'm twenty-eight," she said gaily. "Isn't it awful? But I'd sooner have a birthday here than home, for our house is strict T.T. If my father thought I was guzzling champagne he'd come down here and fetch me home with a flea in my ear."

"He could hardly do that to a daughter of twenty-eight, could he?"

"Oh, yes he could. I don't know whether you know the north well but they keep a rare tight rein on the women up there, much tighter than down here. It's still a patriarchal society, and pi-faced with it."

There was something about Betsy that amused him. It was difficult to believe that she was twenty-eight.

"How do you mean, pi-faced?"

"Well, everything revolves round the chapel. No one goes to the theatre, no one is supposed to drink and cards are the Devil's prayerbook. That's why I spend as much time as possible with Auntie Edith. She's fun, but my people don't really know her. They think she's a semi-invalid, and she plays along with it just to get me here. That's jolly sporting of her, don't you think?"

He hardly knew what to think. For the first time despite her ingenuousness, she was registering upon him as a woman, not all that much younger than himself, a woman with an air of a lively, mischievous child about fourteen radiating a boisterous cheerfulness that was difficult to resist. He said, "Well, make the most of it, Betsy. Join me in some sherry before you serve and we'll follow up with the champagne. How long is Edith likely to be?"

"Oh, not more than an hour or so, but she insisted we weren't to wait dinner. I've roasted a duck and it will be spoiled. I'll have the sherry, tho', and then dish up. Shall I put on the gramophone?"

"If you like." He looked across at the big horned phonograph on a side table, noting that it was an American model, an improvement on George's latest and George was an Edison Bell enthusiast. "That's new, isn't it?"

"Auntie Edith gave it to me for my birthday but I'll

346

have to leave it here. A phonograph is only one up from a pack of cards in our house."

"You could get round that. Why not buy a sacred recording and try breaking 'em in with the 'Hallelujah Chorus'?"

It was the closest he had come to making a joke in a long time and she made it seem a better one than it was, exclaiming, "Why, that's a wonderful idea! They might even progress, eventually, to Gilbert and Sullivan. But I've only got the one cylinder and that's ragtime."

"*What* time?"

The word meant nothing to him and she looked surprised. "Ragtime. Bouncy stuff played fast. It's called 'Alexander's Ragtime Band'," and she hummed the first line or two of a jerky little tune that he immediately recognised as a recent vanboys' favourite at the yard. "I'll put it on. If it winds down while I'm dishing up turn the handle quickly for they sound frightful when they run down, like a rhinoceros with the belly-ache."

She switched on, downed her sherry at a gulp and bounced off into the kitchen, where he heard her singing an accompaniment to the whining, oddly fascinating rhythm of the scratchy recording. He thought, pouring himself another sherry, 'She's a rum sort of girl. Her cheerfulness rubs off on a chap somehow yet it doesn't sound as if she has much of a life, poor beggar . . . no idea Edith's folk up north were straitlaced . . .' and as he thought this he felt relaxed and grateful to her for the lift she had given him. For nowadays there seemed to be nothing much in life but work and sleep.

Her home cooking, to a man who lived mostly in chophouses, was a discovery; brown soup, duck, trifle and Stilton cheese, eaten with some crisp brown biscuits she had made Over their second glass of champagne he said; "Don't you have a young man, Betsy? Someone like you should, surely? More than one, maybe."

"Most women are married at my age," she said, "and I've come within shouting distance of hooking someone three or four times in a row, but it always fizzles out. Not on my part, on theirs."

Her honesty made an immediate appeal to him, especially as she illustrated the admission with a wry face but then, as if to demonstrate the fact that she had survived her disappointments, a chuckle.

"I can't understand that. Let's face it, you're pretty, you're good company, you're a first-rate cook."

"Ah, I daresay, kind sir, but I'm also considered flighty," and he had to laugh as she went on, "I am too, but we aren't here for long, are we, and I honestly can't see why most people have to make such heavy going of it." Then with a flicker of embarrassment, "Was Gilda flighty? Surely she must have been to run off like that, all the way to America."

"You know about me and Gilda?"

"Not *you* and Gilda, or only the very little Auntie Edith's told me. But everyone knows Gilda by now, don't they? I mean, she's famous. I saw her in that French Revolution picture at the Bijou, in Peterborough. Auntie Edith took me."

He was jolted by this. It had never occurred to him that other people took Gilda's posturing seriously and as to Gilda de la Rey or whatever she called herself being considered famous it seemed to him quite preposterous. He said, thoughtfully, "What did you think of her?"

"I thought she was awful. I mean, that kind of thing isn't real acting, is it? No more than a lot of put-on eye-rolling and bosom heaving. I'm sure I could do better than that myself, although maybe it isn't her fault."

It struck him then that she must have known Gilda before he did, visiting here as a child and probably being patronised, as by a governessy sort of cousin. It would be difficult, he thought, to think of two more dissimilar women than his wife and Betsy Battersby. He was pondering this when he heard her say, "You don't like talking about her, do you?"

"Not much, but it doesn't matter with someone like

348

you, that is, someone who knew what she was like before
she was married. What *was* she like? When you met her
after she came home from the Continent?"

"Lah-di-dah," Betsy said, promptly. "Very pretty,
of course, and clever, but I never liked her. She wasn't
interested in anyone but herself. Anyone could see that
in a twinkling. I thought then, 'Any man who marries
Gilda Wickstead will be asking for trouble.' I'm sorry if
that offends you but you did ask for the truth."

"It doesn't offend me." He got up. "I'll help you clear
and wash up before Edith gets back."

They cleared the table together and while relieving her
of a heavy tray he noticed the pleasing swell of her breasts.
It made him think fleetingly of Dulcie, the over-ripe
barmaid at The Mitre, where he drank in the evenings
sometimes, and he thought again, 'I'm damned if I know
why some lively spark hasn't snapped her up long ago.
She'd have a lot to offer to the right man.' Far more than
most, he decided, standing beside her at the sink and
watching her closely as she washed dishes, for every time
she straightened up after lifting plates from the water
her fine breasts rippled and the evening sun, filtering
through a side-window, made her hair glow like red-hot
cinders. 'By God,' he told himself, looking away hastily,
'I need a woman and no mistake!'

But when they had gone back into the dining-room she
asked him if he knew the Bunny-hug and the Turkey Trot.
"A girl I know taught me. She goes to all the hops at the
drill hall but there'd be hell's delight in our house if I
went there, with or without an escort. Did you ever learn
to dance?"

"Formal dances," he said, "when we were kids. We
had a teacher call for the girls and she used to rope me
in as a partner. I never took to it."

"I could teach you. You can dance to ragtime; in fact
it's better. Here, roll that rug up and I'll put it on again,"
and mildly surprised at the pleasurable anticipation of
learning the Bunny-hug with Betsy as a tutor he did as she

asked and soon they were prancing around the room to the whine of the phonograph and he realised that she was quite an expert, although the new dances did not seem to consist of more than skipping and jogging, steps that he found no difficulty in improvising.

"I say, you're jolly good!" she said, pausing to rewind the handle. "You've got a natural rhythm and you lead well. We'll show Auntie Edith when she gets back. Come on, let's try again." He put his arms round her and noticed that her cheeks were flushed with the champagne and that she seemed eager that he should hold her close, and soon he began to perspire gently, not so much by reason of cavorting in a confined space but on account of the fact that Betsy's sturdy thighs collided with his at every turn and hover, so that he found it difficult to sustain belief in her innocence. 'She may have been reared in the Baptist tradition,' he told himself, 'but she's picked up the basic technique somewhere.' Then the phonograph ran down again and when she made no move to wind it, but remained in his loose embrace, he thought, 'I'd be a fool not to make the most of this – a man must have a bit of fun sometimes,' and he kissed her mouth, enlarging his grip in a way that supported most of her weight.

She did not seem to mind in the least. On the contrary, when he adjusted his position so that he could run his hand across her breasts, she gave a definite wriggle of approval and it crossed his mind that his next move should be a suggestion that they write a note for Edith and go for a spin in his car as far as the nearest woods.

He had no opportunity to put the question, however, for as soon as his hold relaxed slightly she renewed it and began kissing him back in a way Gilda had never kissed him and then he was sure, somehow, that he had been excessively naïve about her, and that she had almost certainly had a wide experience in this particular pastime. He managed to get as far as "Why don't we . . ." but at that moment the front doorbell rang loudly and she exclaimed petulantly, "Now who on earth can that be . . . ?"

and detached herself and went into the hall, where he heard her talking to someone on the doorstep.

She came back holding a folded note in her hand. "It's from Auntie Edith," she said, triumphantly. "She sent it over by Timothy, Mrs. Burrell's little boy. It's to say Mrs. Burrell can't manage with that leg, and all the children to see to, and wants Auntie to stay over for the night until Mrs. Burrell's sister arrives from Devizes."

"What did you tell the boy?"

"Well, what could I? There's four children to feed and get off to school in the morning."

"You mean you don't mind staying here alone?"

"I'm not alone, am I? Auntie said you intended staying until tomorrow night."

"So I did but – well, in the circumstances . ʼ

"Oh, fiddlesticks to the circumstances," she said emphatically. "If Auntie doesn't mind, I'm sure I don't for I'm enjoying my birthday. How about you, Edward?"

He said, with a laugh, "You're a rare tonic, Betsy, especially to someone down in the dumps. You're sure you don't mind me staying over?"

"I'd like you to. I'll cook you a slap up breakfast in the morning and maybe you'd take me a ride in your car, for I've never ridden in one in my life."

"You mean you want to go now?"

"Oh no, not now. The morning will do. If I've waited twenty-eight years to ride in a motor, I can wait over-night."

There was simply no resisting her and it astonished him that he had hardly noticed her on his previous visits here. He said, "We've had enough dancing on the sort of meal you provide. Let's treat ourselves to a glass of Edith's port and take it in the parlour." He picked up the decanter and two glasses and followed her into Edith's cosily-furnished snuggery where he settled himself on the sofa. It was growing dusk outside now and a feeling of well-being stole over him as she drew the chintz curtains and paused on her way back to him to inhale the perfume from a bowl of roses Edith had set on an occasional table. He had few doubts now as to what was expected of him and when she passed in front of him he reached out and grabbed her, running his hands over her plump bottom and saying, gaily, "Edith's got a nice sense of timing. Sit on my knee, Betsy."

"I'm no light-weight."

"And all the better for it."

She said, teasingly, "I thought you preferred skinny girls. Gilda was skinny."

"Oh, to the devil with Gilda. Let's forget Gilda for a bit."

"All right."

"Any man in his senses would want you, Betsy, and that isn't the champagne talking," he said pulling her down, gathering her up with a kind of desperation so that she laughed.

"Here, hold on lad! We've got all night, haven't we?"

She began to settle herself close to him but he said, running his hand over her hair, "I'd like to see you with those pins out of your hair, Betsy. You've got wonderful hair. Let it loose now. It must look even more wonderful freed of that comb and all those pins," and she looked at him seriously for a moment, her head on one side and then, getting up again, "I'll have to do it upstairs. It's quite a business. Wait here, I won't be five minutes."

He could feel his heart thumping and was aware of the constriction of his starched collar that seemed to be choking him so that he was strongly tempted to take it off, together with his jacket, but he thought; "Here, that's taking too much for granted." But then he heard her step on the stairs and she came in as he was in the act of getting up, her hair cascading over her shoulders and wearing a voluminous pink bathrobe, sashed about her waist and reaching down to her bare feet but sufficiently open at the top to display her breasts.

"I was hot after all that food and drink and dancing," she said, equably, "and you must be too. Why don't you take your jacket and collar off while I pour us some port?"

It was as though she had found some secret spring in his character, releasing a man charged with an abundance of tenderness and affection. He had always been reckoned the most dour and inarticulate of the family, "Closer to old Sam, in his mellow period, than any one of them," Adam would say of him, and then his late-flowering high spirits had been checked and turned back by the monstrous assault on his pride.

What began as a kind of mutual dare, with undertones of body hunger on his part and high spirits on hers, transformed itself, in a matter of seconds, into a genuine giving and receiving.

He said, touching her neck with the tips of his fingers, "You're beautiful, Betsy! You're the most beautiful woman in the world."

"You don't have to say that. In fact, you don't have to say anything. I needed you and you needed me. I've thought about you a lot. You're not feeling guilty about me, are you?"

"I'm not in the least guilty, Betsy. Just grateful. Would you like me to go and come over again when Edith's back?"

"You want to?"

"No, I don't want to. I want this to happen again as often as you want it to. But I can't expect that in the circumstances."

"You mean Gilda?"

"I mean Gilda. She'll divorce me in time but when I can't say. And I wouldn't want you to be mixed up in a divorce."

She considered this a moment, looking thoughtful, but the strain of concentration was too much for her and presently she smiled. "It's late," she said, "too late to go into all that. Would you like some tea?"

He laughed. Always, he thought, she would demonstrate this priceless gift of being able to sidestep the imponderables and find fulfilment in the moment, and the small change that emerged from the moment. "No," he said, "I don't want tea, Betsy. The only thing I want is you."

3

It was doubtful, Rory Clarke had once told his English wife, whether Ireland would ever be free without more blood-letting and that meant getting arms for the South. Watching, clause by clause, the tempestuous progress of the Home Rule Bill, she had argued, "But if it goes through, if you get what you've been fighting for all this time, would you ever vote for bloodshed, Rory?" and he replied, gravely, "No. I'd do all I could to stop it. We're not assassins."

They were not so squeamish in the Balkans.

At dusk on June 27th, about the time Lieutenant-Colonel Swann was watching Lance-Corporal Hunter strip and reassemble a Vickers machine-gun, and while his brother Edward, abed in England, was discovering the hitherto unimagined charms of Edith Wickstead's hoydenish niece Betsy, five students, the eldest of them no more than twenty, met their schoolteacher mentor, twenty-three-year-old Danilo Ilić in the park at Serajevo, after a final consultation at a neighbouring coffee house.

Ilić handed four of them a bomb, a revolver and a dose of cyanide. To the fifth, Cabrinović, he gave a bomb and a phial of poison. The poison, as it turned out, was all but harmless but the bombs and guns were lethal, even in the hands of amateurs. Their use on the Appel Quay a few hours later were to herald a million fusillades clear across the world. Not least in Ireland, where bombs would burst and guns blaze long after the rest of Europe had sickened of killing.

Helen's humiliating failure to serve Sinn Fein interests in the matter of the stolen brief case had effectively blocked her admission into the inner councils, but it had one bonus. It had strengthened her relationship with Rory for he was all too aware that she had at least tried, that she had been prepared to jettison family loyalties for his sake. And this was all that mattered so far as he was concerned.

From then on she enjoyed his complete confidence, even if she was disbarred from accompanying him on his endless journeyings about the country, and had perforce to remain the far side of a locked door when officers of the movement assembled in her home for conferences. Yet she did not resent this exclusion. Rory trusted her and she resolved to build upon his confidence by what could be described as pursuing an intensive course in Irish grievances, readily available to her in his well-stocked library.

She never read novels or a fashion journal nowadays. Her reading matter was entirely confined to pamphlets, newspaper clippings that Rory had pasted into albums that he referred to as 'The Score', to local histories and government surveys devoted to the economics of Ireland over the last century or so, and she was appalled by what she read.

There were accounts here of evictions, abortive risings, rent strikes, Fenian forays and the savage penalties all forms of protest had provoked. There was the horrifying story of the successive potato famines of the 'forties, and the steady drain of Irish immigrants overseas, mostly via coffin ships sailing out of Cork for the New World where, she imagined, whole areas must now be populated by fugitives from Mayo and Kerry. For those who survived, that is, for it seemed to her, reading grisly accounts of epidemics and ill-found voyages, that only half the emigrants lived to begin life again elsewhere.

It was desperately gloomy reading but it strengthened the bond between man and wife, for he came to see her now as a convert in her own right, brought to the light by her own convictions rather than by wifely obligations. The time would come, he told her, when he would persuade his colleagues to see her in this way, and not as a potential informer in their midst, as they tended to regard every Englishwoman domiciled in Ireland. But it would need ·time, for the long story of revolt in Ireland was blotched with betrayals from within.

This was how matters stood when Rory returned from his survey of Ulster in the early summer of 1914, shortly after the mutiny at the Curragh, where Ulster-born officers succeeded in obtaining from the British Government a guarantee that they would not be called upon to fight fellow Protestants in the north.

He had gone there half-doubting the stories of extreme militancy among the Orange Lodges, and the martial preparations said to be on foot by the Carsonites, aided and abetted by the British Unionists and aimed at re-cruiting an army capable of resisting Home Rule by force of arms. He returned a despondent man, his worst fears confirmed, he told her on the night he came home to find her waiting for him. Ulster was virtually mobilised and it was high time – almost too late, maybe – to take this undeniable fact into the strategical considerations of Sinn Fein.

"I went there supposing they had a few hundred sporting guns and surplus Continental discards," he said, "but our sources in Belfast soon changed that view. In April, over at Larne, they ran in thirty thousand rifles and bayonets and three million rounds of ammunition. Right under the noses of the police and coastguards, and Carson, they say, now has a hundred thousand volunteers pledged to fight. How will the National Volunteers stand up to that?"

"By running in an equivalent armament you've always said," she reminded him, but he replied, with an impatient gesture, "Aye, that's what I said, Princess, but I spoke out of turn. Our Continental agents tell us they can lay hands on enough rifles to equip the Dublin brigades now drilling with broomsticks but in our case, without big money interests behind us, it'll always be cash in advance. Where would we lay our hands on that kind of money? For my part I'm bled white, and so are the few of us who started out with capital. It costs a great deal to raise and equip an army of starvelings."

"I have money, Rory."

He looked at her with a half-smile. "Your private nest-egg, hatching in an English bank? No, Princess, we're not that straitened . . ." But then, his grey eyes regarding her with a curious intentness, "I've never asked about your means. It wasn't my business, for I had more than enough before all these demands were made on me. I know of your father's marriage settlement but as to capital – how much have you got under your own name?"

"Fourteen thousand," and judging by his expression it was a far larger sum than he had anticipated. "Mostly it's my share of Grandfather Sam's legacy and I've never touched it. It's grown over the years."

She rose and rummaged in the top drawer of her bureau, returning with her bankbook and a typewritten list of investments that George's lawyers sent her each quarter. The bank statement showed a credit balance of over eight thousand. The last quarter's estimate of investment yielded another six thousand, four hundred and eighty pounds. He returned the documents. "I couldn't accept this. It represents all you've got, doesn't it?"

"No, Rory, not nearly all. I've got you."

"But, God in heaven, woman, this isn't your quarrel."

"If it's yours, it's mine. What would that money have done for me if you hadn't rescued me from myself a dozen years ago? Arrange for that shipment in cash. By the time it arrives I'll guarantee you fourteen thousand. I don't know what a shipload of German arms would cost, and I don't suppose you do at this stage. But it's a sizeable contribution by any standards, isn't it?"

He said, taking her hand and studying it, much as a fortune-teller might, "You're a strange creature, Princess. I've always thought so, ever since you told me about that part you played in the Peking shindig. But I love you and need you, as few men ever loved or needed a woman," and he raised her hand to his lips and kissed it. "I'll make no promises one way or the other until I've put your offer before them, but I'll tell you this. Spurn it or accept it as manna from heaven, I'll never forget you offered it." And then, with the ardour and despatch of a groom carrying his bride over the threshold he scooped her into his arms and marched out of the room and up the broad staircase. It was ample reward for the money, she reflected. Particularly for a woman who had recently overlooked her forty-fourth birthday.

*   *   *

The Appel Quay ran above the river Miljacka, dividing the ancient city of Serajevo and on the morning of June 28th, St. Vitus's Day, both sides of the thoroughfare were lined with spectators, assembled there to see the Archduke's motorcade pass on its way to the City Hall.

Spectators were more numerous on the north side, for there was shade here. On the river side the crowd stood in blazing sunshine, heads turned west towards the station as the first of the six cars came in view. It was here, close together, that three conspirators were positioned, Mehmedbasić, the one Mohammedan in the plot, young Cabrinović and Cubrinović, both nineteen-year-old Serbs. Across the road stood Popović, the fourth assassin. Further along, again on the river side, Gavrilo Princip was posted. Ilić, the mentor, moved among the five, keeping up their courage, urging them to be firm and sure-handed.

The procession passed Mehmedbasić unscathed. The Mohammedan boy fumbled, or lost his nerve, thinking himself watched by a policeman. But when the second car, containing the Archduke and his wife Sophie drew level with Cabrinović, next of the group, a small black object sailed in an arc to pitch on the folded hood of the car, roll off and explode with shattering force. The procession halted abruptly and the Archduke stepped out unharmed, hurrying back to inspect the damage done to the following car, where one of his entourage was bleeding profusely from bomb splinters.

Further along, beside the Lateiner Bridge, Princip continued to wait but he, too, had no luck. The procession restarted and passed him at speed. The other assassins, with the exception of Cabrinović, who was hauled, vomiting, from the river into which he had jumped, dispersed. Bombs and revolvers were discarded as Serajevo's one hundred and eleven policemen moved in, broadcasting news of the heir-apparent's miraculous escape. But Princip retained his weapons. He had the nerve of a dedicated revolutionary but what was more important, at this juncture, he had more patience than his fellow-conspirators.

*   *   *

Far away to the north-west, where the Kentish Weald was dreaming under sunshine as hot as that flooding the Appel Quay, Adam Swann, a few days beyond his eighty-seventh birthday, took it into his head to take his daily constitutional on horseback.

Only when the temperatures were high, and he found walking excessively tiring, did he venture afield mounted nowadays. In the spring and autumn he could walk, indeed, he preferred walking, and in the winter he stayed indoors. But sometimes in the summer the fancy would take him to feel a horse between his knees again and Henrietta, watching him from the terrace, shook her head at this exhibition of an old man's obstinacy as she saw him ride his mare down the drive as far as the old mill house, then over the low bank, into the coppice that marked the northern boundary of the estate.

He rode well and confidently, she thought, for so old a man but then he had never liked to be driven, not in carriage or dogcart, and certainly not in one of George's motors.

"When a man has to depend on others to get him around

he's done for," he told her, the last time she suggested it was time he put his mare out to grass. She did not argue with him. She was well aware, as indeed were all who knew him well, that he had always accepted the loss of a leg, at the age of thirty-eight, as a personal challenge to his mobility.

He rode north-east along bridle paths and through a stretch of woodland in the general direction of Dewponds, looking about him with satisfaction and noting not merely the quality of his son-in-law's crops but the profusion of what farmers would call weeds but what he thought of, these days, as the summer finery of the Weald. Charlock glowed among the barley and here and there a cornflower added its splash of blue to a patchwork of green and gold. And on higher ground, where a straggle of oaks and beeches crowned the hogsback that separated farm and estate, the woods were en fête with a hundred thousand wild flowers, from foxgloves taller than himself, to tiny outcroppings of bugloss and toadflax under the hooves of the mare.

He thought, with satisfaction, 'I notice these things now. Years ago, when I used to ride this way to East Croydon Station I took little heed of them. The scent, maybe, but not the sparkle and glory of it all.' But that, he recalled, had been a time when he despised the city gent who made his pile, kissed his farewell to the counting-house, and set about turning himself into a country squire. He was far more tolerant now, far more appreciative of the fact that Kent, the oldest settled shire in the islands, was still largely rural, with its panoramas of field, coppice and wood, its red-tiled oast-houses and hopfields, its old, crouching farmhouses that had been supporting life hereabouts since the days of the Plantagenets. Men who worked the land, men like his son-in-law Denzil, and his grandson, Robert, were not qualified to judge their heritage, save in terms of what it would yield. But to a townee like himself it was a rare privilege to be here, with strength enough to sit a horse and savour the richness of the countryside.

He had a mind, as he descended the slope beyond the woods and glimpsed the roof of Dewponds among its screen of elms, to pay a friendly call on Denzil, and drink some of his cider, but he thought better of it on meeting Robert, driving a wain up to higher pastures east of 'Tryst'.

He called, "Hello there! You've got a fine crop, Robert. The weather's been good to you this year."

Robert, reining in, replied, "Arr, it's fair to middling. If we don't pay for it in July, as we generally do."

Adam smiled, reflecting that he had yet to meet an optimistic farmer. He said, changing the subject, "How's your father, my boy?" Robert said he was well enough but not as active as he had been in happier days at Dewponds, and as he said this he looked speculatively at his grandfather, probably reflecting that his eighty-seven years sat upon him more gracefully than his father's fifty-four. He said, however, noticing Adam's jaded mare, "Isn't it time you put that old nag out to grass, Granfer?"

"We'll be put out together," Adam told him, genially, as he swung about and rode alongside the creaking wain. "In a year or so maybe, depending upon how much we get of this kind of weather."

Robert glanced at the clear blue sky. "It'll hold for a time yet," he said, phlegmatically, and lifted his hand as their ways parted and Adam moved back into the shade of the woods, letting his mare crop wherever she felt inclined and easing his legs from the stirrups. 'That's the trouble with being Robert's age,' he reflected. 'You think it's there for good and you don't appreciate it, any more than I did at his time of life. But now, with no more than a summer or two ahead, you hoard it, ticking off each week as a score against time.'

Away in the direction of the village the sound of church bells reached him, intruding, though not discordantly, on the murmur of the woods. He thought, 'I've been lucky, I suppose. Luckier than most, despite this damned leg and that frightful packload of work I carried all those years. I've survived and that's about all a man can expect at my time of life.' And then, glancing at his watch, he saw that it was coming up to eleven and his newspapers would be coming up from the village. It was time, perhaps, to see what was afoot elsewhere, for keeping pace with events was always important to him. He gathered up his reins and set off up the winding bridle path to the summit where, a mile below, he could see 'Tryst' dreaming its way through another June.

*   *   *

The Serajevo dignitaries, putting as bold a face as possible upon the outrage on the Appel Quay, had their fulsome say, trying to look as if they did not comprehend their distinguished guest's comment, beginning, "I come here to pay you a visit and I'm greeted by bombs . . . !"

There would be no more bombs, Governor Potiorek assured him. The Bosnian capital was not swarming with assassins, and the young madman who had thrown the bomb was now under lock and key. The route for the visit to the museum had been changed. There would be no tour of the narrow streets and, after lunch and a brief visit to the hospital to see how the wounded officer was faring, the Archducal couple would entrain for home. To interpose between any potential assassin and the heir-apparent, however, Count Harrach surrendered his seat and took his stand on the running-board. He would have done better to inform the Archduke's chauffeur of the change of route.

For a second time that morning the fate of the world rested at point of balance. Then the chauffeur made a right turn into Franz Joseph Street and Governor Potiorek, realising the driver was in error, shouted that this was the wrong way and the driver stepped on the brake, preparatory to reversing.

It was, to the hovering Princip, a heaven-sent opportunity. He was standing within yards of the stationary car and he acted with the promptitude of a trained soldier, stepping forward and firing two shots before he was seized and overwhelmed. The car reversed, straightened up and sped away down the Appel Quay. The Archducal couple remained sitting bolt upright so that it seemed yet another assassination attempt had been foiled. But then Sophie, shot through the stomach, collapsed and a thin stream of blood spurted from the mouth of the Archduke. Seeing it, Count Harrach enquired anxiously if His Imperial Highness was suffering badly. Franz Ferdinand sagged murmuring *"Es ist nichts . . . es ist nichts . . ."* repeating the three words over and over again. They were the last he uttered. The door had slammed on an era. At eleven a.m., fifteen minutes after his wife had died, His Imperial Highness, heir to the Austro-Hungarian Empire was dead.

*　　　*　　　*

At the precise moment the physicians were probing the fatal wound in an attempt to extract the bullet, Adam Swann, founder of an empire more in tune with the times, opened the first of his Sunday newspapers. There was plenty there to interest him but little he did not expect to find. Jo Chamberlain, unforgiven arch-enemy of the radicals, and scapegoat of the whole sorry mess that had emerged from his policy in South Africa, was ill and not expected to live. Repercussions of the master-builders' lock-out in January were still reverberating round the industrial world. Madame Caillaux, wife of the ex-premier of France, and last in the long line of French *femmes fatales*, was to stand trial for the murder of the editor of *Le Figaro*. The wildest speculations were being made as regards Ulster's threat to fight rather than accept the Home Rule Bill, that had passed its third reading in the Commons a month ago.

He had followed the recurrent Irish crises of the last few months with keen attention, salted with the pinch of cynicism he reserved for Irish affairs. There was not much, he decided, that he didn't know and couldn't predict about that particular witches' brew. In response to the shipment of arms at Larne, or so the Dublin correspondent claimed, Irish Nationalists were now drilling openly in the capital's parks and public squares. Everybody over there was huffing and puffing and what seemed to him a disproportionate amount of space was devoted to the prospect of civil war. There would be no war in Ireland. Neither, in his view, would the northern Protestants be bludgeoned into accepting the Bill for a united and independent dominion, with freedom to go her own way in all matters but defence and a small British military presence would be maintained at strategic points. The Ulstermen had too much money and influence behind them and some kind of compromise would be struck in the end. He thought, remembering the music-hall Ireland of his garrison days in the early 'fifties, 'The whole damned lot of 'em are bored stiff without something to encourage them to strike attitudes and write their maudlin ballads. Wouldn't surprise me if local blacksmiths in the south weren't being sounded on the prospect of manufacturing pikes and much good they'd be, facing the Mausers that idiot Carson has shipped into the north.' Impatiently he turned the page devoted to the impassioned pleas of correspondents on both sides of the Ulster border and passed on to scrutinise the latest Stock Exchange quotations.

In many ways he was a sage and prescient judge of other people's quarrels but he could be forgiven for having no inkling that one of his children, who had sunned herself on the very spot through lazy summers more than three decades behind her, had squandered her entire inheritance in an attempt to equalise the spurs of the two fighting-cocks beyond the Irish Sea.

IO

Heatwave

ROBERT FAWCETT WAS A GOOD WEATHER PRO-
phet. "It'll hold for a spell yet," he had told Adam, looking at his barley crop ripening under a June sun and so it
did, right on through the succeeding month and into that
new phenomenon on the calendar, the seaside holiday
season, commencing with Bank Holiday.

Day after day the sun blazed across the Weald, temperatures soaring into the eighties on the Fawcett pastures, where cattle browsed in the shade of the field coppice, tails swishing, heads down to parry the swarm of fat
flies. Day after day the heat haze hung over the teeming
capitals of the Swann regions – Edinburgh, Cardiff,
Dublin, Birmingham and Manchester – the sun baking the
slippery pavements and the water-carts, abroad at first
light, doing little or nothing to lay the dust swirls raised by
Swann tyres and Swann hooves, so that work in the high
population areas became a penance and the viceroys
(being of the minority who could anticipate the seasonal
rush) slipped away telling one another and their families
that it was wise to take a break while the splendid weather
held.

George and Gisela, the youngest of their family long
since off their hands, went abroad to visit Gisela's sisters
and brothers-in-law south of Vienna, before moving on
into the Tyrol for a breath of mountain air. They were
just in time to see the Archducal catafalque leave for

Artstettin, surrounded by far less pomp than usually attended the obsequies of a Habsburg. Gisela's brother-in-law, who stood with them to watch it pass, explained the modesty of the display.

"They've never forgiven him for marrying a commoner," he told George, mildly interested in yet another Balkan furore. "They're saying here that those anarchists will get a medal from Prince Montenuova, the Lord Chamberlain and a rare stickler for protocol." And when George, a fluent German speaker, reminded him of the newspaper headlines, he declared, "Oh, there's talk of bringing Serbia to book for her share in the conspiracy but it won't amount to anything. The court party is relieved to see the back of Ferdinand and that woman he would marry, despite all the fuss there was here at the time."

George, watching the coffins trundle by on their way to the Westbankhof, attended only by such nobility of the realm who chose to defy the Chamberlain's posthumous snub, thought, 'I remember old Maximilien Körner telling me that Flunkeydom would choke the Empire in the end and it seems he was right. These fellows look more like a troupe from a musical comedy than soldiers,' and he turned away to retrace his steps to the hotel, where Gisela was packing for the Tyrolean expedition.

*   *   *

Mid-July also saw Giles playing truant, despite the backlog of parliamentary business that had accumulated as the summer recess loomed. He had urgent business in the valley, where yet another strike threatened, and when he had done what he could to head it off until tempers cooled, he stole an extra day and used it to drive his new wife, Gwyneth, into Pembroke, that little England beyond Wales, where they walked over the stretch of coastline that had seen the last invasion of England at a time when his grandfather, the old Colonel, was still a boy.

Hand in hand, they explored the Pencaer peninsula

jutting from the North Coast and he told her something of the forlorn descent of a few hundred French starvelings in February, 1897. He seemed more relaxed these days and the expedition emboldened her to ask a question that had been dormant in her mind ever since their marriage, just a year ago. Reminding him that he still held the lease on his first wife's house in the mountains at Beddgelert, and that he had not revisited North Wales since Romayne's death, she said: "Would it distress you, Giles, to take a holiday there with me? I'm as Welsh as a leek but the truth is I've never been to the mountains."

He replied, with a smile, "I've no melancholy memories of Romayne, as she was then, when I met her up there thirty years ago. Nor as the woman she became, when we started from scratch down here in the south. Yes, I'll take you there during the next recess if you've a fancy to see Snowdonia. I'll show you the very spot where we met at the bridge over the River Glasn when I was eighteen. For the fact is, I don't really see you as two women in that sense."

"How then?"

"More as the complement of one another, I suppose. You began where Romayne left off and I sometimes half-believe that it was meant to happen that way. How else did it come about that our paths recrossed an hour or so before she died?"

She thought about that all the way back to London and it did not strike her as fanciful. She had but two memories of Romayne Swann. One of a spoiled and pettish young madam, standing at her counter just before closing time on a Saturday night and demanding the window display should be half-dismantled in order that she could buy a hat; the other of a wan, waxen little figure in soiled clothes, rushed into her casualty ward after a street riot in Whitehall. A willing sacrifice, she would always think of her, to male intolerance, and the way things were shared in a man's world and in a way the impressions fused, especially here in Wales, the ancestral home of both his wives. She supposed something of this kind lay behind his remark. As a champion both of Wales and women, he could not be unaware of the fusion and she thought, gratefully, 'He's almost over it now, and I've helped in an odd sort of way. It really does look as if it was planned.'

George was home in time to stand in for his son Rudi, viceroy of The Polygon, who decided, in the last week of July, to take his wife and young family on a trip to the Isle of Man. He did this each year and had come to regard it as an extension of his own holiday, for up here, among the shippers and the textile men, he could feel the peripheral pulse of the network better than anywhere outside the capital, The Polygon having been his youthful stamping ground and one of the oldest of the Swann manors.

Young Rudi, a dynamo hereabouts, left his father a string of last-minute instructions, just as if George had been an apprentice to the trade to whom had been granted a little brief authority, but he did not complain. The boy was shaping up well after that furtive marriage of his and he wasn't surprised when Rudi was back a day before he was due with a new idea and a rumour that a Continental war was brewing.

Rudi, it seems, had run into old Albert Tasker in a Douglas hotel and had learned from him that there was every likelihood of a boom in textiles by the time harvest was in.

"Tasker is one of the biggest shippers about here," Rudi told him, "and he's given me good information on foreign markets in the past. 'If you hold any Continental stocks unload 'em, Young Swann,' he told me. 'If you don't the bottom will fall out of 'em inside a month.' "

But George, recalling his Austrian brother-in-law's comments on the occasion of the Archduke's funeral, replied, "My advice to you, Rudi, is stick to hauling and don't dabble in stocks. If you've money to invest plough it back in the business, as I do. And you can tell old Moneybags Tasker next time you run across him that your father had his ear to the ground on the Continent less than a month ago. There'll be plenty of huffing and puffing but no more than a skirmish or two, this year or next year. It's all bluff on Austria's part and I daresay the Serbs will call it. What was the other revelation granted to you in the Isle of Man?"

"Oh, that," said Rudi, grinning, "that's more in your line. Why have we never opened an Isle of Man depot? The name 'Swann' doesn't mean a row of beans over there and the local hauliers have it all their own way."

It was true. In the original and successive partitions of Britain the Isle of Man had been overlooked by both his father and himself, and he saw at once what Rudi was angling for, a Polygon concession, based on Douglas, with H.Q.'s authority to expand.

"What have you in mind? Two or three teams to break the ground?"

"Teams my eye and Betty Martin," retorted Rudi, using one of the Lancastrian expressions picked up from his wife, "over there they have a road trial course and no one so much as looks up when a motor passes. Let's start off with a brace of Swann-Maxies for house removals. I've got an option on a depot in Douglas at a hundred a year. A brewery that's being wound up."

"Then cost it and send it down by tomorrow's post. I'll talk it over with the head clerk."

"I costed it on the boat," Rudi said, handing his father three handwritten sheets clipped together. "It's legible. The crossing was flat calm."

He took the papers, forbearing to say what came to mind, that Rudi, at twenty-seven, was barking at his heels even more impatiently than he, in his own day as heir-apparent, had barked at Adam's. The boy was cocky enough and needed no further encouragement from him, but it was a story to make the Old Gaffer chuckle the next time he looked in at 'Tryst'.

*　　　*　　　*

Edward Swann was another who succumbed to the lure of the heatwave. On his mother-in-law's advice he took Betsy Battersby down to Cornwall for a week – "In order to get to know the girl," she added, "for you seem very much taken with her and I'll not have you blaming me for a second fiasco."

Edward, sharp enough in matters of business, entertained no suspicion at all that she and Betsy had been plotting since the night she absented herself from home leaving Betsy to make the running. Betsy had worked a miracle on him and he had already asked Edith to write to Gilda in California, telling her she could have her divorce as soon as possible.

They drove down to the Westcountry in his new Lanchester, travelling as Mr. and Mrs. Swann and exchanging a wink every time they signed the hotel registers. He wondered sometimes what his circumspect mother, and Betsy's chapel-going family, would make of it if news of the liaison reached them but the prospect did not bother him much. Somehow, come hell or high water, he intended to marry Betsy Battersby and neither he nor she was prepared to wait on the law's delays. As he reminded himself more than once during that hilarious trip, at twenty-eight she was old enough to know her own mind. As for him, life owed him a ration of fun.

*   *   *

There was one Swann who did not respond to the brilliant weather but sat it out in his private Mount Olympus, scanning bundles of newspapers and occupied, for the most part, with his own sombre reflections.

Adam Swann had never been one for holidays and it would not have occurred to him to uproot himself and travel in a stuffy railway carriage to the coast. Or cross the Channel in search of a change of scene. Up here on his knoll, with every tree in full leaf, and the scent of honeysuckle coming out of the woods, he had all the pastoral pleasures on tap, plus his own bed to sleep in at nights. He had, too, all his treasures to hand, and his wife by his side. Indeed, the only thing he did not have to cushion his old age was peace of mind, for, despite everyone's dismissal of the European crisis as just one more display of Balkan fireworks, he sensed, deep in his heart, that things were drifting in a way that promised trouble. The newspaper editors, it seemed, did not share his sense of unease but his famous 'little man', who still lived an inch or so above his navel, was agitated. He supposed that Sir Edward Grey was as familiar with the antics of foreign diplomats as he was himself, but there seemed to him a very ominous note in Russia's championship of the Serbs and Germany's encouragement of Austria to use the assassination as an excuse to overawe Belgrade. The devil of it was, France was closely involved too, and seemed likely to exploit the crisis in order to reopen her eternal inquest on the provinces torn from her in 1870, and while he agreed with the wiseacres that no responsible statesman would be such a fool as to use a Balkan assassination to promote a European war, an upset on this scale could play havoc with trade.

And then there was Ireland, where almost everybody was acting the goat, and that solemn ass Balfour, leader of the Opposition, seeing political advantages in backing Ulster, was encouraging army officers to defy a law approved by a majority of nearly a hundred in the House. If they didn't watch out over there those crazy Fenian outrages would begin again, followed by repression and an end to all hope of peace.

It was not the slightest use confiding his misgivings to Henrietta (she probably did not know where Serbia was) and everyone else seemed to be off on holiday somewhere. Towards the end of the month he had to take himself to task, reasoning – 'Why the devil should I lose any sleep over their concerns at my time of life? I've so short a time left!' And so, in the end, he left his newspapers unread and concentrated on his own borders, now a riot of colour and scent and a beanfeast for the bumble bees, whose drone was continuous every time he pottered to and fro about the more regimented sectors of his estate.

He was here, on a morning in late July, admiring some particularly fine clumps of lupins west of the forecourt, when Giles drove up and, without bothering to go into the house, left his motor at the head of the drive and hurried over to him looking, thought Adam, more pre-occupied than usual. Adam spared the boy a sympathetic thought, reflecting, 'He's the only one among 'em inclined to shoulder everyone's troubles but his own. But I'm glad he had the sense to marry that woman and start again.' As he thought this he did his usual little sum about the age of such sons and daughters who visited him, surprised to realise that the grave-looking, soberly attired 'boy' now approaching him was well into his forty-eighth year.

Giles said, "I looked in at The Hermitage on the way up. You're usually there at this time of day reading your papers, aren't you?"

"Indeed I am," Adam said, "but I've given myself a holiday from them. To tell the truth I can't make head or tail of what's happening any more, can you?"

"Russia's mobilising," Giles said, grimly. "That's official, although it missed the morning papers. I'm very concerned, Father. Things are getting out of hand, and I . . . well, the truth is I find it helps talking to you. That's why I drove over. I only got back from the valleys yesterday. Shall we take a turn in the rose-garden before lunch?"

"By all means. There's a rare show this year. Every-thing is responding to this sunshine. So that fool of a Czar has given way, has he? Well, that'll set the cat among the pigeons and no mistake, for as like as not the Kaiser will follow suit, and after him, France." He checked his stride, contemplating for a moment the result of full-scale mobilisation across Europe. "You think there'll be war?"

"Grey seems to think there might be. Some of our people are beginning to hedge."

"You mean the Cabinet is divided?"

"Right down the middle, I gather from the people I talked to last night."

"But good God, boy! If she's fool enough to square up to Germany without provocation, why should it concern us?"

"We're under an obligation to protect France's Channel coast. Not an alliance, a military arrangement. No more and no less, so far as I can discover, for they've kept very quiet about it. Nobody seems to know the true nature of the understanding, not even Asquith, and Lloyd George himself is confused. He told me last week all would depend on what happened to Belgium if the Germans attack France."

It struck him then, as it had many times over the last few weeks, that politics lacked the precision of business, that hardly anyone practising politics had the ability, or even the wish, to think things through, as he and George and the regional managers were required to do when confronted with a choice of alternatives on a haul or contract. They invariably followed a policy of drift, leaving all the final decisions to civil servants and soldiers.

"What you're saying," he said, slowly, "is this. If Germany tries to get at France through Belgium, we're in, like it or not?"

"That's the general opinion at Westminster," Giles said. "What would you make of it in those circumstances?"

He was a long time answering. He had seen many battlefields, had experienced the dragging pain of wounds, had witnessed, in the Crimea and India, scenes that would turn the stomach of the most enthusiastic flag-flapper in the country. Yet he realised that here was a question of principle that could not be dismissed in the way both he and Giles had opposed the South African War. The German Junker was a bully and a brute. Three limited wars, against Denmark, Austria and France, had established that beyond doubt, and an easy victory following an invasion of Belgium would prove fatal to smaller nations and the security of the world in the years ahead. Beyond that, what would it feel like to sit here in Kent, with a triumphant Germany dictating peace terms in Paris and her jackboots stomping in Channel ports only a few miles away?

He said, at length, "I hate wars. Always have and always will. Small and local, or as big as this promises to be. But there are times when a man has to fight, as we found in India in '57. You can't stand aside and let might take over from right. If it was anything more than a straightforward confrontation between jingoes in Potsdam and Paris, I'd fight and so will Grey if I know the man. You say the Liberals are split. Where do you find yourself, Giles?"

Giles replied, unhappily, "With you, Father, in those circumstances, and I told L.G. as much."

The sound of the lunch gong reached them from the house, telling him that Henrietta must have seen Giles' car and hustled. Adam rose stiffly from the arbour seat and paused to inhale the scent of a full-blown rose cresting the trellis work of the pergola. "That's a smell of youth," he said. "Youth and renewal."

They sat on after lunch, mulling over one thing and another. The navy's preparedness. The part, if any, a small professional army like Britain's could play in a war involving the clash of millions. How the Empire was likely to respond. What a professional like Alex would make of it and how long it was likely to last, and Adam snorted when Giles said a matter of weeks was the general estimate.

"Why do they say that?"

"The cost. The City men say nobody could face expenditure on that scale for long."

"That's damned nonsense," Adam said. "Once war hysteria is aroused they'll find the money to keep it going, and anyone who supposes modern Germany isn't a tough nut to crack is a fool. We were bogged down for months before Sebastopol and half a century later it took us three years to round up sixty thousand Boer farmers. No, my boy, once it gets going it'll be a fight to the finish, with half the world involved and casualties running into millions. The pity of it is that most of those damned fools poised on the brink have never heard a shot fired outside their game preserves. You saw what a local war cost Hugo."

Giles said nothing and Adam changed the subject.

"How are you and that nice woman getting along, eh? They say second marriages stand a good chance if one of the partners has been happy in the past. You were always very much in love with Romayne. Does that make it easier?"

"I've been lucky," Giles said, and then, with a smile, "Luckier than you in one respect. For I've run across two women who were prepared to take me on trust." He got up. "It's time I got back."

"There'll be a debate in a day or so, I imagine?"

"On Monday, depending on circumstances. I think Grey will make a statement to the House."

He said, on impulse, "Could you use your influence to get me a seat in the Members' Galleries if I come up to town? The public gallery will be packed."

"I'd do my best, providing you don't think . . ."

"That it would put too much strain on me? You let me worry about that. If that chap Grey speaks I'd like to hear him." His eyes filmed over and Giles, watching him closely, wondered what he was thinking. He went on, after a moment, "I've seen pretty well everything that's happened in the last seventy years or so. Three monarchs buried, two Jubilees, the Charge of the Light Brigade, the fall of Sebastopol, the well at Cawnpore. This will reduce 'em all to a sideshow. I'll see you to the door, boy."

They passed out into the blazing sunshine and he watched Giles manoeuvre the car in a tight circle to descend the drive. Soon the only evidence of his visit was a small dustcloud hanging over the old mill house. Henrietta came out and stood beside him.

"He looked very worried," she said. "It isn't his marriage, is it?", and suddenly, mercifully, he was able to make a grab at his vanishing sense of humour as he said, with a chuckle, "You have a way, my dear, of reminding one of essentials. No, no, it isn't his marriage. That's booming along, just as I predicted as soon as I set eyes on that woman. It's other people's worries, Hetty, and that's Giles – too old to mend his ways."

2

Despite Giles, who had sat here ten years now, Adam did not often honour the House with his presence. It had never, at any time in his life, had majesty for him and latterly he had come to regard it as a kind of clearing-house for specialised interests. But today was different. Old and cynical as he was, he was caught and held by the terrible tensions of the Chamber, sensing all about him a strain that had nothing to do with the high temperature outside, or the presence, in Whitehall and all the converging thoroughfares, of the crowds drawn there by the mounting expectancy of some cataclysmic change in their lives.

He glanced about him, his keen eye ranging the Government benches immediately below where he could spot a few of the men who had contributed to his daily ration of news this century, isolating the bland, slightly clownish face of Asquith. Beside Asquith, fidgeting a great deal, was the familiar figure of Lloyd George, a man he had never trusted, despite his patronage of Giles, and beside L.G., Sir Edward Grey, on whom most of the attention would be focused today.

Grey looked his part. A patrician, whose handsome profile had survived on into middle-age, and who was clearly under very considerable strain for every now and again, glancing at his notes, he tightened his mouth, as though what he was about to say was distasteful to someone who took his pleasures quietly beside English trout-streams and who was said (it was hard to believe) to be able to imitate over a hundred English bird calls.

Winston Churchill was down there, looking cheerful and slightly roguish. Haldane was there, champion of his son Alex, still far away in India, a rather Prussian-looking fellow, who had once made the statement that Germany was his spiritual home and was almost certainly regretting it today. And across the floor, crowded today with extra chairs, the lions of the Opposition, Balfour and Bonar Law, who had made fools of themselves over Ireland, and among the small Labour cohort, two men who stood out, Ramsay MacDonald and Keir Hardie, one looking like an arrogant young clansman, the other, whose integrity had always earned Adam's respect, like the prophet Elijah ascending to heaven in a chariot.

Those fellows will oppose war, he supposed, Belgium or no Belgium, but they already had the look of men who had enlisted in a lost cause. MacDonald looked fierce and defiant but there was tragedy in the eyes of Hardie.

The place was packed to the doors, every gallery full to overflowing, there had never been so many assembled under this roof since Gladstone's day. Well, that was war and the rumour of war.

Grey was on his feet now and there was stillness, shattered momentarily by the sudden and distracting clatter of the Chaplain's stumble against the extra chairs as he backed away from the Speaker. In a clear, level voice, and with no more than an occasional glance at his notes, he began by asking the House to approach the crisis from the standpoint of British interests, British obligations, British honour, proceeding from there, in the same measured tone, to describe the nature of the military 'conversations' with France. No secret engagement existed. No agreement had been entered into to bind or restrict Britain's course of action if France found herself at war with Germany on account of her treaty obligations to Russia. "We are not partners to the Franco-Russian alliance . . . we do not even know the terms of their alliance. What does exist is our naval agreement with France in consequence of which the French fleet is concentrated in the Mediterranean, leaving her northern and western coasts absolutely undefended . . ."

*   *   *

George Swann, at that precise moment, had made his initial dispositions, had descended from his tower and was sunning himself in the yard, all but empty seeing this was a Bank Holiday.

There was nothing more he could do.

For who among his competitors, he reflected, had been granted a kerbside view of the Archduke's funeral in Vienna over a month ago? Or how many had received a direct tip from a source as reliable as old Albert Tasker up in The Polygon, to unload stocks before they plummeted? Yet he had ignored both warnings and it had fallen to his aged father to remind him that, in the event of war, a firm owning a fleet of heavy transport vehicles, and relying on three hundred trained mechanics to drive and service them, was a likely candidate for either bankruptcy or millionaires' row, depending upon how he disposed himself.

Within ten minutes of hanging up his receiver George was on his way to the yard. Within an hour of arriving there he had drafted a comprehensive telegram, running to three hundred words, to every viceroy in the network, giving them basic instructions about stockpiling motor spirit, conserving of machines and manpower, and half a dozen other matters that would alert them to the situation. Most of them (excluding young Rudi) would be as bemused as he had been by the long spell of blazing sunshine.

His imagination, once alerted, worked like a shower of sparks on a scatter of combustibles. In a memorandum, designed to follow his telegram by express post, he covered every conceivable contingency, from the commandeering of his vehicles by government agents, to the mass enlistment of his mechanics in one or other of the specialised army units that had proliferated since the General Staff had conceded the self-propelled vehicle a place among their priorities. He thought, sitting on a makeshift seat used by waggoners for their lunch break, 'That's about it, until I can see Scottie Quirt and get an estimate of future production out of him. They can't close us now, providing those chaps out in the shires follow my guidelines. Given luck, we might even squeeze some contracts from the military and make a killing out of it . . .'

*　　*　　*

There was no doubt now which side of the fence would see Grey's elegantly trousered leg first. The cheers, breaking from the ranks of the Tories opposite, confirmed as much when he asked what attitude the country might take to the presence of the German fleet bombarding French ports a few miles away and then, borrowing lavishly from Gladstone's oratory, he underlined his point by declaring unequivocally: "Could England fail to take her stand against the unmeasured aggrandisement of any power whatsoever?"

Adam, his eyes focused unwinkingly on the elegant figure at the despatch box, thought: 'It's all over now . . . we're in it sure enough . . .' And then, as Grey reiterated our pledge in favour of Belgian neutrality, 'And why not? Had the fellow any real alternative? Has any one of them down there, including that leathery old fox Earl Roberts, perched up there in the Strangers' Gallery?' And suddenly he felt old and tired. He extricated himself from his cramped seat and made his way into the lobby and thence into the yard where the sun beat upon the necks of ten thousand Londoners almost blocking the movement of vehicles.

Giles must have seen him go and caught up with him as he stood with head bowed beside the plinth of

Cromwell's statue. "Are you all right, Father? Can you get back to your hotel alone . . . ? I can't leave now but I warned Arscott, George's chauffeur . . ." But Adam, straightening himself, muttered savagely, "It's the heat. No air in there . . . I'll be all right, my boy. Get about your business." But Giles would not and hurried off to the place where Arscott had promised to wait. Within minutes Arscott was back and helping Adam into the seat beside the driver's, with Giles standing by anxiously. He said to the chauffeur, "To the Norfolk, if you can get there, and then home," and to himself, 'I'm too old for crowds,' as the car nosed its way south-west through thinning crowds, circling Victoria to approach the Strand from Piccadilly and Haymarket, for it was useless to attempt a more direct route.

He thought, watching the surge up and down the pavements, 'They're with Grey, every last one of 'em. You've only got to look at their faces to see that and it's curious, really, when the very lives of some of 'em are at stake.' But then it occurred to him that it was not so curious after all, for the country, apart from that South African business and a string of tinpot colonial wars fought by professionals, had been at peace for ninety-nine years. Too long, maybe, for anyone but old stagers like himself to understand what there was to war beyond cheering and bugle calls and an escape from office drudgery.

3

The news reached them all in driblets. Via the shrill cries of newsboys, via the clatter of the telegraph, via the measured predictability of the post, or the timeless wag of tongues.

Alexander Swann, far away on the Indian plains, heard it with relief, for he had been sure the Liberals would rat at the last minute.

Edward Swann learned it from the banner headlines of his evening newspaper, carelessly scanned while he was awaiting his turn in the bathroom at a Bristol hotel, where he and Betsy had stopped off for the night on the final evening of their Westcountry jaunt. He called through the open door where, a moment ago, he had heard her splashing and singing, "Change your tune, Betsy! There's going to be a war after all," and her tousled red head appeared round the door-frame.

"Will you be going for a soldier, Edward?"

"Not so long as you're available," he said, and she came in, pink and naked, and went to drying her hair as he read her Sir Edward Grey's speech, adding a few random comments of his own.

She did not seem interested and neither, for that matter, was he. With a woman of Betsy's proportions standing there without a stitch to cover her it was difficult to get excited about the tread of armed hosts. She said, "It could make a difference to us, couldn't it? I mean, nobody will bother much with divorces if there's a war to write about. Not that I care, mind. They could say what they liked about me, so long as I was sure about you in here," and she lowered the towel and touched her breast.

He thought about that a moment and then decided that she was laughing at him, so that instead of assurances he gave her a smart slap on the behind and spun her round, saying, "Get dressed, woman, while I have my scrub. I reserved a table for seven and the head waiter said he couldn't promise to hold it. It seems everybody's celebrating as well as us."

*　　*　　*

"England's peril is Ireland's opportunity," Rory had told Helen more than once but she had thought of it as a sentiment that belonged to Napoleonic times and the abortive rising of '98. Until the Bachelor's Wall affair that is, for that, more than any tribulation out of the past, impinged upon patriots in a way that penetrated the haze of ballad and legend. Rory and his friends were now facing a straight choice; submission, and a compromise with Ulster, or militancy of the kind British troops had showed when they tried to capture the arms landed at Howth in the last week of July. Three civilians killed and thirty-eight wounded, half of them seriously. Surely an outrage deserving of a dozen ballads, justifying an equal ruthlessness on the part of the Volunteers.

They got most of the guns away in the mêlée. Over a hundred of them lay snug in her own cellar at this moment but then, it seemed, an appeal to arms suddenly became the currency of politicians all over Europe and the Bachelor's Walk massacre was forgotten by the British. She said, when confirmation came that England considered herself at war with Germany and Austria, "Will the Irish fight too, Rory? Will your people put away their private quarrel until there's an end to it in France, or wherever they fight?"

"Here's one who won't, by God! I hope the Kaiser gives them a drubbing and then, maybe, we can make terms with the Germans."

She said nothing to this. Away in the back of her mind issues that had once been stark and clear were getting blurred. It was not easy for anyone growing up in Victoria's England to visualise the English at the mercy of a conqueror, any more than it was credible to contemplate a man like Rory taking a pot shot with one of those contraband rifles at, say, Alex, over here to keep the peace. And apart from that, having lived among the Irish for so long, she could not bring herself to believe that a fight of that magnitude would not encourage them to think of Ulster and Ulster's Volunteers as small beer. All the same, the news increased her sense of isolation over here and sometimes she yearned, more than anything in the world, to slip into town and make her peace with Joanna, to sit down in her drawing-room and have a good old family gossip.

*   *   *

For the rest, in the enduring blaze of sunshine, the news touched them but lightly. Joanna, in Dublin, Margaret, in the valleys, Deborah in London and Lady Sybil in her elegant house overlooking Southampton Water, may have reflected, with a certain amount of relief, that their husbands were too old, and their sons too young, to be eligible for service in the field, and in any case it seemed unlikely to last more than a month or two. Or so all the experts were saying. They were not the kind of women to take war-fever seriously. Joanna was too placid and Margaret, with Huw for a husband and Giles for a brother, too indoctrinated with anti-militarist theories to wave Union Jacks, or buy wool for soldiers' socks. Deborah, who for years now had suffered physical affront at the hands of men, was inclined to regard the entire male sex as too pig-headed to deserve sympathy and even said so on a postcard to Henrietta from Folkestone, where she heard the news during their annual holiday. "Let them discover what it's like to be hounded," she wrote. "Maybe it will teach them something." And as for Lady Sybil, busy, as usual, organising garden parties and theatricals for Hugo's patients, she had reservations on the subject of patriotic displays, remembering, possibly, a tented hospital in South Africa and a young man on a bed with bandages over his eyes.

*   *   *

It was otherwise with Adam. For a day or so after that spell of dizziness in the House towards the end of Sir Edward Grey's speech, he rested, saying very little and responding hardly at all to Hetty's flow of speculations about the likely involvement of her tribe of descendants, now totalling some thirty-odd. Alex would be home earlier than expected, no doubt, and some of the grand-children might be silly enough to offer Lord Kitchener their services but it would be over by Christmas, wouldn't it? He said, briefly, that he hoped so and bestirred himself, going out on to the terrace and taking the winding path up to the summit of the spur where the old Colonel's summerhouse, constructed of half an up-ended whaler, still stood. The path was steep and taxed him severely but he managed it somehow and sat gratefully on the plank seat, wheezing slightly and resting his mottled hands on his knees as he surveyed the north-western segment of the Weald basking in its sixth week of unbroken sunshine.

It was cooler up here. A faint and welcome breeze rustled the leaves of the beeches and oaks behind him and jostled the pink and white bells of the tall foxglove spires. Blackbirds sang and finches quarrelled in the thickets left and right of the shelter, and away across the full expanse of his estate, beyond the larch coppice where his third son had been sired, beyond the white blur of the old mill house, where, years ago, his second son had lived with his Austrian wife, he could just glimpse, through the shimmer of heat, the grey-brown blob that was the capital of the world, now feverishly involved with the concerns of lesser capitals across the water.

For a while his imagination conjured with those far-off places, so that he saw, in his mind's eye, endless columns of encumbered men marching, marching, marching towards points of collision with one another. As a man of war he could identify with them at all levels. With the braided generals, with sweating privates, wondering when the next ten-minute halt would be called and they could ease the dragging weight of the equipment from their shoulders; with cannoneers riding their limbers and light horsemen freeing their feet from stirrups and flexing their thigh muscles; with toiling teamsters half-asleep on the box-seats of their waggons and even with the clamorous children lining the dusty roads to witness the passage of the cavalcades.

It was so old a pageant and so poor a cause. Poorer than ever in this day and age, when men should have learned the art of governing themselves without resorting to chaos. And yet . . . there was the kernel of that chap

Grey's speech: "If France is beaten to her knees, if Belgium fell under the same dominating influence, then Holland and Denmark, I do not believe we should be able to undo what had happened to prevent the whole of the west of Europe falling under the domination of a single power . . . we should, I believe, sacrifice our respect and good name and reputation before the world and should not escape the most serious and grave economic consequences . . ."

He was right, of course, particularly his reference to economics, for that was what it amounted to in the end. Economics. In other words, to pounds, shillings and pence, to marks, roubles, dollars, francs and kroner, by which men lived and died and without which, with a world population running into hundreds of millions, everything would come to a halt.

Well, they would have to make what they could of it without his help, for it was doubtful indeed if he would live to hear a cease-fire and that, when you thought about it, was a comfort at eighty-seven. In the meantime he would seek his comfort elsewhere. In the movement of those mottled foxglove bells ringing a noiseless peal across the Weald. In the society of Hetty who, like himself, belonged to an older world. And in the contemplation, perhaps, of having done his stint as best he could, without treading the next man underfoot.

He inhaled the rich scent of summer and reminded himself that this, at all events, qualified as something eternal.

He closed his eyes.

A TOP SELECTION OF CORONET NOVELS

R. F. DELDERFIELD

A Horseman Riding By

☐	04360 1	Book 1—Long Summer Day	50p
☐	04361 X	Book 2—Post of Honour	50p
☐	12971 9	Book 3—The Green Gauntlet	50p
☐	15092 0	The Dreaming Suburb	50p
☐	15093 9	The Avenue Goes to War	50p
☐	15623 6	God is an Englishman	60p
☐	16225 2	Theirs Was The Kingdom	60p
☐	02787 8	Farewell The Tranquil Mind	35p
☐	17420 X	Seven Men Of Gascony	40p

To Serve Them All My Days

☐	17599 0	Book 1—Late Spring	40p
☐	16709 2	Book 2—The Headmaster	40p

Give Us This Day

☐	18818 9	Book I—Three Score Years and Ten	50p

NORAH LOFTS

☐	17826 4	Charlotte	40p
☐	19352 2	Crown Of Aloes	40p

KEITH ROBERTS

☐	18805 7	Boat Of Fate	60p

ELIZABETH GOUDGE

☐	15105 6	Green Dolphin Country	75p
☐	15104 8	Scent Of Water	40p

NIGEL TRANTER

☐	16213 9	Montrose—The Young Montrose	50p
☐	18619 4	Montrose—The Captain-General	50p

All these books are available at your bookshop or newsagent, or can be ordered direct from the publisher. Just tick the titles you want and fill in the form below.

....

CORONET BOOKS, P.O. Box 11, Falmouth, Cornwall.

Please send cheque or postal order. No currency, and allow the following for postage and packing:

1 book—10p, 2 books—15p, 3 books—20p, 4–5 books—25p, 6–9 books—4p per copy, 10–15 books—2½p per copy, 16–30 books—2p per copy, over 30 books free within the U.K.
Overseas—please allow 10p for the first book and 5p per copy for each additional book.

Name..

Address..

....